Red Sulphur

THE GREATEST MYSTERY IN ALCHEMY

A Saga by Robert Bosnak
Books I and II

Revised Second Edition

EMPRESS
PUBLICATIONS

WWW.EMPRESSPUBLICATIONS.COM

For

Jonathan Lipsky
Playwright, Dreamer, Friend

James Hillman
Teacher, Alchemist, Friend

Eddie Michaels
Life Enthusiast, Friend

"All that is without thee
Also is within."

- Salomon Trismosin

Fra Mauro map (1460)

The Fra Mauro Map orientation (South at the top) is considered the greatest memorial of medieval cartography by the Venetian monk Fra Mauro.

This period is the zenith of alchemy when Red Sulphur was last made. To us it looks upside down, as does the entire blossom-period of alchemical research.

The year is 1666, the Year of the Beast, seen by many as the year the Devil will appear on earth.

Science is in ascendance, crowding out other systems of thought. The ancient art of alchemy is in retreat.

No one has been able to make the Philosopher'sStone for over a hundred years, but many of the best minds of the age are still in a desperate search for it. Stories vividly abound how alchemists of yore had created a mysterious stone of sorcery, rejuvenating all it touches, the source of life everlasting – turning decrepit old lead into precious fresh gold. A universal medicine known to the alchemists by its true name: Red Sulphur.

But the Divine Art is receding from the memory of humankind. Science is bought at a price.

What follows is based on the last verified reports by credible witnesses. This is the story of the final embers of the long gone days when the Magi could still do what we, children of Science, hold to be impossible.

It has been written down to honor the Ancestors.

Book One

The Helvetius Affair

Historical Document (non-fiction):

From a March 25, 1667 letter (letter 40) written by Benedict de Spinoza, published in *SPINOZA; The Letters*, Translated by Samuel Shirley, Hackett Publishing Company, Inc., Indianapolis/Cambridge

> ... With regard to **the Helvetius affair**, ... I went to the silversmith named Brechtelt, who tested the gold. ... he said that between the melting and the separation the gold had increased in weight, and had become much heavier as was the weight of the silver he had introduced into the crucible to effect the separation. So he firmly believed that the gold which had transmuted his silver into gold contained something singular. He was not the only one of this opinion; various other persons present at the time also found that this was so. Thereupon I went to Helvetius himself, who showed me the gold and the crucible with its interior still covered with a film of gold, and told me that he had introduced into the molten lead scarcely more than a quarter of a grain of barley or of mustard-seed. ...

Part One

Mundanus

Chapter One

The Hague, Holland, December 1666

My clothes are soaked, my back is bent, and the satchel from my shoulder weighs heavier with each step as I drag myself along the cobblestones. It is drizzling wet snow. It always seems to be raining in this wretched country. I find the smell of the city disgusting after having spent weeks at sea on my voyage back from London, where everything reeks like burn, a city in ashes. The London flames haunt me to the far side of my nightmares, mixing with memories of raging mobs calling out for revenge against foreigners. They came for me especially, the Italian alchemist with hot blasting furnaces, artist of the fire. All I have left is on my back.

I usually am aware of new odors for a week or so, and then the particular stench disappears behind the din. After months away from cities I now inhale a human cesspool of stale sweat and urine mixed in with the excrements of animals. Somehow people stink more than pigs. I can almost taste the reek of my own rancid self as I hurry along the streets, on guard against those who want to steal the box in my satchel.

My London days had been numbered anyway, even without the fire. James, Duke of York, brother to the King, is hungry for gold. His bandits in England are many, and all were searching for me. Even here, in Holland, I look around me expecting to see them at any moment. I hug the satchel and feel the small ivory box everyone wants. Besides it, I own Trismosin's book of alchemical recipes and spells, and a loaf of moldy bread. A three-month-old beard and potato sack rags hide me from view. Most people here look like me, hurrying the streets, scared of each other. They are from all over Europe; I hear shards of foreign tongues through the drab atmosphere of thick gray soup making the figures liquid as if made of wet clay. Last year's plague has moved out to sea, to England. But people here still avoid one another.

To my left, rooftop facades of quaint two story homes rise like stairs up to the sulking sky. Well-appointed pane glass windows proclaim the solid square self-satisfaction of the burgherdom I can't stand in these parts. From their cozy living rooms devoid of curtains nosy folk spy the street scene outside suspiciously. A forest of smoking chimneys keeps them warm. I am cold and worn out. I didn't know so much of me could ache and breathing heavily I curse my mission. This has to end – I'm losing faith. Let James of York come and get this treasure off my back and turn it into vulgar gold once and for all - I don't give a damn! But then the stones in my box talk back as they always do. They tell me to do just one more transmutation in front of the most influential physician in these lands now at war with England. The enemies of York need to be enlisted. I want to tell my satchel that then I will be chased by both England *and* the Dutch Republic. But I've given up arguing with the Stone. Its purposes are never obvious. Who *is* this Doctor Helvetius I have to find anyway?

All these damned cities! Long ago they started calling me Mundanus, world-traveler. At 42 years of age I have lived longer than some, and I can feel the weight of my years begin to bear down on me. My hips scowl sharply, shooting spasms through my back. A cart rides by, a puddle splashes; I hardly notice. I don't remember the last time I saw anything soft, fit for a good night's sleep. Tonight will be no different.

Halting my labored pace, I view the entry to a hazy town square in the melancholy afternoon light. From the corner of my eye I see a young man in elegant dress staring at me. With a shock of recognition, I see a large silver Ottoman crescent dagger on his hip. But when I turn my head, the man isn't there.

I'm sure I've seen that dagger on a man. Could he be one of York's adventurers sent to shadow me? Yet now there is no sign of him. One moment he was in plain sight, pale and striking, seeming to almost emit light, and then he's gone. No one can disappear that fast. I shake my head ferociously: I'm beginning to see things, imagining enemies everywhere. Come get me, you bastards! I peer defiantly into the hazy mist around. But no one appears. I sigh and continue walking. A sour taste remains as the non-encounter fades.

An even colder fog has set in to freeze what is left of my lungs. These lands are so joyless compared to Venice. This is the most elegant part of town, and look at it! If it were my Venice there would be marvelous Palazzos. Here, at the center of political power of golden Holland, the grand colonizer of the world with a fleet that is the envy of all, the modest homes push together like bowling pins in a coffin. I wish I could be home. No chance getting back to England; York will have put spies at every port to hunt me down. Getting out of there after the London fires this September had been impossible enough. I had to travel as far north as Denmark. I need to set up a laboratory as soon as possible and replenish my supply of the *Panacea*.

I suddenly see it rise out of the fog: the home of Helvetius, physician to the rulers. It is much larger than the houses in the street leading up to it, with three stories and large windows on both sides of an impressive portico entrance. We face one another, the great burgher home and I. Over the door the builders have placed a family crest in stone bas relief with a large ox pulling a plow. I wonder how a foreign physician, even one to the great and mighty, might end up living in such grand state, and ring the bell.

&

When she opens the door the pretty girl's face is diffident. She tries to close the door instantly when she sees me, apparently expecting an ambush.

"I've come to see Doctor Johann Friedrich Schweitzer, called Helvetius," I say quickly, horrified by the quiver in my voice. I know my Dutch is heavily accented in the way of the Italians. As she closes the door on my foot I wince. Her grey blue eyes are wide with alarm and a bright blush flushes her cheeks. She can't be more than 18 years of age.

"You may close the door on me, but *please* tell Doctor Helvetius I was sent here by Doctor Edmund Dickinson from the College of Physicians in England," I implore.

She looks startled. Clearly the lofty English name confuses her even more that my shabby appearance.

&

"Who is it, Clara?" a melodious older woman's voice asks from the back.

"Some beggar who says he comes from England," Clara calls.

"Send him on his way. No wait, ask him to come to the back and have Mina give him some bread."

Her voice is kind.

"I was sent here from England by Doctor Edmund Dickinson of Oxford. I come here with his greetings," I yell towards the back from where the kindly voice had spoken.

I hear a shuffle of garments. My ears tell me the lady of the house must be wearing a long rustling skirt across a marble floor. White and black checkered marble, my eyes confirm as the door opens up.

Behind the young maid I see a matron in her mid-thirties with a patrician face in the habit of being obeyed. Her eyes too are grey blue, her features sharp: Helvetius is a lucky man.

"*Who* sent you?" she inquires, curiosity straining her voice. This must not be your everyday occurrence, someone coming from England at a time of war.

"Doctor Edmund Dickinson, honorary fellow of the English College of Physicians," I repeat.

She frowns. I can see that the name means something to her. She must be a woman of learning to know of this distinguished doctor. With an imperious gesture she shoves the girl to the side, who in obvious relief flees down the hall and up the stairs.

"It is an urgent matter," I insist.

She nods, and opens the door more widely. I realize that I have not smelled feminine perfume for ages...

As I step in I hear noise coming from the stairs where the girl had fled. A man in dark velvet clothes descends. I see instantly that this man is vain and I smile. Vain people are easy to deal with. They are the most predictable of all. He speaks to me in Dutch with a heavy German accent.

"Who did you say you were?" he asks gruffly.

"They call me Mundanus," I say, loathe to reveal my identity.

"And you were sent by?"

"Doctor Edmund Dickinson."

"How is it that you saw him?" he asks harshly. "No one can cross the North Sea at a time of war. Only spies do. Why should I let you into my house? How do I know that the whole admiralty won't be after me?"

"I'm sure they are your patients, all of them." I stroke his pride with a sense of mischief. "And besides, there is no reason to fear. I have come to talk alchemy. And as we are in a free country, there is no law against it, as there is in England."

"Why talk alchemy to me?" he asks aggressively. His wife puts her hand on his sleeve to calm him.

"Because you wrote against it and you have influence. The philosophers in England need your help to repeal the ban on alchemy so they can experiment freely. They're forming a Royal Society and need your illustrious support."

"I think alchemy is hogwash," Helvetius exclaims, and turns around, indicating to his wife to close the door. The meeting is over. No more audience granted.

She looks at me apologetically.

"Please come to the back," she says gently. "We'll give you a meal."

"What if I carried the Red Sulphur on my person?" I ask Helvetius. Vain men have scared hearts, so I add: "I carry with me enough Red Sulphur to make 20 tons of gold. Enough to finance several wars with England. Your masters would be very annoyed if they heard you had sent me away..." Then, to whet the appetite of this foe of the Great Art whose bluster may hide a secret fascination, I say, "And aren't you even a bit curious to behold the true Philosopher's Stone?"

I hear his pace slacken. A decision is being made in his conceited scull. I despise him. But his lovely wife looks kindly and very curious. She understands. He may just be a dullard who lives by her wits. So I turn to her.

"Maybe the Lady wishes to see the Stone?" I inquire in my most salubrious voice. The promise of health and fortune is dripping from my tongue. I feel irresistible. In the background even the young maid is enthralled. My voice is now in the lowest of registers with a timbre of silver strings, each heard resonating individually: the voice of the Magus. I am pleased with myself.

Helvetius' footsteps stop. I hear him turn.

Then he continues up the stairs.

"Send him up to the study," he instructs the wife, who inaudibly sighs with relief. Her curiosity has been aroused. Madam Schweitzer's fragrance is distracting.

"Marianne Schweitzer-Van Os," she holds out her hand courteously.

"Mundanus," I repeat, bowing and instinctively clicking my heels. I am suddenly very aware of the smelly clothes behind which I hide my identity. I take her ivory hand and kiss it. To my surprise these aren't smooth hands without character of an upper class lady of leisure ruling her palazzo from her boudoir, but dexterous fingers with telling calluses. Behind the lady I see the maid giggle at the comical sight of the malodorous man in beggars' clothes kissing her mistress' hand as if he were a gentleman. Madam Schweitzer turns around and I notice in the young girl's eyes that the mistress' look must have been stern since her giggle dies a sudden death. I cross the checkered marble floor towards the stairs in the back. My footsteps cast a hollow echo. Inside the building feels even bigger than it looks from outside; I realize that I must be feeling more expansive and sense that the woman preceding me up the creaking steep stairs has something to do with it. At the top of the stairs I inhale tones of wax polish and wood fire mixed with a familiar laboratory smell. I step into his study, following the mistress of the house.

Helvetius stands with his back to the fire. The fireplace is large and a pot hangs on a metal hanger. Something is boiling, and it is not soup. It has a sulfuric smell. I instantly recognize the unmistakable odor of ground cinnabar, red quicksilver sulfate. What is he doing boiling cinnabar, the first stage of the Stone? Might he have a laboratory elsewhere in the house? But then why is he writing against alchemy? Suddenly *I* am the fool. Have I underestimated this man? I look back and forth from the cauldron to Helvetius and must display a confused expression, if judged by the wide grin on his face.

"Do you think you have to be dressed in rags to be a Magus?" he asks slyly.

I bow, first to the cauldron and then to him. All the vanity I saw in him I know to have been my own. I bow for a third time, for this lesson.

There is a silence between us. We have to start again.

At this point the young maid enters with a pot of boiling water. An unfamiliar aroma pervades the room.

"Cocoa," Madam Schweitzer replies to my unanswered question. "Chocolatl from the New World. They say it's made by Aztec people. It is all the rage here in the Low Lands. You must have been away for a long time." I nod, inhaling some of the bitter smell. "We mix it with sugar-cane juice, water and warm milk. It tastes delicious."

"You must think highly of our visitor," remarks Helvetius dryly. I've heard of the chocolatl of the Aztecs. It is expensive. It is rumored to give great sexual stamina. I look at Madam Marianne Schweitzer with increasing appreciation.

Madam Schweitzer, in the way of spouses, pretends not to have heard him. She begins to pour me a cup of deep brown liquid, and her quiet activity fills our awkward silence with an exotic bouquet. When I taste the warm chocolatl my eyes roll back into my head in a momentary swoon. My palate has never hosted such richness, like a sweet bitter wine but entirely different: too new for words. I feel my body instantly becoming its slave. As I open my eyes Madam Schweitzer smiles enticingly.

"I so enjoy seeing people drink chocolatl for the first time!" she exclaims, unselfconscious as a young girl, not at all like the serious mistress of a grand burgher home.

"You must be a poor Magus after all," Helvetius remarks dryly. "You know the smell of cinnabar but not of cocoa."

The man is so much sharper than I had given him credit for. I can't but appear a bit sheepish and shamefaced.

"Then why did you write against alchemy?" I ask. "Why did you say that alchemy is an error of the past and has no place in the world of today?"

Helvetius takes the cup of cocoa from his wife without acknowledging her presence, performing the ritual of that particular familiarity which creates mutual invisibility. He takes a sip.

"And why should I tell you this?" he asks in a sudden challenge and a thrust of the neck towards me.

I recoil and remain silent, having no answer to his question.

A long pause follows.

"Do tell us about Oxford," the Lady of the house inquires after some time, a diplomatic undertone in her simple question.

"The atmosphere is much improved since Cromwell's death and the Restoration of the Kingdom." I stare openly at Helvetius to gauge his response.

"So I hear," he replies in a measured fashion. He is obviously a royalist, even in respect to a country at war with his own. I remember that he is physician to the princely family of Orange, the former rulers of this prosperous country, now replaced by burgher regents akin to Cromwell. For the first time I realize the true importance of this man standing with his back to the fire. I realize the wisdom of Dickinson to send me to him. I feel stupid that I had been lulled into a sense of superiority by the coldness of my bones. A sense of gravity descends on me, as I feel the weight of the mantel bequeathed to me by my illustrious ancestor Salomon Trismosin.

"Do you know Doctor Dickinson?" I ask, regaining my composure.

"We have corresponded some years ago," Helvetius says haughtily. "How do you know him?" he asks, as though he couldn't imagine that I would have any business with such a great personage.

"I performed a projection for him," I reply, annoyed. "He was like you, convinced that it was all hogwash."

Helvetius looks at me with fierce suspicion. "You imply that you can perform a projection of the Stone on lead so it will transmute into gold?"

I ignore his tone. "He became a convert to our cause and an avid experimenter. He showed the gold I had made to his Royal Society fellows, who in turn became fascinated. They want to experiment and for that purpose they need to have the ancient laws against the practice of alchemy revoked. They require support from as many great minds in Europe as can be assembled." I notice my voice raised by an octave, the very thought of these matters transports me. "He suggested I perform a projection for you, so you could have it thoroughly checked and report back to him on your findings. He is well aware of the central position you hold in this country among physicians."

To my surprise Helvetius stumbles back to the leather chair by the fire and crumples down unceremoniously. I feel gratified that I have been able to take him off guard. So I push on.

"I have the Stone on my person," I conclude.

Beautiful Madam Schweitzer is now very excited; a burst of her perfume erupts into the room. She gasps, "Will you show us?"

I look at Helvetius for a clue. But he appears dumbstruck. I hesitate. I do not understand why he suddenly appears to surrender. I had expected him to remonstrate. I myself would not have believed me.

"Show us the Stone, if it truly is the Red Sulphur," Helvetius mutters softly after having re-found his tongue.

I look questioningly at Marianne. She has a pay-no-attention-to-him look on her face, eagerly staring at the satchel on my back, moving her lips as if in prayer.

Suddenly I suspect she is not just his wife. She must be his *soror mystica*, the mystical sister with whom an alchemist generates his passion in order to copulate with the metals. I don't have such a beloved and I feel hollow.

I look around the room for signs that they are Adepts, like me. I notice several tomes by Paracelsus, the pupil of my ancestor Salomon Trismosin. Many half burnt candles are strewn around on tables and desks, proof of work till deep into the night. But where are the alembics, where is the oven? I see a door.

"Is the laboratory in there?" I ask Mistress Marianne.

"Across the hall," she replies.

"Then why the article? Why debase the Art?" I turn to Helvetius, my voice icy. Here is a man of great influence, whose words are respected by scientists, turning the harshest critic of the true philosophy.

Helvetius has his eyes closed. "Show me the projection and I'll tell you."

It sounds fair so I shrug, take the satchel off my back, take out the small ivory box and put it on the desk. A scent of moldy bread spreads from my bag. Helvetius gets up from his chair. His face looks as eager now as Marianne's. "I have been dreaming dreams of the Stone of late," he says, his pale eyes dreamy.

 howeq

"Hurry slowly," I repeat the adage of our alchemist trade and allow my movements to linger. I'm also longing to see the Red Sulphur again. I only allow myself to see it sporadically, so as not to be too fiercely in love with the source of all creation and thus become its slave. Every time it is about to come out of its box, my heart beats loudly like a besotted lover. Since my father first showed me this Stone aglow with magic when I was seven years old, I have been in love with it. It commands my life, it decides my steps; it is my past, my future, my very lifeblood. I pause to steady myself.

"Open the box!" Helvetius commands rudely. His patience has been tested long enough.

I slowly open the box and lower it to their gaze. We view three lumps of a yellowish glassy substance.

Helvetius looks disappointed. "The color is wrong," he mutters.

"You've heard the old wives tale that it should be red like cinnabar," I counter. "The color doesn't matter to its potency. This is the most virile sulphur in the world. It is enough to turn 20 tons of diseased metal into pure gold. And it does more. It can heal the plague. I have seen it with my own eyes."

"Heal the plague?" the physician asks. I can see in his eyes that he wants to believe me – that he hopes that this is indeed the *Panacea* all doctors search for but never find: the universal medicine that cures all illness.

"I have been experimenting with it since the outbreak began here in Holland early last year and when the plague moved to England I travelled with it to continue my experiments in London. My laboratory there burnt down in the great fires last September. Mobs stole all the medicine I had saved from the flames. I barely survived their madness. Close the curtains and please cover the fire with ashes."

With a few quick motions Helvetius smothers the flames under the pot of boiling cinnabar. Marianne goes over to the window. There are thick red velvet curtains, very unusual in this land where the windows are never covered to the world. I suspect they do not want themselves exposed to curious viewers, even if it is on the second floor. The room goes dark. The thick Persian carpet, the desk and the bookshelves, everything disappears. All that remains is a green glow from the yellow bars of glassy Sulphur and the smell of bread gone green. "The glow is what makes it real." I explain. "Not the color you see by daylight. This is the glow that makes everything turn green in springtime. This is the greening power of nature herself, condensed and coagulated." There is enough light emitted by the ivory box to show the greed on his face. His fingers curl. I notice his long fingernails for the first time, strange for a physician, more like the hands of a scholar. Marianne stands transfixed in awe, a beatific smile on her face. *She* is devoutly present to the Stone, while *he* wants to possess it. My own heart is full of bluster and bliss, both their feelings mixed into one: the claws of passion mixed with the clear breath of life. I blush and avert my eyes from Madam Schweitzer. I might have been staring at her. I need to find a *soror* of my own, a mystical sister with whom to dwell in passion. The work cannot be done without. I shake my head to rid myself of the vision of the woman standing next to me in adoration of the magic Stone. The words of my ancestor return to me: "No Opus without Woman." The Art is not a lofty pursuit. It is sweaty and desperate. Why am I still holding back?

"May I light a candle?" Marianne Schweitzer asks me, as if I were the master of the house. I feel a momentary flush of intimacy between us, and again I shake my head.

"Why not?" asks Helvetius, thinking I meant the candle.

"Oh, please, by all means, light candles," I say quickly, blessing my beard for hiding my sweat.

The green glow disappears behind the yellow flicker of candlelight. A heady smell of ashes, cinnabar, mold and wax mixes with a sultry air given off by the Stone, like nightfall after a lightning storm. My work here is done for today. I need to make them long to see more so our joint passion will inspire the projection. I begin to close the box.

"I will return in three weeks to perform the projection on 30 drachms of lead of your own preparation."

Helvetius looks very disappointed and so does Marianne.

"Could I hold it for just a moment, feel it in my hands. I have dreamt of this moment," he implores.

I look from one to the other. Then I decide, and lift out two lumps, handing one to Marianne and one to Helvetius.

"It is so heavy!" Marianne exclaims, "much heavier than lead."

"At the root of creation moisture is dense," I quote my ancestor. "It is as concentrated as the womb of the Lord pregnant with our Cosmos."

Helvetius has his eyes closed, his fingers clawing like a cat.

"How do I know I am holding the Stone?" he contemplates out loud.

"Because it fills your soul with rapture," replies Marianne Schweitzer. She knows! I think to myself and am envious of her clarity.

Helvetius puts the stone back into its box. He too is moved by her simple words.

He drops down into the brown leather overstuffed chair by the fire, and pokes absentmindedly into the ashes.

"My whole life I have been tormented by a vision of the magic Stone, convinced it could never exist," he says. "I went to the University of Wittenberg so I could study the science method. I wanted to rid my mind forever of these visions and superstitions. My teachers maligned alchemy as the pinnacle of blindness. I was enthralled by their words and slowly my visions vanished behind walls of learning." He looks sad. "I married my wife and we had many discussions about the Art." He gestures with his head towards Madam Schweitzer who is listening intently. "I could argue both sides of the issue with ease. But then, about half a year ago, the dreams began. At first they were just half forgotten shards. But then they became more and more insistent. My visions returned from behind the bulwarks of Wittenberg. I saw the Stone enter in its chariot of glory like a Roman emperor on his triumphal procession. At first I ran away, hiding from its majesty. But wherever I went it followed me. I began a correspondence with some of my old professors at Wittenberg to soothe my madness. Then the Stone receded again, like a spent storm. And now you are here to confuse me further, to have my dreams chase me in broad daylight. I hope equally strongly that you are able to do what you say, and that I can chase you from my home an impostor."

Then he sinks into a silence so deep it feels primordial.

I look around the room until my eye rests on a carafe filled with deep red wine beside an ornate green stem glass. I fill the glass to the brim and gulp it down till my head swoons.

Madam Schweitzer looks at me with an expression I can only interpret as gratitude.

"I was taught alchemy by my father and together with him I have looked for the Stone since I was 11 years old. The mere possibility that you bring us the Red Sulphur makes me miss my father more than I can say."

I am surprised by her sudden intimate effusion and look at both husband and wife, he in the grip of a leaden gloom, she transported to a world beyond. And I know that *she*, not Helvetius, is the true alchemist. My heart rushes towards this woman with eyes so spacious I could travel within them forever.

I quickly take my leave. Helvetius no longer acknowledges me and I let myself out of the study before Madam Schweitzer has a further chance to talk.

Night descends early in these Northern lands. When I come outside I can barely see.

In darkness I wander the streets, eating my bread and avoiding the enticing calls of the ladies of the night. I dare not sleep for fear of my enemies. But this time, the tantalizing vision of the woman I just met keeps me warm.

When there is sufficient light outside, I leave town for the long walk to where the peasants live in hovels. Though adjacent to the city, in spirit it is as far away from the houses on Helvetius' grand square near the Parliament Court as is Venice: a perfect place to hide out and prepare myself for the Projection. I will need a laboratory to activate the Red Sulphur, to increase its spirits to their highest potency so it can make the medicine, the magical gold. This prospect hastens my step.

Soon I near the home of the blacksmith whose family I cured during the plague last year.

On a wall, stretched by its hind legs, is a hog cut open while a peasant with an ax is butchering it. It must have been slaughtered minutes go. The blood is still flowing. Several children stand around absorbed in the spectacle. The blood is caught in a wooden bucket. The butcher with his huge mustache, a cap diagonally on his head and a blue short tunic over frayed pants, holds his ax in both hands and swings it down with great force. Blood splatters everywhere and covers the faces of the nearby children, who shriek with delight. The work stops as I approach. They all look at me with suspicion. Strangers are not welcomed in these parts. They may carry the plague; a superstition of course, because as everyone knows the plague is spread by cats. In London, all cats have been destroyed.

It is raining again.

Smith's little house is made of red brick, stuccoed over in parts. I see some barrels and a scrawny tree under the grey sky. I knock on the door. When I cured his family from the plague last year, the blacksmith had offered me the use of his brother's smithy in gratitude, since his kin had perished some months before. I have come to collect.

Even with my beard and scruffy look he recognizes me instantly and exclaims, "Doctor Mundanus!" He is a burly fellow with arms like tree trunks and a neck as thick as his head. His black leather apron sticks out over a jolly belly and he wipes his hands on a cloth to shake mine. There is a big fire in the shop and he is working on horseshoes, lots of them. One glows red in the fire. My heart skips a beat and an acute longing for a laboratory rushes through me. He shakes my hand as if he won't let go. "Everyone has been healthier than ever," he booms with his large bass voice. "You have special connections to our Lord." He grins broadly. "Let me get the wife." He calls out to his apprentice to go to the house and get the mistress. "Do you still want to use the blacksmith shop across the field?" he asks. "I haven't rented it to anyone. It's yours for the taking. I don't want to lose my health by not giving you what is your due!"

That was easy! He is a good man. I don't even have to repeat my line that the cure reverses if the payment isn't made. He remembers it from last year. The wife comes out with the four children I saved.

"God bless your soul," she calls out. "Doctor Mundanus, God bless you. My, you look horrid! Come in and I'll get you a pint of ale." She beams at me as if I am her Savior come down in the world. No escaping her or her ale.

The ground around is mud. My boots sink in two inches. I can hear the suction as I walk. I almost stumble over a pig, who is just as surprised as I am. He squeals and I swear. The matron looks surprised as though the Lord himself had just uttered a curse. The three children run ahead, followed by a brown mutt with light brown legs who once had a hound in his ancestry.

Mistress Smith opens the Dutch door in a hospitable gesture. "Will you please come in, Doctor Mundanus? You know the way." I pass under a precarious awning into the house. After my eyes adjust to the relative dark I realize that the light outside had been much brighter than I had been aware. The light in these Low Lands by the sea has a silver tone, like the flash of reflected light from a sword through a haze.

The children run ahead and start playing near a fireplace the height of a grown man standing. This time the cast iron cauldron over the fire is actually boiling broth, not cinnabar, and the fragrances waft towards me. I am indeed starving. The wood fire crackles. In the back of the fireplace, under a protruding arc of red brick is a bread oven. Now I notice the aroma of fresh bread mixing in with the broth. I salivate. Mistress Smith pushes the children out of the way, goes over to a big barrel next to the fireplace and fills a large red earthenware mug with ale from the tap. She hands it to me and I gulp it down, more for hunger than thirst. Inside the structure looks much firmer than outside. The roof is high, held up by roughly hewn beams. The hard dirt floor is swept in the orderly local way. I sit down on a stool by the fire, next to the kids. I see a crib to the side and hear the baby cry. She picks it up and takes it to her full breast in one swoop. I doubt she even notices what she does. Her conversation continues with an unbroken stream of memories of the horrid year when all had died from the plague and doctor Mundanus had come to save them. She looks down and now seems to see the baby for the first time.

"We've decided to start again," she smiles at me through her tears. "He also goes to your account," she says as she lifts the baby to give him to me. I recoil in the slightest of ways but she notices, hurt. After a hesitation she forces the baby on me anyway. I can't refuse. She wants me to hold the baby as a blessing. I look into the face of a screaming infant enraged at having been interrupted from his meal. "His name is Daan, after Mundanus," she mentions simply. Suddenly the baby stops and looks through me intently. I feel a pang of guilt. I should have had my own son by now to pass on the Stone. It has gone from father to son since it had been created almost exactly seven score years ago. For reasons I don't understand the Stone moves through history by way of our bloodline. And at 42 I still have no offspring. The baby seems to see all this on my mind and holds very still for a moment. Then he shrieks louder than before and I quickly hand him back to the breast.

Outside the rain has stopped and a beam of pale sunlight comes in through the large window on the south wall. It lights up the room with a bright yellow cone, giving a greenish hue to the surrounding shadows. I stare at the back of a tow-headed boy in the center of the room whose hair lights up like a ball of gold. For a moment it pulls the whole room together into the single vanishing point of my perspective.

∞

After several helpings of broth, bread and ale have revived me, we walk across the field followed by a loud throng of children. She shoos them away when we reach her brother-in-law's black-smith shop. An uncut trunk of a gnarly tree like the caricature of a flying buttress props up the forward tipping mud brick wall in a permanently temporary measure. Next to it the shed itself struts forward like a cripple on crutches. The best part of the hovel is the roof with fairly new thatching.

"I have cleaned it up for you," Mistress Smith tells me. "I knew you would come back," she says with steely faith in her voice. "You can use it for as long as you please. If you want to stay here for the rest of your life it will be fine."

"Oh no," I reply quickly. "Only a few months. It's all I need, just a short while. I'll be gone by spring."

Inside, the first thing I see is the giant fireplace, big enough to forge large metal equipment. The rounded sand-colored hood projects at least three yards into the room, held up by two support pillars with unexpectedly elegant shapes. The base for the fire also protrudes some yards into the large open space and rests upon a knee-high arched oven under the fire pit.

Some blacksmith equipment is still hanging from the wall. The colors around are dominated by a moldy green and the space smells dank. Next to the giant hood is a cavernous bedstead, filled with a large straw mattress. In this bedstead, her entire in-law family had succumbed last year to the bubonic plague that had ravaged the country and changed all of our lives so completely. Next to the bedstead a simple ladder stands waiting. The frequently patched slats of ceiling suggest an attic. A large window casts its grey muted light into the empty space.

"Perfect!" I say.

Mistress Smith looks sad. "They were good people," she tells no one in particular. "They served the Lord and worked hard. Five children! Five children!" In her voice is a mixture of incomprehension and an unselfconscious accusation of her Lord. I stay very still, not even breathing, in an attempt not to obstruct her sorrow passing through the room.

Then suddenly she turns to me. "Without you we would have gone that same way. My children already had the boils. But you gave them the drops and they were cured overnight. My husband had the chills and your drops cured him too. We have not been sick ever since. Not even the usual colds. I didn't dare to tell no one at the time, afraid they might burn you as a sorcerer."

I smile, knowing she is right. Salomon Trismosin had almost been burnt on the stake three times while sojourning in the states of Bologna, Florence and Venice. What people do not understand, they call witchcraft.

"Is there anything you need?" she inquires. I hesitate, wondering if I can trust her. Then I decide to do so. "I will need bellows and apothecary tools to make more medicine. Some cast iron pots and flasks. And a distiller." She looks worried that I might be a sorcerer after all.

I allay her unspoken fear. "You must have heard of apothecaries. I'm an apothecary, making medicine. I need to make more drops. The plague might return and I want to be prepared. I especially need a distiller."

She nods, suddenly fully grasping the importance of my mission.

"I will send over an apprentice who can get you what you need. I'll get you some furniture as well," she says, surveying the damp empty barnlike space.

"I have to burn the mattress. I will need fresh straw." She looks at me quizzically. "There still may be disease in the mattress. The plague sometimes stays dormant for some time before it flares up again. All cloth and bed straw needs burning." I am met with a look of solid incomprehension.

"I will send over the apprentice," she repeats. She turns around and leaves through the barn door.

౮

She sends me all that I have asked for, and more. I have pots and bowls, glassware, a tripod stool with a green cloth cover, baskets, linen – her gratitude knows no bounds. I have a barrel of ale and a long stem white foam pipe with a pot of fragrant tobacco, and five buckets of water in a large earthenware cistern. Meat from the pig slaughtered this morning hangs from the crossbeam. Alongside the Lord they thank *me*, with all the goods they can spare. The apprentice brought more firewood than needed for a week. He promised to return in the morning with more supplies. I feel rich like a king, eating the cake she made for me by the light of some of the seven candles I requested and received from Mistress Smith.

Then I heat up enough water for the first decent wash since last August just before the London fires. I take some sesame oil, a sprinkle of potash, alkali, and some fragrant essence I have brought with me in a tiny flask from my last trip to Venice. I mix them all together in a large cauldron full of clean rain water, and boil them on a fire made from the embers I have taken along from Mistress Smith's fireplace. I always carry with me ingredients to make soap. The perfume makes my body languid in anticipation of feeling the warm water all over my itching skin. When the water is just at the right temperature, I take off my clothes, all of them, a habit many in these Northern Lands find utterly indecent. But I follow the tradition of the ancient Romans, who knew more about health than anyone today. With a large ladle I scoop out the water and sprinkle it lavishly over my aching body. The heat of the water melts my soul and mollifies my muscles. I sigh loudly. My delicious soap washes away months of hardship and grief. I wash and scrub until my whole body steams with delight, filling the air with a vaporous cloud. Then I wash my clothes in the soapy cauldron water, which instantly turns black. Stark naked, I push the cauldron outside and throw the black water dregs onto the soggy brown slush beside the door. Back inside, I wrap myself tightly in a blanket and repeat the process. After several iterations the water in which I clean my garments remains clear. I put them to dry in the oven under the fire pit, leaving the metal door open for the moisture to evaporate into the room. Inhaling the steam of clean garments mixed with Venetian perfume, I sit dreaming away by the blazing fire. It is then I see Salomon Trismosin. He walks towards me out of the fire.

He has visited me in this manner since I was a boy, clear as a dream. I hear his voice calling my name: "Giovanni Theodore, listen carefully." That's how he usually begins. My heart flows over with affection. The melting is complete and my being has become completely fluid – my soul a thick liquid, like quicksilver blood. Salomon Trismosin always looks the same to me: fleshed out in the way he had drawn himself next to the First Treatise of his book *Splendor Solis*, a tall man with grey curls down to his shoulder blades, and the long thin fingers of a lute player. A blue toga is draped around him in many folds and a cape hangs from his shoulders. He has a long beard like God the Father and melancholy dark eyes under a brown magus hat, and looks at me intently.

> "Go to the house of ox pulled plow
> In a carriage fetchest thou
> The one to heal
> who is no other

Than thine offspring's future mother."

He always talks incomprehensibly at first. I never ask questions.

"At the dark moon take a quarter grain of my Red Sulphur and melt it in a fire of the fourth degree. Then build in your mind the naked form of a woman you desire until she will not leave. Enter the molten sulphur in her belly and let it cook in a fire of the first degree. Do you understand?"

I shake my head, having no full understanding of his words. Then he vanishes, until all that remains is the kindest of smiles and the confident words "You will understand." As always, a momentary parchment scroll in his handwriting from his manuscript *Golden Treasure and Art Room* drifts on my eyeballs, in the shape of a goblet, like a picture dwelling on the dark eye after having seen brightness. It says

> Study what thou art,
> Whereof thou art a part,
> What thou knowest of this art,
> This is really what thou art.
> All that is without thee
> Also is within,
> Thus wrote Trismosin.

I always carry with me a list of new moons for the next 10 years. The new moon is auspicious in starting any alchemical procedure. The next new moon is on Christmas Eve, two days from now: *very* auspicious.

I know that the fire has nine degrees, ranging from the heat of the belly, which incubates, to the great fire which is the master of all fires and melts, burns, dissolves, expels what is bad and saves what is good. The fourth fire is made in the fixating furnace. It melts the metal and lets it run, then fixes it into a malleable substance like wax. I smell the Venetian perfume I used in the water while washing my clothes fill the room and realize that the compartment below the fire pit can be made into a perfect fixating furnace. I have to run a high fire for some hours, heating up the stones enough so they radiate down into the lower oven to the point when the Red Sulphur melts to a fixed fluidity just before coagulation. Then I have to perform the practice of desire.

I know the procedure of creating the naked woman of desire. I learned the art in India, where they call it Tantra. I remember my days in the East, having travelled to the lands of the Hindu by way of poetic Persia where I taught their chemysts much of what I knew while hiding in cryptic images the vast abyss of my ignorance. With some effort I force my mind back to the lands of the Hindu.

I have practiced the procedure many times. I will focus on light, shapes and sound and let them travel through the ancient channels of my body, up from my groin throughout every pathway of my being. Through breathing I will build up the pressure, as in the alchemical laboratory, until the passion breaks all boundaries and a great storm rages. Then I will call in Woman.

On the physical plane I shall create a fire of the first degree, the heat of the belly. This is obtained by wrapping the material in fresh horse manure, which is easy to get around here. After the tantric practice I will wrap the drop of waxen Stone in soft leather and cover it with horse dung from all sides.

But which procedure is meant by
"Go to the house of ox pulled plow
In a carriage fetchest thou
The one to heal
who is no other
Than thine offspring's future mother?"

I have never read any alchemical text with a reference to this. It could mean anything at all. I curse the cryptic language of my ancestor and am ready to curse the whole enterprise of alchemy altogether. Could it refer to Christmas? To mother and child?

Then I put it out of my mind, knowing it will drive me to distraction. I will take it with me to my dreams and sit quietly, staring at the fire, consciously keeping my mind utterly blank. Maybe Salomon Trismosin will return... He does not. But my clothes are dry. I put them on, climb up the ladder to the bedstead with the fresh straw mattress and fall deeply into a dreamless void.

₠ℂ

I wake up disoriented, not knowing where I am, smelling dry ashes and mold. I could be anywhere. Then I realize that I have woken to an insistent knocking on the door.

"Come in," I yell, and a young man enters, fiddling with the rope which holds together his short green tunic fastened over his frayed potato sack pants.

"Doctor Mundanus," he says with a sheepish grin, displaying several missing teeth, "I didn't want to wake you, but you have slept around the sun twice and the mistress was beginning to worry. It is Christmas Eve after noon."

"No!" I yell out loud.

The apprentice takes a step back.

"Not you!" I scramble out of the bedstead, not realizing it is several feet off the ground. I almost come crashing down and at the last minute grab the unsteady ladder, which falls over. I tumble down to the floor holding on the side of the bedstead wall. The crash fully wakes me.

Hanging off by one arm I ask him, incredulously: "Christmas Eve after noon?"

He nods awkwardly, obviously wishing to be back in the blacksmith shop. I must look like a madman to him, with my hair standing on end having gone all curly from the wash.

I will just have a few hours before the new moon night.

Near the fireplace there still is some water in a large wooden bucket. I stick my head down into it and look at the wood slats around me under the water. For some reason that balances me.

When I come up for air I see the apprentice staring at me in horror. He must never have seen a man with his head in a bucket of water.

I drip all over. "After you finish, fetch me a few more buckets of water." I notice the authority in my voice and realize I am coming to my senses. He quickly brings in the firewood, piling it next to the fireplace. I see that an intoxicatingly fragrant fresh loaf of bread has been placed on my green-cushioned tripod stool next to a roast chicken.

"Bring in firewood for three days!" I yell out. He nods, turns on his heels and runs out.

I follow him outside. I can't believe I slept for two nights and a day! Through squinted eyes I see a cloudy sky and feel the wet, cold December wind. Suddenly I remember and call after him: "I will need a bag of fresh horse manure before the night. And a bottle of gin!" He turns his head indicating he has heard me. I go back in to make the biggest roaring fire the large hooded pit will suffer.

I construct the logs like a native tent I've seen etched by travelers to the New World. Much air has to draw into the heart of the fire to make it blaze. I pile up kindling in the center. Soon the roar of fresh flames begins to fill the room. I keep on adding wood and pumping large bellows to raise the highest flame I dare to evoke without burning down the hovel. When the fire has become steady I take some hay from the mattress and put in the fixing furnace below. The moment the straw begins to singe the temperature will be perfect. I sit back on my green cushioned stool and ravenously wolf down half the loaf of fragrant bread and much of the roast chicken. Then I light up the long stem sea foam pipe and deeply inhale the sweet tobacco. My lungs fill with pleasure as I recall my days in the lands of the Hindu. There I met a man who had command of the *nagas*, the Cobra brood who dance near streams and make the land fertile. They are the guardians of treasure and the makers of rain. From him I learned to concentrate the tantric love body into a powerful elixir, much like the Stone. After this he taught me the

Cobra dance to guard the Red Sulphur and to help me find my way to its treasured heart.

The furnace heats slowly, as the roof of the oven under the fire pit is three stone thick. That means the heat will be even and lasting. Around nightfall I notice a whiff of singed straw hover over the strong smell of burning wood. From the metal door of the fixing furnace, left purposely slightly ajar, smoke emerges. I remove the straw and cast it into the flames, where it sparks directly up the chimney. Now I will prepare for the Red Sulphur and the dance of desire.

I light all seven candles and arrange them around the fire-place. Then I go over to the bedstead and lift out my satchel to open the ivory box and take out one of the heavy lumps of Red Sulphur. My blood heats up at the touch. With my razor sharp knife, I cut off a piece the size of one barley grain. Then I divide the grain into four pieces and put them on a hard metal dish, where they glimmer like golden tears.

I take them outside to show them to the cosmos. The stars are bright in the pitch darkness. All clouds have disappeared and the Milky Way coils like a giant serpent through the icy sky. All stars gaze at me, holding their breath, hovering very still. These golden tears are the solid intelligence of Genesis as it still lives invisibly in the roots of metals from the time the world came into being. The night is pregnant with her own beginnings. Sat-isfied, I go back in, followed by the steam arising from my breath like the smoke of a fire -breathing dragon. I close the door behind me, and delight in the heat of the room. By now the fire is needed only to keep the room warm and to distill gin into the pure alcohol in which to dissolve the activated Red Sul-phur for the medicine. Where she got it I don't know, but Mis-tress Smith came up with a perfect glass distiller. There must be an apothecary nearby who uses horses, so she might have gotten it in exchange for horseshoes. It looks like a glass stork with a perfect round head and a long straight beak feeding into an on-ion shaped glass vessel. After taking a swig, I pour Old Dutch gin into the belly of the stork and place it in a pot of boiling water hanging to the side of the fire. Its beak reaches far enough outside of the moderate flames to drip the steam from its head as it cools into the waiting onion vessel. Now I can pay all my attention to the small grains of Red Sulphur. I inspect the bag of horse manure the apprentice has brought together with the clay bottle of Dutch gin I use for distilling. It is still steaming and reeks strongly. Perfect! I quickly close the bag.

I place myself in front of the fire, focused in fixed concentration, and start my trance evoking dance: feet tapping, head back, right arm writhing up in the way of the serpent, feeling my neck flare like a cobra hood. I am drawn into the world of the *naga* brood. I see rivers flowing out of the fire and a rain coming down from the chimney. The dance reaches deeper and deeper into *naga* spirit until I <u>am</u> *naga*, one with the serpent. I feel my affinity with treasure; feel how I am its protector. With my left arm I raise the metal plate with the Red Sulphur drops and place it in the fixing furnace and close the metal door. The tapping slows, the dance dwindles down; I sink to the floor. The activation of the Stone has begun.

I rise and position myself on the green cushioned stool, straighten my back and for a long while purposefully think of nothing. After a long time I open the metal door of the furnace and instantly smell the melting Red Sulphur. Unlike the rotten egg smell of raw sulfur, active Red Sulphur smells like male seed. I feel the familiar swoon of the whiff of Stone filling my empty soul with its presence. Then I close the metal door again.

Now I have to I wait until I see her, the naked woman of desire, the incarnation of the goddess Diana. Each time she appears in a different form. Sometimes she is blond and pale satin, like Freya of the North; sometimes dark like an Ethiopian queen with skin of black velvet . To my great surprise the face that appears in the fire is Madam Marianne Schweitzer's. Her blond hair pulled back from her face has a reddish glow. It reveals her high forehead and the brown eyebrows pulled up in a questioning challenge. Her face is bent down slightly and tilted to the right so her wide-open grey blue eyes look up at me, the whites aglow. A hint of rings under her eyes attests to her maturity. Her nose has a pleasant slight curve at the bridge. But it is her small mouth that stands out most. The sensuous lips wear a shy sneer of irony, reflective to the left and seductive to the right. Her cheeks are round with a faint fullness under her chin, completing the look of mature womanhood. The flames' flickering hues wash over her fair skin and make her appear both solid and transparent. Light bounces off her, taut nipples boldly asserting their presence. Her breasts never suckled a child, though they are lower than the breasts of a maiden. Their roundness overwhelms me. I swallow, feeling desire rise. For a brief moment I am taken aback by the fact that she hails from this world. Until now the Stone has only sent consorts not found on this plane. I know I must see her again in the flesh and I foresee the endless complications of my future.

But my surprise vanishes as swiftly as it came, leaving only Red Sulphur passion burning at the ninth degree. I know that I shall be consumed. I am being lifted and thrown into the fire. I can feel her pliant skin arc under me as I grab with my hand under her buttocks pulling her towards me with my left hand grasping her back. Her undulating flesh writhes like a serpent up to my lips while her head is thrown back in abandon. I plant the force of Red Sulphur deeply inside her, and feel how we both awaken to another dimension where the stars curl in dazzling patterns, turning to color in swirls of desire. Travelling together at breakneck speed the flower opens as we fuse down a spiral toward the first seed of Cosmos: Red Sulphur fulfilled. I begin to feel her body weight lessen and I know she is taking flight, leaving me behind devastated by ecstasy and loss.

After I lie around for some time in the ruins of myself, I hear Salomon Trismosin's voice, reminding me of the fixing furnace. With slow movements, I open the door. The whole oven is aglow with supernal green light. The green glow is dazzling, like the eerie light of a hundred glowworms suffused with a thousand fireflies. The greening force of nature is fully awake.

I quickly take out the quarter grains with a leather strip, and hold them. I take the onion glass vessel, which now carries several spoons full of fresh alcohol, and drop one-quarter grain of the live Stone into it. There is a bright green flash as is sometimes seen at the conclusion of sunset, then a moment of froth and the fluid clarifies. There are enough drops here to heal scores of people.

After wrapping the other three live quarter grains in the boot leather strip, I open the bag near the door. The stench of the horse manure in which I wrap both the onion vessel and the leather pouch brings me back to my senses.

I feel depleted and I tremble. I know the change in me is irrevocable. A woman of this world has entered my soul.

Chapter Two

Mid-January 1667

1666, the Year of the Beast, is behind us, and the Devil has apparently not come. The world is still familiar, lovely and rotten. I wake up three times from the same dream: I ride in a carriage to a house in the city. It looks like Helvetius' home. I am reminded of my ancestor and his cryptic statement about a carriage and the mother of my offspring.

When dreams come in three I take notice. I still have no idea what Salomon Trismosin meant with his statement. But maybe I should just take it face value and get a cart to ride into town. The peasant I met Christmas day after church at the home of the smith had also been a patient of mine in '65 - that's why he had been invited. I know he has a horse drawn cart that he does not use in winter. He also very much wants to do me a favor.

So I set out early in the morning on the road to The Hague, wading through ankle deep snow on the ground. The sky is the lightest of blue. I have left the ivory box with three lumps of dormant Red Sulphur, and two quarter grains of the live Stone wrapped in leather, under the mattress. In my pocket I carry a small flask filled with the Medicine and a quarter grain of live Sulphur in a brown leather pouch: a gift for Madam Marianne, though Helvetius will think it for him.

I like the sandpaper crush of my soles on the snow mixed in with the soft crunch of straw in my boots to keep my feet warm, a very effective trick used in these parts. After plowing my way through the white cover I get to the wide road along the canal called the Vliet. This path is used for horses pulling the barge between Leyden and the Hague. The Romans dug this ancient canal when our Lord was still walking the earth. It is frozen over and people walk and skate on the ice. A peasant half bent by the weight of the sack on his back moves carefully along the path. A horse-pulled sleigh passes by me on the canal in the opposite direction, carrying three passengers covered by a colorful array of blankets. One of them has a long whip. A flock of birds swarms overhead, hungry for food now that everything is under snow cover. I have walked for the better part of the morning on my long detour to get to town. Had I gone in a straight line I would have been there already; but without a carriage. For some reason I need to get to town in a carriage...

I reach a place where the Vliet is hugged by dikes because the land is below water level. The Dutch have skillfully managed to pump out lakes to create dry land, a task usually left to God. On my left, opposite the dikes, are wooden farm houses under rickety roofs. They look more charming than usual, all covered by white caps. I'm trying to remember the farm of the peasant with the cart, recalling mainly how I arrived at his home too late last time. Most of his family had perished already, and I was able to save only him and his elder son. Then I recognize it, just past the old mill, which looks like a box on a pedestal with its four wings going in circles.

The farmhouse stands on the dike next to a bare winter tree. A peasant with a red cap is whipping a white horse pulling a large wooden sleigh up the steep incline to the barn. I hear laughter and the excited shouts of children; a whip cracks.

Then I see him again, the young man who glows eerily, the man from York. He's wearing the same elegant clothes, the large crescent silver Ottoman dagger gleams on his side, and this time I'm not going to lose him. He's on the ice, staring at me, with eyes so terribly familiar. I step towards him but am cut off by four children making a lot of raucous rushing down the dyke with a sled made of a box looking like a tiny barge, two pushing, one in it, one hanging over the side, sliding down to the frozen

canal. I'm almost run over and have to jump out of the way.
When I get back my balance he is gone. I look for him everywhere. He must be a phantom. There is no place to hide out in
this ice-scape. All I see is some men fishing through a hole in
the ice, looking down intently. Behind them a barge lies
stranded in the ice floor. In the background a horse pulled sleigh
transports barrels, the driver huddled into a ball against the cold.
The man from York is nowhere. Either he is a master in the art
of vanishing or I am having delusions. My heart beats like an
African drum in my throat. I'm suddenly freezing cold. Who is
this man York has sent to follow me and why does he look so
familiar?

I walk over to the house and call out. There is no answer.
Friendly dogs barking loudly run towards me and escort me to
the barn. I glance inside, heart pounding, skin crawling, shivering feverishly. The phantom is still hovering in my mind. After
my eyes get used to the dark I see a large open structure held up
in makeshift ways like a limping soldier patched up many a time.
Looking around I see a pile of peat stacked high, enough fuel to
last all winter. To my right I notice Klaas huddled by a peat fire.
He must have come in from heavy work because he looks bent
and tired. "Doctor!" he exclaims, happy to see me. With the
utmost respect he offers me his half broken chair and a bottle
of gin. I sit down with care and trepidation. The gin warms my
grateful gut. Behind us light streams in through the open door
brightening the otherwise forlorn atmosphere with a silver-gold
glow. The sun has come out. The light and the gin slowly drive
out my vision of York's man.

Klaas has not recovered from the loss of his family. He has
the drawn face and collapsed shoulders of a dispirited creature
waiting to die.

The man with the red cap enters leading the white horse by
a rope. He looks at me quizzically.

"Don't you remember Doctor Mundanus, Henk? He saved
your life and mine the year of the plague." Henk's bright face
lights up and he holds out his hand to greet me. His hand is

strong. He must be around twenty and obviously in charge, taking care of the farm and his listless father. Behind him enters a shy young woman. He turns in her direction: "Doctor Mundanus, meet my wife," and gestures for to her to come over. "Gerda, this is the man who saved us. This is the miracle maker we told you about. Everyone still talks about you, Mundanus. I would have hardly recognized you with your beard." He looks down at my clothes, puzzled. When I doctored around these parts I was wearing the garb of a well-heeled city man. This time I did not want to be recognized, so I am hiding behind my beard and shabby costume.

I hear screaming behind me. Children come running in one after the other, two of the four badly bruised and crying. One of the children has an arm folding in places where it shouldn't. The wrist seems broken and the shoulder dislocated. "The sled turned over," the eldest one cries, her dirty face streaming with tears over a mask of fear. She is afraid of being punished. Now I recognize the children and my fear of the Duke of York returns momentarily. I feel angry with them for preventing me from confronting my persecutor. Unexpectedly my mood changes: to Hell with the phantoms of York!

"It *was* a bit steep," I say, to save her from a beating. As the eldest she is being held responsible. Henk begins to scream at her, and the girl cries louder. Before this turns into mayhem I go over to the boy with the broken arm. I motion to Gerda to help me. The frightened young girl instantly retreats to the back of the barn. Henk glares after her. "Gerda's sibs," he explains. "Her parents died in the plague too." A shadow runs across his brow and he forgets his anger. At my behest Gerda loosens the boy's coat and takes it off with care, while soothing the boy so that he calms down instantly. I admire her nursing skills from the very first moment. He wears a coarse undergarment under his olive green coat and I smile at his long bright red stockings. "The under garment too," I say. Gerda hesitates. I get the slightest stir of annoyance against this Northern prudishness. A child, for God's sake! But she follows my orders and the boy lies before me shivering. With one quick movement, before he notices, I manipulate his shoulder back in place. He shrieks with pain. I have taken out the medicine flask, and now I tip it against my middle finger, just slightly wetting it. I rub it into his shoulder and the boy quiets down. A momentary green glow arises from the skin, so slight that most people would only notice if they knew to look for it. But Gerda sees it. I can see it in the startled look on her face. Then I set the wrist. The boy screams again and I repeat the application of the Medicine. Again I see Gerda noticing the fleeting green flash. A special young woman! I ask for two pieces of kindling and some rags, and style a makeshift splint as I have done so many times in my life as a doctor. Then I give him a liberal helping of gin. Within minutes the boy, with his arms in a sling and wrapped in a blanket, is playing again, shouting out loud and singing with the others, proudly showing off his mended arm. Gerda looks at me with gratitude and admiration. "I've seen folk lose an arm for less," she says. "My uncle was a sailor in the war with England. He came back with his arm smashed up like this little one. The barber in town had to take it off. Miracle worker you are alright. Thank you for my brother Peter."

"Don't let them sled down the steep part of the dike," I warn. Another round of gin passes and we begin to talk about the harvest of '66.

"The fields were rich," says Henk. Old Klaas nods. The gin is bringing him back to life. "But we had no families to bring them in. So many had died in '65 … Then Gerda organized groups of families to work on each other's fields. So we got the whole crop in." He sounds mighty proud of his clever wife. Gerda stares down, embarrassed. "What was I to do?" she remarks. "I was responsible for my siblings and the fields were aplenty. I did it for them," she concludes simply.

"Why did you come to see me?" Klaas asks me after some time.

"I need a carriage and horse for a day to go into town."

"You've come to the right place," Klaas exclaims heated by the gin. "You can take Belle," he points at the horse by the door. "We don't need her. And the cart we don't need either."

"I'll come with you," says Henk decisively. "It is a good time for selling wool. Gerda's sheep had more wool on them than we know what to do with. I'll bring it to market. It should fetch a good price in this cold. Gerda said we should hold on to it till winter."

"That's what my father used to do," she explains. "He used to say that wool is dearer in the winter cold, so hold on to it till then."

I look around and see many bales of wool in the back of the barn next to the cart – a large wooden platform surrounded by railings resting on two great wooden wheels shod with metal strips. They have thick spokes, are well crafted, and the axle looks sturdy. Two strong poles sticking out the front are to rest in the horse's harness. In my endless travels I have broken down with carts too often to trust them right off. I go over to the bales, looking at them admiringly, feeling the wool, and inspecting the cart all the while. "Beautiful wool," I praise them as I finish my inspection. The wood of the cart is in excellent shape and the axle well-greased. I can discover no fault.

"We'll go on the Vliet," Says Henk. "It's solid. My friend just came back from The Hague and told me his horse cart was fine all the way. The road is too heavy with slush. It started to melt right after snowfall and then it froze up again, so the ice is clear as glass. We'll leave when the cock crows," he decides.

"The kids will load up the wool. Just half, mind you. It will fetch even more next month," Gerda commands.

෨

They insist I sit in the cart, warmed by the bales of wool, while Henk leads the horse walking beside it. I feel like an old man, but I know it is a sign of respect, so I don't protest too much. It is a very comfortable way of travel, I must admit. Henk is holding a walking stick with a metal ice pick bottom. Belle is well shod and ready for the outing. As we start moving on the ice we see them all wave us out. Little Peter is singing at the top of his lungs.

Henk leads Belle carefully; the ice is slippery and sometimes gives an ominous cracking sound. I sit up in the cart, high off the ground, the large wheels coming up to near my shoulders. The poles are fastened to both sides of the horse with a leather contraption over a blanket to keep Belle warm. She seems not to mind the cold much, though her nose fumes with blows of steam. Henk, sure footed on enviable boots, is wearing his bright red cap and a thick yellow tunic over an old brown sweater and dark green pants. I breathe in the cold moist air and am surprised to feel myself being excited. Then I realize I am about to see Madam Marianne Schweitzer-Van Os. I'm both eager and apprehensive which translates into a sharp feeling of happiness and I give in to an urge to sing out loud. Henk joins in.

The city draws near. We ride beside the first houses along the canal. The ice here is used as a regular roadway, with many carts and people carrying heavy burdens. Donkeys with barrels on either side labor heavily. The steep roofs are laden with ice-crusted snow, and trees with frozen white trunks stand orderly along the canal, like guardsmen of winter. Activity bustles everywhere. Next to us a giant man is straining to pull a horse-cart stacked high with firewood. His animal must have perished. Belle slips for a moment but Henk holds her steady. A large barge dreaming of summer lies frozen in the ice, like an incongruous remnant of another era. There are dozens of people now, some skating, and some pushing barrels. People in city garb, incongruous with their dainty shoes and colorful capes, and hats designed for elegance, not for the razor sharp cold, are shivering among the more appropriately clad lower classes with their many layers of warm rags.

I find myself looking for my pursuer with the Ottoman dagger, expecting him to turn up around every corner. York must have sent others besides just him, but this one frightens me down to my soul. There is something profoundly threatening about this glowing man with his invisibility cloak that seems to make him appear and disappear at will.

Now we are passing a wall of houses. The buildings stand shoulder to shoulder, a symphony of roofs, never repeating, though harmonious in a haphazard kind of way. Some are as high as five stories, counting the large attics, and look like warehouses for the many goods a big city requires. It is as though the air itself has changed, with the red brick presences solemnly proclaiming the urban conquest over the rural grassland from which they arose.

Before us, streets of many houses lead to the heart of town. We enter a labyrinth of increasingly narrow corridors where the sounds of our metal wheel-covers on cobble stones echo back at us from all sides. These dark urban passages are framed by homes and shops. Women with brooms tidy up the streets while house-proud wives and maids wash windows leaving sheets of ice on the windowpanes.

As we near our goal the buildings become statelier, built to impress. Soon I see Helvetius' home, like a giant in a crowd, defending itself proudly against its encroaching stone neighbors. My heart beats in my throat as I approach the flesh of my vision.

Henk agrees to come and pick me up in the early afternoon so that we may return before nightfall, and he sets off to the market to find cold buyers for his warm wool.

Resisting a childish desire to run away, I drop the large knocker loudly on its metal plate. The door opens and an unknown young woman in a blue frock and a sand colored top stands before me with the challenging look of a domestic defending the integrity of her mistress' home. Behind her I see Marianne standing by the large lead paned window reading a letter. Her low cut top reveals the intoxicating luminescence of her skin. She looks up and sees me. "Mundanus!" She exclaims, pleased. The maid looks surprised. My rags contrast sharply with the elegance inside the black and white marbled interior. An open door gives a view into a sumptuous red room I have not seen before. Ahead of me a pendulum clock – high up with its weights hanging down low, next to a rich gold-framed painting of an unimaginative hunting scene – chimes 10 times. Madam Marianne comes up to me and warmly shakes my hand. "I'm so glad you returned. So eager to talk with you and witness your Art! Let me get Helvetius. He has been waiting for you with great expectation."

I have trouble breathing. Her presence in the flesh is even more intoxicating than her apparition as the goddess Diana called forth by the Stone. "But I need to talk to you first," she whispers and motions for me to follow her to the red room. After I enter she closes the door. I am alone with her and breathe her perfume. It is hard to concentrate. Then I notice she has tears in her eyes.

"It concerns my niece, Clara. You met her last time you were here. She is very ill. I'm afraid she is dying. Helvetius is treating her without success. I know him, he becomes stubborn. When he gets that look in his eyes he will be unyielding until the patient dies. It is his pride." Marianne is rambling, obviously both upset and relieved that she can talk to me. "I so hoped you would come. I know you are a doctor. You are a true Magus. I just know. Please take her away from here before my husband bleeds her to death. I trust you more than I do my husband. It is as if I have known you forever. Really known you!" The moment is intimate as her hand lingers on my sleeve. I am holding my breath, quieting myself under her touch, which to me feels like a brief caress. Her distress softens my passion. Suddenly I understand: the carriage. I have to take the young niece with me in the carriage.

"Where is she?" I ask.

Marianne leads me to the back of the house, to a bright ochre room lit by a pale winter morning's light. To my right is a wood stove with a large black belly, to the left a large loom with a remarkable unfinished cloth, the weaving having stopped

in mid-stream. The room is stuffy and overheated. In the bedstead draped with green curtains lies the young woman shivering. Her teeth are clattering. I see immediately that the girl is far
gone. I don't know if even the Panacea I carry with me can restore her to life.

"How long has this been going on?" I ask while I put my
hand on her forehead. It is burning like an out of control fire of
the ninth degree.

"For about a week. Helvetius has been bleeding her every
day. And he has been giving her all sorts of medicine. But she
is not responding."

I suppress a curse as I remove the pile of blankets which
cover her and make her inner furnace burn even brighter. "Is
she drinking?" I inquire.

"Very little," replies Marianne. "It hurts her to drink. We try
to get fluids into her but she cannot swallow. It is hard to get
the medicine into her."

"And still he bleeds her?" I ask incredulously.

"That's what the physicians do," Marianne says, with open
despair. "The barber comes every day to draw the bad blood.
And every day she is getting weaker. I can hardly look at her
anymore. She is so pale. Look! Her skin is almost transparent."

"Fools," I mutter. These physicians with their ideas about
drawing out the weakened blood and their barbers with tourni-
quets opening the veins to breathe them, they don't know that
what it really drains out is the invisible spirit born with each one
of us.

I ask for some white wine, and within moments a servant
called Mina brings me a large carafe. I go to the bowl next to
the bed, empty and clean. I wash my hands with the wine, something I learned from a doctor in Venice who insisted on cleansing with spirits before every medical procedure. Marianne looks
startled. No physician she has seen washes his hands with alcohol. I don't take time to explain, but take the flask with the universal medicine out of my pocket and shake it, looking intently
at Marianne in order to enhance the attraction of the elixir, (and

because it is hard for me to keep my eyes off her.) She looks away, shy. I open Clara's mouth, which clatters in her freezing heat, and squeeze three drops under her tongue. The flash of green is very pronounced, and I wonder if it is because the medicine can feel the crackling atmosphere of Marianne's presence, or if Red Sulphur unveils its healing love more ardently to Clara than to other mortals.

Within minutes Clara begins to breathe more deeply. At that moment the barber comes to the back door for the daily bloodletting. I motion to Marianne to send him away.

"Doctor's orders!" he exclaims and pushes his way through.

"Get out of my house!" Marianne calls out in a staccato threat, emphasizing each word. But the barber clearly does not take orders from a woman. I step in, but my shabby presence does not impress him. He is a burly man of considerable strength, able to pull even the most reluctant tooth, displaying an ardent pride in his surgery. He takes out his tourniquet and his venipuncture knife to open poor Clara's vein. If he does so the elixir may turn against her, feeling betrayed. I have to stop him.

"Get Helvetius!" I exclaim and Marianne rushes out. That stops the barber for a moment. "No need, Mistress," he yells after her. "The doctor has given very clear instructions."

"Could you please hold off for just a moment," I implore.

"I have a busy morning, many more patients to bleed," he says, holding up his sharp knife, the blood of the previous person still smeared along the blade. He takes a rag to wipe it off. Suddenly I feel a powerful authority enter my being.

"Stop!" I say, and step between him and Clara.

"And who are you," he replies scornfully. "An insolent beggar?"

"I'm a doctor," I counter.

He looks me up and down, incredulously. Then he is convinced that I'm just a nuisance and he wipes me away like a buzzing fly. But I feel myself get larger, my eyes aflame. No one will come between me and my patient! With a lightning quick movement I press a place in his neck shown to me by a doctor in India, used by him to paralyze patients momentarily before surgery. The barber sinks to the floor.

"I am sorry to do this," I apologize. "But you need to learn to listen. My next touch will make you sleep for an hour." He looks at me in sudden awe, unable to move.

At this point Helvetius enters. He calls off the barber's surgery and I touch the frozen puncturist in the release point. He flees, terrified.

"What did you do to him?" Helvetius asks, both curious and annoyed. I don't respond to his inquiry. I just want to get him out before his professional jealousy kicks in and he claims the patient for himself, which would be the end of Clara. I know I will have to take her with me. Helvetius goes over to Clara, his face expressing a profound love for his niece. He looks worried as he feels her pulse. Then he turns to me. "What happened?" he asks, dumbfounded. "Her pulse is regular. When I saw her early this morning she was close to death. I didn't want to tell you," he continues, talking to Marianne, "but I was frightened. The odor of death was all over her. But it is gone." He looks torn between disbelief and relief.

Both Marianne and I are silent. He looks imploringly back and forth at each of us.

"I don't understand!" he insists.

"Come upstairs," I coax him to seduce him away from Clara, "and I'll give you a piece of the Stone you desire. I will perform a projection on lead." He wavers, not knowing whether to leave his niece right this moment. He looks at her with deep concern, bends over and gently kisses her forehead. Then his curiosity gets the better of him and he rushes ahead of me up the stairs to a room diagonally across the hall from the study I visited last time.

I am very surprised to see an entire alchemy workshop. The shelves are lined with dozens of medicines like a rich apothecary. A great many alchemical instruments are neatly arranged on shelves. Excellent distillers and pelican flasks are waiting for an alchemist. The cauldron of cinnabar hangs in the fire, moved here from his study.

"You have a complete Vulcanian shop here!" I exclaim in admiration. "You who scorns the Art!"

Helvetius points distractedly to Marianne. "It's her workshop." Now it is my turn to be stunned. I could never have expected a woman to have such a grand laboratory. Helvetius still looks shocked by what he witnessed downstairs with Clara. Then he appears to make a decision. "I suspect you have something to do with Clara's miraculous recovery." He concludes thoughtfully. I hear traces of gratitude, love and envy. "And I still owe you my explanation from last time, why I wrote my treatise so critical of the Art in response to Sir Kenelm Digbys *Sympathetick Powder.*"

I am truly curious about this and my attitude shifts from competition – which might be due to the scent of Marianne Schweitzer-Van Os – to the call of Trismosin's mission. It is my task to demonstrate to philosophic leaders of my generation the verity of Red Sulphur in order to make them honor their ancestors' wisdom and keep searching for the Stone and the verity of the universal medicine. Human wisdom does not move forward; it shifts sideways along a cosmic spectrum. New discoveries are made while ancient knowledge is forgotten.

"In this day and age," says Helvetius, "if you confess to an interest in the spagyric arts physicians heap you with scorn. They call you Bombastic, a follower of Paracelsus," whose actual name, I'm well aware, is Theophrastus Bombastus von Hohenheim. "Today we have surpassed his skills and he is considered old fashioned. I am the physician to the young Prince of Orange. If I were to confess to my love of the Art I would lose my position."

"So you bleed people to death because it is more fashionable!" I exclaim. Paracelsus was a star pupil of Salomon Trismosin, and the modern certainty of progress enrages me.

I see Helvetius stare behind me and I turn. Marianne is looking at him with derision in her eyes. I have apparently said what she, as a true adept of the Great Art, had long thought.

"One year's fashion is another year's folly," I lecture him disdainfully. "Today we believe in progression. We believe we get wiser by the day. We have faith in the future. Yesterday they sought all wisdom in the past. And tomorrow they may think yet something completely different altogether. But you can't profess against the Art just because it goes against fashion!"

"If it is to diminish a grand reputation you do," Marianne says from behind me, quiet and without accusation.

To change the subject I point to the many flasks of drops, pots of herbs and vials of pills.

"To what end so many Medicaments?" I inquire. "Unless the days of your life have reached their pre-ordained number, against which all medicines are powerless, the spagyric arts know only of one medicine, the Panacea." I sound terribly pompous, a true Bombastic for sure, but I know it will get him going. I need some time to make up my mind as to what to do next with Clara. It works.

"You are talking about the universal medicament that is said to rejuvenate, prolong life, cure all diseases otherwise incurable, and many other such things," Helvetius holds forth in a voice matching mine in sheer pomp. "But I have never met a man who can lead us to that fountain of youth. No man at all." I turn my head and smile at Marianne behind me who has just witnessed the power of the Panacea. She acknowledges me with gratitude. Helvetius doesn't notice our brief exchange. He is fully absorbed in his argument. "And from the books the ancients left behind you cannot learn it. It is like drawing water with a sieve. Anyway, I don't believe in universal medicine. For each patient medicine works differently. Paul drinking wine gets filled with fear, but Matthias sings and Luke weeps. So they need different medication. Paul's blood turns bitter, his skin prickles like flea bites and in pestilential times he gets blistering chilblains. Matthias blood is sweet and putrid and during the plague he gets tumors. Luke's blood is salty and during the plague he goes mad till he dies. Each needs a different treatment," Helvetius rattles off the familiar arguments of contemporary physicians against their alchemist forebears. "No one medicine can cure them all. For Paul I use the salt of the herb sorrel; for Matthias the herb fumitory, for Luke I employ the help of the sweet moistening *mercury* of the herb brook-lime, or red colewort. So a prudent physician doubts the universal medicine," he concludes, combative.

"I have seen a needle soaked in the Great Medicine pierce the heart of a man thought dead by physicians, and he revived," I remark, remembering my Lazarus moment last year when a farmer's wife with ten children implored me to revive her dead husband.

"Did that really happen, Mundanus," Marianne asks me in awe. "Did you really see this happen? A needle to the heart?"

"Of course not," Helvetius exclaims with conviction. "He just says that for the sake of the argument." He continues to hold forth with increasing eloquence, forgetting entirely about his niece downstairs in dire condition. Marianne and I look at one another and I can feel her admiration as well as the urgency that we take care of Clara. She has just witnessed the green flash of the Elixir. She knows more than he. In order to not embarrass her with my staring eyes I turn back to him and argue further about the nature of the Panacea. Then I conclude that the Elixir and the Stone are one and the same.

"You promised me a piece of the Stone," he says.

I nod.

He looks embarrassed. I wait.

He looks down at the floor. It is obvious that it is not easy for him to say what he is about to. I expect a confession of some sort.

"When last you were here and gave me the stone to hold…" He pauses. I look over at Marianne. She seems embarrassed too. "I attempted to raze some of it with my finger nail." I remember him clawing like a cat, and smile. "I got no more than an invisible atom from under my nail after you left. I wrapped it in paper and injected it on the molten lead. Almost all of the lead vanished into the air. I was surprised that such a small amount was capable of doing that. What was left behind had been transmuted into some kind of glassy earth." He looks sheepishly. I can't help but laugh out loud.

"You're more dexterous a thief than an expert of the fire," I say with as much humor as the serious moment allows. Saving Clara is foremost in my mind. "You seem to have no understanding of the fuming nature of lead." Both Helvetius and Marianne exhale audibly, relieved that I seem to be so casual about the matter. I appreciate his honesty. I am well aware of his two mistakes. One I will tell him about. The other, the fact that he was using inactivated, dormant Red Sulphur, is my business. I am not going to initiate him into the ritual unveiling of the goddess; no casting pearls before swine – and especially not with Marianne standing right here with us in the room. "Had you wrapped your theft in yellow wax, so it would have been conserved from the fume of lead," I lecture him, "it would have penetrated into the lead and transmuted the lead into gold. But since you performed the operation directly in the fume, the medicine flew away. All gold, silver, tin, mercury, and the like are corrupted by lead vapors and likewise converted into brittle glass. Vitrification, we call it." I hear the clock downstairs chime 12 times and I know that Henk will be coming within two hours to get back to his home. In these parts winter twilight starts at 4.

"I will come back tomorrow to perform the transmutation. I will give you the stone now so you can study it." I take the leather pouch out of my pocket and open it, revealing the narcissus yellow glassy teardrop not much larger than a mustard seed. I put it in the palm of my hand and hand it to Marianne. Our hands touch and a bright green flash blushes through the activated live Sulphur which appears thrilled with our connection. She stares at the Stone in awe. Helvetius looks disappointed. I know that he cannot look to the hidden spark and only sees the apparent shell. He is not a true Artist. I have seen so many seekers after the Art. They see only the crust, and do not know that deep within the crust resides the brilliance of the sun, *Splendor Solis*. They remain disappointed and end their lives as bitter men. For an instant I can see Helvetius' future. Then I become wrapped up in his myriad questions about the Stone and its making. Did it take seven or nine months? I do not know where to begin. I know that all I say will bounce off the glassy surface of his mind which is as vitrified as his failed projection. I speak anyway, but my words are destined for Marianne, to momentarily distract her mind from her worries about Clara.

"The whole operation is performed in a crucible on an open fire and ends in no longer than four days."

He looks incredulous. "But all talk of seven or nine months to make the Stone!" he exclaims.

"Only Adepts can read the texts and understand their meaning. Therefore they say nothing certain about the true time it takes to prepare the mystery."

"But could you tell me some of its secret?" he implores me. I know that even if I tried I couldn't. His mind has closed around him like a vault. He is a man of his age, a child of Salomon Trismosin's prophecy that men of the future would no longer be able to see the spark of genesis that inspires all matter. Wittenberg has taught him well.

I speak lyrically to Marianne while looking at him, my heart aflame like a furnace. Transported by the fire within I express my passion in the language of the metals, directly quoting Trismosin: "I can't begin to tell you how the Stone of the Philosophers is made, or how the virginal glassy seal of *mercury* is broken inside which *the sun* emits its metallic splendor in golden rays, wonderfully colored like the eye of narcissus from which the Adepts gather their fire." I take a deep breath inhaling her intoxicating perfume. "With the help of the splendor of the sun within, volatile metals are fixed into gold." He looks at me in solid incomprehension.

Marianne is still holding the Stone in the palm of her hand. My words have penetrated her heart and she looks rapturous; our substances are fusing whether we want it or not. Then I see a gust of worry blow across her face. We need to act on Clara's behalf.

"But enough at this time and more in the morning." I hold up the leather pouch and she drops the seed of Red Sulphur back into it. I hand the pouch to her. "Hold it close to your body and feed it with your warmth until I return."

Downstairs a knock is heard. A servant comes up and whispers to Helvetius. He nods and turns to me.

"The young Prince needs my attention," he explains. "I have to leave right away." As he turns I sense my relief at seeing him go. His deaf ears have made me aware once again of our age of ignorance. Deep down, we are the same, he and I, each of us dealing with our benightedness in our own particular way. Neither of us could fashion the Stone. Despondent feelings like this are never far from the surface. I turn to Marianne. She smiles faintly. My eyes are attracted to her radiant shoulders and I avert my gaze.

Having seen Helvetius' inability to grasp the nature of the universal medicine I know that Marianne is right. If Clara stays here she will die.

An hour later Henk carries Clara to the cart out front while Marianne covers her with blankets where the bales of wool have been – Henk had a good day at market. Marianne had sent the servants off on errands so we are alone in our abduction.

"Where will you take her?" Marianne asks me. Henk explains the way to his house in such detail that she could backtrack every step if she so wished. "Clara is my sole family. She is my sister's daughter and all other members of my family have perished. Please, Mundanus, save her!"

"Come on," Henk exhorts me. "We need to leave, or we will travel by dark. And I don't like losing the cart and the horse to bandits." I nod. Unexpectedly Marianne embraces me. "Thank you, Mundanus. Save her." I am immobilized for a moment. In her mouth my moniker sounds like a caress. Henk looks at me with the sly smarts of a peasant who knows which way the wind blows. He smiles broadly showing a missing tooth. Embarrassed, I climb into the cart with Clara, keeping her warm with my body. I squeeze two more drops under her tongue. Her skin is no longer a transparent grey and I have some confidence she will pull through. Feeling the pulse in her neck I know that her heart is strong. The afterglow of Marianne's embrace stays with me until we pull into the barn at nightfall and Gerda puts Clara onto a makeshift mattress near the fire in the barn. I don't trust any of the existing beds. I had told all my patients to burn the bedding of their deceased, but I don't know how many have done so since linens are dear. I make a bed next to her and keep vigil through the night. Now that I know she is precious to Marianne, Clara is worth more to me than all but the Stone itself. I press my body against her to let her partake of my heat. My heart beats strongly as warm affection streams through me into the young woman's body.

∞

Gerda turns out to be a superlative nurse. Her touch heals. I have rarely seen such aptitude. After a day I can safely leave Clara in her care. The medicine is doing its work and any more drops would be harmful. I need to get back to my blacksmith shop and prepare my own projection. I have suddenly decided to buy a home around here. For this, I need gold.

I don't want to go back to my home in Venice until I get irrefutable news that my grandfather is truly dead. He's my sworn enemy. I'm repulsed by him and don't want to spend a moment in his presence. I despise what he did to my parents and I hold him responsible for their deaths. For no reason at all I miss my mother: her laughter, her beauty and her loneliness. I remember my father's many goodbyes as he would travel the world for her father Giovanni Dolfin, after whom I was given my Christian name. My grandfather hated my father, so he continuously sent him on long perilous journeys. I'm convinced my Grandfather is dead, or he'd be well over a century old, but there is no one to ask. And as for Trismosin's mission, being a stranger is an advantage. I'd rather not admit to myself that Marianne Schweitzer is the true reason for my sudden decision to stay in these otherwise drab overcast lands.

I toy with the idea of asking Marianne to attend the projection, since I know that her presence will double the amount of gold I can convert from lead. The laws of attraction govern the cosmos: the higher the flame, the greater the force of transmutation.

In the morning as I'm packing my satchel to set out on my long walk back to the smithy I hear a carriage rattle up the ice. It had been a quiet morning, so the noise is crisp. My first response is to hide. A fright of York's men makes the pit of my stomach go faint. I see a vision of the phantom youth with his crescent dagger.

"How is she?" I hear Marianne's eager voice entering the barn. In a complete reversal my soul now dances through my blood. I rush out of hiding to embrace her, but realize that Gerda is around. Marianne is obviously very pleased to see me, though her main expression is worry. I introduce them. "Clara is doing very well," Gerda states with confidence. "She is drinking milk and has eaten several eggs. But her mind is still like a fog on the meadow before dawn." I am startled by her simple peasant poetry. Marianne begins to sob, the tension of her fear for Clara's life finally breaking after a week of despair.

"Helvetius has gone off to treat the young Prince for his lungs. He will stay at the North-End Palace for some days," she tells me softly after some time, drinking the warm milk Gerda has served her. The children have all come in to gawk at Marianne. Her splendid city clothes and her wealthy carriage have created a stir. She smiles at them. "My siblings," Gerda explains and pauses, looking intently from Clara – still sleeping on the mattress by the fire, with a glow on her face which makes her look healthier than she is – to Marianne, who has glistening cheeks from her recent tears. Written on Gerda's high round forehead under the white cap which covers her hair is a studying frown. Her lips, displaying the faintest of smiles, look both shy and reflective. Her obvious intelligence is striking. "The Lady must be her sister," she concludes. Only now do I see the striking resemblance hidden under a thin veneer of difference.

"She is the daughter of my elder sister," says Marianne. "She is all the family I have in the world."

"The pestilence," Gerda remarks calmly. Marianne nods, quieting immediately from her anxious memories by Gerda's simple acceptance of facts. The plague is the great equalizer; it binds the classes in the same experience.

Clara stirs. In a medical reflex I go over to her and look closely into her eyes as they open. Her grey blue eyes are like Marianne's, I now notice. Confusion covers them like shreds of mist. Gerda's description is accurate. Clara stares straight at me, startled. Then some kind of recognition flickers, not of me, but of someone she sees through me. I instinctively look behind me to see if someone is standing there. I understand the religious fervor in her looks as that of a woman who beholds her Savior. The blush on her cheeks is not just from the glow of the fire. A smile of comprehension dawns all over Clara's dewy face. She instinctively knows she has returned from the dead and that it was I who saved her. Her adoration makes me uncomfortable, yet I stare back at her. Her lips aren't as full as Marianne's, her nose is more even and the chin carries less of the pleasing flesh which makes Marianne look like the ripe fruit of summer. But through the clarity of Gerda's vision I now see the resemblance, instantly visible in her countenance, as if she and her aunt had been glossed individually over identical layers of under painting.

Marianne bends over Clara from the other side of the mattress and hugs her tightly. "I am so glad, so glad! I thought I had lost you."

"Aunt Marianne," she whispers, full of affection. Then she looks around, puzzled.

"You are at the farm of friends," I reply to her puzzlement. "We brought you to the country to heal from an illness that almost took you from us." Marianne begins to cry for utter relief. "Doctor Mundanus saved you," she adds looking at me with gratitude. Gerda has taken a clean moist rag to wash down Clara's sweaty brow. The ecstatic transport on the patient's face returns as she looks at me. I quickly pivot away and pretend to be doing something important behind me, feeling quite foolish.

"This is Gerda," I say turning back. "She is nursing you back to health. She is the best nurse anyone could want. You're lucky," I say in heartfelt praise.

Marianne now looks at Gerda, as if for the first time. "Thank you," she whispers.

"Sleep for a bit longer, and when you wake again you will be fully restored," I say in a voice of medical authority.

Clara nods, her eyes flutter and roll up as she drifts away again into the mists of healing. I take out the dropper and pour a drop in a large, red earthenware pitcher of clear water. I take a ladle and mix it in for a long time. Then I siphon up a drop of the water from the pitcher and spill it on her half open lips. She licks it with her tongue without waking. "This will make her sleep for some time more," I explain to Gerda. "When she wakes, give her one small spoon full with every glass of milk she drinks."

"Here," says Marianne, giving her five silver guilders, "Please take this. It isn't much, but it is all I have on me." Gerda accepts it without eagerness or hesitation. This is more than she will get for most of her wool. She stuffs the coins in her rolled up yellow sleeve. I am certain Henk will never know. Gerda runs all the finances in their household. Then Marianne turns to me. "I don't know how to repay you," she mutters. I know how, but I dare not say. To have her present at the projection would increase the amount of lead I will be able to transmute into gold by a factor of two. I'm directly aware of this calculus by way of my inner thirst and dry throat as the heat of her presence desiccates me. We sit around in silence.

After some time I ask Gerda, "Is there a roof maker nearby?" Gerda nods and explains in detail where to go. It is a place close to town, more than an hour by foot. "Take Belle," she adds.

"I have to go on an errant," I explain to Marianne. "I need to buy lead."

Marianne instantly understands and her eyes display total attention. I don't explain further. "I will return before the end of the morning." Marianne nods, a momentary overcast of disappointment darkening her face. I take my leave to find a roof maker and buy six pounds of lead used for gutters.

ಬಿ

When I return the scene has not changed much except for the fact that Klaas and Henk are talking animatedly among themselves, oblivious of the three women. They look at me eagerly. I know they want me to decide in an argument they are having.

"My son here insists to buy more sheep with the money he made from the wool. I say we should put it away for hard times," Klaas bursts out.

"Gerda agrees with me," Henk retorts. Her words carry much weight. But Klaas' caution outweighs his respect for her in this instance. I witness the struggle between the expansion of strong youth and the fearful contraction of devastated age.

"Trust your children, Klaas. They are the future. You can't forever be frightened of the pestilence. It will kill your spirit and that will make you die before your day. Health of spirit matters most. And anyway, a fire does not care for a forest it already consumed. The charred remnants are too hearty. The pestilence won't return any time soon. Trust the future."

Henk looks at Gerda, satisfied. Klaas still hesitates.

"Don't worry, Father. You will never want," Gerda adds with a certainty which would convince even the fiercest doubt. Klaas sighs in surrender. A fresh breeze of youth washes through the barn.

Right on cue, Clara wakes, as if she had sensed the spirit of renewal.

I unload the lead from Belle's back.

"What is that for?" Henk asks curiously.

"Gutters," I reply without further explanation.

Marianne looks back and forth between her niece and the lead with equal love. The alchemical longing of her spirit enflames me even more. Distractedly I look at the pearls of her necklace on the vulnerable throat like bubbles of moon drops.

"I am hungry," says Clara. We all laugh for various reasons of relief. Gerda takes a large ham from the ceiling. "It's Christmas again," she exclaims. "Joy is born in the manger." I marvel at her wisdom.

ॐ

Toward the middle of the afternoon Marianne announces that she has to leave back for the city. Clara is in good hands and there is nothing more for her to do here. "I could give you a ride to your laboratory; the lead is heavy," she offers to me. After heartfelt goodbyes, with Clara crying but comfortable, we step outside where her carriage had been waiting. The black-glazed coach has doors in the side with an iron step protected by leather. The old driver, who had been waiting by an outside makeshift fire guarding the coach, already sits on a coachman's seat out front. We climb in behind him and I marvel at the steel spring suspension, a recent invention. I place the lead in front of us and we cover ourselves with thick blankets and furs. The ride is like floating compared to the motion of Henk's cart, which had rocked my guts. As we pass along the Vliet towards my smithy, huddled together under the same covers, warming one another with our bodies, I get up my courage to ask her.

"Do you trust the coachman?" I ask.

"With my life," she responds. "Hendrik was a groom in my father's stables and my grandfather's groom before him. He is the only servant to survive. Why do you ask?"

"I want you to come to my laboratory and assist me with a projection," I explain, pointing at the lead. "Send him home and ask him to return in the morning."

Marianne looks at me with sparkling excitement. Without hesitation she opens the small cabin window up front and speaks loudly, with the easy authority of a woman used to giving orders. "Hendrik, a change of plans," she says. "I will stay at the shop of doctor Mundanus. He needs my assistance. You drop us off and pick me up in the afternoon tomorrow."

Hendrik turns around without surprise or suspicion and nods briefly. There is complete trust between them.

Chapter Three

We're sitting in the back of the smithy at a low table made from some half rotten slats on a barrel. I have made a quick and pathetic effort to clean up the place, which is a labor like Hercules', who had to clean up 30 years of cow manure from the Augean stables. It is as humiliating a task for me as it had been for the great hero of old. I give it up almost instantly as futile. It smells like mold and disrepair. Marianne looks like a radiant white lotus surrounded by a fetid pool. When I pause my frantic activities I am aware of the cacophony of odors battling their way through the air: the mold mixed with the sweet spermatic smell of the activated Red Sulphur not quite drowning out years of wood rot and wet thatching; and lurking underneath, the deadly breath of mercury which was released when its seal was broken by Diana's bath. I have lit six candles and have cut the seventh in half for the yellow wax needed to protect the Stone from the fumes of the lead, mindful of the mistake Helvetius had made in his ignorance. In the flickering light my companion looks more alluring than ever.

Sipping her ale from the one mug Mistress Smith has given to me, she says: "I am of course most eager to see the projection. Nothing is nearer to my heart now that Clara is better. But my curiosity has the better of me. I can't stop thinking of who you are."

"I feel the same," I reply. "I wish nothing more than to know your history." I wait and realize that the polite course of action is to tell her my story first. I don't know if I should give her the long or the short version and decide somewhere in between.

I light up the long sea foam pipe with fragrant tobacco and pass it to her. She takes it, surprised. This is not the custom between gentlemen and ladies. I don't know if it is the custom anywhere, but I feel an impulse to share. After a puff she coughs uncontrollably and we both laugh.

"Your first?" I ask.

She nods, still coughing.

"You'll get used to it." I assure her. "It is actually delicious in the mouth and fills the lungs with courage."

She takes another puff, and then another. It is not courage she lacks.

After some time she nods: "Indeed."

"My real name is Giovanni Theodore, but they call me Mundanus, Theodore Mundanus, since I have spent my life traveling the world, searching for the mystery of the Stone."

"And you found it," she concludes.

"No, I did not. Not yet, at least."

"But you showed us the Red Sulphur?!" she exclaims with a slight undertone of exasperation. I pass the pipe to her again and she takes a thoughtful puff.

"The Red Sulphur I carry was handed down in my family from father to son for 160 years. It was made by my illustrious ancestor Salomon Trismosin."

"The author of *Splendor Solis?*" she asks in awe.

"You know it?" I return in surprise.

"The original 1598 Rorschach edition was my father's prize possession. He bequeathed it to Leyden University in his testament. I know it by heart!"

"Did you also read his diaries?" They were published with that same 1598 edition.

She nods, dazzled. "I could recite them to you word for word." I have the sudden urge to hear my ancestor's story spoken in the melodious alto of this woman who has entered my life in the surreptitious way of dreams. What woman inspiring

Diana in my soul would I meet in this day and age who can recite Salomon Trismosin's work?

"I am a man alone, not having heard the music of a woman's voice for a decade. Could you recite it to me?"

She hesitates. "Splendor Solis or the Diaries?" she asks.

"The diaries maybe?" I carry with me the leather bound copy of his detailed handwritten diaries – one of the two Trismosin family treasures. My great-grandfather had made a brief innocuous excerpt available for publication in the Rorschach edition.

I hand her the manuscript. "This is the original," I say. She takes it as if it were the Holy Grail. The smile on my face comes up straight from the earth through my feet by way of my heart to my lips. The world is alight with the presence of Woman.

"When I was a young fellow," she intones like a rhythmic chant from the Vespers, in a voice of the finest copper, "I came to a Miner named Flocker, who was also an Alchemist, but he kept his knowledge secret, and I could get nothing out of him. He used a Process with common Lead, adding to it a peculiar Sulphur, or Brimstone, he fixed the Lead until it became hard, then fluid, and later on soft like Wax. Of this prepared Lead, he took 20 Loth or 10 ounces, and 1 mark pure unalloyed Silver, put both materials in flux and kept the composition in fusion for half an hour. Thereupon he parted the Silver, cast it in an ingot, when half of it was Gold." I poor her another mug of ale, enchanted by her recital. I know this text will forever be linked to the sound of her fine copper voice etched upon my blissful soul.

She begins to narrate Trismosin's adventures in Venice where he finally learned the Art at the large laboratory of a Venetian Grandee who later drowned in the Adriatic. The Laboratory was then shut up by the family, but they kept the Chief Chemist. "Then I went away from Venice, to a still better place for my purpose, where Cabalistic and Magical books in Egyptian language were entrusted to my care, these I had carefully translated into Greek, and then again retranslated into Latin. There I found and captured the Treasure of the Egyptians."

I have searched in that way, trying to recapture Trismosin's knowledge; to no avail. Now, however, I consider myself fortunate. Without my quest, I would never have been in the company of this woman whose enchanting voice is as much a herald of my destiny as were the clumps of Red Sulphur I received from my father.

I can hear in her voice that she is coming to the end of the section she is reading. "After a while I saw the fundamental principles of this art, then I began working out the Best Tincture (but they all proceed, in a most indescribable manner from the same root), when I came to end of the Work I found such a beautiful red color as no scarlet can compare with, and such a treasure as words cannot tell, and which can be infinitely augmented. One part tinged 1,500 pages Silver into Gold. I will not tell how after manifold augmentation what quantities of Silver and other metal I tinged after the Multiplicatio. I was amazed.

Marianne sinks back, the leather bound folio at rest on her lap, and closes her eyes. The strain of the concentration of reading Salomon Trismosin's minuscule hand has engraved a frown on her forehead, which is now slowly lifting. I am acutely aware that this woman is the wife of another.

"How are you able to recite so directly without fault," I ask, stunned. "You read it as if from memory!"

"My father was an adept who looked for the Stone all his life." Her voice drops to soft velvet. "He always thought fulfillment to be just around the corner. When he died from the pestilence he was mainly amazed that he would pass before being initiated to the mysteries of the Stone." I have found my mystical sister, the lover of the Opus and of my soul, and she belongs to another. It hurts.

She hesitates. "But that is my story; you gave me Trismosin's, not yours." I feel caught in my habit of listening to others without divulging my own history. So I continue the tale:

"Trismosin died in Venice and our family stayed there in the German community. He had fashioned a Stone without equal. Trismosin knew that the age of his knowledge was about to go into eclipse and he wanted to make sure that later generations knew that once, in another age, this magical Stone had been made."

"Couldn't he have just told us how he made it?"

"In my family we have asked ourselves this question generation after generation. I think I have an inkling of his reasoning."

"What do you think?"

"Trismosin says that when you work the Stone you see ever further into time. Your mind opens up and time loses its river-like boundaries and becomes one simultaneous sea. He was among the last of his kind, the select brethren of Adepts who see great distances into the future like Master Nostradamus. In his diaries my family did not publish he speaks of his knowledge that soon the Art will be lost forever. Soon so-called adepts were to speak in riddles full of pretense about matters they have no direct knowledge of, the wisest among them confused like a blabbering child. He knew that an era of the world was ending. What still was clear to Trismosin's generation was to be vanishing before the rise of Natural Philosophy. Trismosin met the future and it was Copernicus. Trismosin's long conversations with Copernicus convinced him that the nature of natural philosophy was about to change from the inner spark of creation around which matter coagulates to the opaque external crust, from inside to outside. His descendants would look but not see. At the same time they were to see new things Trismosin's generation could never have seen. One vision replaces another like the constellations in the skies. And he knew that in those days to come, the days in which we now live, the vision of his era would be scorned and derided as superstition without worth. That's why he left us the Stone." I pause to gather my thoughts. "Our understanding does not just rely on logic. Our soul receives in the ardent embrace of love. She sees with lover's eyes.

And when our soul falls out of love, what once was apparent to her becomes immaterial. She longs for new embraces and finds new paramours. I think Trismosin's generation was the last to adore without question the Elixir from which the universe sprang. They could see it within every stone of nature, the way we see colors. Instead, Soul fell in love with Reason, with the direct perception of light; the sun became the center and measurement our passion. We fell in love with proportion, with numbers and with calculus. Even our best can no longer perceive the Elixir at the heart of all matter. I have tried my whole life to see it beneath the surface, but it repels me, eludes me, remains stubbornly invisible. It is the sting that scratches my soul and torments me. So I am like your father, but worse. For I carry the Stone with me every day. I know it exists for a fact, but I have lost its secret."

"You look sad," Marianne remarks.

"Whenever I'm present to the mystery of the Stone, like when the Stone healed Clara, I palpably feel the great mystery and how I am excluded from its essence. It makes me feel desolate."

"But you are closer to it than anyone; doesn't that give you any solace?"

"It makes the pain more acute. I think no one feels the loss of Trismosin's vision more painfully than I do. I carry around my constant undoing in an ivory box."

"But at least you get to act in the mysteries," she insists.

"As an actor, yes; but not as an author."

"Are you greedy?" she asks.

Her question silences me. I have had this thought myself many times. Why isn't my mission enough? But it just isn't. My heart is hollow, down deep. I feel pathetic. Here I am with the woman of my dreams...

"You are much like my father," she begins suddenly, as if she wants to give me something in return for my confessions. "From my earliest days I was like a son to him. Two of my three brothers had died as children and only the youngest boy, my elder sister Johanna, Clara's mother, and I survived to adult-hood. But neither my young brother nor Johanna had any inter-est in his laboratory. After mother died when I was ten I became very close to my father. He treated me like an equal and always told me to search diligently and learn all the alchemical texts by heart, like one does the Bible. Helvetius was a young friend of my father's." She pauses, strain emerging in her expression. "His wife and infant son had died in childbirth, which made me feel caring toward him. It reminded me of losing my mother when I was a child. He was exotic and he professed great inter-est in the Art. We had long conversations and I was taken with his eloquence. He was nine years my senior. I was young, not yet 18." Then, with a note of bitterness she adds: "But I found out later that it was not the philosophical gold he was after, but my father's. I am from a Dutch merchant family. Sixty years ago my great-grandfather Dirck van Os was one of the founders of the V.O.C., the Dutch United East-India Company, the trading company that now rules the world." I can see she has no pleas-ure in her fortune. "That was the gold Helvetius was after, that and the glory of being the physician to the Prince of Orange. By being married to me the elite became his clientele."

"You despise him," I conclude, not knowing whether to be elated for myself, or sad for her.

"No I do not," she replies with certainty, her face displaying a proud smile. "I was blinded by his appearance, his quick mind and his apparent knowledge of the Art. My father gave me free choice, though he warned me of his suspicions about Helvetius' intent. He told me the wealthy can never be sure of the source of the affection directed at them. I was disappointed, I must admit; horribly so. But I found that if I despised Helvetius, my life held no meaning and I would descend into a hatred of my own being. I began to focus on his kindness instead. After he got what he wanted he was kind to me. He knew that he had used me for his betterment and to make up for that he treated me with respect even though I could give him no children. I found solace for my barren life in his library, containing many books unavailable to my father. Helvetius had brought them with him to Holland from Wittenberg. At first I studied with the help of my father, and then on my own. I learned scores of Latin and German books by heart, hoping that their recitation would open the mysteries. But they did not. So I know in some small part the pain of which you speak. I built a laboratory with the best equipment money could buy. When we moved to our Van Os family home after Father passed I merged my state of the art equipment with my father's laboratory. You saw the result in our home." Again I am struck by my own certainty that it had been Helvetius' laboratory and could never have imagined it to be a woman's, even though I had read the works of Maria the Jewess, the much admired woman alchemist who had aptly remarked that the best souls have the stretch of rubber. In this case it had been *my* soul that was vitrified in a glass cage of preconceptions. I am reminded of the present by the beauty of her voice resuming her story.

"But I ended up where my father had, seduced but not fulfilled. That's why my encounter with you fills me with hope. Even if you yourself can't make it, the Stone itself matters more than either of us." She looks at me, her face aglow. To her the Stone is the fulfillment of two generations of anxious dreaming. In silence I prepare another pipe.

"What else is in the book?" she asks, eagerly. The book looks larger in her delicate lap than it usually does in my satchel.

"These are Salomon Trismosin's diaries, the full version. My family just allowed a few pages to reach publication in the edition you have in your library. Trismosin wanted to keep it in the family. Like the stone, it has to go from father to son in an endless chain."

"Do you have a son?" she asks me directly.

"No," I say and look at the ground. "No, I do not."

We silently share the tobacco.

"Tell me more about the Stone and tell me about yourself." She looks at me with an unavoidable quiet gaze which makes me feel uncomfortable. I'd much rather start the work of projection, but she seems to have forgotten all about that. Deep down I am flattered that her interest in me is even greater than her longing to witness the transmutation after two lifetimes of fruitless searching.

"The Stone is alive and always in danger, because it is the last of its kind like a fugitive from a distant past. It has not been made for more than a hundred years and all modern adepts end their lives like your father, like me. Or they write books to mislead others. I carry enough Red Sulphur to make more gold, if properly applied, than a whole country will need in a lifetime. Therefore the Stone is always incognito, forever unknown but to a few. Currently I'm being chased by the Duke of York, who wants it to finance his adventures in Africa. There's always someone hot on my heels. Trismosin's diary spells out my mission: in every generation some men of influence need to be shown the power of the Stone so they keep the memory alive of his world's accomplishment. Trismosin admits that it may be vain pride, yet he can't help himself. He needs the respect of his descendants. But he also alludes to something else. A mysterious matter he doesn't spell out; a revelation to take place after generations. It has to do with the life of the Stone. But he doesn't say more as if he carefully shrouds his knowledge. He only tells us that history travels in cycles of vision. And his cycle is ending. I am reminded of a sailor who had rounded the Cape of Good Hope once telling me that the night sky in the southern hemisphere is completely different from our own. Trismosin's firmament is no longer showing itself to us. His diaries are full of melancholy, like the voice of Jeremiah looking back at Jerusalem ravaged by time. Do you understand what I am trying to say?"

She nods, looking sad. "I don't know what saddens me more: my father's and my own fruitless search for what could never be recovered, or Trismosin' world ending. It feels as though we suffered similarly." She is transported back to Trismosin's loss. I know instantly that it will never let go of her. She has been inducted forever into the aching awareness of our inability to remedy the inexorable chasm in the fabric of time. I am grateful to my ancestor to have left us the signpost that reminds us that this rip had actually occurred. We now think that time runs steadily like a pendulum clock once set in motion. But that is not so. Each era has its own vision, time its own quality, and the continuity of the ages is an illusion.

We share the pipe in silence.

"I lost my mother when I was ten," I hear myself say. "Just like you. She's coming back to me all the time since first I met you. Not that you remind me of her. But you bring me a solace I have not felt since she passed."

Marianne has tears in her eyes. "I feel the same," she responds.

The orphan intimacy between us feels both familiar and fresh.

ℂℂ

I have explained to Marianne that Diana's bath – when the goddess disrobes and the inner spark of the metals rises to the naked surface as the world turns inside out – is governed by the laws of attraction. This holds the whole cosmos together and makes man and woman long for one another. She grasps that in order to have the greatest amount of lead transmute into gold the attraction should be raised to its highest potency. I remain silent until the full realization of this fact has sunk in.

"It is the true meaning of the mystical sister, isn't it?" she says to no one in particular. "So it truly *is* about the desire between man and woman, I never knew! I always thought these pictures were just emblems," she adds. I nod, holding my breath. "You mean that the more we allow ourselves to desire one another, the greater the power of the Red Sulphur?" I nod once more.

"Then that is what will happen," she concludes simply.

My heart beats more fully than ever before as I feel love pulse through me. We pause and look at one another for a long time. Her face is serious, then breaks into a mischievous smile.

"I do not mind," she laughs. "Not at all!" I want to embrace her yet do not, held back by an inexpressible modesty between us.

After a while I continue my explanation.

"Trismosin has set clear rules about how much Red Sulphur may be used for each generation: 3 grains for demonstration, which yields 12 demonstrations, and 3 grains for personal material purposes. That way the Stone will last for 700 years. I have used 2 of the personal grains to make tinctures I have used during the plague and have conducted 8 demonstrations to date. Tonight I will use half a grain to make enough gold to buy a house and household. I will need it for the woman who will bear me a child. Boy or girl, it does not matter to me. But I am 42 years of age and the next link in the living chain must be born soon. Trismosin is adamant for reasons he doesn't spell out that the Stone can only pass through our bloodline. I think it must be related to this mysterious future to which he alludes that is to reveal itself after generations."

"Do you have such a woman?" she asks with the directness I so appreciate in her.

I shake my head. "I wish it could be you."

"I am barren," she says, with muted iron in her voice.

"And you are married," I add.

"And I am married," she agrees with a nod.

"But you can be my *soror mystica* forever," I say with certainty.

"So I shall be," she concurs. I look at her and see peace in her eyes. I had not noticed before that her eyes were never quite still, as if they were always searching for something. These are the eyes of a woman who has – and has been – found.

"Thank you," I say, grateful from the bottom of my heart. A long chapter of endless wandering is behind me.

"So what's next?" she asks very practically, belying the atmosphere of romance which gives the disorderly smithy a beguiling appearance. I feel like a knight with his lady, like Lancelot and Guinevere. She catches me looking at her low cut top. She has taken off the blankets, now that the room has been heated by the high fire I built upon arriving. She looks down at her bosom and smiles. "Do I undo my bodice for this adventure?" she asks with a faint smile of seduction. I know she is teasing me.

"If you wish," I reply playfully. "But it will not be necessary."

"Such a pity," she laughs.

"I would like you to, to be honest. But maybe not."

"We shall see," she replies. Her openness to come what may enchants me ever further. The hunter goddess Diana is beginning to inhabit her forest long before the stone is reactivated. That bodes well. I could of course use the stone as is, since I brought it to life just two days ago. But I am convinced that fixing it once more in Marianne's physical presence will revive it in a way I have never witnessed before. The scent of her body will reveal the Goddess in Her most translucent state of nakedness and arouse the loins of the Stone to penetrating potency. The more potent the Red Sulphur, the deeper it infuses sick lead with its mystery of radiant health. I put some hay in the oven below the fire pit.

"You use the lower oven for fixation?" she asks astutely.

"For the fourth grade of fire," I explain. "When the hay singes the heat will be perfect." She nods, needing no further explanation.

I reflect scornfully that Helvetius has no affinity whatsoever to alchemy. The quarter grain I gave him has been a waste for my Ancestor's project because of Helvetius' ineptitude. No one will believe him if he comes out as an advocate of the Art. His peers will deem him a charlatan; not because of the Art, but because he just *is*! I drift off in dark thoughts about the futility of my mission, until I realize that I am horribly jealous of Helvetius and want to destroy him and his reputation.

"May I have the honor to work the bellows?" she asks me.

I silently pass her the instrument for pumping up fire. It is a privilege to work with another adept. She bends forward and I see the pink nipple of her heaving breast as she pumps with vigor. For a moment I swoon, unable to avert my gaze. She looks at me and grins. "The Red Sulphur needs fixation, not your face!" I laugh as I'm brought back to my senses and take the leather pouch with two quarter-grains of the Stone from my coat. In a silence sparkling with fire we wait for the hay to start smoking. The flames rise up high in the chimney. I tell her to reduce the heat, as I don't want to burn down the thatched roof. She stands up, her blushing skin glistening with a haze of fresh dew. My mouth waters and I feel like a beast, not knowing if the crackling I hear arises from the fire pit.

"The hay is ready," she remarks, noticing my distraction. I shake my head to cast off my mood and bend to remove the smoking grasses. Then I hand her the metal plate, which she holds with reverence as I place the Red Sulphur upon it. "Please place it in the fixing furnace," I say softly. As she does so with the care of a mother putting her baby in the crib, I deposit all of the lead in the large cast iron cauldron and place the cauldron directly in the fire. Very shortly the lead melts and begins to bubble. Fumes arise and I begin to feel my usual lightheadedness as I breathe the life of saturnine lead.

"The fumes of lead usually drive me to melancholy and a burning head ache," she says. "But now they just fill me with longing."

I look at her and see untouchable Diana, the virgin huntress deep in her woods, ready for bathing. With her naked arrows she will hunt down her leaden quarry and suffuse it with the sun of Apollo her twin. The lead won't stand up to her furious passion and must transform into gold. Her divine hair glows like fire and her eyes gaze at me fiercely. I need to wrap her arrowhead in wax or it will consume me. I remove the Red Sulphur from the fixing oven, take the yellow wax I have prepared, and knead the activated Stone into it. Marianne's face emerges from behind the Virgin Goddess and I extend my open hand to her, presenting the seed as an offering. She takes the yellow lump and for a moment stands in deep contemplation as if saying a prayer; then she casts it into the cauldron of primordial bubbling lead. A brief sizzle and it disappears. I close the cauldron with a lid. Upon the lid I put heavy stones. I sit down on a barrel in front of the fire and offer her my stool.

We wait as the room fills with subtle odors and fragrances. I can feel everything change in my insides.

"My body melts," she says calmly. "It melts into yours." And I know she is right. I close my eyes in bliss as my body magnetizes into in the purest attraction. I hear her sigh. The radiant Stone and the leprous lead make love in ever expanding circles of passion until they encompass the cosmos. A guttural cry erupts from Marianne's throat as she throws her neck back in transport. The gold is done.

I rise up to remove the cauldron and let it cool down away from the fire.

We are both breathing deeply, embraced by the radiant splendor of the sun.

Chapter Four

As the cauldron is cooling, so are we. I notice that the bright blush on her skin is receding back to the color of milk under a faint glow of strawberry. We remain silent. I give her a mug of ale, which she swallows down in one long draft. Some of the beer runs down her chin and drips between her breasts. I follow the course of the drops and dream away into her body. I know that tonight is not the night, but it will come, I'm sure. I know my reckless heart and it has completely surrendered to this woman. She smiles at me, seemingly guessing my thoughts.

"Me too," is all she says. We both know we have set out on the path of danger and will not turn back.

I take her in my arms and feel her dewy skin against mine. I touch her face and have a sudden desire to rid myself of my beard. I want to sense her face against my cheek. I want to come out of hiding.

"You can sleep in the bedstead," I suggest. "I will stay here near the fire."

"I want to sleep in your arms," she replies with certainty. "I do not want to make love with you yet, but I want to feel your body around me. I need to be held. You have just fulfilled everything I have been searching for my entire life. I want to be close."

I nod silently and guide her to the bedstead where we fall asleep instantly, limbs entwined and souls entangled.

જી

When I awake she is not next to me. I look around with fuzzy view. Daylight brightens up the room and in the center Marianne is standing by the cauldron, the lid lifted off staring down, her face lit by the glow of gold. There is an awestruck look on her face. I move and she looks at me, then back at the golden glow.

"It is fully fixed," she says in a strangled voice, barely able to make her words rise up through her windpipe, as in an anxious dream when words have been arrested and we attempt convulsively to utter sound without result. I jump down the bedstead to the ground and take her in my arms again. She is instantly released from her spasm and begins to sob uncontrollably. I rock her slowly, smelling the gold of the metal and of her hair.

"I never thought I'd ever witness this!" she exclaims after a while. "I'm weeping for my father. I am heartbroken he is not here with me." I suddenly realize that in Trismosin's days we would have been forced to our knees and sing hallelujah to a Father divine. The fathers have changed as the divine has moved into the endless distance, leaving us behind in our personal lives.

We sit down by the last glow of the embers from last night, drinking large amounts of water as if our fluids had been taken out by the projection and we need to replenish our blood. I break the last of the bread Gerda has given Marianne for the journey back home and hand her a piece, which brings us back to the present.

I marvel at the fact that all six pounds of lead have been converted. I had expected to find just some veins of gold inside the lead as I had before when projecting upon large amounts of Saturn's metal. The potency of the half-grain must have been of enormous concentration to transmute 82,000 times its own weight, ten times the amount of the usual number of 8200 mentioned by the Magi. Sandivogius himself tells us without doubt that the seed is always the 8200th part.

"What will you do with it?" she asks, returning to the practical.

"I don't know," I reply. "If I try to sell the lot I will cause suspicion. And with this country at war with England I will have all the spies in the Low Lands after me on top of York's men. I have no idea at the moment. I haven't thought it through yet."

"I'll do it," she says with calm conviction as she looks at the cauldron full of radiant gold. Seeing large quantities of gold is nothing new to her. "No one will doubt a daughter of Maarten van Os and the ring of his fortune. Melt it down into briquettes and I will bring it to our family goldsmiths who will pay me in silver guilders without asking questions. It will be enough to buy you and your wife-to-be a lovely home." Do I hear a mocking tone of regret in her voice? "I must leave," she adds quickly. "Hendrik will be here soon and I still want to see Clara before going back to The Hague."

I feel a sudden distance yawning between us.

After we have finished the bread and Marianne has gone to a chaste corner to freshen herself with the rest of the melted fresh snow from the buckets close to the fire pit, I hear the tell-tale click clack sounds of Hendrik's arrival.

"When can I see you again?" I ask.

"I'll return to Clara in two days after Helvetius comes home. I will tell him I brought Clara to the country to heal. We can meet there." She gets up and comes over to me. Her mouth presses into mine in a fleeting kiss, and I briefly find rest in the flesh of her lips – so ephemeral a moment, I almost don't know if it truly happened. Then she rushes out to the waiting carriage. I wait till it is just a speck in the white distance and go back inside to begin making molds for the briquettes of gold.

એૐ

The fifteen briquettes of gold, weighing about one hundred drachms each, made from the six pounds of lead, are stacked carefully next to the ivory box in the cool fixing oven under the fire pit behind a pile of firewood hiding its existence. Only one who knew it was there might look for it. I trust Smith's family. I sit down on the tripod chair and stare into space, my whole body feeling Marianne as if we had been physical lovers. I remember that when I saw my father last, before he went on the journey from which he did not return, he told me to find a woman, and not just to have offspring. I needed to find a woman with whom to dwell in desire. That's when he told me the Magi insist that the transformative power of Red Sulphur depends upon the force of attraction to the naked Goddess.

I can only guess at the heat of magnetism between Marianne and myself, which must be ten times greater than average. I smile to myself, realizing that the hot reality of our passion is disappearing behind a cold veil of calculus.

ℰℭ

I find Clara in very good shape. She is sitting up, drinking broth. Henk and Klaas, with the help of several other families, have made the main room of the decrepit farmhouse livable again. Gerda has decided that the stables are no place for a Lady and she has quietly commanded the troops, who by now are used to doing her bidding. It seems the work has just finished because there still are eight adults around and a large crop of children. Clara has been placed near the fireplace wrapped in warm sheep skins. Next to her a man in a green coat and hat wearing grey pants over sullied socks is seriously drinking. The room is thick with smoke. Four of the men smoke tobacco from their long-stem white pipes. A large woman with a white cap and dirty white apron is talking to Clara. Gerda is nowhere to be seen. Henk gets up, still sporting his red cap which I suspect has not left his head since last I saw him, "Mundanus!" he says. Clara seems to have trouble remembering who I am. "He saved you," Henk says loudly. "He saved all of us." The room grows uncomfortably silent. Much to my relief Gerda enters. She seems to be agitated. "He's nowhere to be found!"

"He'll turn up," Henk comforts her. "He's probably just playing somewhere."

"That's not like him. He's usually with the others. Has any of you seen Peter?" she asks the children. They shake their heads. "He's been missing since the morning," Gerda utters anxiously. No one else seems much perturbed. Then she notices me. "Doctor," she says respectfully and comes over to shake my hand firmly. I am aware that all who don't know me, including Clara, look me over. I am conscious of my scraggly beard and torn clothes, not the garb of a physician. But in Gerda's eyes it matters not a bit. She sees only essentials, it seems. She goes over to Clara and strokes the curls of her strawberry blonde hair. Clara looks at her with great affection. Gerda and the others must have taken excellent care of her. "Doctor Mundanus' medicine saved your life," Gerda says simply. "When you came here you were almost gone. He brought you back."

"I'm sorry," says Clara in a weak voice, "but I do not remember." I make a sign indicating that it does not matter. This is much more comfortable to me than the fervor of her adoration. Now she looks even more like Marianne, just a few shades darker in complexion and with more regular features. But there is a note of diffidence in her face which contrasts decidedly from Marianne's confidence. Her grey blue eyes are withdrawn, not open as wide as her aunt's. Something in her face looks as if she has been beaten down by the fates. I remember Marianne telling me that her mother had died in the plague. But it seems to me that under her look of a shy little bird lays a lively spirit. The combination of her traits and moods invigorates me: it makes me want to protect her like a daughter. I hold her wrist, thin like the blonde bamboo I have seen on my travels, and I take her various pulses as I have been taught in the Orient.

Her kidneys are still very weak and her liver full of toxins, which explains the faint yellow hue in her eyes. She has an excess of black bile which could explain her melancholy mood weighing down her bright spirit. But her heart is strong, though pumping very slowly. Underneath her sadness there is courage, a lion heart. I ask her to open her mouth and hold my nose close. Her breath still reeks a wee sour and I recommend to Gerda that Clara should drink cream to soothe her wild stomach and tell her to add a drop of the diluted essence of Red Sulphur I had given her when we brought Clara in. I had noticed a freshly slaughtered goat on my way in and ask Gerda to prepare the testicles for Clara to heat her stagnant blood. Everyone is standing around us, listening to my orders with gravity. My final words cause hilarity among the men and they leer at the women around, especially at Clara, who indeed looks very appealing wrapped in the sheepskins, which give her an animal appearance. "Off you go," Gerda shoos them out, "The show is over. Thank you for coming to clean up the place. Next we meet to fix Adrian's roof," she commands, pointing to the man with the green coat. The fat woman with the dirty apron looks pleased. I bet she is living with him under that same roof. The visitors file out, followed by rowdy children. "And please everyone, look out for Peter and send him home at once," Gerda calls after them.

"I'll bring some more peat in the house," says Henk, taking his father with him.

"How do you feel?" I ask when all have left. Clara smiles faintly and mutters, "Fairly well for a corpse."

"A pretty pink corpse," I respond. "I wish all corpses looked like you. They would all be like Lazarus."

"I'm deadly tired," she adds. "I feel I could sleep for a month." This alarms me. She should want to get up at this point. Her blood is still sluggish. "Let's get her up and walk her around a bit," I say to Gerda.

"She is wearing no clothes," Gerda responds. "We had to undress her with the women after you left, to sponge her down with cold water. She was burning up." Again I am impressed with Gerda's instinctive initiative. Most people would have tried to keep a sick person warm. I had found her in the bedstead in The Hague under piles of blankets. Cooling her down had been just the right thing to do.

"Well done," I say admiringly. "Could you help her get dressed? I will go outside for a moment."

Clara looks very unhappy. She does not want to get up at all. But I know she has to walk a few steps to get the blood flowing more freely.

"I cannot lift her by myself," Gerda says simply. "All the other women are gone." Her silence is neutral. I can do as I wish. I'm flustered.

"Why do I need to get up?" Clara asks me with more firmness in her voice.

"You have been lying down for many days and the surgeon has bled you half to death," I explain. "Your blood flows like molasses. It needs to run thinner. The best way to get the blood moving is by walking."

Clara's eyes display Marianne's intelligence and she nods. She begins to push herself up. The sheepskins fall off and her flushed body reveals itself to my unprepared eyes. Taken aback I move a step backwards, off balance. Gerda, seeing the fluster in my face, grins in spite of herself. Clara has Marianne's body at a younger age. I feel thrown back into the past. The cold makes her nipples stand out and her skin is a fluid rose gold; her shoulders are firm and thighs ample. I avert my face to find back my physician's dispassion. Gerda covers Clara with the sheepskins as she helps her up. But the skins cover her back, leaving the front exposed as my eyes are drawn back to a stare. I remind myself that I am a physician, for God's sake! But I seem to have no resistance to female descendants of Maarten van Os. I am filled with her ravishing presence like a lad. I take her by the arm, thinking with great focus of only her wellbeing, but fail miserably. The touch of her skin transports me back to last night and the Goddess is with me again, this time without the mediation of metal. Clara looks at me in gratitude and trust. Shamefaced I feel like a hidden lecher, no better than the leering men with testicles on their minds. Her hands are refined, fit for needlepoint, and I am surprised I could ever have taken her for a maid. We walk the room with increasing vigor, Gerda under one, I under the other arm. The hair of her armpit against the back of my neck is soft like the head of a baby. I see storms in my future.

છ

Young Peter, whose arm I'd set with the medicine, has not returned. A search party goes out looking all over the ice for a hole he could have fallen through.

At midnight Henk returns, weeping. Walking slowly as in a dirge, arms outstretched, he carries a gruesome bloody load.

"Wild dogs," he mutters between sobs, "They've devoured his heart and liver."

Gerda screeches, an inhuman wail. Henk gently puts the desecrated body on the table. I rush over and immediately see that the heart and liver have been cut out with a knife, a very sharp pointed knife, more likely a dagger; and very skillfully at that, in one fell swoop. I see a vision of the phantom youth and the long pointed Ottoman dagger on his belt. What kind of ghoul is this? Such vengefulness I can't even ascribe to bandits sent out by the Duke of York to haunt me. A child, for God's sake! Then I shake off this chimera and prepare young Peter for his journey home. I close the wounds as best I can. There still is a hint of green glow about his corpse, as if the medicine I gave him some time ago has been reactivated. Gerda sobs, angry with herself, calling out to her parents with remorse about not having taken care of her brother. Henk holds her as she shakes with heartbreak and guilt. I can see his love for her light up every inch of his being. After a while Gerda calms down. Henk quickly fashions a casket. The corpse of the child is too horrible to behold. Men from the search party have returned and are now digging a grave in the field out back. Even though the boy is no longer alive, the green glow has gotten stronger as we put him to rest in the simple wooden box. Gerda notices it and asks me.

"The medicine must have tried to defend his life. I really don't understand, but that's all I can imagine," I muse.

"Who would do a thing like that - mutilate a little boy?" Her distress is hard to bear.

I have a vision of the liver and heart being devoured and I'm sickened by the certainty that this is what happened to Peter. "Has there been Devil worship in these parts?" I ask Gerda. "No," she replies, "There has never been anything like this. It could be the Jews. They eat Christian children!"

"No, that's not true," I say with certainty. If that rumor isn't stopped right off terrible slaughter may result. I've seen it in other parts. "No Gerda, I'm sure that isn't it. I don't know what happened, but I'm sure it's not Jews!" Gerda is still dubious. But her respect for me makes her contain her need to quickly blame someone.

"We should not let Miss Clara know," Gerda says. "It might set her back." I'm astonished that she can think of Clara when her little brother has just been so gruesomely murdered.

Gerda tells Henk to keep silent about what happened to Peter. The neighbors digging the grave are told that he had fallen through the ice and drowned. The mourning is quick and passes rapidly in this community so numbingly familiar with death.

In my heart a little boy sings at the top of his lungs as I ride on the ice to The Hague in a cart.

୫୦

Marianne returns two days later. She looks lovely in a simple red dress of thick wool high up to a white lace neck showing off her bright hair in sunny curls. As she embraces Clara tightly with tears of relief, I can clearly see the difference in their appearance and realize that a gloss of her aunt's being had covered Clara, reflecting Marianne's image back to me while I had walked with Clara in a state of undress. I can feel without doubt – or do I really? – that my primary attraction is to the mature woman, as Clara now looks like a mere child in Marianne's arms. They hold one another for the longest time. Gerda and I walk outside to give them time alone.

"Doctor Mundanus," Gerda tells me calmly, "I feel the Lord has called me to heal the sick. With my brother's death I've suddenly become certain."

I nod without surprise, knowing it to be a genuine calling.

"Can you teach me?" she asks. I am taken aback, not knowing what to say. I know Gerda has the makings of a remarkable healer, but I don't know how to go about training her.

"You have a family to care for, and I will move on soon."

She has clearly thought it over carefully. "I will arrange matters here. I'll find a solution." I know she will. I want to help her, but I hesitate.

"Will you be moving far?" she asks.

"Amsterdam," I reply. A cloud covers her face. Amsterdam is far away. Then she makes her decision. "I'll manage," she concludes simply. I feel a rush of gratitude to be able to teach what I learned in the East and during the years of horror when the plague devoured us *en masse*, to someone as worthy as Gerda. Salomon Trismosin would agree. Within me I can feel the stirrings of a teacher.

"I'll think about it," I hear myself respond as if reciting well-rehearsed lines in a preordained play.

She smiles, gratified, yet still with the pall that has come over her since Peter's murder. I turn to go back in. It is a bone-chilling day outside.

Marianne looks as if she has been waiting for me. Both she and Clara are happy to see me. She is holding her niece's hand.

"We did a projection the night before last," she rushes in, her words almost tumbling over one another. "Helvetius came back from the Prince in great excitement. Grand Pensionary Johan de Witt had been there and Helvetius told him about the Red Sulphur and that a man had visited him who said he could make 20 tons of gold. De Witt had asked if he believed this man and Helvetius replied he would not know until he had tried a projection himself. De Witt is open- minded towards anything capable of filling the coffers of state."

"That's been my fear all along," I sigh. Now York, De Witt and the Devil are after me.

"I know," she continues breathlessly with a shade of anguish. "I know. So I told Helvetius I would not give him the pouch of Red Sulphur until he promised me that he would not betray you to the Grand Pensionary. De Witt's power over Holland is absolute and he won't leave a stone unturned until he has found you. I have known him for a long time. He was a friend of my family. He was a great admirer of my father's. We move in the same circles in The Hague. He's Johanna's age."

Clara looks sad at the mention of her mother's name.

I nod, anxious. Johan de Witt is the most powerful man in the land, equal to what Oliver Cromwell had been in England a decade ago. And Holland is as powerful now as the English, locked as they are in battles over the hegemony at sea. He needs all the money he can get his hands on for the war. He would make a most formidable adversary. He is a total pragmatist, ready to use anything that works. He would instantly throw aside all contemporary derision of Chrysopoeia, gold making, if it would serve his purposes. In that way he's just like York, who wants the gold to pay for their ships to take African colonies from the Dutch and get a slice of the slave trade. Their fortunes are down and they're facing insolvency.

"At first Helvetius was suspicious as to why I was so eager to protect you. I told him I knew Johan de Witt and I would find it unconscionable to deliver a man who had done us a good turn into his claws. Helvetius believed my high mindedness and agreed." Marianne looks for an instant at Clara and I see her worrying that Clara might guess our relationship. But Clara is drifting in and out, listening to the story with clouded ears.

"He melted six drachms of lead in my furnace," she continues.

"Six drachms!" I exclaim.

Marianne looks at me, puzzled.

"The Red Sulphur I gave you could have transmuted 30 drachms under normal circumstances. I had said 30 drachms, not six!" I decide not to mention, because of Clara's presence, that yesterday we had transmuted 750 drachms with the equivalent amount.

"It was already hard to convince Helvetius that he should use more than one drachm. He believed that the amount was so small that it could never transmute more."

"He's an ignorant fool. Six drachms will leave the gold highly activated. If you use too little material to be transmuted with too much Red Sulphur you get an unstable metal, like a mare in heat desiring copulation. It will affect all metals it touches." I shake my head.

"Well," Marianne says, slightly irritated. "We didn't know. So we did the projection and it worked like a charm. The gold is beautiful. He didn't wait for a moment to tell his friends. By yesterday afternoon, the rumor of this wonderful metallic Transmutation had spread all over The Hague. Many men of importance – some lovers of the Art, some skeptical scientists, others surely spies for Johan de Witt – came to Helvetius. They requested he would give them some small particle of our artificial gold, to prove it by legitimate examination. Knowing this to be important, probably to prove it to Johan de Witt – for I don't trust Helvetius in matters of fortune and glory – he gave them two drachms of our gold. I insisted to come along with them. At first they were reluctant to have a woman among them, but they couldn't refuse me because of my rank, since they all admire my family. We went together to the house of a famous silversmith, by the name of Brechtelt, in whose workhouse the excellent nature of our gold was evidenced. Brechtelt's grandfather was a famous apothecary and a free spirited investigator of nature. His written works were worthy of blacklisting by the Inquisition, a badge of honor in these parts. His grandson is as curious as he. We hold him in high esteem."

I don't know whether to be elated or terrified: I have achieved exactly what my ancestor had demanded and simultaneously I have become the most sought after fugitive in all of Europe. Most of all I am very curious to know what happened. "How did they test it?" I inquire eagerly.

"They used the form of probation called quartation, that is when they melt three or four parts of silver with one part of gold in a crucible, and then, by hammering reduce that mixture into thin plates, on which they pour a sufficient quantity of aquafortis. By this the silver is dissolved, but the gold settles to the bottom, like a black powder. Afterward, the aquafortis is poured off, and the golden powder is again put into a crucible and by strong fire reduced to gold."

I nod, having seen this test performed several times, having used it myself to test artificial gold other adepts brought me.

"But when this work ended they supposed that one half of the gold would have vanished to prove it a fraud. And then comes the strangest part: we found that the gold, besides its own weight, had transmuted some part of the silver into gold. Two drachms of the gold transmuted two scruples of the silver into gold of its own nature. There was one third more gold than when we started out!"

"That's because Helvetius projected too much Red Sulfur on too small a dose of lead. His gold was still activated and famished," I say.

"To his credit I must say that Helvetius suggested that the gold must have contained an abundance of its tincture, transmuting the silver into its own nature. But the others, including Brechtelt, assumed a mistake had been made, and General Examiner of the Moneys, Mint-master Porelius, ordered a further examination since he suspected that the silver was not well separated from the gold. So Brechtelt made a mixture with seven times as much antimony. And after this test, we lost eight grains of gold. But when we again evaporated the antimony, we found nine grains of Gold, yet in color somewhat pale. Thus, in the best trial of fire, we lost nothing of this Gold. Porelius ordered this infallible kind of test to be repeated three times and Brechtelt did so to ever greater excitement of the illustrious observers. And three times we found that every dram of gold acquired from the silver an augmentation of one scruple of gold. Brechtelt assured us that the silver had been tested by him before and found to be pure good, and very flexible. So the five drams of gold attracted to itself five scruples from the silver. And when Helvetius explained again the way of projection they all were amazed that such an exceedingly small amount of Red Sulphur did transmute six drams and two scruples, of a more vile metal into gold, fixed to the point it was able to sustain the most intense torture of fire. The men were most surprised however that before their very eyes the gold had transformed one third of its weight in silver into its own kind. Mint-master Porelius admitted that he had suspected foul play on the part of Helvetius, but that now he was convinced, as was Brechtelt. I am sure by now Johan de Witt is hunting for the adept who gave the Red Sulphur to Helvetius, casting his nets for as far as a man can travel in a week."

"That is you," Clara says, now wide awake, nodding in my direction. "You came to us telling us you were sent by some great Doctor from England. I remember, it was you!" Clara seems to be more relieved that her memory is returning than concerned with its contents.

"I have to leave immediately," I say with certainty. "Every moment longer endangers these families here." I already feel horribly responsible for young Peter's mutilation. "The spies will soon find my tracks. Neighbors must have seen us leave with the cart with Clara. In Holland everyone spies on the other. They have spy mirrors on their windows to see what is going on in the street. De Witt's men must be hot on my heels."

I rush out, and Marianne follows me.

"What will you do?" she asks, unable to mask her fear for my safety.

"We will go back to the smithy and get you the gold. I will cut off my beard and wait for you to return from The Hague with silver guilders and an excellent suit of clothes with a simple wig like the courtiers wear. Then I will travel by horse-pulled boat to Amsterdam. I am sure they will be checking all the roads and waterways. But the papers of passage I carry are flawless. Better to confront them soon. I will be glad to stop traveling incognito. I was beginning to hate my beard," I add truthfully and in order to make light.

Marianne looks unconvinced. "These men are ruthless," she says. "We are in a country at war and they will stop at nothing."

"I have been hunted before," I say, though I know this time is different. I'm a man with the Devil on my heels.

"So you are leaving?" Clara asks in a small voice, having come outside for the first time since her illness. I feel concerned she may catch a cold.

"Please go in, Clara. Your aunt will help me escape and then she will take you home in a few days."

Marianne takes Clara in her arms, pressing her close, soothing the fear in them both; then she takes her back in. I follow them. As Gerda comes in with a bowl of broth for Clara, I take the opportunity to whisk Marianne outside again.

"I am telling everyone I'm off to Amsterdam. But I'm going to Leyden. It is closer. I don't want to be too far away from you. My family owns a home near the old courthouse next to the Church of St. Peter. I'll move in and set myself up as a tutor of medicine under the name of Giovanni Theodore. I have very convincing papers if anyone asks. No one will suspect me." I embrace her tightly and feel her tears. "I never want to be too far away from you," I repeat. "Not ever!"

"Same," she whispers.

Part Two

Marianne

Chapter Five

Mundanus and I ride in my carriage from Gerda's farm to his smithy to pick up the briquettes of gold. My heart is in turmoil from what I've just witnessed. For decades I have kept my father's faith that the transmutation of lead into gold was possible, yet when I saw it happen before my own eyes it had not been the gold in the cauldron that had startled me most. I was overtaken by a passion in my body as if I was alive for the first time, as though the soaring spirit of the metals was air to my lungs. I have been living my life in the dull narrows of expectation and predictability. But now everything is blown open. My past receded in an instant, sliding away from me down a steep incline behind my back. I'm a different woman now. I can feel my skin flushed, my eyes burn, living in a world inhabited by only one man. I look at Mundanus sitting next to me. His outlines are a blur. I remember the preacher say how when the Lord returns the air will taste different, that we would not recognize what had been familiar but a moment ago. I had nodded together with the rest of the congregation. But the transport had been in the poetry of his words, nothing like the reality I am now living. I force myself to focus on the familiar carriage. I call upon my memories to ease my breathing, to remove me from the Promised Land into which I have been so harshly cast, tumbling down a funnel of unknowing. I look at Hendrik on the box of the coach. I squint to see him in his younger days, when first he rode us out and the carriage had been new. Father had bought it when Mother was still alive. It had been a gift for her. I see us all go out for a ride: Father, Mother, Johanna, my twin Young

Dirck and I. We are ten, each dressed in bright yellow summer costumes. I can smell the starch. Young Dirck is excited and Mother has a bright blush on her face. It is my last memory of her and of my twin. Hendrik gives me a sense of home. I can smell my recollections, and am enveloped by a protective past. Then suddenly Mundanus comes into focus. The whole world looks back at me in deeply saturated colors. I feel my breasts and know I am a woman in a way I have never been before. Mundanus looks ridiculous in his knotted beard, this theater prop behind which he hides. I envision him clean shaven. That's how he is supposed to look, even with his disfiguring pock marks. His beggar garb is incongruous under the hidden outlines of the face of a Mediterranean nobleman. Old Salomon Trismosin must have loved a Venetian woman, as did his offspring while they stayed on the Adriatic for generations. One could easily think Mundanus a Spaniard, a hated occupier from the southern provinces, a nobleman from Castile. I now appreciate his wisdom to travel thus hidden. Only the eye of love can see his true face behind his foul exterior. I envision the suit of clothes I will buy for him: a dream of black velvet. My lips tingle. He can either wear the costume of a beggar or be elegant, but he could never be dressed in one of Helvetius' dour frocks. Sitting close to him, feeling his warmth, the screaming fact that he will be the most hunted man in the land has receded behind clouds of wellbeing. I don't recognize my world. My head leans on his shoulder while I wonder why I trust him so profoundly. I muse how Father has always treated me the same way he had Young Dirck; but even more like a boy than my brother. He had taught me mathematics and languages. My twin had no interest in these matters. He liked mischief and was always in trouble. The school taught us to tame our unruly nature, to become the Regents of the land. At Father's death, Young Dirck was to become the single largest stockholder in the United East-Indies Company, inheriting the substantial percentage of family stock Dirck van Os had obtained when the Company was formed many decades ago, combined with the dramatic augmentation of our fortune under Father's expert ministrations. Mother always protected Dirck's disrespectful behavior and took him to her quarters after he had been punished at school, his hands whipped ferociously. The more Young Dirck had become Mother's, I became Father's. I was the *famula*, his close attendant in his laboratory from the time I was seven. I looked through the books and searched for answers with him, reading Latin more fluently than Dutch. It had been my pride that I was like his boy. I felt awkward with my female body, especially when the moon cycles began. They were a rude interruption to my studies, a time of change when my blood flowed in the wrong direction, away from my head. And here, at this moment, I feel like a woman leaning against her man. I am happy with each curve of my female body, with all the accidents of my flesh. I have loosened a waterfall of blonde hair to flow over his shoulder and through his beard in strands of gold. I treasure the hot transmutation in my moist place of secrets. Yet at the same time I have a compelling sense that this, my man, is not mine. And it is not because I am married to Helvetius. It is because Mundanus belongs to the greater world of legend: the legend of Trismosin, the tale of the Red Sulphur to be carried through the ages by a man who does not belong to himself, a messenger without a life of his own.

I could have predicted Helvetius' vain boasts to Johan de Witt. He is a dangerous man, Johan. When he came to the house as a young man-on-the-rise to discuss the mathematics of taxes and bonds with Father – in his early days as Grand Pensionary before he rose to the pinnacle of power – and he looked at me with inappropriate frankness, I knew that I never wanted to be his enemy. He admired Father, who had studied mathematics with Rene Descartes in Leyden. They would discuss the new philosophy and how the world exists in the mind of God. I was still very young, but instinctively I knew that this man with the long face and the hawk's nose had quiet eyes of total determination which could wait for the right moment to swoop down upon his prey. And now I am his opponent, playing a game with him to evade his grip. I find it strangely exciting. It is good Mundanus is going to Leyden. The tensions in Holland are between the Princely family of Orange, which bestowed its University upon Leyden in 1575 as a reward for its resistance against the Spanish oppressor, and on the other side, the Regents, who are the real rulers of the Netherlands. Leyden is the Orangist stronghold and people despise us Regents led by Johan and his older brother Cornelis. The coming game of cat and mouse with the rulers of my Regent class rouses my blood, and I feel briskly alive in this new world which has unexpectedly been foisted upon me.

For the first time in my life I wish for a child: Mundanus' child. I drown momentarily in the wild hope that my body had just been waiting for Mundanus, and had protected my insides from Helvetius' seed. But then, deep down, I know it not to be so. An illness I contracted at 20 left me forever barren. The doctors, including poor Helvetius, told me that the high fevers must have destroyed my womb, and I knew they were right. I have not had my moon cycle since. Even now that my blood is quickened to a torrent, the dead spot inside me is still cold as ice; colder than usual even, with all the heat coursing through me.

"Why are you crying?" Mundanus asks, concern in his kind eyes.

I cannot tell him the truth, ashamed as I am about my barrenness. When I told him before it was in defiance.

"I am afraid for you. I know Johan de Witt," I break the silence.

Mundanus smiles. He is a man who likes danger, though he is not reckless. His eyes make me feel safe in the way Father's used to, but in a radically different way. They don't make me long back for childhood; these eyes make me feel like his equal. I take his hand and we continue our silence through the cold windy winter around us, floating inside a bubble of heat.

I am glad the hovel Mundanus lives in has not in the meantime collapsed, as it stands on its crutches waiting to succumb.

I give a sign to Hendrik no other might have noticed to indicate that I'll just be inside for a minute. He nods as his deeply grooved face casts me a brief toothless smile, his beetroot red nose betraying his love of Dutch gin.

Inside the smithy the memories of the last time in this place swamp me instantly. I remember the glow of gold bathing my soul, and notice an ache of restrained desire. I feel how a mother must experience the birth of her first healthy baby, a mixture of elated love, pain and deliverance – and catch a glimpse of an ordinary world Mundanus and I will never inhabit. My heart breaks again, as it did the morning after our dance of desire. I want to press him to me, feel him inside and taste his sweetness with my whole body. It is not to be. Our love must be curtailed so he can marry a woman who will give him the child he needs to carry Salomon's mission into the future through his blood-line. Yet at this instant I do not care. At this moment I want him just for myself; I don't care a damn for the future.

He is taking down the logs stacked in front of the fireplace. I walk up to him, my hips heavy with longing. All of this is new to me. I was brought up by stern French governesses to be a proper patrician lady and studied the world of the mind with Father; but no one raised me for love. And absolutely no person in the world could have ever prepared me for a love as impossible as this. Am I to be the chaste sister consumed by a burning thirst quenched only by the copulation of metals? I hear my shrill laughter. So does Mundanus. He looks at me quizzically.

"I want to love you right here and right now!" I whisper with force.

He drops the logs and takes me in his arms, his kiss gentle. That is not enough. I pull him towards me and feel the harsh prickles of his beard rough my mouth as I reach into him with my tongue. I don't know what is coming over me. My hands are exploring his chest under the rags. I want to discover all of him, take him by the waistband and pull him to the bedstead, up the ladder and almost throw him onto the mattress. My open hand strokes the hair on his skin and feels the strong muscles of a man used to physical labor. His hand, big and sure, touches my breast firmly and I sense the melting funneling down to my belly as ocean waves rush up my thighs. For the first time I want to hold a man in my hands, feel the thrust of his desire, increase it with my movements. I adore the throbbing sensations as he gasps in surprise and mounting elation. My clothes have fallen off me in a mysterious way, as have his, and our skin kisses and writhes. I caress him into my lust and absorb him within as I become a single pool of sensation. Our motions dance and I hear a voice I have never heard before moan up my throat. My boundaries vanish and in a space that is both wild and still we plunge as one into the pulse of divine attraction.

ॐ

I'm rocking in the carriage back to The Hague, next to a potato sack filled with briquettes of gold, a small ivory box and a thick leather-bound diary, 160 years old. It is the first time Mundanus has ever parted with these items and he gave them to me as a matter of course. The trust between us is as complete as the one I have with Hendrik on the box in front of me, steering the coach through a land made of silver. Our horse is not in any hurry, click-clacking a rhythm conducive to thought. My skin is singing and I still feel the weight of his body as he fell upon me, shipwrecked on my beach. Now I know what it is to be woman. It took this transport to the sea-beyond no one ever mentions, to teach me the love that is hidden from view. Slowly the rhythm of the carriage brings me back to the world I inhabit with others besides him, and I think what I will do with the valuables my beloved handed over into my trust.

When we moved into the Van Os family home after Father and Johanna died two years ago from the plague, I had a secret compartment built behind the fireplace in Father's laboratory which not even Helvetius knows about. I keep Father's papers there together with an overview of Clara and my financial records. The gold, Red Sulphur, and Trismosin's diaries are much safer there than on Mundanus, who is now being hunted by the spies of De Witt. A moment of fear for his life passes through me. Then I see the strong smile on the face that now is my world and I calm. Like a drift of fresh snow, my mind floats towards Helvetius. He trusts me completely and this is the first time in 16 years that I have betrayed his trust. I feel curiously unmoved by this. I feel neither the guilt nor the shame I had foreseen. I'm just aware of an unexpected fondness I feel for my husband, thinking of his pale blue eyes, seductive in their melancholy, his sensuous lips, the self-indulgent round jaw and mischievous dimple in his chin. He gives off an air of femininity and our love was never ardent. Now I know that I much prefer more manly lovers such as Mundanus. I don't know if Helvetius' dreams of desire are filled with women or with the men in whose direction his gaze sometimes wanders. We do not talk about it. I prefer it that way, as long as he feels no need to enter my bed chamber. Our safe ground is his study where we talk about the spagyric arts and about the mysteries of medicine. Since the end of our courtship he has always been critical of alchemical thought. His sharp critique of Sir *Kenelm Digby's Sympathetick Powder* was not just for the purpose of distancing himself from the Art. His mind truly *is* more excited by the inventions of his friend Anthonie van Leeuwenhoek, who stares through a magnifying glass so strong he sees all kinds of invisible life-forms he calls *animalcules*. Helvetius and his overly serious Jewish comrade Benedict de Spinoza, a lens maker himself, swear by Van Leeuwenhoek's visions, having seen these creatures themselves through the looking glass. The three of them scorn alchemy as a superannuated delirium from a benighted age. Like my father and Johan de Witt, they follow the Frenchman Rene Descartes of Leyden, who died almost a decade ago, but whose work is still gaining in influence. But while my father could hold two mutually exclusive realities at once, they made their choice, and to their loss, have cast off the past. Therefore I do not really understand why Helvetius was *so* sure that Mundanus' Red Sulphur actually *had* the power to transmute lead into gold, and that he risked talking about it with Johan de Witt. I want to ask him as soon as I am home.

Breathing the brisk air of a bright winter day, I marvel at the beauty of the flat rural landscape with horizons far off to all sides, like the view from a ship on a calm silver ocean. Squinting against the glare off the icy snow I realize with a pang of regret that I spend too much time in the city, in my windowless laboratory, straining my eyes by the light of candles. Noticing my relief over Clara's recovery and marveling at Mundanus' miracle, I am grateful that he has used his allotted personal supply of the Stone to devise ways of curing. His heart is humane. Wrapped in a maternal smile, I remember Clara's dewy eyes reflecting the vernal devotion of a maiden who has met her Savior as she gazed at Mundanus. Suddenly I gasp, fall back in my seat and black out momentarily. The absolute conviction that Clara is meant to bear Mundanus' children rips through my heart. I squeeze my eyes shut, but Mundanus and Clara stand ever closer together before me. It is unmistakable. I know it to be true, like the pain from a blow is unmistakable, while my mind does all it can to avoid this dread vision of future. I make a solemn decision that I will never tell Mundanus, yet I know I will do so the first time we meet. My ardent desire to see him as soon as possible turns into a wish to never see him again, and gloom fills my soul like clouds before thunder.

As we arrive at home I tell Hendrik to drop me off at the front door and take the potato sack with him to the stables in the back. "I trust you to not look inside and have no one else do so either. Keep it hidden till I pick it up." He looks at me with reassurance in his old eyes. Since Father's death his devotion to me has become even more absolute. I respond to his expression with gratitude, feeling the bonds of family.

In the hall of my home, I see Helvetius in heated conversation with the General Examiner of Moneys, Mint-master Porelius. The latter is an unattractive man with a dry-skin face flaking with a red rash. His lips are always pursed as if he is weighing things, finding them lacking; a good character trait for his exalted profession. Today he looks uncharacteristically shaken. I would have thought nothing could throw the Mint-master off track. A fixture in The Residence (as our little Hague is usually called,) I have known him for a long time and his un-flappable nature makes him a most boring companion.

They stop talking respectfully when I enter; then Porelius pulls me into the discussion in a conspiratorial fashion with a hushed undertone.

"Madam Schweitzer, I am telling your husband that every-one in The Hague is after me to give them the story. Some are laughing in my face, saying that I have been duped. But I saw with my own eyes how the gold transmuted the silver. Could you tell me once more what you noticed at the time of the pro-jection? I've been ordered by the Grand Pensionary to investi-gate this matter carefully."

I offer the Mint-master a cup of tea from China, brought to Holland by our East India Trading Company. He looks pleased. We go to the parlor with the Bordeaux-red wallpaper and sit down. Porelius is looking at me anxiously. I see the man is greatly disturbed. His orderly life has been harshly disrupted and he wants it to be over as soon as possible.

"What do you wish me to tell you?" I ask him, innocently.

"Tell me about the projection from the moment you added the tincture. What happened?"

I begin talking matter-of-factly. "Well, I wrapped the Red Sulphur in wax, and Helvetius cut half an ounce of lead, and put it into a crucible in the fire upstairs in the laboratory where my husband prepares his medicines." He doesn't need to know that I in fact am the laborant. "After it had melted I kneaded the rape seed of medicine into the yellow wax until it was a small pill and cast it into the molten lead. It made a hissing noise, and in a quarter of an hour the mass of lead was totally transmuted into the best and finest gold, which amazed us. We could not stop gazing upon this miracle. The melted lead, after projection, showed the rarest and most beautiful colors imaginable, settling in green, and when poured into an ingot, it had the lively fresh color of blood. When cooled it shone as the purest and most splendid gold." I cannot help my enthusiasm breaking through. I attempt talking about it in a distant way; to no avail. The Projection has turned my soul to gold and it can never be undone. I know my face is flush, shining with the memory. I get up and the gentlemen rise as well.

"Is there anything else you need to ask me?"

"Yes," Mint-master Porelius responds. "You have known the Grand Pensionary for many years. He was a friend of your esteemed father. He trusts you. Would you be willing to tell him the story yourself?"

I shiver; remembering his direct gaze that could always see deeply into me, Johan de Witt is last person I want to see right now. But I know that this is not a request, but an order. No one can defy Johan de Witt, not even parliament.

So I nod politely and leave as quickly as possible, going upstairs to my laboratory. This summons has come earlier than I expected. I sit down and look around aimlessly, knowing I have to carefully seal off the place in my soul where Mundanus lives, or Johan de Witt will surely find it.

Thinking of nothing is hard. Mundanus' face wants to intrude and I find no way to resist it. How can I live when Clara is the mother of his children? Clara who is like a daughter to me… A curse escapes from my lips, and I look around anxiously to see if any of the servants may have heard me. It is greatly out of character for me to swear. After some time of static fidgeting I decide to go down to the stables and get the bag from Hendrik.

℘

I find Hendrik in the stable in the back where we keep our two horses. Helvetius' horse and carriage are out so I know he will not be back for some time, probably doing his physician rounds along the wealthy homes in The Residence. His marriage to me came with a rich dowry: all of Father's friends and acquaintances wanted to try out this new German doctor who had landed a daughter of Maarten Van Os. I notice I am sour with Helvetius and realize that I'm angry with everyone. It is hard not to growl at Hendrik and treat him like a lowly servant. Enraged with my fate, which left me barren and will steer the man I love into the arms of one who is virtually my daughter, I notice my thoughts have become repetitive. I'm stuck, which makes me even more furious. "Nothing is pre-ordained!" I hear Father's voice. He would tell me that over and over, in private, insisting that every course, no matter how likely, was open to alteration. It was a dangerous faith, at odds with his Calvinist environment; he believed in the essential freedom of spirit. His peers were convinced that God predestined everyone's course, knowing in advance whose path led to Heaven, and whose to Hell.

And according to my vision of Mundanus and Clara, I am on my way to Hell. But I could just tell Clara not to come close to Mundanus, that he is a dangerous man, and in the meantime find him another broodmare. I can feel the bitterness on my tongue and shake my head violently to rid myself of my thinking. Hendrik is taking a deep draw from his long white pipe, looking at me with an expression I cannot read. As he exhales the smoke he turns around and goes over to stacked bales of hay. From behind them he pulls out the potato bag. I can see instantly that it has not been opened, Mundanus having tied it carefully with a complicated knot.

"Are you alright, Miss Marianne?" he asks me, concerned. That makes me even more annoyed and I don't even reply. I turn on my heels to lead the way to my laboratory, Hendrik carrying the bag. Halfway the stairs I turn around. "No, Hendrik, actually I'm not feeling well. Thank you for your concern." I look at the old man below me carrying my burden and I bite my lip in order not to cry. I miss my father. I need to talk to someone, but I have no friends close enough. I tell Hendrik to put the sack in the middle of the laboratory next to the fireplace. As I cast him an uncertain smile he looks at me quizzically, but when I don't give any indication of an intention to speak, he bows almost imperceptibly, turns around and leaves. When I lock the door behind him I feel terribly lonely.

Mundanus' knot, however complex, is easy to undo. Inside the bag, the gold is in yet another knotted sack with the ivory box. Only the leather bound diaries are visible. They are written on folio leafs, four pages to a leaf, folded in the middle so each parchment page is written in two columns. Salomon Trismosin's handwriting is very small, hard to decipher. Opening the book, I begin to read, translate from the German. I sit down on the floor and become entirely engrossed in a voice 160 years old, forgetting all my concerns.

"March 9, 1498.

I was invited to Domenico Maria Novara da Ferrara's home for observations of the stars. He is more interested in the location of the stars in the natural sky than in the way they rule our destiny. Had a long conversation with his assistant, a young scholar called Copernicus from Poland. Novara began teaching him to look at the sky exactly one year ago and the two of them were celebrating this anniversary with excellent wine. They believe that the sun is at the heart of the cosmos even though this goes against all clear observation. We spoke of how hard it is for us to believe that we are not at the center of the cosmos. I was trying to stay open to their thoughts, which are mainly based on mathematics, but I cannot believe them. How can I disbelieve what all my senses tell me? Yet, in their eyes I see a vision of the future. A future I do not understand. A future so different from who or what I am, that I cannot fathom it."

∞

I put down the heavy book and stare aimlessly. 'A future I do not understand.' There is a difference between predestination and a true vision of the future, I argue with the ghost of Father in the laboratory. In Copernicus' vision Galileo's observations were foreshadowed. Father had explained this to me, with great reverence towards Galileo. So couldn't it be that I see the true future in Mundanus and Clara? That this future is contained in the seed of their meeting and that my clear eye of jealous envy can see the outcome in those beginnings?

I hear the front door open and recognize Helvetius' footsteps and quickly put the book back in the sack and place it in the secret compartment. I'm happy I was wrong about Helvetius' whereabouts. He did not go out on his rounds. He must have run some kind of errant. 'Maybe I'm wrong about more important matters as well,' I mutter in self-conscious childish superstition. For the first time in years I am very happy to see my husband.

ₘₓ

We sit in his study with a cup of hot chocolatl and milk. Mina the maid does not prepare it as well as did Clara – she does not add enough juice of sugarcane – but the smell gives one a sense of well-being.

"I have wanted to know why you trusted Mundanus the alchemist. Your assessment of the Art has been rather scathing over many years, and sometimes I felt that you mocked me."

Helvetius is silent for a while. "After seeing Mundanus I had another dream: a dream of cinnabar and of the Stone."

He looks very uncomfortable. It obviously is an effort for him to talk about this.

"Could you tell me the dream?" I inquire respectfully.

He pauses, unsure whether to proceed. Then he seems to make a decision.

"I heard the Stone speak to me. It is very confusing." He looks disoriented, his full lips mumbling to himself inaudibly. I stare at his mouth distractedly, wondering why I've never liked kissing him. Something repulses me.

"Remember you asking me why I was boiling the cinnabar in the study and not in the laboratory?"

"You evaded me, giving me all kinds of implausible reasons," I reply.

"It was because of these dreams about boiling cinnabar in my study. I had the dream twice before. They were just a silent tableau of my study with the cauldron and a green radiance spreading throughout the room. But in this last one I come into my study and see the cinnabar boiling bright red. Suddenly the vessel turns over and I scream. Then on the floor, in the middle of my study is a stone, shining with green effulgence. I approach it in awe and just before I touch it I feel myself waking up."

He stops, clearly shaken by the events as they return to him while he describes them to me. "After the first dream I felt I had to do something. I knew you had cinnabar in your laboratory and I took it." Discomfort contorts his face. I almost burst out laughing but manage to restrain myself.

"I thought so when I saw it boiling in your study," I admit with forced neutrality. "I was wondering because you didn't tell me about taking it. But I had this strong feeling that I shouldn't ask."

He looks lost. "After the first dream I boiled the cinnabar in my study, day after day, hoping to understand it. Then a second dream appeared, identical to the first. But still nothing happened. And then Mundanus turned up and showed me the Red Sulphur while the cinnabar boils. And when you closed the curtains it shone with green radiance. That's when I knew my life had changed. That night I dreamt the Stone spoke to me."

I understand him fully. It is how I felt when I took the lid off the cauldron in Mundanus' smithy. I knew for sure that life itself had transmuted, never to be the same again.

"Since then I've been overcome by a strange excitement, a new kind of courage. It was as though my constant need to understand vanished from me like shackles falling off a prisoner and I knew that life is brewing in every grain of the world; in a different way from Leeuwenhoek's *animalcules* under the 'microscope', very different. It has nothing to do with smallness; it is about essence."

I nod in agreement, understanding him fully.

"And since the transmutation I see the world with the same clarity I once experienced high up in the mountains, when the light was crisp and breath was sharp. Everything around me sparkles with spirit; it is as if the world talks to me and my ears can hear. I remember you telling me once that an alchemist exclaimed that the Magus had to *become* the Stone. 'Transform yourselves into living Stones!' you quoted. That's what I feel has happened. The Stone has spoken. And I am dumbfounded."

"And you don't know if you altogether like it."

"No, I love it. But what bothers me is that minute by minute, the old world is taking me back and the shimmering veil of the Stone diminishes. I am waking from the dream of the Stone and this time I can't pull myself back in, however much I try. I saw the vision and I wasn't prepared. But the one thing that stays with me, Marianne, is that I've done wrong by you. I married you for your fortune," he admits in a grand gesture, "whereas I should have married you for your vision and your heart. I am deeply sorry. Please forgive me."

I am taken aback by his non sequitur confession and squeeze his hand gently to convey my complete absolution. I am aware that I, too, can feel the world of Red Sulphur slipping from view. I too was unprepared, even though I had tried to find it all of my life. I realize that this feeling of a brilliant world slipping through my fingers must be the undercurrent of what Mundanus senses all the time. I feel close to both men.

We sit in silence. I think of the passion for mathematics Helvetius has, just like my father, Johan de Witt, and Spinoza the Jew. There is a hush of admiration in their voices when they talk about Descartes, the French mathematician from Leyden who found the secret of life in his personal existence. '*I* think therefore *I* am.'

We are the generation *between*, no longer able to fashion the Stone from the vibrancy of the world, nor yet fully aware of what is about to be revealed through our findings by way of mathematical measurements. We exist between magic and ratio, between the visible world as a thin veil over divine essence and the rationale of calculus.

છ

"Whatever it is," he continues after some time, "it is infectious. The Grand Pensionary is a Calvinist as devoted as I was to the rational idea that the world was created once and for all by a God who withdrew to the heavens. But he was instantly curious when I told him of the possibility of godlike spontaneous creation." I can hear in his crisp formulation that Helvetius has thought about this over and over again.

"All he thinks about is money," I say scornfully. "Anything affecting his fiscal policy matters to him. It has nothing to do with his being infected with your dreams."

Helvetius looks hurt. I know I have stepped on his heart and feel bad that I attack him because of my fear of Johan de Witt and my imminent meeting with him.

"It felt different," Helvetius replies. "It felt as if he saw something."

I don't believe a word of it, but I stay silent in order not to hurt him again. What matters is that both his world and mine have been shaken to the core and we are each moving towards an uncertain future. Suddenly I feel a great tenderness towards him. I go over and kiss him on the forehead. He closes his eyes and sighs deeply.

"I will have to publish all this," he says softly. "I know I will have to."

I am instantly alarmed.

"It will make me the laughing stock of the world," he adds apprehensively. "My reputation will be shattered. They will call me a benighted alchemist and no one will believe me. They all are convinced of the world as I knew it too, before those cinnabar dreams and before the projection."

I can see how his vanity is about to be crushed by the ridicule of a hostile society and how much simpler it would be to forget the affair. I am surprised that Helvetius has more courage than I have imagined and, incongruously, I am proud of him, while at the same time wishing he would never write about this. A man I thought vapid turns out to have fiber. I stroke his hair softly; he looks bereft.

"Please remember to hide Mundanus' identity. You promised."

Helvetius nods in agreement.

୫୬

Benedict de Spinoza seems not to care what people think of him, which I am sure is the quality that caused him to be exiled from the community of Jews in Amsterdam ten years ago. He started visiting the house as a friend of Anthonie van Leeuwenhoek. They are the same age, around 34, and share an interest in optics. Leeuwenhoek's lenses are far more advanced than anyone else's. Helvetius has told me that Leeuwenhoek has several looking glasses by way of which Helvetius has seen the inner life of blood and other human tissue. That's when he saw the invisible *animalcules* as Anthonie calls them. He is about to take some of the alchemical gold to Leeuwenhoek to compare it with natural gold under his powerful lenses.

Spinoza is a private man who naturally keeps a distance. He is extremely modest in his demeanor. His egg-shaped face has the sharp protruding beak-like nose of his people, curly dark hair down to his shoulders, and the most remarkable set of eyes. His right eye looks at you with contemplative dispassion, while his left drifts off to sights unseen by others. His lips seem to constantly curtail a desire to smile at the world. I like him and find his awkwardness amusing. Conversations with him are invariably delightful. He treats me like his equal and I don't feel like a woman in his company.

"Respectfully, Madam Schweitzer, I do not believe there are miracles. If a transmutation *did* take place, the potential for transmutations from lead to gold must be inherent in nature itself. In that case all metal must consist of a common essence, which the Red Sulphur you mention brings out and transforms. So I'm of a different opinion than men who ridicule the possibility of such a transmutation are completely convinced that Helvetius was out to fool us all – yet they write with conviction about such unnatural things as birth by a virgin and the resurrection of the dead. Men only believe in their own line of incredible events. They heap all manner of scorn upon Helvetius – which leads me to believe that the matter threatens ideas they hold dear. Their ardent disavowal interests me." Spinoza allows himself a brief, rather melancholy smile and I wonder if his left eye sees a memory of his expulsion by the narrow-minded Jews with the same calcified spirit as the men to whom he refers. Smug blindness may arise from any provenance.

"Benedict! So glad you came!" Helvetius' jovial voice comes from behind us, using the informal term for 'you' in his address. "Have you spoken to Anthonie?"

Spinoza rises, and uses the formal 'you' in his return greeting. Then he adds, "No, but I have come to see the gold for myself. An esteemed friend of mine asked me to look into the matter and see if there is truth to it."

"Well, you can tell him every word of it is according to the facts," Helvetius shakes Spinoza's hand with obvious relish. "You can ask Mint-master Porelius or goldsmith Brechtelt himself."

"I went to see Brechtelt," Spinoza replies, with his customary measured earnestness. "He told me that he could not explain why there was 30% more gold after the assay than before. The only way it could have happened was if the gold had something within it capable of transmuting the silver into gold. He admits that it is utterly impossible but it is the only way to explain the facts." I had found it rather amusing when I saw Brechtelt's face of a man whose certainties had been trampled by out of control facts.

"I can show you the cauldron in which the transmutation happened. You might want to inspect it," Helvetius suggests gently to his friend.

Helvetius leads us in procession up the stairs. There is pride in his footstep. It is connected to his immense admiration for his young friend, whom he calls the smartest man he has ever encountered.

My father's laboratory is in its usually untidy state, the only room in the house allowed to exist in the wild without much restraint. All other rooms have been tamed into ordered domesticity. Here, flasks on shelves are randomly mixed in with open books, a skull, and snakeskin in a jar. It is the one room in the house where servants are rarely allowed access and the dust has settled on old half-forgotten experiments. Spinoza has never been here and he looks around with disapproval. His orderly mind abhors chaos. I am secretly pleased to have upset his monk-like austerity and feel like teasing him mercilessly.

"Excuse our dust and disorder," I say in mock seriousness. "But you must be used to it, given that you breathe glass dust all day long." Spinoza's grimace is full of distaste, as if the odors of the laboratory and the state of its dissonance assaults his nostrils and sours his tongue. He takes out a white handkerchief and holds it in front of his nose, trying to be inconspicuous.

"Well now," I say, "It's not all that bad. It's the smell of nature. You write about Nature as Divine. Well, this is what it looks and smells like when left to its own devices." I am sure he has never smelled cow dung and that he somehow avoids the stench of ordinary bodies clad in clothes drenched in months' worth of sweat and mud mixed with urine. I wonder if his virgin distaste for the passions has to do with an oversensitive nose. If he were not a man of such obviously impeccable character, I wouldn't trust him a bit.

"She does not allow this room to be cleaned. She is afraid it will endanger her experiments," Helvetius tells him with a grin on his face. He is proud of me; and exasperated. He can talk this way to Spinoza who knows that I am an experimentalist. Spinoza likes unusual people, and I qualify. "But then she comes up with medicines which often work better than those of the 'learned' pharmacists," Helvetius adds, soaking the word 'learned' in a marinade of irony. "Here is the *vas*, the vessel of the transmutation." There is a hush of awe in his voice as he picks up the small black iron pot and hands it to Spinoza. Inside the glow of gold is clearly visible, as it has fused to the metal of the vessel. Helvetius points at it. "That used to be lead," he says simply.

I notice a brief tremble in Spinoza's hands, very unusual for a lens maker used to manual precision. He holds his breath, unable to curtail the excitement overrunning the city-walled safety of his enormous intellect. I had never thought the day would come I'd see Spinoza shaken.

"There must be an explanation," he mutters.

"Well, it looks pretty miraculous to me!" exclaims Helvetius.

"The affect caused by its miraculous appearance does not mean it is a miracle," Spinoza says sharply. A bit too pointedly methinks. He seems to be trying to convince himself. "Lead must contain the essence of gold and the powder must unlock it."

"You're speaking like a true alchemist," I comment. "That's how they explain the tincture. My father studied alchemy for many years and so did I. I never thought I would actually see it before my eyes. I was beginning to think alchemy some kind of poetic fancy. I was beginning to believe that the imagination of the metals alchemist talk about is not in the metals but in our minds. But here it is, right in front of us in physical space, for all of us to see. So what do we do now?" I ask, serious.

"We be shocked," Helvetius grins out loud. "That's all we can be."

"I must agree," Spinoza admits against his nature. "I'm shocked."

"Or maybe there is no such clear separation between the world of thought and the world of things that take up space; maybe a physical object is under a different aspect a thought, and vice versa," I say.

Spinoza looks at me with admiration. "I have been thinking this for some time now. I am trying to formulate it but have not yet as concisely as you just did. Thoughts and things in space are caused by the same underlying nature I call 'substance'."

"Being a woman has its advantages," I tease him. "You must think succinctly, in brief intervals while running a household and taking care of others."

൭

When Mint-master Porelius is at our door first thing the next morning, I'm not surprised. Johan de Witt is a man who won't be kept waiting. It had been no fluke that 13 years ago, in '53, he had risen to the highest rank in Holland at the age of 28. No one before him ever had. In most places one could not even become mayor of the city until 40 years of age. His power had grown in direct proportion with his greatness ever since. A mathematician at heart, Johan de Witt is particularly interested in the algebra of finances and carefully oversees all monetary transactions of the Republic. No one in the world knows more about state bonds than does he. I have always known that he instinctively knows the smell of gold.

"Tell the Grand Pensionary that I can't come today," I say to the Mint-master.

Porelius perspires, taken aback by my intentional arrogance. I look at him down my nose, stretched to my full height wearing shoes with very high heels from Paris. "Tell the Grand Pensionary that the daughter of my sister Johanna van Os has been severely ill and is recovering in the country, and that I am her guardian and am going to visit her. I will contact him upon my return." De Witt knew Johanna. They were the same age. Clara had played on his lap in my father's house. I pull out all the stops, not ready to face De Witt's supreme power while I feel confused and weak. I turn around with elegant aplomb and can't help being pleased with myself. I know that De Witt won't have me arrested or escorted to his offices. His deep respect for my father will give me a day or so of respite. But after that the game is up and I will have to go see him. Ignoring Porelius' presence, I call out to Hendrik to prepare the carriage.

Diffidently the Mint-master bows in order to leave and I acknowledge him with a cold stare intended for De Witt. Then, sorry for his discomfort, I smile as sweetly as I am able to smile in the face of a toad, while feeling womanly and superior. In a sudden reversal, I am excited by the adventure that is my life. The pain in my heart is well worth it, when compared to the dull existence of a money counter. I sigh with relief when the slam of the door drums goodbye to Mint-master Porelius.

Then reality sets in. I had not planned to go and visit Clara for some time, not until I had some grip on myself, but now I am forced. I feel a bit guilty that I did not want to see her right now. I'm sure she is eagerly awaiting my coming, not aware of the chimeras in my mind. I go upstairs to my bedroom and search for better shoes to walk the slush. I find boots my father had bought from some Russian traders in exchange for spices. They had also sold him a full length thick coat made of soft white lynx fur, illustrating their stories of the steppes from where they hailed, and I remember Johanna's intense pride when she first wore her white lynx in the snowy streets of The Residence. I miss my sister.

&

I'm snug in Johanna's fur and blankets as the carriage moves slowly through the brown mud. Hendrik's face is bright red. I have been thinking of Johanna constantly since putting on my boots. I also realize that I feel warmer towards Johann Friedrich, whose first names I only use when I feel kindly towards Helvetius. We are in a conspiracy together to protect Mundanus' identity from Johan de Witt, which puts both of us in danger. One word from De Witt and Helvetius stops being the physician to young Prince William of Orange and loses most of his medical clientele among the Regents. It would matter little from a financial perspective, since I have enough money to last us several lifetimes, as long as our Dutch East-India Trading Company keeps bringing in the spices and other goods. They call ours the Golden Age; it certainly has been for my family. Thirty years ago, just before the prices collapsed, Father had sold all his positions in tulip bulbs for a tremendous price which he then used to buy more stock in the East-India Trading Company. His extraordinary financial canniness had earned him the admiration of a wealthy Amsterdam investment banker, the brother-in-law and principal financial advisor of Johan de Witt. That's how our family got to know De Witt. He would come to the house to talk finances. Johanna had always had strong feelings towards De Witt from the first days they met ten years ago, even though Johan to his advantage had married young Wendela Bicker from the powerful Amsterdam family the year before. De Witt had been warmly gallant towards Johanna, a kindness I appreciated. Everyone knew that Johan de Witt was besotted with his wife and had no eye for other women. Her impossible affections had cast a new pallor over Johanna's already joyless life. Not even Clara's thriving as her only surviving child had given her pleasure. She had always been sad for as long as I remember, and her moods were not much helped by the loveless marriage to a man who had married her for her money. It was a relief when he died in 1650, three years after Clara was born, and they moved back to Father's house. Those had been the only years when my sister had shown a pale version of happiness; that is, until Johan de Witt came into our lives ten years ago in '56. I am thinking of the years when Clara would be in my home for months while Johanna would not leave her darkened room, pining away under down covers. It had driven Father to distraction. Every day he had her chambermaid get Johanna dressed and then he would take her for a ride along the Lange Voorhout with Hendrik, sometimes in the same coat I am currently wearing. Clara was a cheerful child, seemingly oblivious to the leaden moods of her mother, a dancing wood sprite stealing everyone's heart without effort, including Johan de Witt's. She was always humming songs and her blond curls gave her a cherubic aspect which she danced before us unselfconsciously. I would enjoy the times with her as a child and was always heartbroken for some days when she had to return to Johanna. I could not admit to myself that I hoped Johanna would never recover so Clara would be in my home forever. Until she died, that is. Then her loss burst over me in torrents of guilt and for months I could find no pleasure in Clara's presence. I relegated her to some kind of servant role; maybe it had made her sick at heart and that's why she fell ill. So when her condition deteriorated I had become desperate with premonitions of another loss caused by my wishes, which would make Johanna depart altogether and sew me permanently into a tight bag of self-recrimination. And then, as Mundanus revived her and a blush came back to her cheeks, so did my love for Clara, in waves of joy which felt like grief. I sit back and let the memories wash over me, feeling gratitude that Clara is alive and I will imminently get to see her. I watch the passers-by distractedly. A young man wears a fascinating exotic silver dagger on his belt. I stare at it and think of Mundanus' travels.

℥

"Madam Marianne!" Gerda exclaims with obvious delight, standing in the front door of the old farm on the dyke along the Vliet. "I hadn't expected you back for days. What a wonderful surprise. Clara will be so happy. She is getting restless. A farm is no place for her. She is such a city lady. She wants to go back to The Hague. I think she is well enough." Her words tumble over one another in her excitement over seeing me. I rush inside to see Clara. She's in the very back of the large room, bending over the large table, going through Gerda's wool which she is preparing for the spinning wheel. From early childhood on Clara has always been a weaver at heart. I wait, enjoying looking at her in the distance, taking pleasure in her concentrated gaze and the soft sound of her voice humming a popular melody. Her flowing gold curls and slender frame in Gerda's warm coarse yellow dress gives her the look of an angel lost on earth by accident. She looks up, sees me and exclaims at the top of her lungs, as she runs towards me with a vigor belying the fact that she has just returned from the dead:

"Aunt Marianne! You came!"

I stand still, arms wide open, letting her find her way home to my embrace. As I hold her, all the madness around Mundanus drops off me. I inhale her fragrance and feel my family surrounding me, as if the entire Van Os clan is gathering to protect us from the dangers to come. We are of one body, a single bloodline. Under Clara's frail exterior, I can feel the tenacity I know so well from my own tribulations. That's why she is alive, this daughter of ours, our flesh. Then, from below, the shrill crooked voice of jealousy rears up. I can't hold it down. I envy her youth and her fertility. So here I stand, with Clara in my arms, mother and rival folded into one. All I can do is feel it, praying for the wisdom to deal with the volatile amalgam. I realize this alchemy is going to be harder even than projecting the gold. I hold Clara by the shoulders and look into her face, a youthful reflection of mine.

"You've come back to health," I say softly, and am relieved by my unadulterated happiness over this. "You've come back to us." I watch the tears on her cheeks.

"Please take me home, Aunt Marianne. I like it here with Gerda but I would so much rather be with you and Uncle Johann." Her use of Helvetius' first name brings back Johan de Witt. I shudder briefly, wanting to elude him for as long as I can. Being away from The Hague gives me respite.

"I could use some country air myself," I mutter disingenuously. "I'll stay here with you for a day or so if Gerda will have me, and then we'll go back."

Clara looks disappointed and happy at the same time.

"We could spin wool together and take it home with us to weave cloth." Clara's passion for weaving has made exceptional at it. Her teacher, old Elspeth, marvels at it every day. "How one so young can weave so old," I hear her mutter incredulously, shaking her head with the violet widow's cap which indicates a late stage of mourning. She had come to us in black, a forlorn member of a Regent family destroyed by the pestilence, last in a renowned line of women famous for their ravishing weavings. When she took Clara on as an apprentice, within months Clara had been weaving to such a level of complicated artistry that only a natural talent could explain her excellence.

"Gerda's wool is very fine and strong. I've been spinning the thinnest of threads, very sturdy. It would be wonderful if you could help me!" she exclaims, her desire for home instantly forgotten. A child she is, a nineteen-year-old woman child. "And then we can make dyes in your laboratory when we get home, and we can visit the dye masters!" Her excitement is infectious.

"Gerda," she calls out happily, "Aunt Marianne will stay and help us with the wool."

"I'll pay you the price it would fetch in the heart of winter," I smile.

Gerda nods and brings in a second spinning wheel from somewhere in the back. We are three happy women around a roughhewn table laden with wool.

Clara's hands get busy instantly and I admire her natural dexterity. The thread from her wheel is so much finer than what I can do. I feel clumsy next to her.

"You should do the spinning, Clara. I just ruin the wool."

Gerda smiles broadly. "I gave up too," she says. "Miss Clara performs miracles at the wheel."

I nod and remark with restrained pride "We all marvel at her mastery."

"Have you heard from doctor Mundanus?" Gerda asks. I hear Clara's spinning wheel slow down and stop. The question hangs pregnant in the room.

"No, no I haven't. He went to Amsterdam," I lie, "and he has not sent a missive yet," I add truthfully. "He is going to set up practice there."

"I know," Gerda says, serious. "He is considering taking me on as an apprentice. I want to learn to heal the way *he* does. I want to bring that to my kinfolk here so they will not have to die when the next pestilence hits. All doctors are useless except for him."

I see Clara nodding adamantly. The look on Clara's face combines the ecstatic transport of the mystic with the surrender of love. Shrillness shreds my heart. A volatile mixture of my emotions fills the room and I have a sudden urge to take Gerda into my confidence. I resist it. It is too dangerous.

Clara's long fingers resume their work at the wheel. Slender and dexterous, they dance along the strands with inimitable grace. I can feel how our relationship has changed. A subtle shift has taken place in which I am no longer just her Aunt Marianne, her surrogate mother. Her mature mastery at the spinning wheel displays her adulthood: the child I had imagined just moments before is an afterglow of a past now gone. She has been changed by this illness, just as I have been changed by my encounter with Mundanus and his Red Sulphur.

Together we have to play the game to save Mundanus and his future generations of Red Sulphur progeny. I intuit that Red Sulphur has its own intentions and Trismosin's remarks about a future generation when its mysteries will be revealed refer to us. The pain in my heart recedes, yet without diminishing, as if attention has shifted away from it without affecting either its heat or intensity. On the stage of my soul a new play takes shape, one in which I am cast in a supporting role. My personal pain, though in no way insignificant, has been reconfigured.

Clara and I are equal pawns in a greater story than our own. I realize that we do not know one another, that we are now familiar strangers. I have to tell her what is happening to Mundanus, the man who has transmuted us both.

I speak with sudden resolution. "Mundanus is being chased by the Grand Pensionary."

Gerda grows pale; Clara looks non-comprehending, the wheel still whirring absentmindedly. My next words are lies, which I must tell to hide Mundanus' connection to the rumors of gold making which are rumbling throughout the United Provinces.

"Johan de Witt wants to prevent him from treating the Prince of Orange. He has heard that Mundanus can cure him from his asthma and his headaches and De Witt does not want a healthy prince."

Gerda responds with predictable fury. The peasants are usually Orangists, fiercely protective of their young Prince, whom they consider the true Viceroy of the land. The rabble violently opposes our current regime of Regents, an alliance of ruling burgher families like my own Van Os clan.

In this play I am an Orangist, protecting the sickly young Prince of Orange from the claws of the Regent of Regents, Johan de Witt. "De Witt has demanded that Uncle Johann Friedrich bring him Mundanus." I pause. "My husband is the Prince's physician," I explain to Gerda as an aside.

Then I turn to Clara. "Both your Uncle and Mundanus are in danger. Helvetius would never practice medicine again and Mundanus would hang." At first Clara looks aghast, but her expression rapidly shifts to firm determination.

"We have to let Mundanus know!" she exclaims, and Gerda nods fervently.

"That's what I'm trying to do," I reply, "but I don't know where he is."

"But you said he'd gone to Amsterdam!" she reminds me.

I blush silently.

"Didn't he tell you where he went?" Surprise makes Clara's voice raise an octave.

"No," I lie again, "He knows De Witt has ways to make people talk and he didn't want to endanger me by knowing his whereabouts. And he is right. It is better for the moment for none of us to know where he is."

"So what can we do?" asks Clara, tremulous, in a tone of despair.

"Regents, tax collectors, they're all out for themselves. They hang us by the dozen. The Prince will stand over them and save us," says Gerda with angry conviction. I know the romance of the masses with the House of Orange. This Prince's father had hanged Regents like me indiscriminately for no reason at all – but I play my part, and nod.

"I think I know how to find him. I can't tell you how but I will. For the time being, I have been ordered to De Witt's offices. He wants to talk about Mundanus. I'm sure a slew of spies have already been dispatched. They will trace Mundanus to this farm. He's been seen by many people here *and* he is famous in these parts for his work during the pestilence."

Gerda nods, her face flushed.

"That's why I came: to warn you, Gerda. Pretend you know nothing. And by all means, don't tell them of your conversation with him about an apprenticeship."

"Is my family in danger?" Gerda's acute fear takes me by surprise. I've not yet heard that tone in her voice. She had always been the calm beacon in the room. It seems as if something has already happened to her that now makes her fear for her family. Her distress makes me falter for a moment.

"I am sorry we got you into this trouble," I say. "I didn't know."

"Of course you didn't," Gerda responds, visibly pulling herself together. "Doctor Mundanus is worth the trouble, Madam, thousand times over. He and our Prince! If you will excuse me, I must warn Klaas and the men before," (unspeakable scorn and disgust enter her voice,) "the Balthasars are here." Balthasar

Gerard, the stealthy murderer almost a century ago of our liberator William the Silent, first Prince of Orange, was more hated by the Orangists than the Devil himself. Seeing my worry, she quickly adds: "I know how to talk to the men here, Madam Marianne, leave it to me." With her Orangist hatred of the Regent regime the tone of confidence has returned to her voice and I know that she is right about her ability to handle the peasant folk. They respect her more than anyone. We smile at one another: the Regent and the peasant, equals. I have never felt this before. In our society everyone knows his or her station from birth. I feel this breaking of the boundaries to be oddly exhilarating. Gerda leaves through the barn doors next to the great fireplace.

Clara stares at her wheel, despondent. The pale window light gives her face a silver glow.

"May I tell you something, Aunt Marianne," she says, after a long silence.

"Of course darling, of course you may," I say, the intimacy between us returning like a warm wind.

"It is very private," she adds, looking at me intently.

I remember times when she would speak to me about her life without any reservation, telling me things she could not tell her mother. It had been one of the most exquisite pleasures in my existence. Yet now I feel a foreboding.

"You know you can tell me anything, Clara. You always have."

Clara smiles shyly, her face angelic. Then she blushes crimson. "I have strong affections for Doctor Mundanus. Very strong! I've never felt this before," she blurts.

My heart burns with the acid certainty that the vision I had seen of our future had not been a chimera with which to torture myself, but the foreshadowing of matters to come. The Gordian knot within me draws tight, looking for a sword to slice it open. Jealousy shrieks its desire to cover Clara with the burning pitch of Hell while fighting a bloody battle with the fierce angel of Mother-love.

Suddenly a vision of Mundanus stands before me, his apparition towering all the way up to the ceiling. Then he vanishes. His presence pushes me backwards and I have to hold on to a chair to keep my balance.

"What's happening, Aunt Marianne," Clara exclaims. "You look like you're about to faint."

I rub my forehead, trying to dispel the swoon which has come over me, the muscles in my body melting, no longer able to keep me upright. I sink onto the chair before I melt all the way down to the floor. The world swims in front of my eyes. I see Clara as through a sea of waves.

ॐ

I need to decide. I need to decide which side to choose in this battle for my soul. My stoic education teaches me to rule my affections, to master the turmoil of the heart. I must choose family over all else. And I must throw my weight behind the Red Sulphur vision of Salomon Trismosin. My personal pain must be conquered. It must! But jealousy parries, with the scrappy determination of a street fighter who has the advantage of passion over the cool aristocratic forces of duty. I can no longer look at Clara, as my insides have it out.

"Here, Aunt Marianne, drink this." I can smell the burning spirit of Old Dutch gin under my nose. Without a thought I obey. The flames pouring down my throat wake me. Clara gives me a second glass and it too finds its fiery way to my innards. Its fire stills my turbulence and clears the sea foam from my mind. Determination wins out, and the agents of jealousy are locked away into the deepest dungeons of my heart. I know they will escape from there, but for now we are safe. I stretch my back and stand.

"I was overcome with worry for the future," I say stiffly to Clara; she nods. I add, "But I did hear your words, my darling. We should find Mundanus so you may declare your affection.

He is a good man of considerable riches from a good family, I know. He is a worthy candidate for your love."

Clara smiles eagerly. "It feels like I have always known him, Aunt Marianne. It is as if he has returned home to me from a long journey." I know exactly what she means. I have another shot of gin.

We hear excited voices outside. Gerda breaks in, followed by muscled men carrying pitchforks and shovels. "Orange above all!" someone yells. I'm suddenly afraid of having incited a riot.

The disorderly mob spreads through the barn. I motion to Gerda to come outside with me.

The cold outside air washes off my lingering distress. I hear it echo away, like the wild voices of the men inside after the barn door closes.

"Gerda, this is a very bad idea. I'm sorry. I should have explained myself better." Gerda looks at me intently, caution in her eyes. The distinction of our birth reasserts itself. I know I do have to take her into my confidence. We all play our predestined roles in this drama of the Gold.

"Johan de Witt will not send a force of arms at first. He'll be sending spies. If they report back to him that the peasants encountered them in arms, he will escalate his response. Then he *will* send federal troops." Gerda looks unconvinced. Her suspicion of the Regents has been aroused and won't quiet down in a hurry.

"You must trust me as I trust you." I wait and notice her tight muscles soften for an instant, which I take as my cue.

"Mundanus is in Leyden. You must go see him and tell him De Witt is after him. Tell the men to disperse and be ready. Someone has to go to the smithy up the road where he stayed for some time. No one there is to breathe a word about Mundanus. Do you think your people here can keep silent? Even on gin?"

Gerda is fully convinced by my openness, a flush of excitement on her face. "No offence, Madam Marianne, but we hate the Regents around here. They've let us rot. We love the Prince. We'd give our lives for the House of Orange. Mundanus' secret is safe with us." Her conviction inspires me. I have crossed the chasm of birth for good, thereby committing the gravest sin known to our carefully stratified society: a Regent-born conspiring with the peasant rabble. The distinction between lead and gold has blurred.

"Tell Mundanus to stay in Leyden. He is safe there. They are fierce Orangists." I still have a hard time believing that I have switched sides after what the young Prince's father did 16 years ago, taking the federal army to the walls of Amsterdam to subjugate the Regent families. It had broken through the equanimity of even a man like my father, and had evoked outrage in us all. We had rejoiced (in a well-mannered, dignified fashion) when the aggressor Prince died of the pox that same year.

"Give Mundanus the message to not contact me," I add, a momentary pang taking me by surprise. Gerda nods, her sharp eyes registering my brief lapse. My stoic education, which has trained me from childhood to keep my face in line, fails me miserably. I smile at Gerda. I can't keep it hidden from her. I love the alchemist and I know she does too in her way. Thirty-four years of the most careful training as a plant in a hothouse has gone by the wayside in meeting the man who has turned my matter to gold.

"But won't I be under surveillance too?" she asks.

"Not if you have not seen a stranger in these parts."

"No one was spotted," she replies.

"Then you should leave right away, before they come. But tell Henk to beware: Johan de Witt will put a bounty on Mundanus' head, and gold is hard to resist."

"The Prince matters more to us than their gold," Gerda says, proudly. I feel unconvinced, but there is nothing I can do.

"Leave immediately," I repeat and I give her Giovanni Theodore's whereabouts.

Against all social protocol, Gerda hugs me briefly before she goes inside to talk to the men.

I stand alone and look out over the dirty white landscape with patches of mud and De Vliet with large puddles on top of the melting ice. I shiver, knowing that I have just taken on the most powerful man in our world.

Chapter Six

The meeting was set for this Monday afternoon at De Witt's office. Poor Mint-master Porelius had been perspiring profusely on the ice-cold morning when he came to the house with the Grand Pensionary's summons. He pushed it into my hands and before I could finish reading it he was gone, escaping with a speed that belied his corpulence. I immediately recognized Johan de Witt's handwriting. Many letters about matters of finance and taxes had passed between de Witt and my father, who always allowed me to read them. He would come to the house to get Father's advice on the abstruse arithmetic of bond issues, the lifeblood of the Republic. Father had a multi-layered understanding of these matters, and De Witt treated him as a student would treat a grand teacher. In this way I had come to know Johan de Witt in a different way from most people. To everyone else, he was the great leader, whom they called 'the Schoolmaster'. To me, he was a pupil, full of deference to my father.

The tone of his letter today was respectful, yet suffering no contradiction. This was an order, not a request. The time for delaying was done.

Hendrik brings me half an hour early to the large courtyard of the Inner Court one block away from our house, where all the carriages of dignitaries are parked. I walk across the yard to the Great Hall of Knights, a churchlike structure with two high, pointed towers. I go to the stalls of booksellers in the anteroom to get a paper and inform myself about the dire political situation of the moment. I haven't read the news since Mundanus has entered my life. I buy a *Hollandsche Mercurius* and read about the tensions between Spain and France at our Southern borders; and about final details of the peace treaty with the Bishop of Munster a year ago February after his invasion of the eastern provinces in '65. Today the war with England is on the inside page. The African Adventurers of James Duke of York – brother to King Charles II of England – who had started this war in '64 by attacking our African trading posts and gold mines, was reportedly in financial ruins. It is gold that will win this war. I know that De Witt needs money to defend the country. What a windfall it would be for the entire Regent government if I were to deliver them the Red Sulphur from its hiding place in my laboratory. For an instant I feel Regent solidarity weaken my resolve. I breathe in deep and shake my head free from the vise grip of my social background.

To distract myself I look through the many pamphlets, critical of our Regent government, some even talking about its overthrow in favor of the young Prince. I hear my Father's voice quote his revered teacher in mathematics and philosophy, Rene Descartes of Leyden: "In what other country could one enjoy freedom so completely and where could one sleep with less worry?" Here, at the center of Regent power, pamphlets are being tolerated advocating its demise. No other country would allow that. For a moment I can feel again my father's pride in Holland's tolerance, which is based on privileges wrested away from the feudal nobility by cities ruled by the burghers themselves. These burgher rulers of the citadels of freedom are organized in families of Regents calling themselves collectively the party of *True Freedom*. They control the gray masses with an iron fist of burgher discipline and are ardent republicans, critical of all royalty. Johan de Witt is our undisputed leader. I can't help feeling like a renegade. Following one's heart over one's duty to family and the public good is anathema to our stoic upbringing, which teaches us to live in a web of social obligations. Our republic is in dire straits. A short while back James Duke of York's *'Company of Royal Adventurers of England Trading to Africa'* had begun a campaign of systematic attacks on our colonies, and two years ago in '64, they had overrun Nieuw Amsterdam, re-naming it New York after James. England had been demanding rulership over the seas. I know that Johan de Witt needs gold to build up the fleet. The populace has been taxed to the hilt and they are tapped out. If you eat fish at a tavern around here you have to pay thirty different kinds of taxes. One more cent and De Witt would have mutiny on his hands.

Lost in thought I suddenly notice an elaborate carriage surrounded by men at arms. At the door I see a hunchback boy I recognize as my husband's illustrious patient leaving the premises. Instinctively I curtsy to him. His youthful face is crafted of hard steel, looking me over briefly. Then he bows imperceptibly and steps into the waiting grand carriage. Johan de Witt has followed the Prince to the door, and sees me.

"Marianne van Os," he says, with unexpected spontaneity. Among Regents we never use our personal names without titles like 'Highly Esteemed Lady.'

"Grand Pensionary," I reply, and curtsy once more, though less deeply.

"I have not seen you since your esteemed Father's funeral. A great loss to us all." He looks sincere and I am taken off guard by his friendliness. "Please follow me up to my quarters," he invites. People around look at me curiously, realizing that the Grand Pensionary is acting in an unusual manner towards a lady they don't know. They may be burghers, but they are courtiers as well. He turns to his secretary: "No callers." The man bows briefly. This raises even more eyebrows, and I wonder why De Witt wants to get the word out about our meeting. Maybe it is because our encounter will be unchaperoned, and open curtains with a plain view are the best defense against rumors. Indeed, no one else enters his study at the top of the stairs, just he and I. He points towards the leather chair across his desk and waits for me to sit down.

"How is Clara?" he asks, with genuine concern. Here a father speaks, not a statesman.

"Thank God, she is doing much better."

"This Doctor Mundanus, he cured her?" he inquires, letting me know he is well-informed. I blush and nod. His directness confuses me. I had expected an elaborate cat and mouse game.

"Where could I find him?" he asks without further ado.

"I don't know," I say sweetly, regaining the impenetrable mask I have learned to maintain.

"He just left after treating Clara."

"You know that I don't believe you, with all due respect. I know you and Helvetius are protecting him for some indubitably noble reason. But as your Grand Pensionary, I do need to know where he is." Now there is an unmistakable tone of threat in his voice. Instantly I feel much more comfortable. This I have expected.

"All I know is that he was going to Amsterdam."

"I am aware of that. I have been told that he performed another projection there." I am surprised that he uses correct alchemical terminology. "The Mint-master tells me that this man can make gold and has done so twice: once in your presence and once in Amsterdam. But Amsterdam is a very big city. Where do I find him?"

"You want his Red Sulphur," I state calmly.

"You must know that we are at war, potentially with three countries at the same time. We need gold. As the daughter to one of our great minds of finance, you should be aware of this." He reels me in with a line of loyalty.

"Mundanus told me that you would be after him and his Red Sulphur so he made a point of not telling me." De Witt looks at me with intent eyes. I don't flinch, having prepared myself for this very moment over a matter of days. "I know your men are following every step I take, but you might as well call them off. I know nothing. If I knew where to find him I would contact him this instant, begging him for his secrets. You know my father, you know about his passion for the Great Art."

"No, you would not. You are protecting him and you would not betray him by leading us to him. Let us assume for the moment that we are equally intelligent so we do not have to weave improbable tales. It is not becoming." He pauses, pensive. "I must admit I never understood this passion for medieval pre-occupations from such an eminently rational man as your father. But now I'm no longer as sure as I was since Mint-master Porelius' story. It came so well verified that even I begin to doubt my certainty."

"Radical doubt is a good start, Master Descartes would say." I know De Witt to be a follower of the great mathematician.

"Indeed it is," he smiles. "That's why I shall begin with doubting every word you say."

"Your privilege, Grand Pensionary. By all means."

We have arrived at the predictable stalemate. If we keep it this way I will forever be under the curse of his suspicion. So here I must play my card of utter bluff.

"Have we come to the end of our conversation?" I ask him, transgressing all form. He is supposed to indicate the termination of our talk. He looks surprised. Then he nods.

"You know that you and your husband will be under continuous surveillance," he concludes. "I apologize for this." I bow slightly, indicating both understanding and forgiveness.

He begins to rise. I stay seated, so he sits back down.

"I have a personal request, coming directly from the Van Os family." De Witt listens intently. Unexpected matters put him on alert.

"My niece Clara wishes to marry. For the sake of my father I would request your presence at the ceremony."

"With pleasure!" he exclaims. "It would be an honor for me to return to your father a fraction of the great favors he did me. When is it to be?" he asks.

"This summer, early August," I reply. "On a date that would suit your calendar."

He nods and leads me out of the room. "You can arrange it with my secretary when the time comes." I curtsy once more and he bows. I notice how he looks at me with pleasure. He likes to fence with a woman.

I feel myself running down the stairs, trying to slow down my steps. I hardly notice people staring at me. As if Hendrik has anticipated my needs, the carriage pulls up right in front of De Witt's office door. I don't remember how I enter. The first thing I know is that we are riding and my sobs behind the drawn curtains are drowned out by the racket of wheels on cobblestones. I am terrified. It is insane to take this risk. Of course De Witt will find out who this Signor Theodore really is. Mundanus should flee the country, go down to Venice and stay there. But my heart tears; I can't be without him. I can't let him go. And I can't go with him to Venice or a city like it. De Witt's power extends over all points of trade in Europe.

Suddenly I hear Mundanus' voice emerge from behind my right shoulder. His presence calms me down instantly. I note a glow of gold and the faint smell of male seed which accompanies the great transmutation. "You did well," says Mundanus' voice. "It had to be done. Only in broad daylight can we hide. He will search each rabbit hole in the Lowlands but he won't see me when I am the groom and he is the guest of honor." Then the glow disappears; only the fragrance of transmutation stays behind. I feel weak as if my muscles have been drained of life. I have placed my bet - to be with Mundanus forever, in whatever capacity. Together we will fulfill the Trismosin mission: Mundanus, Clara and I. My breath slows down, leaving a great lassitude behind. I barely hear the metal sound of jealousy rattling the dungeon door.

Clara is in the red room when I come home. She's brought her spinning wheel from her room in the back, innocently unaware that she has reclaimed her central place in the household, which my guilt had taken from her after her mother died. A large wicker basket filled with Gerda's wool takes up a corner of the room and blocks her from my view. I hear the whirring of the wheel stop before I see her.

"How was it?" she asks with anxious curiosity.

I know I should not lie to her, even though the truth may be quite shocking.

"I told him that you were going to marry Mundanus this summer in August and that he would be the guest of honor. He accepted. The only thing he does not know is that Mundanus is actually the man you will marry. To him it will be a stranger called Signor Theodore. We will need to find a plausible story about how the two of you met." Now that I have blurted it all out, I feel a modicum of relief.

Clara looks run over. Several emotions wrestle for precedence, her face a waterfall of expressions. "Me, marrying Mundanus?" she finally exclaims in disbelief.

I sit as motionless as I can. I don't know what to hope for. I wish she'd run like lightning and never involve herself with Mundanus again; I wish Mundanus would never marry her. At the same time I know it will be the only solution.

I wait. Clara is still wrestling with various storms, her eyes like saucers. I wish I could help her, but sit frozen, waiting for the verdict of her soul.

"But they will recognize him; someone will." Her voice is almost pleading.

Now I know that she wishes to marry Mundanus, but sees the obstacles. Sadness dissolves my last hope, that Clara would wish no part of this. I speak slowly, thinking of my vision in the carriage. Mundanus had assured me that this mad plan would work. "I'm sure Mundanus can disguise himself beyond recognition. Only the heart will know him. Only you and I will recognize him." At once I have the shocking sense that I have given away my secret, and I rush to cover my tracks. "It will all depend if Mundanus has the same affections towards you that you feel for him."

"I know he does," Clara utters with certainty. My heart drops down a chasm as I try to force a smile.

"I'm sure he does," I manage, "who wouldn't: a lovely girl like you. He would be blind."

"I have seen it in his eyes," she remarks calmly.

My fate is sealed. I wish I were dead.

"What makes you so sure of his love?" I ask her.

Clara searches for words, unable to find a way to give expression to her certainty. "It was something about the shelter of his arms when he held me," she muses. "He talked to me without words. He let me know that I could count on him always."

"He was your doctor," I hear myself try.

"It was more than that," Clara replies with solid conviction. "We were like birds in perfect formation sailing through a single affection, carried by the wind." I can't help but be surprised by Clara's soaring burst of poetry. I feel part of that same flock, flying. Clara's words release my own love for Mundanus as I had felt it during the transmutation. We sit together in silent rapture.

"So what do we do now?" asks Clara in a practical voice. We both laugh out too loud at her nosedive down from the sublime. "I think Mundanus should be told he's about to get married; it would only be fair that he know," she continues in the same dry tone. We laugh uncontrollably.

"Mundanus doesn't know what he is in for," I conclude. Clara responds with a radiant smile which cuts right through me. I have to be alone.

"I think I'll go up to the laboratory for a bit." I rise. Clara nods and resumes her spinning. I see her face is flushed. Hurriedly I walk out of the room and go upstairs. My heart aches as if it has been compressed into a leaden ball, heavy and dense.

The atmosphere in my laboratory is smoky brown. The ornate beams across the square-paneled ceiling are shining with wax, reflecting the flames from the fireplace. Since the maids can't touch the rest of the room they insist on waxing the ceiling.

Looking around the room, I feel myself surrounded by decades of futility. On a lectern sits a useless alchemical text, impressive in its leather-bound grandeur. Now I know the content to be incomprehensible to those of us born after the permanent setting of the constellations by which the alchemists steered their experiments. Hanging from a wooden shelf along the wall are glass flasks of different shapes, pointed and bulbous like tulips in winter, next to mortars and pestles, leaden ladles, spoons and earthenware pots: the leftovers of Father's search for the Elixir.

I need to touch the Red Sulphur, return to its reality I need to connect to the Stone which might give value to the pain of a woman who has to send the man she loves to her daughter's bed. I am grief-stricken. My Regent upbringing calls this effusiveness 'self-pity.' I hear derogatory laughter echo through the inner chambers of my skull: 'Look how seriously she takes herself. Shape up!'

Then a voice speaks to me from *outside* my head. As with the apparition of Mundanus in the carriage earlier on, the voice comes from behind. Startled, I look around, but see no one. The odor of transmutational sperm is intense, making me feel slightly nauseous. Just a moment before the room had been suffused with the pleasant fragrances of wood fire and fresh ceiling wax.

"Don't be afraid." I hear words spoken in a Latin heavy with German accent.

"I am terrified," I reply honestly. I feel the flesh shudder under my skin as if pierced from within by icy nails. Oppression all but flattens me.

"What can I do?" I ask out loud.

"Take out the Red Sulphur from its hiding place, my daughter," the reply comes, in its gothic voice. "I shall teach you. You are overcome by dread of your own bravery. My gratitude to you is boundless."

I feel a rush of recognition and know I am being seen deep down to my roots. I am aware this instant that I'm hearing the spirit of Salomon Trismosin and realize he is watching over his creation to make sure it reaches its destined future and I know I'm part of it.

The secret compartment containing the Red Sulphur is hidden behind the fireplace, next to shelves of failed experiments and useless potions.

I take out the ivory box and put it on a table, my hands shaking.

"Open it!" commands the voice. I do so. The greenish glow of the three Red Sulphur stones reaches up towards me like a giant breath. I am instantly at peace.

"From the smallest stone scrape off a flake no bigger than one tenth the size of a barley grain. Use the sharpest knife you have." I follow his orders like one walking in her sleep. I find the knife my Father had kept sharpened to the point where it could split a hair. With a sureness of hand I do not know of myself, I slice off the exact amount required. "Now mix it with 100 drops of the purest alcohol you have distilled." I look around the flasks and find a little brown vial filled with 15 times distilled alcohol, its purity unquestioned. "Now mix it with the spirit of *Lunaria*, the moon plant."

Here I am stymied. "What is the moon plant?" I ask. The voice does not answer, and I can feel disbelief hanging in the room that I don't know the nature of the moon plant. I had never expected that a disembodied voice could be perplexed and at a loss for words. It is actually quite comical. I smile at his momentary discomfiture that bridges centuries. "It has round silver mirror pods, flat like the disc of the moon. It flowers purple or white," he tries. Now I understand, "Oh, you mean 'Honesty', that's what we call it in our time, 'Honesty'. I have it somewhere around here."

"It must be made from pods that can reflect the face like mirrors do," he continues with audible relief. I nod. The pods turn silver after they've spent their seed. I have ground them myself using moon-disc pods I had purchased from dye makers for silvering the threads of silk Clara uses for weaving. I remember marveling at seeing my face reflected in a silver plant pod.

I find the pearl dust powder in a round-bellied pot. "Add 7 barley grains of the Lunaria and shake it well in a glass vessel at night. Hold it up to the moon outside so that her rays can activate its transmutation power. Then send it off to my descendent Giovanni Theodore and instruct him to take three drops before

retiring at night for three nights." His voice reaches its crescendo like the spire of a Gothic cathedral. I am amused by his
sense of theater – he obviously is Mundanus' ancestor – while
being filled with respect simultaneously. "What does it serve?"
I ask, but get no answer. The room smells once again like ceiling
wax.

I check my lunar calendar and find that the next full moon
is on February 8, in two days. From the laws of correspondence,
which are based on similarity, I have concluded that because the
Lunaria pod looks like a full moon, this must be the phase corresponding to its essence. So in blind faith I have to wait for a
full moon night to create Trismosin's potion. In the meantime
I have to find a way to get the mixture to Mundanus with an
accompanying note explaining the correct dosage and composition of this medicine whose purpose I don't know. I remember De Witt's warning that we are under surveillance. I know of
no solution to this problem.

Downstairs I hear Helvetius' voice talking excitedly with
Clara. With trepidation I close the ivory box and put it with
Trismosin's potion in the rear of the secret compartment. I want
to stay upstairs but I hear the maid rush up, no doubt to invite
me down to see my husband. I've been in my laboratory for
much longer than I thought. It is dark outside. Communing
with the spirits twists time out of all proportion.

ℬ

"… he said. He thought she was an impressive lady," I hear
Helvetius finish his sentence when I enter the red room.

Clara jumps up, excited: "Aunt Marianne, you've made quite
an impression on the Prince of Orange." I must look surprised.
It was the last thing I had expected.

"He said that he had seen you, and found out you were my
wife. He called me a man of good fortune with a wife of your
beauty," Helvetius says proudly.

"Our young Prince is not a child anymore," I respond. "I didn't know he looked at women this way. Maybe he should meet our Clara. She is truly beautiful." I hope my voice does not display traces of bitterness. I had tried to be jovial. I smile with a placid mask over churning feelings. "How is his health?" I inquire.

"It's on a down turn," Helvetius continues in a serious tone.

"Doctor Mundanus could help him," Clara suggests innocently.

"Mundanus is the most wanted man in Holland," Helvetius mutters, annoyed. I can sense that De Witt has already put him under the pressure. Helvetius is the weak link in our plan. If he recognizes Mundanus, Johan de Witt will get the information out of him without much effort. A mild threat to Helvetius' prestige would do it. I have not yet solved that part of the puzzle either.

"And the Grand Pensionary tells me that congratulations are in order. It was a bit embarrassing. He specially sought me out after I had finished my medical examination of the Prince. I pretended I knew the man in question, but you could have told me. I asked Clara just now about this mystery fiancé who has not even asked my permission for her hand in marriage."

"I gave him my permission," I say coldly. "Clara is a Van Os, not a Schweitzer."

"It is the prerogative of the head of the household," Helvetius counters with the pomp of pride.

"That is open to question," I rebut. "Legally, I am her sole guardian by explicit testament of my sister."

"Anyway," Helvetius folds turning to Clara, "whatever the case may be, I think I should meet this new man of yours as soon as possible." His tone is conciliatory and I let it ride.

"I think you should indeed meet Signor Theodore," I further decompress the atmosphere. "He is from Venice and converses in either Latin or Italian." Both Clara's education and mine had taken place in Latin. From age eight the only language spoken in our home by my Father was Latin, and I conversed in French with our governesses. Girls usually went to the French school, and boys to the Latin school. But Father had insisted that Latin was the global language of the intellect and we were tutored three hours every day except for Sunday in Latin, over and above all of our schoolwork from the French Lyceum. I loved the Classics and studied with a passion. Soon my Latin was as good as Father's. Johanna preferred French. I spoke Dutch only with mother and outside the home. Dutch was my intimate mother tongue and Latin the formal language of my father.

Helvetius' Latin is of the written kind. He reads and writes well in Latin but in speaking he is considerably less fluent than Clara and I. He is at a disadvantage in the Regent world where every man is educated in spoken Latin. This might serve us well. Helvetius doesn't speak any Italian at all. If we could trick him into not recognizing Mundanus, the latter's language wouldn't give him away. I trust that Mundanus, coming from an illustrious line of alchemists, speaks Latin effortlessly.

"He is currently traveling," Clara says without blinking. "He will be back in The Hague in March. I am sure he will be honored to make your acquaintance."

Helvetius nods, and changes the subject.

"I saw Anthonie van Leeuwenhoek today. I've asked him to come by tomorrow and look at our gold through one of his 'microscopes.' I want to see if there is any difference between our gold and natural gold. I have ground a gold coin and some of our transmuted gold. We'll compare them."

"That's a great idea! I want to look through that 'microscope' of his and see for myself," I say with enthusiasm.

"He promised to come by tomorrow afternoon with one of his best lenses," Helvetius responds, excited. I feel very close to him at this moment and wonder about the great fluctuations of my affects. I no longer recognize myself.

After Helvetius retires to his chambers for the night, I go to my laboratory to read from Solomon Trismosin's diaries. Closely nestled in my father's overstuffed leather chair by the fire, after having fixed myself a delicious cup of chocolatl and cream in the kitchen, I take out Trismosin's diary from its secret compartment behind the fireplace. I'm looking for anything more he can tell me about *lunaria*, but soon find myself absorbed in his contemplations on the nature of time. His long conversations with Copernicus echo back over the chasm of history. Reading their thoughts coming to me through the ages makes me marvel at our human ability to relay images to one another over vast spans of time. Language is a miracle; recorded words a miracle squared. I can participate in Trismosin's conversations with young Copernicus, almost two centuries ago. I can hear the philosopher of the stars tell Mundanus' ancestor that time is created by the movement of the planets around the sun. Trismosin is perplexed by this idea, because it contradicts our direct observation that the sun is rising and setting in a course around the earth. In the margin of the conversations he writes in a hand that betrays alarm that if Copernicus is right then we can't trust our direct observations anymore. I put down the diaries and realize that Master Descartes had codified Trismosin's fears by stating that indeed our senses could not be trusted to portray reality. I look up at the waxed ceiling where the flames reflect in luminous patterns and wonder if there is anything I can trust at all, and I know for a fact that my love for Mundanus is real.

When I pick up the diaries again I read how Copernicus told Trismosin that time was sectioned systematically by the orbits of the earth and planets. He thinks of time as a clock inside of which we live where the sun chimes out the hours at steady intervals. Trismosin could not believe this, though he knew that he was hearing the thoughts of the future. To him time was alive and could dance in rhythms of music which could fold back on itself, slowing down and reversing, bringing itself to a halt, or rush out to the horizon in a flash when time could be here and there simultaneously. This is what the Red Sulphur can do: make two moments in time – which in Copernicus' revolutions of the spheres are vastly different, thousands of years apart –

occur at once. To him time is a living force, an ever-changing dancer.

I am walking in a high mountain landscape. There is not much here other than rock face and wind. In the distance, darkly silhouetted against the full moon night sky, stands one lone tree. I know that I have to go towards it.

The path, which appears straight and level at first, seems to rise up as I walk it. I find myself climbing over rocks and bemoan the fact that I am not wearing the right shoes. At one point I fall and almost tumble down into a chasm. Finally, exhausted, I come to the tree.

There I see a man, though he is not a man. Everything about him is pearl, like the powder of Honesty. Yet I know it is Mundanus; my heart tells me so. I want to embrace him, but I know I would only hold cloud.

Up in the tree sits an owl, shining green from within like Red Sulphur. "Listen," the owl conveys to us in a language unspoken. "A man's white silk shirt will be brought to the seamstress and there will be stolen." The wisp of Mundanus bows deeply towards the owl.

I wake up in my laboratory, where I had fallen asleep in the chair by the fire with Trismosin's diaries on my lap. ...

I get up and carefully place the diaries next to the ivory box and the unfinished medicine of Honesty. I go downstairs through the quiet house to the laundry room. There I pick out one of Helvetius' white silk shirts and take it back to my laboratory. I tear the shirt carefully along a seam and place it in my secret compartment. Then I lock the door and retire to my bedroom.

ॐ

I have only seen Van Leeuwenhoek once or twice before when he came among many other guests to parties Father would give for the natural philosophers of his day. Everyone greatly respected his remarkable lenses, though they made fun of his

observations of invisible *animalcules*. To them he was a crafts-
man, not a scientist; to make matters worse, he was not connected to the Academy but was a canny businessman, a wealthy
shopkeeper, seller of cloth. He was a man of the merchant
Guilds, and the social separation between the Regents and the
Guilds was absolute.

He never told a soul how he made his remarkable lenses,
high quality glass spheres, with the smallest providing the highest magnification. He led all of us to think that he was labori-
ously spending most of his nights and free time grinding increasingly tiny lenses to use in microscopes. This was hard to
believe, because Helvetius told me that Leeuwenhoek had constructed hundreds of microscopes and had a habit of building a
new microscope whenever he chanced upon an interesting
specimen he wanted to study. Leeuwenhoek had only taken lens
grinder Benedict de Spinoza into his confidence, and Spinoza's
oath of secrecy could be fully trusted.

Van Leeuwenhoek has arrived early, just before fourteen
o'clock. When I come down to meet him, Helvetius is already
showing him Clara's weavings with great pride. Clara herself
stands in a corner, blushing crimson, while Leeuwenhoek lav-
ishes her with praises. He is looking at the wool thread she has
spun from Gerda's wool under a peculiar looking magnifying
glass. "You spin wool fine as silk," he keeps saying. "And look
at that cloth! It has more threads per square inch than ever I
have seen made here in Holland!" He turns around and says,
"Helvetius, if ever your niece wants to make gold, have her send
her cloth to my store in Delft and I'll make her a fortune." His
words sound gregarious and crass. His thin-lipped round face
under a tiny moustache and a broad nose are the scaffolding for
his great gray eyes, which look into the world with discerning
curiosity. His cheeks are flushed with indomitable health and
stamina. The thick halo of brown curls reaching down below
his shoulders look like his own, not a wig. Van Leeuwenhoek's
robust presence makes us all look a bit sickly in comparison.

"Is that what you call a 'microscope'?" I ask him, pointing at the lens by means of which he inspects Clara's exceptional cloth. At first he looks a bit confused, not knowing what I mean. Then, suddenly understanding, he laughs heartily.

"Oh, no Madam Schweitzer," he bellows in a voice too loud for the room, "this is just a clothier's lens through which we check the number of threads per square inch. Through one of my microscopes I would see *animalcules* walking on top of each hair. This magnifies 10 times, my microscope 500 times. Let me show you." He walks over to a carrying case and takes out a rectangular copper plate, about 2 inches in length, mounted on a two screw mechanism leading up to a needle point in front of the tiniest of lenses.

"The object I want to examine is raised, lowered or rotated by these threaded screws attached to the plate." He points them out with his fleshy fingers. "I hold it close to the eye," he demonstrates. "It takes some practice and good eyesight. But just in case, I have brought some corrective lenses ground by our friend Spinoza. You grip the plate between your eyebrow and cheek in a horizontal position, in the manner of a jeweler's loupe. Then you hold the microscope with this especially de-signed set of pincers." He hands the lens contraption to me to-gether with an elegant long-armed pincette. It feels pleasantly solid and I note that the lens is being captured between two thin copper plates welded together with remarkable precision. The lens is even smaller than I had first realized. It is no more than a globe the size of a pinhead. The small instrument makes my eyes grow wide with admiration. I know the tools of the alche-mists' trade, but this is an entirely new level of craftsmanship. I wish I could show it to Salomon Trismosin so he can see the glory of our Copernican world. The separation between ob-server and observed has created miracles of measurement.

"I need good light," Van Leeuwenhoek continues. "The best is a grey day without direct sunlight. Today is perfect." Then he adds with pride: "I constructed this microscope spe-cifically for the gold."

"I don't know where you find the time to grind these lenses down to such minuscule sizes, Anthonie," says Helvetius, shaking his head. Then he suggests, "Let's go up to my study. We can open the large front-facing window." The three of us nod. "May I suggest you all wear comfortable upper clothing so nothing constricts the movement of your arms?" I take Clara up to my laboratory where we undo our fashionable French corsets with their rigid flatness of the bodice front to offset our curving breasts peeking over the top, an uncomfortable undergarment, and don my loosely fitting laboratory frocks over our bare skin. We giggle with anticipation. Suddenly she embraces me with ardor. "I love you so much, Aunt Marianne. So very much!" I feel my reservations melt and give in fully to maternal affection.

When we enter Leeuwenhoek is already seated on a purple leather desk chair by the window. In front of him stands Helvetius' desk, covered with a billiard-green cloth. On the desk are two white porcelain plates, each covered with a small amount of gold dust. Helvetius is just closing the window as we come in. When I regard him with a questioning look, he points with one hand at the gold dust and the other at the window: "Wind," he explains.

The silver gray light streaming in from outside brightens the colors of the otherwise dark and gloomy room. Helvetius usually keeps his curtains drawn, against Dutch custom. "No one needs to know when I'm working," he always counters my remarks that on the second floor no one can see him anyway. I don't spend much time here. The floor is of the same black and white marble checker pattern as downstairs. But here it looks a bit out of place.

"I will demonstrate the viewing position to you," Leeuwenhoek expounds. He is wearing an orange robe which lends a warm southern hue to the cold Nordic room. He straightens his shoulders and reclines slightly so his back makes a ninety degree angle with his bottom.

He plants his left foot firmly on the ground and crosses his right leg over it. With his right hand he takes the pincers from the table, clips them onto the microscope and pushes the entire contraption almost against his right eyeball. His left hand grabs his right arm firmly under the wrist and he looks steady as a rock. "You see?" he asks, holding the position for a few more seconds. Then he takes from another small pouch two tiny black slate platforms, each with a hole at the bottom just large enough to fasten it on top of the pinhead in front of the lens. After tightening one micro platform onto the pinhead, he twists the screw mechanism until the small horizontal surface is right in front of the vertical lens holder. "Helvetius shall put natural gold dust on one plate and your artificial gold on the other. Then we adjust it until the image is as sharp as we can get it and we describe to each other exactly what we observe. I'll go first, and then the Ladies; Helvetius, you go last since you know which is which."

He hands Helvetius the little black slate platforms and invites him to put the two different kinds of gold dust on each platform. Then he resumes the viewing posture and stares for a full minute at the gold Helvetius has handed him. In a practiced single move he unhooks the platform, replacing it with the other slate Helvetius has prepared. He closes his eyes for a minute and looks at the next gold dust.

"And?" Helvetius inquires eagerly when Leeuwenhoek puts down the microscope.

"I saw no difference," Leeuwenhoek responds. "They both look exactly the same. The two kinds of gold are indistinguishable."

Helvetius looks disappointed. I am as well. I had secretly hoped that there would be some kind of distinction between the natural gold and the transmuted metal.

"Madam," Leeuwenhoek makes a gesture towards me. For a moment I am aware that I am naked under the laboratory frock, but that disappears when I hold the instrument in the required position. I keep my eyes closed until my breath is even and slow and my grip is firm. Then I open my right eye. In front of me I see a treasure chamber of hazy shapes of light. I manipulate the lens slightly until the dust comes into focus... I see great boulders of gold piled one on top of the other. I gasp and lose my focus. I close my eyes until I regain my self-control. Once I have the golden rocks back into focus again, I begin to study the surface of the rock face. I understand why gold is called *aurum*, meaning 'shining dawn,' in Latin. The rough facets meet one another at all angles like a snowball of sunlight at dawn. I look more intently and am overcome by the stillness of this microsphere. It is perfectly at rest. I am astounded and very grateful to Leeuwenhoek for this world of the infinitely small which he has opened up to me. Now he commands me to close my eyes, and takes the microscope from me. A moment later the pincette is put back into my right hand, and he guides my left to grasp below my wrist. I look again. Again I see the gorgeous formation of rock, raw crystals of early morning sunlight. Leeuwenhoek is right; there is no difference. I keep staring, absorbed in an esthetic trance, having given up my search for distinction. Suddenly I notice that the atmosphere I am seeing is far from still. Though nothing moves, it vibrates with a breath of its own. Even though the shapes are identical, I'm looking at a life form here, not an object. I notice a vitality which connects to mine in a way the dead gold did not. They are in shape identical - in the way a corpse looks the same as the living body did the instant before it was drained of life. But the feeling of the two states is vastly different. This gold has invisible soul breathing through it. "This is our gold," I exclaim with certainty. "It is alive."

"It is indeed our gold," Helvetius concurs.

Leeuwenhoek takes the microscope from me and looks for himself. "Now I see it!" he exclaims surprised. "You are right, Madam. The metallic structure of this gold is identical to natural gold but it has some of the same motion patterns as the *animalcules* in a drop of water. I don't know how I could have overlooked it. It teems with life! It behaves like a growing plant!"

In a flash I understand Red Sulphur in a way I never have before. In the world of Red Sulphur, time speeds up, making processes leap from the infinite time frame of minerals, to the growth rate of weeds, which mature in a day. Minerals live in an inconceivably much larger time scale than do plants. *Metals are exceedingly slow-growing plants maturing into gold!* To us this seems utterly impossible because in our days we firmly believe in one single time which is uniform, moving inexorably into the future to the steady rhythm of a pendulum clock which never varies its endlessly even tick-tock. Red Sulphur compresses time frames: it is the master of time. I hear Trismosin's voice echo through my head. He and Copernicus are both right!

ॐ

The next day the sun breaks through the clouds and by the evening there is no cover in sight. My ephemeris tells me the moon will be full at 21 hours 57 minutes. At 21 o'clock I go outside to the stables. I'm dressed again in Johanna's Russian furs. On a chair in front of the stable Hendrik is drinking his gin. The full moon is already over the horizon and I can see enough to discern his bright red nose. I ask him to continue his drinking in his quarters above the stables. He offers me a shot which I kindly decline. "I was thinking of your father," he says. "You look more and more like him every day." He pauses, and then adds quickly in order not to give offense, "That is meant as a compliment Miss Marianne, a great compliment." I am moved by his simple words, grateful that he is a part of my life as a living reminder of days gone by.

"I'll be going up then," he concludes, tipping his hat. "Goodnight Miss Marianne." Hendrik has never gotten into the habit of calling me Madam, which irritates Helvetius no end.

"Good night, Hendrik. May the Lord watch over your sleep."

He bows slightly and stumbles towards the stairs in the back of the stables.

I sink down into the vacated chair. The smell of foreign furs evokes in me a sense of wildness as I look up at the pearl radiance of the moon. I reach into my pocket and feel the little vial with the not yet activated mixture and think back to the many times Father and I performed alchemical procedures by the light of the full moon. I can feel his spirit close to me, watching over me, giving my unhinged life a semblance of security. I remember the intense anticipation and our inevitable disappointment when the elixir did not activate yet again. I asked him once how he could stand all the disappointment, year after year, striving for a goal which always eluded him. "It is the passion of my expectation which drives the transmutation, expectation against all hope. Once I become detached, it's over. Disappointment is the fee I pay to stay in the game."

"But why stay in the game at all?" I asked.

He pointed at the night sky and moved his arm expansively to encompass its swoop. "The whole cosmos is alive. We are being envisioned by it. If it is a world of clockwork we see, we are cogs; if we apprehend a world of breathing life, we are part of its soul. Vision chooses you, it overtakes you. This vision dreams me. And I would not exchange it for a certainty that makes the fact of my thinking proof of my existence." I could hear the echoes of his nightly debates with Descartes, his great French teacher in Leyden, about the latter's 'I think therefore I am' vision. "I choose disappointment," my father concluded.

And now here I sit, once again distilling my dreams into a potion, led by a spirit from the past who claims me with his absolute conviction. Did I see the life in our gold through Leeuwenhoek's microscope because Trismosin has captured my eyes? Am I locked into the same futility as were Father and I during all our previous experiments? But what more proof do I need than the Red Sulphur itself? I saw the transmutation with my own eyes. Yet were these eyes my own? Am I being dreamed by the legend of Trismosin? I know I am not in an ordinary dream. So much has happened since the transmutation, and I remember it all. This adventure has far too much continuity over too long a period of time to still be part of my usual nightly dreaming. Have I broken through to the great dream itself in which the moon is the pearl of great power? I feel my familiar confusion and attempt to calm my fluttering breath. Nearby the clock chimes, first four times at a high pitch, then ten times in the deep sound of bigger bells. 22.00 hours. My moon is full.

Full of expectation, I remove the vial from my sleeve. In its clear glass, the potion looks like water. Am I to say an incantation? I remember Plotinus saying that the incantation is as important as is the medicine itself. So I wait for a song to rise up; then I sing, listening to my strange words:

> "Stars you raised me
> Moon you nursed me,
> Father you taught me,
> Mother you took me with you to the world beyond.
> Let the spirit of Honesty
> Become a potion of silver
> That whitens the earth."

I have no idea why I am saying these words. They speak themselves through me. I stand up and turn to all four directions, holding the vial up to the moon. I feel a shaking arise from the earth below, moving through my feet, legs, torso and arm and into the vial, which shudders violently in my hand. I clearly perceive its concentrated longing rise up to the moon. Madness overtakes me as I'm being spun ever faster...

"That must be strong stuff you have in your little flask there, Miss Marianne," says Hendrik as he lifts me up to the chair. I feel a faint smile on my lips and notice how my right hand tightly clasps the vial.

Hendrik insists on guiding me up to my quarters.

�

Mina the maid is crying. "There were five of them, Madam. They scared me so." She is very young and I feel guilty that I sent her on this mission by herself. "They kept bumping into me. I was screaming and they laughed. Then they grabbed all the clothes I was to bring to the seamstress and ran off with them. I really couldn't help it Madam. I really couldn't." She sobs uncontrollably. I silently curse Mundanus for his lack of consideration. "Go to the kitchen and have Cook give you a warm glass of chocolatl. ... Wait, I'll come with you."

As we enter the kitchen the fire in the hearth sparkles with coziness. It is a good place to snuggle on a rainy February morning. We sit down on the wooden bench and watch Cook scrub a large pan, her wide blue skirt under the white apron flowing around her body in the movement of her metal brush. The white cap on her stringy dark hair bobs up and down as she bends over the pan to add pressure. She looks up and wipes her brow. "What can I do for you, Madam?"

"Could you make Mina and me a large cup of chocolatl. And have yourself one too." Cook looks very pleased. She walks over to the wall next to the Dutch door to the outside, and carefully picks a tin jar from a shelf. She makes it her pride to check the jar every week to see if anyone has taken out chocolatl without her explicit permission. I always tell her when I take a cup. With a big smile on her face, she hangs a kettle over the fire and scoops a generous amount of cream from the bucket of milk. Her eyes tell me that this is a feast. Mina calms down at the prospect of the cherished drink she only gets for Christmas.

I am amazed that the plan worked. Mundanus must indeed have had the same dream and took these admittedly brutal measures to get hold of the silk shirt the day after the full moon. It is well worth three cups of chocolatl.

"They were after the silks, Madam," says Mina. "I'm sure of it. One of the men pulled out the Doctor's white silk shirt, the one with the tear at the seam; they took it from the basket and held it up to the others. They all applauded like it was a performance at the play house," she ends her story, indignant. I try a concerned look, while inside I am just as pleased as were these men with their trophy. I deeply inhale the pleasant fragrances spreading through this warm environment.

&

Two weeks have gone by and still no word from Mundanus. My impatience becomes unbearable. I spend my time reading papers I have Hendrik pick up at the Inner Court. Finally France has come to our aid and Louis XIV has declared war on our enemy, Charles II of England. Preparations are being made to meet in Breda to sue for peace. All parties are jockeying for position. Pamphletists are spouting theories, negotiators remain silent: Johan de Witt must be very busy.

For the first time since Father's death I perform a thorough laboratory cleaning. It is a ritual to mark the next phase of my life. I spend time reading in Trismosin's diary, but feel listless. Not even touching the Red Sulphur enlivens me.

Clara is spending her days with old Elspeth, concentrating on the intricacies of spinning wool like silk and making more of the cloth Leeuwenhoek so admired. They want to start selling it to him. He is a very successful cloth merchant with a thriving shop in Delft, and Elspeth can use the money now that her family fortunes are down. Clara's agile hands are more nimble than old Elspeth's and her thread is unequalled. Soon she will have to get more of Gerda's excellent wool. I send out a message with Hendrik to Henk and Klaas to reserve all the wool they still have, hoping to get news from Gerda who must have contacted Mundanus by now. I let them know that I will pay well above top winter prices. We receive word from Henk as Hendrik returns. He will come by with all the rest of the wool the next day. Clara and Elspeth are ecstatic. I can't wait. The cleaning in my laboratory gets increasingly frenzied and I find myself enter Helvetius' study to stare out the window. I have taken to pacing.

When Henk arrives he tells us to pay special attention to the second bale of wool. Gerda has said it is of a particularly fine kind. He tells me she is well and has taken up visiting Leyden in the horse pulled barge along the Vliet, making contact with cloth makers and buying more sheep. He speaks about her with admiration and absolute trust. Her ability to make money astounds the peasantry; they usually can't see beyond the fruits of the land. Leyden has become the center of cloth-making since most of the cloth manufacturers fled religious persecution in Habsburg-ruled Flanders earlier this century. It has made Leyden the prosperous giant it now is, second only to Amsterdam, with over 70,000 inhabitants and a university which has become one of the most respected in the scholarly world, with great minds flocking to it from all over Christendom. Religious tolerance has paid off handsomely in this golden age of Leyden.

"Please tell me more about your wife," I ask innocently. "We owe her greatly."

"Gerda looks better than ever," says Henk with poorly hidden innuendo. Clara laughs out loud and a conspiratorial look passes between the two young people.

"I assume children will be on the way then," I respond drily.

Now even Henk blushes. We all laugh and I offer him a bottle of the best old gin we have, together with a princely sum in silver guilders for their wool. He looks exceedingly pleased. Better to keep him on our good side, I think. He can be had for a good ransom. And when Johan de Witt gets more desperate for gold, the price on Mundanus' head may rise.

After he leaves we find a note in the second bale.

All it says is "Friday 16 o'clock."

Chapter Seven

I wake on Friday before dawn and go over all my dresses, deciding what I am going to wear. I feel giddy as a schoolgirl and have been avoiding Clara, who has her own share of romantic expectation. Now that a meeting between the three of us has become imminent and our impossible future has blown wide open, I have more trouble reining in my jealousy. It has broken out of its dungeon and threatens to burn down the building. I have nowhere to go for advice, not daring to even talk to Father, in whose spirit I usually confide with ease. Salomon Trismosin remains conspicuously silent. I feel abandoned in my hour of need. Again my Regent-self abhors all this effusiveness and I concentrate on the rational task at hand: selecting the appropriate dress. I despair over the cruel limitations of my considerable wardrobe; not even the right pair of shoes seems to offer itself. I finally decide on a modest dress of black velvet, stern but inviting. I am convinced Helvetius will not notice my affections: men have no feeling for these matters. But Clara is another story altogether.

We gather in the red room at 15.30 hours. Clara looks stunning; I am taken aback for an instant. She is wearing a yellow long dress with gold stitching and a plunging neckline to drive any man to distraction. Helvetius hardly notices. He is fidgeting uncomfortably, unused to be head of the family.

"Your father should have been here," he says softly. I go over to him and squeeze his arm gently, my eyes moist.

"I miss Grandfather," Clara whispers wistfully. All my jealousy recedes behind the moat of kinship.

"Anyone for a glass of wine?" I inquire. "It may be too early but the occasion asks for celebration." I pour three glasses from the crystal carafe before the others can answer and raise mine. "To Clara's future!"

I note that Clara is very nervous. I have to be the adult in this situation, so I button up my heart and go over to put my arm around her shoulder. We walk into the hall, leaving Helvetius behind.

"What if Uncle Johann recognizes him?" Clara asks in a small voice.

"We'll deal with that *if* it arrives. Your uncle can be fooled." She looks at me with questioning eyes, but I have no inclination to explain my words.

Then the doorbell rings. A shock goes through my system and I herd Clara back into the red room.

From behind the closed door we hear the manly sound of an unknown bronze voice a full octave lower than Mundanus'. Clara looks confused. I am baffled.

The door opens and Mina lets in an utter stranger.

The tall thin man has long angel-white hair and skin pale as snow, as if the sun has never touched his flesh and he lives by night. His expressive eyes are striking, light grey with a hue of red under an absence of eyebrows. He looks less than thirty years of age.

"My name is Theodore," he says in a melodious baritone, speaking Latin with a strong Italic accent.

Clara faints. Helvetius tends to her, forgetting about the stranger.

I look at the white man and feel a strange disparity between my eyes and my heart. My heart dances with recognition while my eyes behold a total stranger.

"Trismosin's blanching formula is startling, I know," he whispers. "It creates the albino overnight."

I am suddenly nauseous with confusion as my world of perception shatters like a mirror and all that remains is distortion.

My rational world is dissolved by the unquestionable presence
of magic.

He turns to Clara as she comes to, looking deeply into her
eyes. "Good afternoon, Miss Clara, you look lovely today." At
first Clara has the air of a frightened deer, but then comprehension creeps up on her. She is silent for a moment as a lexicon of
unreadable expressions configures her face.

"Good afternoon, Signor Theodore," she replies in a shaky
voice. "Your journey seems to have changed you."

"For the better, I hope," he counters with elegance.

Clara is at a loss for words. "It is the inner man that counts,"
I respond for her. "This is my husband Doctor Schweitzer, better known as Helvetius."

"I have heard great things about you, Doctor Helvetius,"
Mundanus speaks in flawless Latin. "Your reputation has spread
all the way to Venice." The compliment makes Helvetius ebul-
lient. Even his rudimentary spoken Latin does not hold him
back.

"I welcome to my house the fiancé of my niece," he says in
stilted language.

Now it is Mundanus' turn to be surprised. But he hides it
well. All I notice is a drop of perspiration on his upper lip.

"We have invited the Grand Pensionary as a guest of honor
to the wedding," I confound him further. His transformation
has unsettled me and made me cross with him.

"That is indeed an honor," he says slowly, some sweat showing on his snow-white forehead as well. I notice a crack in his
voice and feel a desire to torture him.

"I am so glad that a scion of such an illustrious family has
deigned us worthy to ask my niece's hand in marriage." My
voice is condescending. A flash of fear runs over Mundanus'
face. I instantly regret my inappropriate behavior. "May I offer
you a glass of wine, from the Prosecco region, in your honor?"
Mundanus bows, relieved by my conciliatory offering of Venetian wine.

"I had a long journey by horse-drawn barge from Leyden where I make my home, is there a place where I can refresh myself?" he inquires stiffly.

"Of course," I say. "How inhospitable of me! We have a water closet in the hall."

"With a modern French *Angrez* flush toilet," Helvetius adds proudly. I can't stand his boorishness.

"I'll show you," I offer. "Clara, could you please pour your fiancé a glass of wine?"

Mundanus confronts me in the hallway. "What is this about me being Clara's fiancé?"

"I love you, Mundanus, more that I could ever tell you. But this is the only way you can have an heir, Johan de Witt will be thrown off your track, we can live at close quarters, and I can give you your gold in the form of Clara's dowry without arousing suspicion," I rattle off the reasons.

Mundanus recoils in dismay.

"You *must* understand," I plead. "In the name of Salomon Trismosin, please *do* understand!"

Mundanus shakes his head in disbelief as he enters the water closet.

I return to the red room, shaken. Clara looks at me questioningly.

"He is so glad to be here, he told me. So happy to see you again."

Clara smiles.

"He looks like a good man," opines Helvetius. "But you could have told me that he was an albino. That is quite a surprise! I've had albinos in my medical practice. It usually doesn't pass down to the offspring," he tells Clara with kind reassurance.

Mundanus returns. "I am deeply honored to be received with such open arms in my fiancée's family," he bellows out, as if overcoming his trepidations by an overly loud voice.

A radiant smile which would pale the sun by comparison breaks over Clara's face. I realize acutely how much I love her, and exhale deeply. We are silent.

"Maybe you could tell us about your Venetian family," I suggest, breaking the impasse and giving me time to study his new appearance.

"My father's family is not from Venice originally," Mundanus begins. "He was a merchant in the German community in Venice working in the company of my mother's father, the Dolfin family of traders who trace their lineage back directly to Marco Polo by way of his daughter Moreta. My father's marriage into our family was a bit of a scandal, as he was considered to be of much lower rank. He died when I was fourteen and after that I was raised by my grandfather Giovanni Dolfin VI. My grandfather sent me all over the world and that is how I came to meet many of the Dutch United East-Indies Trading Company where I first heard the name Van Os."

I am amazed at Mundanus' aptitude for lying. He tells his story with the utmost conviction.

"After my last journey to India, where I encountered many thoughts I could not explain, I returned home to Venice with a desire to study philosophy. I started out in Padua," he turns to Helvetius, "where the famous medical college is," Helvetius nods, pleased. "But then I realized that all I would learn is the dogma of the Church of Rome and the doctrine of the Inquisition. This brought me to Leyden."

With admiration I hear Mundanus spin his web of lies. I believe every word he says, such is the beguiling certitude with which he presents his fabrications.

"In Leyden your esteemed Father's name still rings with glory," he contrives without hesitation. "He is renowned for his mathematical skills and his understanding of taxation and the issuing of bonds. That's why he was a central advisor to Johan de Witt, I've been told. As a merchant by trade your father intrigued me, as did the family van Os."

I want him to stop. This is going too far. He is telling a much more complicated story than is needed. But Helvetius seems spellbound. "Then how did you meet Clara?" he asks, fascinated. Clara looks with great expectation, tasting each of his words with delight. She believes the reality he paints for them even though she knows it for a fact to be a pack of lies! Who would have thought Mundanus to be such a brilliant impostor? His change into a bleached angel-ghost would not even have been necessary, he can bend the truth with such relish.

Signor Theodore turns to Clara: "Maybe you would like to tell that part of the story, my dear."

Clara gulps. Mundanus waits. This is cruel.

"Maybe I should tell it?" I offer, having no idea what I will say.

"No, please Aunt Marianne, let me." I consent, with intense curiosity as to what her story will be.

She turns to Helvetius. "Do you remember, Uncle Johann, when about three months ago Elspeth took me to Leyden to show me fabrics that couldn't be found here in The Hague?" Helvetius nods. "Well, she had to go on an errand and I had some time to wander through the city by myself. I went to the cloth market and was roaming around when I saw this remarkable looking gentleman. I must have stared at him because he came up to me and introduced himself."

"How could I not?" Mundanus asked. "You looked so lovely surrounded by all this colorful fabric." Clara blushes.

"We got to talk, and somehow I spoke about Grandfather, and then we were in conversation for two hours until Elspeth returned. Since then we have been writing letters."

Helvetius looks annoyed. "I must take Elspeth to task," he says. "Leaving you without chaperone is inexcusable."

"Please, Uncle Johann, please don't. She helped me find the man I shall marry! If you get her in trouble I shall not speak to you for a week!" she threatens in the way of a little girl stomping her foot effectively. "And we never met without chaperone again."

"That is true," I join the liars' ball, "I have been with her every time she met with Signor Theodore since."

Helvetius is mollified. "Let us eat dinner and celebrate the bond between our families," he says haltingly in the best Latin he can muster.

"Shouldn't you ask Signor Theodore about his financial position?" I ask sweetly.

"I'm sure you did so already, my dear," Helvetius responds, teasing me.

"I am like Father, and let Clara marry for love," I reply, reminding him of the love which was once ours. I feel affection for Helvetius and an equally profound contempt. He can be fooled as easily as a scullery maid.

"Don't worry Doctor Schweitzer, the Dolfin Trading Company is one of the largest in Venice," Signor Theodore assures him.

This last bluff frightens me. It can so easily be traced. Especially since Helvetius is sure to boast about it to Johan de Witt!

Mundanus notices the fear rush across my face and understands my worries instantaneously. He pulls a parchment from his pocket and hands it to me. It hails from the Giovanni Dolfin Company, Palazzo Dolfin, Grand Canal, Venice; it is authored by the owner of the company, Giovanni Dolfin VI, recommending his grandson Signor Giovanni Theodore to his banker, Banca Monte dei Paschi di Siena, founded 1472.

I am stunned. "Is this real?" I hear myself exclaim, trying to rein the words back in as I speak them. But it is too late; they have inexorably left the gate.

Helvetius takes the letter, reads it, and is obviously cross with my offensive language to a guest in our home. Such direct and unsubtle expression of doubt about the veracity of a guest's credentials, especially one who is about to marry your niece, is considered highly uncivil and against all laws of hospitality. He is about to make a remark but is held back by his limited Latin.

"You mean if this is the original copy of the document?" Mundanus saves me. "Indeed Madam is *very* perceptive: no it is not. My grandfather had it copied fivefold before I left. The original is with the Banca Monte dei Paschi di Siena. How did you know?"

"My Aunt is an astute observer, Signor Theodore. She is a master of the Great Art."

"It carries no signature," I try to recover.

"It does so!" Helvetius responds, annoyed. "Right here!" He points to the bottom of the letter.

"That is what surprises me about your skills, Madam. It is indeed the signature of my Grandfather's secretary in his stead. My Grandfather had to leave in order to go to Sienna to see his bankers and took the original with him. By the time his copiers had finished the documents he had left. See," he points at the parchment Helvetius is holding, as he moves over to stand behind him, "It says 'by attorney' over the signature. I am very impressed, Madam. You didn't look at this for more than a second!"

I am very grateful for his ingenuity, but still convinced this is a forgery. Mundanus had told me nothing about being a descendant of the great explorer Marco Polo and being a member of one of the princely families of Venice.

"Wasn't there a general Dolfin?" I ask, to regain my composure and credibility.

Now Mundanus is truly impressed. "Yes indeed Madam. Your knowledge is correct and astounding for one living in these parts. The first Giovanni Dolfin became the fifty-seventh Doge of Venice in 1356. He is unfairly known as the general who lost us Dalmatia."

"I read about it recently as one of the cleverest negotiations in history. The article said that while Dolfin was defeated at Nervesa in 1358 and was forced to sue for peace, he gave up Dalmatia in order to maintain naval predominance in the Adriatic by having the King of Hungary accept not to build a fleet of his own. One of the Dutch negotiators in Breda, where we ourselves are negotiating for peace with the English as we speak, brought up this example in the papers lately. The author said

Johan de Witt should study Doge Dolfin's negotiation strategy. But I think De Witt does not want to give up anything, besides maybe Nieuw Amsterdam in the colonies."

"And he is right!" Helvetius interjects emphatically.

"Let's not talk matters of state tonight," Clara intercedes, "This is an evening of celebration, not of politics."

"Signor Giovanni Theodore," Helvetius turns to him in a solemn manner, "I give you the hand of my niece Clara de Chatillon in marriage."

Clara smiles broadly, Signor Theodore politely, and I sourly.

"You are an adept of the Great Art?" asks Mundanus, as we sit down for dinner in the formal dining room.

I gesture dismissively. "I'm just assisting my husband."

"Oh no," Helvetius counters, "I truly am her assistant. She has worked as an alchemist since she was seven years of age."

"My Grandfather was an alchemist," Clara clarifies.

"I heard rumors that you were involved in that famous transmutation last month. It is spoken about all over the Academy." Mundanus directs himself to Helvetius. "Leyden is in fact quite skeptical, if I may use my privilege as a new member of the family to speak openly?"

Helvetius nods emphatically: "By all means, Signor Theodore, tell me what you heard spoken. It may of useful information be to me. I publishing pamphlet about the transmutation, to appear in March." His poor spoken Latin is comical. I suppress a smile.

"The great librarian Isaak Vossius is going around Leyden denouncing the transmutation, saying the ones involved were naïve. He says that these so-called alchemists have more tricks up their sleeves than magicians at a country fair."

"I know," Helvetius confirms. "He said the same to Spinoza."

"The fact that he is an illustrious librarian means of course that he has an intimate knowledge of alchemy," I remark in a sardonic tone.

"Indeed, Madam. Many scholars who have an acclaimed knowledge in their field believe to have authority in many fields they know next to nothing about."

"Vossius has never been outside a library," I continue my scorn.

"He didn't even ask the jeweler or the Mint-master who were there to assay the gold, Spinoza said. He found his attitude less than scholarly. Spinoza keeps an open mind about these things," Helvetius adds.

"There are few people in this world for whom I have a more profound respect than for the great Benedict de Spinoza, though I have never met him."

"He is a friend of Uncle Johann's," Clara tells him proudly. "I'll make sure you meet him well before we get married."

"He is kind of a recluse," I interject.

"They tell me he lives in Voorburg to be close to Leyden but not right there," Mundanus responds.

"I can understand that," says Clara. "I would not want to live in a city as gigantic as Leyden with so many people. I like to visit, but not live there."

"So where *do* you want to live, Clara?" Mundanus asks her with serious interest.

"I want to live close to Aunt Marianne, right here in The Hague. We could maybe find a house nearby. Would you want to live here, Giovanni?" she asks shyly, having found herself to be too forward.

"Signor Theodore might wish to stay in Leyden to continue his studies, Clara. You might have to move there," I dissimulate.

Clara looks sad.

"No Madam Schweitzer, I would gladly move to The Hague if Clara so wishes," Signor Theodore quickly interjects. This is the first moment I allow myself to breathe deeply. The plan is working.

"You are a generous man, Signor Theodore," Helvetius compliments him. "We would be loath to lose the closeness of our niece. She is the only family we have. She is like a daughter to us."

"I hope you will enjoy being part of our family," I remark, feeling horribly disingenuous.

"I might love her family as much as I do Clara."

"Well, not quite, I hope," Clara laughs.

All the muscles in my face tense taut like a mask. "I am sure he will cherish you above everyone," I say softly, looking at Mundanus as my heart cries tears of sorrow.

છ

"Can we show Signor Theodore your laboratory, Aunt Marianne?" Clara asks, as we sit together after dinner. The Gentlemen are up in Helvetius' study to smoke pipes and be men. I consent to Clara because I don't know what else to do.

A knock on the door announces a messenger. We hear the maid run up to the study, then the heavy footsteps of two men rushing down the stairs. "The Prince is having a serious asthma attack and I have to go over to the palace immediately," Helvetius explains.

"Wait!" I say and rush up to the laboratory, where I find the small flask containing the medicine which so miraculously cured Clara. I know Helvetius' medicine to be less than effective. We can't have the young Prince die on us while his uncle Charles II is negotiating with us for a peace settlement. They might think Johan de Witt had him killed, and the war would escalate.

"Here," I say to Helvetius. "Give him three drops of this now and three in the morning. It cured Clara. If you want to, you can do your own medical procedures, but please give him this as well." Helvetius hesitates. I look for Mundanus to come to my aid but instantly realize that he can't.

"Please Uncle Johann! I know for a fact that it works miracles."

Reluctantly Helvetius takes the little bottle from me and puts it in his pocket.

"Have I told you that the Prince has been asking after you?" he says sarcastically. He does not like me to involve myself in his medical practice, especially since his near fatal failure with Clara, a memory he'd rather forget.

After Helvetius leaves, Clara leads us up the stairs, her gold stitched wide dress swooshing against the stairs and wall like wind against rocks. Walking behind Mundanus, I feel as if we are her parents following her up to a room full of Saint Nicholas presents.

She opens the door to the laboratory. "You've been here before when you still were another man," she remarks calmly in Dutch when we are all inside. She is different when she speaks her mother tongue, I notice. More childlike and fluent. I wonder if I'm different as well.

"I remember," he responds in his Italian-accented Dutch.

"Where did you learn Dutch?" I ask him, no longer knowing the way back to what's real.

"On my grandfather's ships. We had Dutch captains because their maps were the best and they sailed with a crew of their own. I was sent along to oversee the trade. They spoke no Italian so I had to learn quickly. And afterwards I lived in the Spanish Netherlands for some years among the Flemish."

"Who are you??" I ask, hoping he can mend my scattered world.

"You tell me," he replies. "You made the potion which turned me into this."

"Trismosin did!" I counter.

"Trismosin has been dead for a century and a half," Mundanus remarks calmly. We sound like a bickering old couple.

"Who is Trismosin and what is the potion?" asks Clara.

We turn to her, almost having forgotten her presence. I wave the attention away from myself to Mundanus with an elegant motion of my wrist and right hand. "Ask him."

The ghostly man looks hesitant at first. "Let me start with the potion." He concludes after some time during which Clara has been waiting impatiently. She is fidgeting and worrying a kerchief in her hands.

"On February 7, the night before the full moon, I have a dream that I am walking in Venice near the Bridge of Sighs. A man comes up to me. He is very old and carries a white ball. He throws it up in the air and it stays in the sky, becoming the full moon shining bright as a pearl. Then I see a skirmish near the quay next to the Doge's Palace. Five men are attacking a young woman carrying a basket with laundry. I rush to come to her aid. They taunt her and steal the basket from her. They put it down and pull out Helvetius in a torn white silk shirt. They hold him up to each other and laugh uproariously. He looks light as a feather. By the time I get to them they are all gone, Venice is gone, and I am in The Hague near Helvetius' home and the white silk shirt lies empty on the cobblestones. Behind me I hear the old man say: "Do this!" then I wake up."

Clara has stopped fiddling, listening in complete rapture entranced by his baritone.

"Even though I have many dreams, this was an unusual one. My unusual dreams often begin near the Bridge of Sighs."

"What is this Bridge of Sighs?" asks Clara. Mundanus closes his eyes and focuses carefully on his memory of the Bridge.

"It is an enclosed lime stone bridge passing over the Rio di Palazzo connecting the prison to the interrogation rooms in the Doge's Palace. Prisoners would pass along it to be judged by the court and then pass back, often seeing the sun for one last time. To us it is the symbol of judgment. So whenever clear judgment is needed in my life and it is a matter of life or death, I find myself looking at the Bridge of Sighs. I know that if I read the dream wrong I may well have seen the sun for the very last time."

"So what did you make of it?" she asks eagerly.

"At first I had no idea. I just knew I had to talk about it with someone. When I tell someone else my dreams I can hear much more. That day Gerda came by. She is helping me set up my laboratory in Leyden so I can start making more medicine to stem the next pestilence. I tell her the dream. She is a very smart young woman. We all know this." We both nod adamantly.

"Gerda just asks me if the old man has come into my dreams before. I tell her, yes, that he had. Then she asks me if he can be trusted. I affirm it again. Then do as he says, she tells me and asks me if I want another cup of tea. That was all we spoke about it."

"So you hired five thugs and had them attack my maid Mina," I say in a mixture of outrage and admiration.

"You did what?" Clara exclaims, incredulous.

"What your aunt said," he smiles sheepishly. Clara is furious. "Mina could have been hurt! She was scared out of her wits."

"I calmed her down," I interject, realizing that I have to be on Mundanus' side or Clara will get worked up. "Nothing bad happened. I gave her two cups of chocolatl and a silver guilder. She was quite pleased."

Mundanus continues quickly: "I told them I'd only pay if nothing bad happened to the laundry maid. I sent an observer with them, to play the role of myself watching the events near the Doge's Palace. And in the collar of the silk shirt I found a minuscule vial with a note saying '3x 3 drops'. So I took three drops morning, noon and night and you can see the result." He spreads out his arms and points to himself.

"That must have been a surprise," I remark, drily. Clara laughs. Then in a flash I realize:

"You took three times the dose! I meant 3 drops 3 nights in a row." Now I am worried.

"You knew about this?" Clara asks me, incredulous.

So I tell her my part of the story: making the potion, wondering how to get it to Mundanus, my dream.

"Do you still have this essence of Honesty?" Mundanus asks me when I finish. "Enough to make an army of ghosts," I respond.

"Clara should use it to blanch her wool. The threads spun from it will be magical. I know the proportions. Trismosin writes about it in his diaries."

"So who is this Trismosin?" Clara wants to know.

"You tell her," I say to Mundanus. For the first time I feel that we are a team, like a span of horses.

All of a sudden I see Mundanus' eyes roll to the back of his head and it looks as if he is going to fall over.

"What's happening, Mundanus; what's happening?!" Clara calls out in fear.

I catch him before he drops and sit him down in a chair by the fire. His eyes are still rolled backward. Then suddenly he looks out again.

"What happened just now?" I ask, worried.

"It's been happening for the past few days," he responds. "I think the tincture of *Lunaria* has affected my spirit. I get moments like this when all I see is a searing white light which envelops me and I feel almost weightless as if I will fall upwards. It is beginning to happen more frequently. I fainted this morning on the barge here from Leyden. It scares me. It really does."

Hearing Mundanus admit to his fear terrifies me. I had hoped for his strength to carry me through, but now I realize that the overdose he took of the tincture I made could kill him. What have I done?

"There is an antidote somewhere in the diaries. I remember reading it years ago. Trismosin says that if the blanching goes too far it can be stopped by something, but I don't remember what."

I had never considered that even the great spirit of Trismosin might be fallible. I had approached him the way I did Father when I was a child, with total trust. Yet, maybe the drops were too poisonous and Trismosin's spirit had made an error. Or possibly my mistake had made Mundanus take the drops in too quick a succession. I feel completely without guidance, rush over to the secret compartment, utterly oblivious of Clara's presence, and pull out the leather bound diaries and the ivory box. There are more than a thousand pages, so where do we find it? Even if I find the page, Trismosin could be wrong again. I feel as if I am in a maelstrom of madness.

"How did you make the potion, Aunt Marianne?" Clara asks with eerie calm.

"I used the Red Sulphur." I take a yellow stone out of its ivory box and show it to Clara. "This is the stone that saved you. It was made by Mundanus' ancestor Salomon Trismosin 150 years ago. It controls time and growth. It contains the force that makes plants turn green."

"Is that all you used?" Clara asks, matter of fact, as if what I told her is a matter of little consequence.

"I mixed it with the powder of the Honesty pods we bought from the dye maker. Trismosin calls it the root of the moon, *lunaria*."

"That's what Elspeth calls it too, *lunaria*. So maybe it can be made to slow down by a color that counters it, like *purpur*. It is a dye extracted from Mediterranean shellfish. Elspeth mixes the smallest dose of *purpur* with Honesty to get a perfect skin tone in the tapestries."

"She is right. That's what it was!" Mundanus mutters. His feeble voice makes me ache inside, draining my spirit. "That's the antidote, the *tincture of purpur*. Now I remember: Ten barley grains of *purpur* mixed with a rape seed of Red Sulphur on the night of the new moon."

For us alchemists, tincture is essence, and tincture means color. I look at the ephemeris. "That is tonight, Friday February 22 at 22.29."

"I have *purpur* in my room. I was just about to use it for dye."

Mundanus' eyes roll back again. "They're coming faster. It's speeding up." He whispers.

☞

As I mix Clara's *purpur* with the rape seed of Red Sulphur I have shaved off with Father's knife, I feel profoundly dispirited. What had felt like a great adventure before, now has an aspect of drowning. If the task of the alchemist is to inspire matter, I

am not up to it. My back is sore and I feel I have been aged by
decades. Were I to look in the mirror it would not surprise me
if my hair was white like Mundanus'. My hands are numb. I look
at Mundanus on his chair by the fire looking ever more ghostly.
I fear that soon he will be a cloud of his former self like the
spectral presence in my dream, and evaporate like mist. I can't
find the passion I have felt for him. I am tired of all this emotion. Better be a gray cog in a clock that ticks away time with
predictable regularity than to live in these rapid reversals of
mood. I am giving up on Father, Trismosin, Mundanus, myself.
Emptiness echoes around me. Yet, deep down somewhere,
deeper than where once jealousy had been incarcerated, there is
an ember. My leaden hands speed up a fraction.

Clara is sitting with the snow white shadow of a man, singing
in his ear, watching his life drain away. Yet her back is straight
and her focus unwavering as she carries the faith for us all. Her
weaver's eye seems to glimpse the fabric of destiny.

Part Three

Clara

Chapter Eight

Doctor Mundanus' skin is a taffeta satin. It catches the glow of the fire like fine alabaster. I am surprised that I am so calm and certain I am not going to lose him. As Aunt Marianne is working on the potion we will activate in less than an hour, I hum lullabies into his ear. I understand nothing of the alchemy about which they are talking. To me it's just magic. I feel no need to understand what has happened or what will happen a moment from now. Being here with him is all that matters to me. I have always lived in a world of textures, seen moments as weavings of light. When I was close to death only weeks ago and floated through shades of delirium there was no particular fear; no ripping of fabric, no tearing of threads, just the feeling of gossamer moments. And so it is now as I stroke his face and stare at his closed eyes. I know he is fading, I know he may pass, but having him with me right now is all that I care about. I have always thought that the game we are playing with Johan de Witt is strange and disturbing, and I write so each day in my diary. I have heard the stories of the transmutation, but I don't care much about gold, beyond the gold dust I have used on the thread of this dress. I feel the sumptuous fabric hugging my body and I want him to touch me, but not as a doctor. I sense his hands in my hair as I touch his, feel him caressing my eyes as my lips kiss his eyelids. I am strangely happy with this man I don't recognize.

Aunt Marianne indicates that the mixture is done and we should go outside and wait for hour 22.27. I understand that we each are threads in the Grand Tapestry and that the hours of the moon are the interlacing of warp and woof. If the intersections are not precise, the weaving is uneven and ugly. The law of the world as I understand it is in the elegance of the loom, the skill of the weaver and the refinement of thread. It has given my life a sense of cool inner precision not found in the world outside; important for a child without parents to speak of, spending much of her time on her own.

We carry Mundanus down the stairs, each holding him under an arm. I hear Aunt Marianne heaving under the burden. In the last few years our strengths have reversed. Though Mundanus seems to be growing lighter he still has weight. I can feel his breathing and savor it.

In the yard by an oil lamp Hendrik is drinking. Since I can remember, there always was Hendrik drinking old gin.

"Can you help us please, Hendrik," asks Aunt Marianne. "Our guest is unwell and the doctor has left for the night." Hendrik carefully puts down his glass and pushes his old body up from the chair. "What do you want me to do, Miss Marianne," he asks. I never get used to him calling her Miss. He makes her and me feel of the same generation.

"Just help us put him down on the grass and then go inside to get a blanket from the linen room." Hendrik disappears into the house.

"What do we do now?" I ask my Aunt.

"We wait for the clock to chime twice."

Hendrik returns with a set of blankets. One we put under Mundanus, one on top. He hardly is breathing by now; at times breath stops altogether. I feel a sudden twist in my body as if my inside is spun around while my outer body is motionless. I am losing my balance.

"Hurry!" I call out to Aunt Marianne. She nods and holds the little flask with the *purpur*-ed Red Sulphur up to the silver sickle edge of the moon, shaking it violently, mumbling incantations I can't understand. A purple glow begins to shine through the mixture. The louder she sings and the more violently she shakes, the wider the aura of purple around the vial.

The magic excites me and I breathe fast. Suddenly she sinks to the ground, exhausted. Hendrik picks her up and puts her on the chair. Then he swallows a large shot of gin.

"Here," says Aunt Marianne feebly. "Take it, and put three drops under his tongue."

All through The Hague clocks chime twice for the half hour. 22.30.

I bend over very close and notice he has stopped breathing. It has all happened so fast.

"He is no longer breathing," I utter vacantly. I feel his heart, but there is no pulse. "He is dead."

My aunt jumps up from her chair and screams loudly. She rushes over and slaps his face hard. "Don't do this to me, Mundanus. Don't you dare die on me!" She whisks the flask out of my hand and pries his jaws open, showering him with glowing purple drops. The aura of purple now glows eerily off his death mask. I turn away, dead inside. Then I see Aunt Marianne fall on top of Mundanus, across his chest. She gets up and jumps on him again.

"Aunt Marianne, please. Leave him in peace."

"No!" she yells loudly, "No-no-no! He is not going to die."

But Mundanus remains lifeless. Aunt Marianne howls her loss into his ear, telling him to wake up in the name of Trismosin. But it is useless. Mundanus has died. The story has stopped in mid-sentence. Even Hendrik has tears in his eyes, the gin bottle next to him draining fast. I feel like I did when I lost Mother and Grandfather during the plague.

"You were supposed to have his children and I killed him," moans Aunt Marianne between sobs.

I nod, oblivious. My Fates have cut the thread: at twenty I have entered my epilogue.

The night grows still around me.

Suddenly I see Aunt Marianne dipping Grandfather's sharpest knife into the radiant tincture. Then without hesitation she plunges it into Mundanus' heart.

I hear myself shrieking, Hendrik yells, and Mundanus' body spasms. "Wake up!" yells Aunt Marianne. I see Mundanus' face contort in pain as my Aunt douses his wound with the tincture. The medicine goes straight to his heart down the wound she inflicted. In awe I realize that she has done the only thing that could have saved him: infuse his heart directly with the medicine.

"You'll be alright," she tells him. Her tone has changed and she sounds like one talking to a small child who is hurt. "We'll get you through this. Just breathe, and focus on the pain. Concentrate on the pain. It will keep you alive."

℣

After we carry him upstairs to the laboratory, Mundanus' skin goes through a myriad of hues. First it turns purple, then wine red, ending in a pale blue like a bright winter sky. I can't stop kissing his face as Aunt Marianne expertly cares for his wound, soaking it with half a bottle of gin. With alum stones in her hands, she presses her weight onto the wound until it stops bleeding. She tells me to run to my cloth storage and find a translucent fabric with a loose open weave, which she continues to cover with honey from the kitchen. After the wound has been dressed not much more can be done except wait. Mundanus is breathing evenly by now.

"Miss Marianne," says Hendrik, who has stayed in the background providing us with the necessary gin for the wound and our spirits. "You called this man Mundanus. But it is not the doctor Mundanus I met before."

"The name 'Mundanus' is a badge of honor. It means as much as 'World Traveler'. This is another great traveler; from the greatest family of travelers in Venice," she adds proudly. "But I would like you to never mention what you saw tonight. To no one, not to doctor Helvetius, not to anyone. You understand?" Her voice stands tall with authority. Hendrik nods, which is enough. He will carry this secret with him to the grave.

ℰℛ

Towards the morning I wake holding Mundanus' head on my lap on an improvised mattress Hendrik made. At the foot Aunt Marianne is watching us with an undecipherable expression on her face.

"He looks much better," she says, sitting on the floor like a tailor, propping up her head with her right hand.

I look down at his face and see it has the same flesh tone as the tapestries Elspeth has made by mixing Honesty and *purpur*. It looks too beautiful to be natural, but no one will notice but us. His hair has also gained a pale reddish hue, not unlike a refined version of the mops of the Irish. I wonder what his eyes will be like. But he remains fast asleep.

"What do we tell Uncle Johann?" I ask. "He no longer looks like an albino. His skin has more the quality of a painting by Master Vermeer."

"I will tell him that I gave him a few drops of Mundanus' medicine and this is the result. He will believe me."

We sit in silence for some time while I savor the breathing of my beloved. I now know for a fact that we are destined for one another.

"You love him," Aunt Marianne remarks, matter of fact.

"Very much so," I reply.

"Well you had better," she responds drily. "A life with a person you don't love is not easy, I can assure you."

I know she refers to her sometimes frosty relations with Uncle Johann, but it is not my place to intimate that I understand her innuendo.

"Do you believe he loves me back?" I ask, disliking my tremulous tone.

Her momentary hesitation alarms me.

"Do you mean that he does not?"

"No, not at all. I am just remembering my own days of love," she muses mysteriously.

I wish she would tell me. I could use guidance. I could use a mother.

"Tell me about love, Aunt Marianne. I know nothing about it."

"You feel it, can you not?"

"I feel that I never want to inhale a breath without this man," I say with certainty. I notice Aunt Marianne flinch. Did I say something wrong?

"I once loved a man," she says, her eyes far away.

"Uncle Johann?" I ask boldly. We have never conversed on this level, as women together.

"I thought I loved Helvetius once. Your Grandfather gave me free choice, but he was skeptical, you know. When he was younger Helvetius was a very charming man; all women flocked to him to be his patients when he came here from Germany. He dazzled me. Looking back, no, I was not in love with your Uncle. But so it goes…" We are silent. I see sorrow on her brow.

"Then who was he?"

She looks at me questioningly.

"This man you once loved?"

She hesitates. I understand she does not feel free to talk with me about matters of love. She is my aunt, after all. And in our circles love is not spoken about directly, only via allusion.

"He was a sea faring man," she begins. "He sailed on our ships to the East: a merchant with a profound interest in alchemy. He taught me more than even your grandfather. He gave me a sense of the great transmutation. When I was with him I could feel…" Here she breaks off. I don't dare to probe any further.

She gets up resolutely. "I hear the carriage. Helvetius has returned from his visit to the Prince. You stay up here with Mundanus. I shall go down to meet him and tell our tale."

I am happy to be left alone with my master who sleeps so peaceably on my lap. His recovery is miraculous. When Aunt Marianne removed the dressing this morning, there was scarcely any blood, and the skin around the stab wound was a healthy pale pink. The healing power of the Red Sulphur is a remarkable blessing.

As if he can hear my longing, Mundanus opens his eyes. They are still a pale grey but the red albino hue has vanished from them.

"What happened?" he asks in confusion. I tell him the story in detail.

"You saved me," he says, gratefully.

"Aunt Marianne did. I would never have dared to stab you in the heart!"

"But *you* thought of the tincture of *purpur*. Together you saved me."

"One is responsible for the life one saves," I say with conviction. "Therefore I will take care of you forever. And you saved my life so I hope you will do the same for me." I grin broadly. He replies with a faint smile. "I will," he whispers. "I will." After a while he asks: "Where is Marianne?" For an instant I am taken aback by his familiar use of her first name, but then I forget.

"She went downstairs to meet with Helvetius who has just returned."

He nods, closes his eyes and drifts off. I rock him in my arms, pressing my face against his. So *this* is what happiness is all about. Up till now I'd just known it from hearsay.

After some time I hear my Uncle and Aunt come up the stairs.

"So how is the patient?" Helvetius asks. Then he stares at Mundanus with complete surprise. "He looks like a new man altogether! This tincture of Red Sulphur is a true miracle, I must say. This doctor Mundanus is a prince among men. I wish I knew where I could find him. We will soon run out of the Panacea. And to think I debated it with him when we first met! I can't believe how ignorant I've been!" Such admissions are highly unusual for Uncle Johann, as is his expansive mood.

"What happened?" I ask.

"The Dowager Princess Amalia van Solms has invited us to the North-End Palace," Aunt Marianne explains, obviously bored with the whole thing. Grand personages always fail to impress her. Princess Amalia is young Prince William's grandmother and guardian, and the undisputed leader of the Orangist faction.

"How did that come about?" I ask, genuinely interested. Princess Amalia has been the central presence in social The Hague for two generations and I have grown up hearing and reading gossip about her royal aspirations.

"When I arrived at the Palace last night, there were already four other physicians in attendance. The Prince couldn't breathe and his asthma was suffocating him. They had started bloodletting in the afternoon but his condition had worsened substantially by the time I arrived. I gave the Prince a few drops of Mundanus' elixir, and within 10 minutes he was breathing regularly again." Now Helvetius is positively flying with pride, as if the elixir had been his own and Aunt Marianne didn't have to force it upon him last night. "All the courtiers were astounded, the other physicians humiliated. It changed my position at the court and among the nobility overnight." I see Aunt Marianne, standing behind him, rolling her eyes in mock exasperation. Uncle Johann is easily flattered. "Now it is *I* who has to find Mundanus. Everyone at the court wants the elixir for sick relatives. Some call it the fountain of youth. Princess Amalia wants to be assured that I keep the elixir for the Prince and wants to forge personal ties with *me*, a commoner! ... I wish I knew where to find this damned Mundanus!"

Mundanus opens his eyes. "Doctor Helvetius," he says. "I am so sorry I have caused worry to your wife and niece. I must have had food poisoning. I feel so much better now!"

"You *do* look remarkably better, indeed," says Helvetius. Then he turns to Marianne. "Don't you have any idea how to find Mundanus?" he asks her.

"Now we have two problems, Johan de Witt and you," she replies, dripping with scorn.

"Do you think we might get the Red Sulphur without giving him away?" Uncle Johann asks, not heeding the tone of her voice.

"You can use my laboratory if you want to make it yourself," she replies haughtily and turns on her heels out the door. Helvetius is left behind with us, shaking his head about his predicament. "The Princess knows your family," he tells Signor Theodore. "Her family has had dealings with Giovanni Dolfin years ago when she and her parents were courtiers with penniless royals. Your family seems to have lent them great sums of money. I am sure you never saw a penny in return. The Princess feels in your debt, and that can only be of help to us. Now she wants the whole family to come to the Palace, ostensibly to meet the lucky Van Os who will marry a Venetian Dolfin. By now the word must be all over town." Uncle Johann is rubbing his hands in beaming delight. I can understand why Aunt Marianne speaks of my uncle as 'oily'.

I turn to my fiancé. "You don't have to do this," I insist.

"It will be my pleasure," he responds to Uncle Johann without hesitation, sitting up with a proudly straight back. I can feel my life becoming increasingly convoluted. "Do you have any idea where Mundanus went after he treated you?" Uncle Johann asks me with an undertone of desperation. I look at Mundanus and restrain my laughter by remembering Aunt Marianne plunging Grandfather's knife into his chest.

෧

Mundanus and I are in the laboratory sipping chocolatl. Mundanus is about to leave, back to Leyden. Aunt Marianne, along with Gerda, will go with him to help him with cases arriving from Venice, containing much of the equipment bequeathed down the lineage by Salomon Trismosin: an entire early 15th century alchemy workshop. Mundanus and Aunt Marianne have formed a strong bond, which makes me happy.

"And when I return we will look for a house nearby to set up our household this summer," he tells me.

"How much can we spend?" I ask, feeling very practical, like a true Van Os.

"I made enough gold to buy you a palace if you wish."

"I want to live in a modest home with enough space to put up several looms for Elspeth and myself. And many rooms for children," I add, blushing.

"Maybe we should get you a cloth dyer's workshop outside the house. The dyes can smell pretty abhorrent," he suggests with enthusiasm. My heart races as I think of all the cloth we can weave, all the beautiful dyes we can make with Mundanus' alchemical expertise. "Before you leave, can you show me how to use the tinctures of Honesty and of purpur to dye Gerda's wool?" I request.

He nods adamantly. "Don't think I forgot. I very much want to have these tinctures find their terminus in wool rather than in unfortunate humans." He grins conspiratorially. I am enthralled by his face. The color of his skin, now three days after the night of horrors, has settled into a faint glow which makes him look permanently radiant. The elixirs have removed all the wrinkles and pock marks from his face and pulled his skin taut, so his 42 years now look less than 30. His hair has turned into a pleasing silver strawberry blonde, a most unnatural color but so delightfully fitting with the tone of his skin that it makes you forget its artificial appearance, which would be instantly visible if it were framing another man's face. The curls he had as the old Mundanus are all gone and in their place is a straight texture of hair seen primarily among the Chinese. When I had asked him how he had lost so much of his body weight, he told me that most of the body is made of water, and after taking Aunt Marianne's tincture of Honesty he had spent hours eliminating fluids. Knowing as a true alchemist that it must be of a special potency, he kept the urine in a vat for later experimentation. After all, he told me, many alchemical recipes begin with cooking youthful urine for its color. "It will not only produce a beautiful shade of gold, it will also make an excellent mordant for dye," he had concluded his remarks. A mordant bites dye into the heart of fabric, preventing a fade. The diaries of Trismosin spoke of the joint origin of dye making and alchemy at the dawn of mysterious Egypt when they embalmed their dead into a permanent twilight state they called a 'mummy'. There will be much to get used to as Mundanus' spouse. I could sit at his feet and hear stories like this for hours. I begin to understand Aunt Marianne's passion for the Great Art, and have all the questions of a novice. Mundanus loves to teach. Aunt Marianne will be his amanuensis and Gerda his apprentice. We will make a remarkable foursome. We will create impossible cloth, produce mysterious healing tinctures, and bring inexhaustible gifts to the world. The future looks magical.

"Let's get your Aunt to help us with the dye making," Mundanus suggests. He has never again used her intimate first name by itself. He now addresses her formally as Aunt Marianne, a comical matter since he is ten years her senior; but these are the curious habits of our land. When entering a family one gets to occupy the same place as does one's spouse.

I go downstairs to call Aunt Marianne and find her in the kitchen, discussing with Cook the meals during her absence. I sit on the wooden bench and wait. The scullery maid brings me a glass of milk. She must be around 14. I notice the details of her traditional costume. She is in the dress of a Zeeland woman wearing a white cap, flanking her ears with small lace sails held together by tiny square gold-tinted mirrors on either side. Under her apron the bodice has diagonal stripes of yellow, and her long sailor-blue skirt coquettishly shows off the hem of a coal black underskirt. She wears thick black stockings and wooden clogs which make a racket on the ochre tile floor. Aunt Marianne likes her maids to wear their traditional dress in the house. She believes it makes them more confident. I think she is right. It is a joy for the eye to see all these different textiles, some very old, having been prized possessions in families for more than one generation. Lovingly cared-for cloth does a woman proud.

"You go back upstairs," says Aunt Marianne. "I will be with you in a moment."

Back up in the laboratory, I cherish having another unchaperoned minute with my fiancé. I find him bent over the thick alchemy tome on the lectern to the left of the doorway.

"They don't know what they are talking about," he shakes his head. "They are groping in the dark. I trust no book after 1500."

"But printing didn't even come *about* till Laurens Jansz Koster invented it. And that was when, 1420?"

"I mean written, not printed. Trismosin's *Splendor Solis* wasn't printed till 1595."

I so love details. They make me happy. Well, to be truthful, at this moment everything makes me happy. But I *do* have a special pleasure in detail. I look at his long fingers lovingly caressing the pages of the open book. Though he does not much like the content, he obviously loves the book as an object onto itself. I can't wait till these long fingers caress my body down to the most secret places where no one has ever lingered. I feel womanly and desirable as I approach him suggestively. He takes me in his arms and holds me very close.

When I open my eyes I look into Aunt Marianne's disapproving face. I quickly disentangle myself from Mundanus, taking two steps back, nearly overthrowing a small table. The silence between us makes it clear to me that she no longer approves of unchaperoned moments. She is right. This is indeed improper. But so delicious!

Mundanus is not fazed by her disapproval. He looks at her frankly, a hint of irony on his tilted face. "Aunt Marianne?" he says with emphasis. She turns away in order not to have us be privy to her expression.

"Aunt Marianne," Mundanus continues, "we still need to make the dye for Clara from the Honesty and the *purpur* tinctures before we leave. Where did you place them?"

Aunt Marianne goes to a big-bellied earthenware jar and takes out a key. Then, behind the fireplace, she opens a small invisible door. I see the shining splendor of stacked gold and some other objects I can't quite make out. She pulls out a small leather pouch and hands it to Mundanus without saying a word. I do not understand the tension between them.

Mundanus takes the two vials out of the leather pouch. They are each still at least three quarter full. He holds them up to the light of the window. One glows silver, the other purple.

"That will do for 30 bales of wool, at least," he mutters, his brow knotted with concentration.

"Marianne, can she use your athanor furnace?" There it is again, this intimacy.

"Of course," Aunt Marianne replies, her face softening into a gentle smile.

"With this tincture the wool needs cooking at a low steady temperature over a long period of time," he tells me.

I nod, pulling myself away from my distraction around the relationship between Mundanus and my aunt.

"Use more water than usual and much less vinegar. You use vinegar as a mordant?" I nod again. "Only use colorless vinegar," he warns me, "and much less than usual," he repeats. "You want the tincture to float on top of each hair like a thin film of oil on water. Use about a quarter of your usual dosage. Ten drops of *purpur* or one drop of Honesty per bale. Or if you mix them together use a ratio of 1:10."

"Why?" Aunt Marianne asks.

"Because the tincture of *Lunaria* is obviously more potent than the tincture of *purpur*. Nine drops almost killed me, and you seem to have sprinkled and stabbed me with liberal doses of *purpur*. Perhaps *Lunaria* gets a greater acceleration from the full moon than *purpur* when the moon is young."

Mundanus sounds reasonable. I will follow his proportions on a few pounds of wool and take it from there. If even Trismosin can err in proportions, so surely can Mundanus. In the realm of dyes and wool, I have some experience of my own. And I may call upon Elspeth's assistance.

"In fact it is best to do the process in two phases. Boil the first batch inside the small egg of the athanor at a very low temperature and wait for it to set. Then, in a large egg use this batch as the sourdough starter to leaven the rest of the wool. Always hold on to a starter batch."

"We need to leave, Mundanus," says Aunt Marianne tersely. "The track boat is on a schedule and is not going to wait."

Mundanus comes over to me and takes me in his arms. It feels uncomfortable in Aunt Marianne's presence. "We'll be back in five days," Mundanus whispers in my ear.

ဢ

I have never worked Aunt Marianne's athanor furnace by myself. I know it is state of the art and can keep steady low temperatures, called the 'immortal fire', over long periods of time: Mundanus told me that when he first saw it he was overcome with envy. He had rarely seen an instrument of such unparalleled precision. It is one of the first furnaces entirely of thick cast iron. It is a tall cylinder covered by a semi-spherical top connected to the body of the furnace by a hinge. When you lift open the top, in the belly of the cooking compartment where the air heats up, a spherical cast iron globe called the 'egg' rests on a low tripod stand. This egg contains the material prepared for transmutation - in my case, the wool. Aunt Marianne has several sizes of such eggs, the largest of which so heavy it takes two strong individuals to lift it. I will use a small one for the starter batch. At the bottom of the cylinder is the fire box that can contain large amounts of charcoal prepared in the fireplace next to it. It is perfectly aerated so the heat glows steady without a need for the bellows. A pipe from the athanor's firebox feeds directly into the flue above the fireplace.

First I filter the water several times through cloth sieves. Then I distill aged vinegar by boiling it in a glass vessel with a long beak which allows the evaporation to condense by natural cooling. A clear and purified liquid, white vinegar, drips out of the beak into a receptacle. This I add to the filtered water and pour the mixture into the egg. Now I wait until I feel the necessary concentration, shake the Honesty tincture three times firmly, add one drop to the contents of the egg, and carefully immerse the first batch of wool I had prepared by washing it several times in cold water. In the meantime the fire in the fireplace has produced several loads of charcoal which I shovel into the firebox of the athanor. I place the egg in the hot air cooking belly, hermetically seal the lid, and spend the next half hour saying elaborate prayers for a good outcome.

At the end of my prayers I feel the silence of the dark laboratory and taste my loneliness in the absence of Mundanus. It is a different kind of loneliness than I have known before. Now a *particular* lack makes my solitude sharply painful. I listen to the faint crackling of the charcoals in the firebox. I wonder how long this will take - I had forgotten to ask Mundanus. If I were boiling a batch of wool this size, I would boil it for no more than half an hour - any longer than that and it would start matting, and after an hour I'd have nothing but felt. But in the hot air heating of the athanor the water will remain below boiling, especially since Mundanus has opened one of the small windows in the air-belly a crack for heat to escape. My guess is that three hours is the maximum. I decide to wait for two hours and check again.

But when I open the hermetic seal at the first check point and look into the egg, nothing seems to have happened. The water is too hot to touch but well below boiling. All I notice is that the hair of the wool is thinner than it had been before, more like silk. But there is no matting whatsoever. So I seal it again and decide to come back after four hours. By now it is deep into the night. Outside I hear the clock chime 11. Uncle Johann has retired an hour ago, exhausted from the excitement of the previous night and apprehensive about finding the elixir.

I check the fire box and add some more charcoal, then I go down to my room in the back where I stare some more, this time at one of the large looms. I look at the thread Master

Leeuwenhoek has praised and note it is much coarser than the wool in the athanor. I lie down in the bedstead for a rest and wake from a most pleasant dream to the clock chiming 5. It is still dark this winter's morning and the room is cold. I startle awake and jump out for a mad dash upstairs to the laboratory. The room is still warm from the embers in the fireplace and the athanor feels hot to the touch. Chiding myself for having wasted a precious drop of the tincture I quickly break the seal, and open the egg in the belly expecting a ball of felt.

Instead, I am gazing into a firefly glow of spider silk locks. Each gossamer hair stands out by itself; no matting at all has occurred. I can't see from where the glow emanates; it seems to be drifting upon the surface of each translucent hair, as Mundanus had predicted, like the sun reflecting in a spider web, emitting a rainbow of colors which are at the same time pure white. I stand back in awe, then sink down to the floor, hearing prayers resound through the room. It takes me a while to note that it is I who sing them. Around me I hear a hallelujah like I once heard in a Catholic church on the Feast of the Annunciation, as I see a halo rise from the egg. I quickly close the lid, in order not to lose any of the potency of the starter batch which now has to leaven the bale of wool I have washed. I don't know if I have to add more water but instinctively sense I should not. I take a thick apron and use it to lift the small egg out of the athanor, then walk over to the largest of Aunt Marianne eggs, a monster almost the size of the hot air belly. Together with its tripod it makes for a very tight fit, just wide enough to have air circulate between its outer shell and the enveloping womb. I have seen Aunt Marianne use it only once in all the years she has allowed me into her laboratory. I remember three servants helping her lift it in. In a trance I walk over to the gigantic egg and lift it without effort. I am not surprised by my miraculous strength but just do what needs to be done, carefully placing the egg into the athanor, noticing neither heat nor weight.

I quickly make a blasting hot fire in the fireplace and wait till enough charcoal is aglow to shovel it into the athanor's firebox.

I put the carefully washed bale into the large adult egg, open the small egg, and quickly transfer its contents. Only after I hermetically seal the semi-spherical cover over the grand egg do I notice that my hands are aglow in the dark, covered with magic film. I sink back to the floor and stare at my hands with a sense of unspeakable lassitude. I fall asleep and dream of clouds and of feather-like angels.

Mina knocks at the door of the laboratory around 16 hours. Again I have slept without intending to do so.

"Madam Elspeth is here, Miss Clara," she calls out. "What should I tell her?"

'What should I tell her?' indeed! What *am* I going to say to Elspeth?

"Could you please say that I will be down in a little while? I'm just finishing work for my aunt up here. Tell her to go to my room. I've started a new cloth on the loom."

"Yes Miss," says Mina and I hear her rush down the stairs. She is an admirer of Elspeth and cherishes each moment she gets to spend with her. "I will be a weaver one day," she told me once. Big dreams for a peasant girl orphaned by the plague at a station one rung above the scullery maid. Since then I have given her little tasks to do and she spends every minute she can be excused from her household tasks near one of the looms.

I rush to the athanor and open it. The white halo of Honesty is blinding at first, bursting out from the egg like lightning. After some time it calms down to an approachable glow. With both hands I pull the gossamer wool out of the egg and spread it all over the floor. I reserve the next starter batch and place it into the little egg. I know Elspeth has to see this. I trust I will find an explanation, some bluff worthy of an alchemist.

"Mina," I call down the stairs. "Could you ask Madam Elspeth to come up?"

I hear the slow footstep of old Elspeth shuffle wearily up the steep stairs so characteristic of our Dutch homes.

As she enters she stops with a gasp, looking at the material spread out on the floor.

"What is that?" she exclaims, incredulous.

"Wool," I respond, not yet knowing how to explain it.

"It doesn't look like wool," she mutters slowly. "I have never seen anything like it."

Suddenly I feel a rush of inspiration. "My fiancé has brought a new dye from Venice. He tells me it was made by chemists there. It strips the wool of all its pigmentation so it looks like hair made of glass, and saturates it with an essence made of glow worms and fire flies. It is extremely costly and he brought it as my engagement gift." It sounds good enough to pass muster. I am beginning to develop a deeper appreciation for the tall tales told by the alchemists.

"Amazing," Elspeth repeats several times. "It is finer than a gossamer veil." She rolls a ball of it between her fingers and notices the glow coming off on her hands.

"It hasn't settled yet," I warn her. "It will take a while."

"Should we wash it?" she asks me, in a reversal of roles. It is usually I who asks her the questions.

"I think we should wait till Signor Theodore returns. He may know the answer."

Elspeth has never been in the laboratory before. Aunt Marianne does not let anyone enter she does not know well. "Did you prepare it in that?" Elspeth asks me, pointing at the opened athanor and the egg without lid. I nod. "It is called an athanor. It can heat very even and slow over long stretches of time. Alchemists call it the immortal fire. It took 6 hours for the starter batch and then 10 for a whole bale of wool. There was no matting whatsoever. Anything else would have turned into felt, even at a slow heat."

"Remarkable." Elspeth pulls at the strands and her eyebrows lift in surprise. "It is very strong; much stronger than wool or silk. And so fine! I want to run a test thread just to see how it will speak to the loom. We can do that before it is fully settled. It doesn't matter if it rubs off some of its glow. Let's use a drop spindle." She selects a thick roving of wool, if it still can be called wool, and with dexterous hands begins to draft it apart to thin out the roving. "This is the finest hair I have ever seen," she mumbles as she drafts it into ever thinner strands.

I call Mina to bring up a drop spindle from my room. I stay at the door because I don't want the maid to enter the laboratory. She does not have to be involved at this point. Elspeth is very discrete and won't talk, but Mina is a chatterbox.

I take the drop spindle from Mina and close the door. It's a long stick with a wooden disc at the bottom. Elspeth takes yarn from her pocket and fastens it just above the disc. She puts the spindle under her right arm and connects a strand of the exceedingly thin roving to the yarn. Then she drops down the spindle so it hangs off the strand of fleece and spins the spindle clockwise between her thumb and forefinger, muttering exclamations of surprise all along. She slowly releases small amounts of fleece into the spun thread which would have been invisible but for its silver glow. It has barely any thickness. Elspeth looks at it with awe. "This can't be true," she says. "I must be dreaming."

"In that case we're in the same dream," I remark.

She yanks up the spindle by the thread in a way that would break yarn several times its girth. The threat is far more elastic than silk, the only material that warrants a comparison.

"This can't be true. Are you sure this is wool?"

"Absolutely," I respond, "I even know the sheep that grew it."

"Your fiancé has gold on his hands."

I smile.

"I can't wait to see what a cloth looks like woven from this angel hair," she exclaims. I have never heard such enthusiasm from Elspeth. In fact I didn't know she was capable of it.

"How much of the dye do you have?"

"It seems that we won't need any more dye," I reply. "It works like sourdough bread. You keep a part of the sourdough to leaven the next batch: ad infinitum. At least it did this time. I already took out the starter batch for the next bale."

Suddenly Elspeth becomes very practical. "Clara, we have work on our hands." We smile broadly at one another, knowing that Elspeth's financial worries are a thing of the past. Leeuwenhoek will pay us a fortune for the cloth we weave from this miracle web.

❧

Two days later we have two spinning wheels running 'round the clock. One third of the bales of Gerda's wool has been dyed, each time with the same result from a starter batch reserved from the previous iteration. Mina is working with us now; the Zeeland scullery maid has taken over Mina's duties. Mina is giddy with pride. Elspeth has found a way to stop the glow coming off on our hands by adding a fraction of alum to the mix as an extra mordant. I have sent Hendrik over to Elspeth's home to pick up her large loom, which we put up in the stable, against Uncle Johann's protestations. Hendrik has made a part of the stalls available to us without inconveniencing the horses. Uncle Johann's carriage is parked under an awning in the yard.

I hardly sleep anymore and have started weaving the cloth on the large loom, an honor Elspeth has bestowed upon me because the miracle dye had been a gift from my fiancé.

"You will have a wedding dress that will make you the envy of the Mother of God," she blasphemes.

Because of the extreme refinement of the thread there are dozens times more threads per square inch, which makes my work slow and arduous. But it matters not a bit as I slide the shuttle back and forth along the warp, dreaming of my radiant future.

❧

After 5 days we get word from a messenger that Signor Theodore and Aunt Marianne have run into some of adversity with the shipment from Venice and they will be away for another few days. This gives me a chance to finish my first five yards of full width 'glow-cloth', as Elspeth has dubbed it.

While weaving I have noticed that the gossamer film of rainbow reflections sometimes will cast images onto my eyes, much like after-images that remain imprinted after you look away from a bright object, like the sun. Dark balls and bright squares will flash along the cloth even if the light in the stables remains unchanged. It is as though my imagination can see itself more clearly by staring at the glow-cloth for long periods of time. It seems much like what I have heard about the art of scrying, used by fortune tellers and adepts of magic who can see past and future in the sphere of a crystal ball. Aunt Marianne had many times told me the famous English folktale of Bloody Mary which would curdle my blood on All Hallows' Eve. She had heard it from the sea faring men she knew. The tale encouraged a young woman to walk up a flight of stairs backwards, holding a candle and a hand mirror, in a darkened house. As she gazed into the mirror, she would be able to catch a view of her future husband's face. If she saw the skull face of the Grim Reaper instead it meant that she would die before marriage. I never tried it and Uncle Johann teasingly called me a coward. The story terrified me, yet each fall just before the onset of winter I would beg her to tell me the story again. And every time I promised myself I would walk the dark stairs with a mirror and candle to see the face of my husband to be, but I never did try.

The larger my weaving the more certain I become that the Red Sulphur has made the glow-cloth into a scrying surface. I never tell Elspeth, but the same fascination and dread of All Hallows' Eve make me shiver inside while my heart turns into a clenched fist of anxiety. I want Mundanus to come back. But then we get word of another delay.

When the sheet is finished I hang it out against the wall of my room like a giant screen for a magic shadow play I have seen at a fair. After dark, when the house is quiet like a tomb, I put a candle on a low stool in the center of my room and lie down in the bedstead, my eyes firmly closed. Finally, overcoming my dread, I open my eyes. First I gaze at the flickering flame dancing a jig with each draft in the house. On top of the purple blue dunce hat around the wick dances the will-o'-the-wisp yellow flickering light, surrounded by a spherical faint orange halo dimming outwards to the invisible. I force myself to stare only at the flame and not at the glow-cloth behind it. But then my vision gets drawn to the background and instead of a flat cloth I see a deep stage like in a playhouse. On this stage a world is being created. At first I see shadows of bodies in air and carriages pulled by dark horses. I have to tame my fear to keep gazing. Then the shell of an egg bulges forward into the room, getting bigger and bigger, until it cracks. Behind it, in full color, a true world emerges. I see a man and a woman standing by an alchemical furnace made of old bronze, green with age. My bedroom and the candle disappear and I am present with the man and the woman in their laboratory. The woman is stirring the black iron cauldron on top of the furnace while the man is using the bellows. The woman is wearing no top and the man looks at her with a desire that fuels the flames in the oven. I hear myself shriek, but they don't know my presence. I see Mundanus, in a transport of passion, stare at Aunt Marianne, her pink skin glowing moist from the heat. I shut my eyes tight, but cannot keep out the after images of the horrible vision. I jump out of the bedstead, kicking wildly around me, and rush toward where I know the candle to be. I don't open my eyes until I hear the little stool on which I had placed the candle shove across the floor. The stage of the spirit of Honesty has vanished and the room is pitch dark.

Chapter Nine

After nine days Mundanus and Aunt Marianne return with a large carriage full of goods, which is brought to a warehouse nearby Mundanus has rented for storage.

I have taken ill with the torment of the vision on the glow cloth, and no longer dare to sleep in fear the tableau will return in my dreams. I keep repeating to myself that what I see in the cloth is a phantasm, just my jealousy over the time Aunt Marianne gets to spend with my fiancé with whom she shares a passion for alchemy.

I remember Grandfather telling me about the difference between true imagination and phantasmagoria. A phantasm differs from a true *imago*, he would try to explain. I was still a child and remember the strain in my head trying to follow his reasoning. How I wish he were with me to guide me through this hall of mirrors.

An *imago*, he told me, comes to us from a world of true dreaming, a real world where beings live whose bodies are more subtle than the thinnest of veils. They have spirits as we do, but not a gross body made of flesh. Their bodies are made of a solid light so dense it looks physical. From their Otherworld, they come to us, in the way of a dream in the night.

But phantasms live behind our eyes; they are the shadow play of our fears and desires, and when we think we see them out in the world, they truly take shape inside of our skulls. How am I to assess if the horrible presence conjured up by the glow cloth is the offspring of phantoms or a display of truth? My

Grandfather's memory cannot answer that question, and the uncertainty drives me to fever.

Aunt Marianne comes to my room the first moment she returns from Leyden, deeply concerned.

"Mina tells me you have taken ill again," she says in a flurry as she takes off my mother's Russian white lynx. I resent her wearing Mother's fur and think I shall ask her for it. But not now: now I just want her to be gone. How can I tell her that she is at the heart of my current distress?

She puts her hand on my forehead and I shiver. "Oh my darling, you are burning up inside. I will get Mundanus to come down from the warehouse."

"Did he bring a furnace from Venice?" I inquire, desperate to *not* hear the answer.

"Everything," she says with a glow of excitement overtaking her worry. "All these tools I have never seen! Wait till you are all better, you will be amazed!"

"What took you so long?" I manage to ask.

"Johan de Witt's men-at-arms looked through everything. They didn't know what they were looking for so it took them forever. It didn't even give us time to assemble any of the tools."

"Not even the furnace?" I ask, not knowing which answer to hope for.

"Nothing! They said we couldn't touch anything until they had cleared it all. I didn't want to involve the Grand Pensionary personally, so we just spent our time reading through all the old manuscripts which came with the shipment. The things we can learn! Life is too short."

I close my eyes in relief. I can deal with the phantasms as long as I know that's what they are. I can feel my fever break instantly. Aunt Marianne looks at me with deep love in her eyes. I realize that I have missed her; my jealousy must have kept me apart from her since the first time Mundanus called her by her Christian name.

She hoists herself up on the bedstead and sits close to me. From this vantage point she notices the great glow cloth thrown over the loom in the corner of the room.

"That is a lovely textile. It looks radiant." Then, in a flash of comprehension she asks with admiration, "Is that from the tincture of Honesty?" She lets herself slide down the bedstead and rushes over to the loom. With her back to me she touches the cloth, letting it slide through her hands like water. "It feels like dry clouds to the touch," she exclaims, "I've never felt anything like it." When she turns back to me she is the one who glows. "It floats!"

Suddenly I know what to do. "I will make you an undergarment from it, Aunt Marianne. Then you will feel like an angel."

"Would you?" she exclaims, like a young girl, excited with an unusual present. As with Elspeth asking me for advice, I feel a reversal of roles: at this instant I am the mature woman and she the child.

I nod, feeling maternal affection towards her, realizing that as I lost my mother, she lost her father.

Now we are living together in the house of Van Os under our family crest, an ox pulling a plow, over the door (since in our language an ox is called '*os.*') This is our family home, just as much mine as it is hers. I feel emancipated from being her ward.

I will make Aunt Marianne an undergarment which will set her body aglow with Honesty. And then we shall see what happens.

Aunt Marianne caresses her cheek with the gossamer fabric and dreams off, spellbound. My body cools down by the second.

❧

When Mundanus returns from the warehouse I am measuring Aunt Marianne for her Honesty slip, so he waits impatiently outside of my quarters. I can hear him pace back and forth. It gives me pleasure to let him wait. For an instant I see Aunt

Marianne through *his* eyes as I take her measurements. While I round the tape measure over her breasts I notice their inviting flesh, undulating upon her accelerated breath. I know that she is aware of Mundanus waiting in the hall. At the same time I remember how as a child I would snuggle up to her in the large four poster bed when I would be staying with them in their home, during one of Mother's many illnesses. Uncle Johann would be out at night with a patient and I'd crawl into bed with Aunt Marianne, enjoying her closeness, her warmth and her scent. She'd take me in her arms and I would rest my head on her quiet breast, feeling the soft skin against my cheek through her nightgown. It would fill me with a rosy sense of wellbeing. By and by the memory evaporates, and this time, touching her skin, I can feel it tingle and sense my aunt's heart beat to the rhythm of her lover's pacing. The vision of the woman by the furnace in a state of undress haunts me once again and I press my eyes closed tightly.

"What's happening Clara, are you unwell?" Aunt Marianne asks me, concern in her voice.

"No, it's nothing," I reply, trying to sound casual. "Just a moment of faintness, that's all."

"If I wouldn't know better I'd think you're with child," she teases halfheartedly in the intimate manner of the days when she was Mother to me.

We both tense up simultaneously and freeze in midair, a silent scene of distress.

I sense the pain in my Aunt's demeanor, and am deeply aware that she can't bear a child. She had confided her misfortune to me just after the deaths which orphaned us both. I am flooded with compassion and find myself caressing her womb as I measure her waist. My jealousy vanishes as we look deep into each other's eyes and feel the vibrant nature of our family bond.

After Aunt Marianne is dressed again and I can dispassionately admire her beauty, Mundanus is allowed to enter. He only has eyes for Aunt Marianne, and the jealousy takes possession of me once more. Inside my soul two people vie to possess me, the way Aunt Marianne and I are competing for Mundanus' affection. I view both Aunt Marianne, slightly flushed, and myself, a bit pale, in the mirror I used for the fitting. Her beauty draws one in, down a whirlpool drowning the eye with seduction, while my face looks pleasant, well-formed, and forgettable. Though our traits are the same and we resemble one another closely, *her* presence impassions the beholder, while *mine* invites esthetic contemplation at best. No wonder Mundanus finds her more beguiling. My cool considerations affect me like a dry breeze; I know that I see by the spirit of Honesty. The turmoil dies down in the face of what's real: I will never have Mundanus all to myself.

After his eyes have feasted themselves on my Aunt's beauty, Mundanus notices the cloth.

"This fabric looks like a sheet made of opal: look how it diffracts the light!" He takes it in his hands and caresses it much the way Aunt Marianne had done just moments ago. "They say opal is the stone of good luck because it possesses the virtues of every gemstone. See how it glows in all colors when you change your position? The Art calls this the 'tail of the peacock.' It is the state of the Stone as it wakes from its slumber." Right now I have no interest whatsoever in Mundanus' teachings.

"I will fashion a shirt out of it for you as well," I offer drily by way of a welcome. He seems to notice me for the first time. "You made this?" he asks, incredulous.

"From the tincture of Honesty," Aunt Marianne says proudly, both of me for dyeing and weaving the cloth, and of herself for making the tincture.

"It worked exactly the way you said," I say diffidently, not knowing what to feel right now. "I did the dye in two phases: first the starter batch, then the leavening. How did you know?"

"After living with the Stone for a long time you can hear it whisper its secrets whenever you need to know," Mundanus says. What a week ago would have enchanted me, now makes me mock him inside. I feel torn between admiration and hatred for this man who saved me and led me to love him, but desires the woman who's like a mother to me.

"Please take off your jerkin and I'll measure you." I watch him take off the light-colored sleeveless leather garment he wears over his doublet, as a fashionable gentleman of the world is wont to do. He is playing his role to the tee, looking the exact opposite of the Mundanus he was in his vagrant days. I see the strawberry hint in his fine long hair and, mildly surprised by my own dispassion, wonder what it would look like spun and woven. As the measuring tape does its work I muse about the *purpur* tincture which awaits me in its flask in the secret compartment of Aunt Marianne's laboratory.

ⅎ

As Mundanus and Aunt Marianne begin their forays into looking for homes in the neighborhood I have no desire to join them. I will take part in the final selection, but right at this moment my interest in the tincture of *purpur* and its potential as a dye holds a far greater fascination. I'm glad they are out together because it gives me time with the athanor. As I am becoming familiar with the immortal fire, I can sense a beginning of my own place in Grandfather's laboratory. Unlike most of his Dutch Calvinist contemporaries, as a man with his heart in the Florentine Renaissance, Grandfather held women in high intellectual esteem, encouraging us to follow the creative spirit to the farthest reaches of our possibilities. "If the fortunate don't quest, society languishes," was his motto. And to him, this was true for men and women alike.

The athanor begins to feel like a friend and I find myself talking to the soul of its cast iron presence, encouraging it as one collaborator does another. I quiet my emotion as I hold the purpur tincture in my hand to listen for its voice. After some time I realize that the spirit of *purpur* is a different being than the spirit of Honesty. The tincture of *purpur* wants to be applied directly, not by way of a starter batch. This red tincture is far less ardent than the white and requires a much greater amount to inspire the fabric with its nature. As I look at the flask I know for a fact that the entire amount will not dye more than a single bale of wool. I am thrilled that I'm becoming conversant with the substances. They have become my teachers. My journey towards emancipation from the guidance of my elders is accelerating.

This time I mix the white vinegar with the alum mordant *before* I add it to the filtered cold water in the great egg. I say my prayers, sinking deep down the well of my heart until I faintly taste my own blood. I shake the red tincture vigorously to awaken its spirit. A halo of cardinal purple emits from the vial, even though the vial is hermetically sealed, enveloping me with a fragrance of the sea salt. The dye is extracted from Mediterranean shellfish; I guess that the Red Sulphur enlivens its essence so subtly that it can pass even through glass.

I observe myself knowing the procedure with a certainty I cannot explain. When the entire laboratory is pervaded by a purple haze, I open the vial and empty its contents into the vinegar water inside the large egg. Then I mix in the wool and seal the grand egg. I heat the athanor's glow box with the slowest embers in the fireplace and know that the ripening process will take a full day and a night. The athanor informs me that it will need three refills of embers. I bow deeply towards it, and leave.

Down in my room, cutting the glow cloth for the slip and the shirt, I remember my mother Johanna van Os. From her I learned the art of dressmaking. It was all she did during her many days in bed, cutting and stitching, sculpting the fabric into beautiful garments alive with sumptuous embroidery, belying the pain from which they emerged. I could never understand how my deathly pale mother could generate such beauty. From her I learned my love of fabric and my care for the spirit of clothes. As I fashion the slip for her sister, I can feel Mother's memory soothing me. I sense her touch in the feel of the cloth. I remember sitting tucked away in a corner, hardly breathing, trying not to be noticed so I wouldn't be sent to my governess to learn irrelevant things. I could stare at her dexterous hands for hours feeling how my fingers learned directly from hers. The cloth was our connection. Sometimes she would spot me, a wan smile on her face, and I knew she would protect me from Grandfather's insistence that I study Latin or some such. My Mother-world is full of exquisite embroideries, musings and faint recollections. I don't know whose hands are making this slip, my mother's or mine.

తు

When Aunt Marianne returns in the evening with Mundanus her face is flushed with vitality. To my surprise I don't feel any jealousy. I'd rather they'd stayed away longer.

"I didn't realize how many beautiful homes are for sale," she says as we sit down for dinner.

"The plague is an excellent purveyor of homes," Uncle Johann remarks drily, a gallows jest. He is heartily eating the partridge Cook has prepared from Aunt Marianne's family recipe. His hands are dripping with fat. I know how Aunt Marianne despises the way he eats birds with his hands and this time I find myself rooting for him.

"*The Golden Calf* pamphlet will appear in a few weeks, toward the end of March," he tells us.

"Did you disguise Mundanus?" Aunt Marianne asks, worry in her voice. I wonder at her false anxiety, since the current Mundanus looks in no way like the one we met on December 27.

"I describe him dressed as a *Mennonite* of a middle stature, his visage somewhat long, his hair very black, yet not curled, little or no hair on his chin, and about 43 years of age. I assume that he hails from North Holland." My Aunt and I laugh at the disfiguration of Mundanus, who at the time had been bearded and tall with curly brown hair and an obvious Italian accent.

"Before publication, my pamphlet is already being denounced by the proponents of natural philosophy. But they

don't bother to ask Brechtelt, who did the assay. They just know
for a fact that my story is a concoction because it cannot be true.
Even if it truly happened, it can't be true. Only Spinoza checked
out my story from all sides."

"The alchemists of old predicted that there would come a
time when the Art would be denounced as a fraud because people would not be able to fathom how the Stone could come into
being," Signor Theodore remarks calmly. "I'm afraid you'll be
the object of derision."

"Not as long as I have Mundanus' medicine. When that runs
out, I'll be in deep trouble." I can sense his apprehension and
feel really sorry for him, wondering if we can't get him some of
the Red Sulphur tincture to save his neck. I decide I will ask
Mundanus for it later.

"You better keep the young Prince healthy, Johann," says
my Aunt. "King Charles' men at the peace talks in Breda will
construct any deterioration of his health as an act of war. The
King uses his nephew for England's purposes."

℣

"But he has asthma!" I exclaim. "De Witt did not cause his
asthma."

"People believe what is convenient to them. Lead can't be
turned into gold; this we know for an absolute fact, reality not-
withstanding." Helvetius smiles sadly, knowing he will be re-
viled. "I was of the same opinion myself when I wrote against
alchemy less than a year ago. Then my friends commended me.
Now they believe I've become feeble minded." I see the tragedy
for a man whose greatest wish is to be accepted by his peers: to
become excommunicated.

"How is it that Spinoza has not been crushed by his excom-
munication?" I ask, non sequitur. Eleven years ago Benedict de
Spinoza had been excommunicated from his Portuguese Jewish
community in Amsterdam when he was just 23 years of age.

"Because truth matters more to him than a community of fools," says Signor Theodore, admiration in his voice. "In Leyden they say it is the best thing that could have happened to Spinoza. He has become one of the most penetrating independent thinkers of our time. He cares not for honors or the judgment of others. That's probably why he is the only one to check out your story without prejudice."

"I wish I had his fortitude," Uncle Johann mutters under his breath.

ॐ

In the morning I place the final load of embers in the athanor. It will burn at low temperature until the afternoon; then I shall open the egg.

I finish the last stitches on the slip and the shirt. Now I am awaiting Aunt Marianne and my fiancé for their fittings. The cloth has made me remember the truth of my childhood. It has excavated the mother I love from under the debris of my resentment over her inability to have me with her for much of the time. After touching and working the cloth for hours, I am beginning to glimpse the nature of the spirit of Honesty. It brings deeply buried images to our unsuspecting awareness.

I wonder what the garments will do to Mundanus and Aunt Marianne when they wear them for the first time.

Aunt Marianne comes first to my room with a Christmas child look of anticipation on her face.

"How lovely, Clara," she says, holding the slip in her hand, touching it with her cheek. "Sometimes you so remind me of Johanna." The expression on her face shows her love for her sister, my mother, and the heat of my displeasure with her dissipates. She hugs me with ardor and takes leave to go change in her room.

Upon leaving, she runs into Mundanus, they each giggle like young lovers, and my anger returns in vicious spurts of acid. I hand him his gift with my face frozen, but he seems not to notice. All he sees is the garment, which I couldn't help but make with deep love. I despise the battle inside me. I have adorned the shirt with an exuberant cravat which ties in a bow in the way of the English, knowing it will look stunning with his strawberry hair. His thanks are sincere and effusive. I turn away so he can't see me blush.

As they try out their clothing, I rush up to the laboratory to open the athanor.

It is already beginning to get dark, and wet snow is drizzling onto the pavement outside the window. The fire in the fireplace has died down and the room is shrouded in dusk. I say a prayer as I break the first seal, hinging the outer semi-spherical cover off the belly. I notice the potholder shake in my hand as I touch the crown of the egg. I have no idea what to expect. As I lift the cover steam escapes with a hiss.

To my deep disappointment, the wool inside shows no trace of dye. It looks like ordinary washed wool. I step back and sink down on the chair near the lectern. I have used up all the purpur tincture, and I feel like a wastrel. I am annoyed with myself that I trusted my communication with the material. I have been fooled by the tricks of Hermes Trismegistos, as Grandfather called the deceptive Thrice Great patron of the Master Art. In his form as Hermes, the trickster, he makes you believe you have gained understanding, only to show you how foolish you truly are. A laugh without pleasure escapes from my lips. I sit in silence for some time, berating myself. Then with effort I rise, feeling old and decrepit, a preview of what life will be one day. I walk over to the egg to feel the wool's texture. When I touch it a flash of red lightning crackles up from the material shocking my body right to the heart; it stops, one beat, then two.

When my heart starts beating again my blood is on fire and my skin smells as if it were seared. I find myself having recoiled several yards from the athanor. I slowly move forward and see that the wool has turned a saturated scarlet. I *have* to touch it again; I am drawn to it as if by a magnet. This time it awakens my most private self, tingling up through my belly. Aware of my womanhood as never before, I close my eyes and know that *this* fabric I want all to myself. I will weave lustrous garments that will make me irresistible to myself and to others.

When I walk down the steep stairs I'm a changed woman. My gait is self-assured as I carry the scarlet wool to the loom in the stables, away from the eyes of Mundanus and my aunt. Crossing the courtyard, I barely feel the drizzling snow.

"Can I help you, Miss Clara?" asks Hendrik, who is sitting on his usual chair under the awning with his habitual bottle of gin.

"No, thank you, Hendrik," I reply, "I will just be dropping this off."

Hendrik looks at me, and in his gaze I can see him realize that I'm no longer Miss Johanna's little girl. His eyes follow me with restrained admiration. I can feel that he appreciates me as a woman; his eyes, clouded by gin, travel along my body in the ways of men. I do not mind; the wool in my arms makes me feel richly sensuous. At the same time I hold my breath and wish to remain invisible.

Only when I'm in the stables with the door closed behind me am I able to exhale. I sink down in the chair facing the loom. It still has the warp of Honesty wool waiting on it, ready to be woven into new glow cloth. I find myself clinging to the scarlet wool as to a source of life itself and repress the urge to burst into uncontrollable laughter. Tears run down my cheeks onto the *purpur*-dyed wool, leaving spots of deep crimson.

After spending some time enjoying this volatile mixture of feelings, I feel a sudden thirst arise. Depositing the wool into one of the empty wooden boxes once used for horse feed, I leave the stables. In the kitchen I drink more than a pint of milk, feeling the warm cream drip down my chin. I wipe my mouth, tell Cook I won't be joining the family for supper and take another swig. Before Cook has time to express concern, I'm off to my quarters. I fetch a light spinning wheel and hurry it over to the stables. Reuniting with the wool as with a lover, I passionately hug it close to my body, feeling its caress, before depositing it next to the wheel. Its softness is intoxicating. In a waking dream, I notice my hands starting the careful process of carding the wool, breaking up the unorganized locks and aligning the individual fibers so they are more or less parallel with each other. The wool roving seems to vibrate, sending a tingling sensation through my hands and arms down my spine to my tailbone while opening my sinuses to let in the clear brisk night air. The wool still smells like the sea. This yarn is more robust than the heavenly thread of Honesty, giving off an earthy feel. I instantly know, with incontrovertible certainty, that it should be woven through the Honesty warp waiting on the loom. In a trance, I spin faster than ever, feeling the force of my spine thrust up into the gathering yarn. Rapt in concentration, I at first do not notice that Aunt Marianne has entered the room and is standing motionless, watching me in my world of wool.

"Do you mind if I just talk?" she asks me. "From one woman to another?"

I'm of two minds. I don't want to be disturbed in my love affair with the wool. But, I know that Aunt Marianne is wearing the slip of Honesty directly on her skin and I am very curious about the sensations she is having.

"How do you like wearing Honesty?" I ask her with intended double meaning.

"From the moment I put it on I felt transported to a world behind appearances. I'm forced to see things stark as they are, stripped bare." She sounds both transported and dismayed.

My trance breaks and I want to know the truth. "You are in love with Mundanus, aren't you?" I ask her in a voice sounding surprisingly neutral.

She blushes, taken off guard by the directness of my words, and nods. The silence between us is miles deep. I wait until words emerge from the chasm.

"When I was sitting between all the crates from the Venetian shipment," she begins, "the excitement over being with the actual laboratory of Salomon Trismosin was close to unbearable. Some of Trismosin's laboratory dated back hundreds of years, bought from Arabic alchemists. I greeted each flask and each pot as though meeting old masters," she recalls. "And finally the green bronze oven was revealed, spread out in parts on the floor - part of the furnace used by the Master himself. The entry of De Witt's men at arms almost felt like a relief to my feverish imagination. Each unfamiliar instrument further invigorated my passion for the Art, and with it, my love for Mundanus."

I have little interest in her uncharacteristically sentimental musings but her admission of love for Mundanus actually feels like a relief. The sense of suspicion had been worse than knowing it all for a fact. I remain silent, my hands caressing the purpur wool.

Aunt Marianne continues in her state of operatic transport – Mundanus' Mediterranean style appears to be rubbing off on her I think laconically – "After he had perfected the transmutation and made large amounts of the Red Sulphur, Trismosin sent out an order to the Venetian traders to bring back any alchemical equipment to be found in the world of the Moors. He kept track of it all in the large leather ledgers, carefully tallying which object originated where and what story was attached to it. De Witt's spies had no interest in the ledgers. Mundanus and I were conversing freely about all of this in Latin, of which the armed intruders of course understood not a word." Now she pauses and looks directly at me. Her tone of voice changes from narrative to difficult confession. "During this ongoing dialogue while the inspectors displayed their incomprehension, a new element entered our relationship. I realized that a life without Mundanus was unimaginable. When I stabbed him in the heart, our destinies had fused. He could feel it too, but neither of us understood. I had done what my whole being resisted when I plunged the knife into his chest. Through that act I became part of him, leaving one heart to beat for us both. At first I tried to be responsible. He was your fiancé for God's sake! But I was overcome by madness and had to surrender: we were one. At that moment I felt the horror of what I had done to you, involving you in my madness. When I first wore the slip of honesty I felt naked, covered in shame, and I wept over the pain I caused you; you who I raised with the love of a mother. And when you didn't appear for dinner I had anxious premonitions and rushed first up to the laboratory, then down to your room, and at last to the stables, where I knew I would find you."

Standing in the doorway she bows her head, awaiting my verdict.

I feel pulled back in by the wool as her words float away to oblivion. The wool matters more to me at this moment than any of the drama between her and Mundanus and myself. I'm immersed in the scarlet spirit of seashells, in a world of Venus rising. Her story actually bores me.

"Aunt Marianne?" I ask.

She lets out a sigh of relief. The silence between us must have been trying.

"Can it wait?" I say dispassionately. "I would like to finish spinning this batch of roving before doing anything else."

She is overcome by the unexpected. She must have been prepared for my judgment or my absolution, but not for an honest absence of interest. Dejected, she turns, then looks back, as if noticing something for the first time. I realize that she had not truly been with me all this time while she was confessing. It had been rehearsed so she would get out the words and overcome her overwhelming shame. Now she truly looks at me and past me to the wool.

"Is that made with the *purpur* dye?"

I nod without inviting her in. But, fascinated, she steps forward into the room and walks right over to the wool. Before I can prevent it she takes the wool in her hands and inspects it. This is my private wool, with feelings just for me; I feel more violated by her touching my wool than by the entire story she's just told me.

"That is very beautiful," Aunt Marianne says after a while. But her praise sounds faint and I know that she doesn't *get* this wool. It doesn't speak to her, doesn't love her. She can't feel its power. I feel enormous relief. I realize that the wool must be like the abandoned duck egg I once found as a child. I kept it warm in my bedstead and when the duckling hatched it followed me around everywhere as if I were the mother duck. All of the adults had made fun of me with my duckling chasing me all through the house. I'm convinced that the feeling I've been having – that the wool belongs only to me – is mutual and fully requited by the scarlet wool. When the flash of red lightning shocked out of the material and stopped my heart, the fabric and I were each imprinted with the other's spirit, both wishing to remain closely together forever. It must have been what Aunt Marianne felt as she sank the knife with the purpur tincture into Mundanus' heart. I profoundly understand it, but it makes me feel my rage as well.

"To tell you the truth," Marianne remarks, "I think the Honesty wool is more magical."

"I'm glad you think so," I reply coldly, feeling no need to explain myself any further.

"Aunt Marianne," I say after some more moments of awkward silence, "I'm a woman and my heart sees clearly. I know Mundanus loves you; I know that he wants to share *your* bed, not mine. I am just the broodmare in your drama." I sound bitterer than I had hoped I would sound, and stop.

Aunt Marianne bows her head in submission, ready to receive her punishment. She is like one of those flagellants during the pestilence who went around whipping themselves, doing penance for their sins. I'm not going to oblige.

"I want his children," I say calmly, knowing this for sure to be true.

Aunt Marianne sinks down to the floor and cries. Punishment would have been so much easier to take. I feel a moment of delicious cruelty. She may love him all she wants but she can't give him offspring. Then I feel myself relenting.

"I have been enraged with you, Aunt Marianne; furious that you put me in this situation; that you encouraged me to be betrothed to the man who loves only you. It made me sick with a fever. I couldn't fathom why you would do that to me."

"I can explain," Marianne interjects feebly, but I raise my hand, silencing her.

"Whatever your reasons may be, they do not matter to me now. When the fever broke, I realized that I had been set on my path. I feel no will of my own in this matter. I sense a greater will guiding me, well beyond Mundanus or you: a destiny I feel when I touch the Honesty cloth. I feel a purpose beyond the question of whether a man loves me or not. Don't get me wrong, Aunt Marianne, I will fight for his love every day of my life. My one demand is that you will never, not ever, share his bed." I feel a sharp steel certainty that connects me to the core of the earth. "I need not know what happened before, but it can never happen again. And then I have one request, which I hope you will honor. When I wed Mundanus, I want you to lead me down the aisle and give him my hand in marriage as my witness before God."

Part Four

Mundanus

Chapter Ten

April 1667

"It smells atrocious!" Gerda tells me.

"It's supposed to," I respond. "You've smelled bad things before. You've lived in a stable full of manure."

"This is much worse! It makes me faint in the head."

"Maybe I kept it too long. But I didn't have a chance to work it."

We are bringing some order in the temporary laboratory I've set up in the warehouse I've rented for the equipment I brought from Leyden to The Hague. The content of the large glass jars looks brown and putrid. It is the urine I saved from the days after I took the blanching elixir. I know there must be something I can do with it. There are rumors that German alchemists have transmuted urine into a mysterious new compound they called 'the Devil's element'. They believe it to be the precursor of the Stone. I hoped that my urine, which had made me lose much of my body weight after taking Marianne's drops, would be the primal material for a very potent Devil's element. All I knew about the preparation of this Devil's substance was that the urine had to rot for a long while before it could be used. Some said the smell must be so bad that an inexperienced adept would faint; at that point it was ready for distillation.

"Breathe in deep," I order Gerda, as we stand close to the malodorous jars. She squirms. "Do it!" I order. This is an alchemical test that needs to be performed. I have smelled all kinds of horrid odors and am used to stench.

Following my orders, Gerda breathes in deep, and instantly wobbles on her legs.

"It's ready," I conclude. I tell her to go outside to breathe some fresh air. But the young woman, stubborn as she is, wants to stay.

I am very fond of Gerda, who is turning into an excellent apprentice. I am reminded of what she told me of the moments after I had taken the blanching formula. Before her eyes she had seen me turn into an albino ghost. Apart from her brother's gruesome murder, it had been the most ghastly experience of her life. She had known horror during the plague, she told me, when everyone around her rotted away in agony, but this had the eerie quality of the supernatural. She had taken to praying devoutly. Walking into my Leyden laboratory that day, she had found me on my bed, impossible to rouse. My face looked as though it were covered by a thin film of melted butter, with ripples passing over it. At first she thought there had been something wrong with her eyes, until she noticed that everything around me was sharp and unmoving as usual. The churning skin of my face slowly clotted into a smooth cream, while my hair went limp and was drained of its darkness into a vision of pure snow. At first she had screeched at the top of her lungs, lost in a live Hieronymus Bosch painting of the tortures of Hell. When the butter ripples began to set, she had stared into the face of a man of an alien race. She had never seen a human being like this, with skin bearing resemblance to the snowmen she would fashion during her winters of childhood. Yet I neither looked like a corpse nor like the ghost of a man; I was more like a body of colorless grass that grew under a stone. When I opened my eyes the irises were bright red as if a brain of fire glowed behind them. Gerda knew brains, having served cow brain delicacies to her family many Sundays after church. They were gray, which made the iris blue, since eyes were the windows into the gelatinous soul alive behind them. Gerda thought my brain was burning with embers so that my eyes shone red into the darkened room. My voice had been weak at first, at a much lower pitch than before, as if I had swallowed heavy bars of silver. And then I had spent hours urinating bucket after bucket which I instructed her to preserve in any jar she could find. I knew this was important, though I didn't know what for.

I had selected a warehouse with a very large fireplace under a mighty chimney and instruct Gerda to make a fire in the ninth degree. Then I send her out to get the largest cauldron she can find that will fit in the grand fire-pit. I manage the fire in her absence. When she returns with three men carrying a huge metal vat, we put it directly on the fire and pour all the horrible-smelling putrid urine into it. The men run off gagging. Gerda has to rush after them to hand them their pay.

It is a cold early April morning. Of course it is raining out-side. We have opened all the windows in the large cavernous space with its red brick walls and high ceilings. Even though most of the stench goes up the chimney, the laboratory reeks like the lowest rungs of Hell. No wonder the element I'm at-tempting to fashion belongs to the Devil himself.

First we boil the urine down to a brown paste. Then I heat this paste to a high temperature and lead the vapors through water to let them condense. I'm left with a white, waxy sub-stance. By now it is twilight. The horrific smell has departed and Gerda and I look at the white cake, the size of a small sausage. We look at it intensely as night falls.

"Look!" Gerda exclaims. The paste glows bright in the dark, giving off a green light even stronger than that of Red Sulphur. I take a piece in my hand and, to see how it responds to fire, cast it onto the last embers. An explosive flash of pure white light shoots up, utterly startling us.

I instantly realize what we have created. I have heard about it on my travels but never witnessed it before. It is the fabled *phosphorus mirabilis,* the miraculous bearer of light. I feel that I have come one step closer to the Stone. I tell Gerda, who smiles broadly.

Exhausted, we fall asleep on our respective mattresses on opposite ends of the room, leaving the phosphor on the table by the fireplace between us.

When we wake the phosphor paste is gone.

We look everywhere, but can't find it. It couldn't have evaporated. It had thickened down to its highest concentration; all non-essential parts had been consumed by the fire. To my dismay, I must conclude that it has been stolen. But who could enter here? I had taken the usual precautions and had provided all the entry ways with intricate locks. I can find no signs of a forced entry. Maybe the substance had been unstable and volatile after all. It is hard to believe. In my mind, I go over each step of the procedure, and find no moment that could have introduced volatility.

Gerda, in her practical manner, leaves to buy bread and cheese, because we're both famished. I follow after her, in need of outside air.

When I leave the front door of the warehouse I see him to my left near the corner. The sun reflects silver on his Ottoman dagger. I'm instantly sure that he is our thief and run after him. He looks back, smiling defiantly, with teeth bared in phosphorescent white and rounds the corner. When I reach it he is gone.

Gerda had gone the other direction and I catch up with her, debating with myself if I should tell her. I decide against it.

When we return, laden with food, he is sitting by the fire on one of Trismosin's Venetian stools. Gerda shrieks and drops the provisions. I draw my knife.

"There is no need for that," he smiles, with feigned kindness. His deep, sonorous voice belies his youth. "I just came to thank you for making the Devil's element for me." In sudden fury, Gerda rushes at him. He doesn't move, does not pull his dagger.

"Gerda!" I yell out, afraid for her life. Her hand reaches out to grab his throat – and passes right through it as her forward movement continues uninterrupted and she stumbles over the empty stool. Yet he is still sitting right there, truly a phantom.

He turns around and looks at the terrified woman. "I'm sorry," he smiles disingenuously.

"Who are you?" I scream at the top of my lungs.

"A Magus like you, Theodore Mundanus," he replies politely, his extremely handsome face breaking into a wide grin. I'm again struck by the shining phosphorescence of his teeth.

"You're a phantom," I exclaim, infuriated by his calm and startled by the fact that he knows my name.

He nods. "I cast my presence where ever I please."

I have heard of this. A Magus lies down in deep contemplation and casts his dreamlike presence elsewhere in space, in a concentration dense enough for others to see. It is said to be done by those who possess the secrets of Red Sulphur, the true master of time and space. It is similar to the power of the glow cloth but without the need for a fabric. He could appear in any form he pleases. His physical being most likely looks entirely different from his cast presence. If I were to meet him I would not recognize him – or her.

"But a phantom cannot lift a cake of the Devil's element. Your body must have done so. Your physical body was in my laboratory last night." He nods again, utterly unperturbed.

Gerda glares at him with poisonous eyes of hot vengeance.

"You killed my little brother," she hisses at him in a voice like a scratching claw.

For a moment it is as if he flickers like the light of a candle: his presence vanishes and materializes again after a second. Her venom has taken the Magus off guard. Gerda pulls the stool from under him and he floats. Then she radiates such passionate hatred at him that she stares him down. He vanishes for several seconds this time.

"You evaporate easily," I say with satisfaction. "You're losing your power. You're out of Red Sulphur, aren't you! Your physical body is weak and you'll consume anything that carries Red Sulphur - Peter who I healed with the elixir, the phosphor that carries the salts of the Stone. You need it because your life is running thin!" This time, as if to prove my point, his presence becomes transparent like a haze.

"You will never get my Red Sulphur. Never!" I exclaim in a voice booming with vigor.

The phantom smiles with melancholy. "We shall see," he whispers, and vanishes.

Gerda runs up to me and sobs uncontrollably as I hold her close to my heart. I am relieved that my true enemy has finally shown his hand, but at the same time I realize that this desperate conjurer dwarfs the combined threat of York and De Witt. I'm hunted by the Devil's three-pronged trident.

"I don't want anyone to know!" I tell her with authority. "Fear will play right into his game. This is between you and me."

She nods with grave determination.

❧

The country is in turmoil. The peace negotiations in Breda are going nowhere and the prospect of never ending war makes the people despondent. In all this turbulence, no one but its detractors notices the publication of Helvetius' Golden Calf. The rumors of gold have receded behind the historic moment as Holland awaits the verdict of the great powers, England and France. A decisive victory is needed to break the deadlock.

Marianne has assented to attend the Palace dinner. She feels the need to support Helvetius, since his publication had received ridicule among the scientists. Princess Dowager Amalia had told Helvetius that she had spoken about him with her old family friend the poet Constantijn Huygens. He had then sent the pamphlet to his son Christiaan, the famous scientist and mathematician who had recently moved to Paris to become a member of the French Academy of Sciences founded last year by King Louis XIV. Christiaan Huygens had written a scathing review of the *Golden Calf* in a letter to his father, who in turn told Princess Amalia that his son had called the pamphlet too puerile to warrant scientific attention. Apprised of this,

Helvetius had become despondent. He eagerly accepted the invitation by Princess Amalia to visit the North-End Palace with his family to celebrate my engagement to Clara, at such time when Christiaan would be visiting his father. I learned that old Constantijn Huygens had built his classicist palazzo thirty years ago diagonally across from the Van Os residence on the Square. I now looked at it with curiosity. It was grand indeed. The Princess Dowager was to invite both Constantijn Huygens and his son Christiaan to join them.

Marianne had told me of her conversation with Clara and made it a point to see less of me. I missed her terribly and had trouble looking Clara in the face. So I spent most of my time in the laboratory, focused on trying to make phosphorus with an admixture of highly diluted Red Sulphur. I hired a guard with a diminished sense of smell to protect our experiments, knowing full well that the conjurer would know every step I took. If he were able to cast his visible presence, he'd be capable of being invisibly present as well. I had the eerie sense that someone was constantly looking over my shoulder. I instructed Gerda to concentrate on her intense rage at her brother's murderer by visualizing a pentagram of flaming hatred around our laboratory, since the conjurer had not been able to withstand it when he had crossed minds with her.

The invitation to the North-End Palace is set for Thursday, April 14, Christiaan Huygens' birthday. Huygens had returned from Paris to invigorate the Dutch cause in the hearts of the French diplomats who were suing the English for peace in Breda as allies of the Dutch Republic. For his birthday he would visit his childhood home for the day, and was eager to attend dinner at the North-End Palace to discuss science and natural philosophy with the doctor who was held in such high esteem at the princely court of Orange, yet published superstitious gibberish. Christiaan had been a diplomat early on in his career, but unlike his father had left politics at a young age to follow a calling in Galileo's new science. His father Constantijn had been secretary to both Princess Amalia's beloved husband, Viceroy

Frederik Hendrik, and to her son Viceroy William II, father to the current Prince William; so Christiaan had been close to the Oranges since birth. I was told that Princess Amalia, a relatively uneducated woman, had always been kind to Christiaan, even when he was just a boy conversing with his father in six languages. It was said that she admired quick wit. Her greatest pleasure was to invite Europe's Royals to her palace, as she always aspired to higher rank, the Princes of Orange being just Viceroys, not Kings. That's how she had been able to marry off her son Viceroy William II to Mary Stuart, sister of King Charles II of England. As the undisputed Matriarch of the House of Orange she was a political power to be reckoned with, the ultimate national opponent of Republican Johan de Witt with whom she maintained a relationship of guarded mutual respect.

ಐ

Marianne, Helvetius, Clara and I are to gather at 15 o'clock to go jointly to the North-End Palace at 16.00 hours. I arrive early on purpose, hoping only Marianne, in the habit of conscientious punctuality, will be ready to meet me. It is the first time in almost a month since I have seen her. I feel nervous as a lovesick lad. I spent much time on my clothing in an effort to steady myself. I had a famous costume maker fashion me an olive green suit with a turquoise sash embroidered with a small Dolfin family crest, (a shield with three breaching dolphins, each above the other and a cross in the left top corner.) A black velvet cape with a silver-blue lining tops it. Under my jerkin with wide-open sleeves, I wear the ruffled Honesty shirt with the jaunty English cravat, to please Clara.

Marianne opens the door herself as if she has been waiting for me. I can see in her eyes that my lovesickness is a fully requited affection. I admire her exquisite dress; it is light ochre with a hint of gold, the plunging neckline covered by a coy mesh of white lace. It flows off her body like waves of water dancing in constantly shifting ripples. She leads me quickly to the

Bordeaux red best room. Helvetius is still perfecting his dress and Clara has not been out of her room yet this morning, so we have a brief stolen moment. Since time is precious, I speak to her at once after the door is closed behind us.

"Why have you not come to be with me?" I asks her, careful to avoid a tone of accusation. Wearing the shirt made of glow cloth, I feel compelled to speak honestly.

"You are about to marry Clara," she replies sadly, eyes brimming.

"I wouldn't have agreed, had I known it meant losing you," I respond passionately.

"You can never lose me, I assure you," she exclaims emphatically. At once she is taken aback by the unintended loudness of her voice. "I love you," she whispers.

"Then why do you stay away? I can think of nothing else. I can't do any work." I feel the despair of the past weeks, which I had covered over with my feverish phosphorus experimentations.

Marianne appears distressed by my pained expression. I know that the last thing she wants is to hurt me. "Please understand," she pleads, "for Clara's sake. She knows about the love between you and me and it drives her to fever. She wants us to never share a bed again, and I have consented to her demand. How could I not?" I audibly groan at the prospect of never holding Marianne close anymore.

"We have to love one another through the metals in the laboratory," she proceeds with deceptive calm. "And at this very moment I am not capable of doing so. I desire you too much to be in the same room with you and not end up in your arms. I can come back to you when I can just be your mystical sister and our love only conjures the bathing Goddess in the alchemical vessel, hermetically sealed, without craving your kisses to the point of madness. Until we can live our passion exclusively in the subtle world without it overwhelming our physical bodies you will have to wait for me. Please! I will come when I can contain myself, but not before. It hurts terribly."

We stare at one another, crestfallen and beset with grief, fully cognizant of the sacrifice we are bringing to the mystery of Trismosin's bloodline that I'm sure will culminate during our lifetime.

"Maybe some good will come from it," I mumble sadly without conviction.

"Maybe we'll understand at some point," she smiles in return, with equal melancholy.

"I'm not sure," I mutter and hold her hand, feeling the rings on her fingers.

We look into one another's eyes and each see hopelessness struggle with passionate love.

When we hear footsteps we quickly step apart, a gulf opening up between us. I despair at it ever being bridged.

Helvetius enters, a nervous expression on his face. His dress looks disheveled and he obviously needs help. Marianne goes over to fuss with his clothes. Under a cape of black satin silk, he wears a button down vest with many cloth buttons, some of which are undone. His broad white silk collar is ruffled where it should be flat because it is tied underneath in a pitiful knot. Under his knee length black breeches he wears stockings of a different black hue than his pants, pointing to a careless choice. Marianne corrects what she can, then sends him back up to get a different pair of stockings.

"How are we going to do this? How are we going to live this life without the other?" I voice.

"It is not going to be without each other, I promise. I will be back and we'll find a way." A cover of soothing certainty masks the raw emotion she is truly experiencing.

Helvetius comes rushing down the stairs again and enters with stockings in hands, changing them in public. Marianne is startled by this lack of decorum. He must be frightened to behave in this way.

"What makes you so frantic?" she asks.

"Christiaan Huygens," he replies, fear in his voice, "he's going to decimate me. He is one of the cleverest men in the world. And in front of the Princess!"

"You have saved her grandson's life. That matters much more to her than the arguments of logic!" Marianne replies forcefully.

"Maybe I can be of some assistance," I intone in my most earnest deep silver baritone. "I have some knowledge of both alchemy and of Galileo's science. I will help you in the conversation."

Helvetius looks unconvinced, but at least he no longer has the air of a beggar.

Light footsteps on the marble floor announce Clara's approach.

I gasp under my breath when she enters, feeling blood rush up to my cheeks. She's been transformed. The girl is gone. Here is a self-confident woman of animal attraction outshining all other light in the room, as if a heavenly body has just entered into our midst. Her dress is a simple design made of silk-like cloth with the shine of pink mother of pearl, like the inside of a large sea shell. It picks up all colors of the rainbow, while continuously shifting back towards blush. It catches the afternoon sunlight, plays with it in various dances of barely perceptible greens, and yet always settles back into a flesh-tone pearl. The waist is set high, just under her diaphragm, the gown flaring out to the floor, giving full range to the life of the textile. The top of the low cut dress follows a crescent curve gathered in the center of her chest by a large silver broche – one of her mother's I had seen Marianne wear before. Clara must have claimed it. The décolleté displays the foothills of bosom and a youthful neckline down to her bare shoulders, which catch the cloth at their outermost curves, holding it delicately. Her sleeves are turned up below the elbow and set off with precious Flanders lace. But what is most striking about Clara's appearance is her bearing. She walks with sensuous self-assurance, taking over the room as if the space she inhabits does her bidding. The change in her being comes from deep within and is as startling as my own exterior transformation had been. Clara's commanding presence is restrained by a natural modesty, which makes it beguiling instead of loud.

Even Helvetius notices. "My, Clara, you look lovely! You do me proud. It will be an honor to present you to the Dowager Princess and to Prince William." Her appearance seems to take his attention away momentarily from the absorbing nature of his worries.

Marianne has been eclipsed by her niece – like a sun by the moon passing before it – and seeing the stunned expression in my gaze, I know she realizes that a new future has just entered the room.

"Signorina…" is all I am able to utter.

Clara acknowledges me politely and walks over to her uncle to kiss his cheek. "It's going to be lovely, Uncle Johann. They are going to be much impressed with you."

"I'm not so sure," counters Helvetius diffidently.

Marianne makes a sudden decision. "You look ravishing, darling," she says, "But it is going to be cold tonight. And with your bare shoulders… I have always wanted to give you your mother's white lynx. It should be yours. You would do me a great favor if you'd wear it tonight … and from now on."

Clara turns to Marianne with tears in her eyes, moved by the peace offering. She walks over to her aunt and embraces her.

Even though it feels intrusive to do so I can't help but notice how Marianne appears torn between maternal love, jealousy, and an envy of youth.

ৰ৩

Hendrik has been told to lay off the gin for the day and the evening. A reeking coachman sours the air of respectability. He is dressed in livery that has not been worn since the days when Marianne's parents would visit other Regent families in their country homes. His black greatcoat with two shoulder capes to lead rain off his shoulders, is embroidered with a modest Ox family crest. He wears his tall hat with pride and his eyes look particularly clear today: a visit to the palace makes him bask in a groom's glory. The carriage has never been glossier; the two horses are brushed to a radiant shine.

Inside the carriage, we Gentlemen ride backwards, allowing us full view of the beautiful Ladies across from us. Helvetius stares out the window, perspiration on his upper lip, seeing nothing but his chimera. I'm unnerved by seeing my young fiancée in the furs usually worn by Marianne, whose presence appears to fade behind Clara's newfound prominence, aging her by comparison. I try not to see how her skin and posture sag in the light of Clara's youthful immortality. Being enveloped in furs makes Clara even more irresistible and I am transported by a flush of lust towards my ravishing fiancée. I feel both guilty and reconciled, to say the least, to be engendering offspring with her. In my mind Trismosin's mysterious command rings loud and clear: "In a carriage fetchest thou – The one to heal who is no other – Than thine offspring's future mother." My body truly grasps the full extent of his instruction. With masked desire, I allow myself the briefest of gazes at her while she stares out the small carriage window into a world of her own. But Marianne notices and hurt displays its inevitable outlines however much she tries to hide it. We look at one another in silent communication. Her facial expression tries to convey surrender to the inevitable while her posture screams 'Don't you touch her!' I close my eyes to avoid reality altogether while feeling acidic guilt about my passions taking their disloyal course towards my magical young bride while at the same time I feel supported by Trismosin's emphatic vision. Marianne and I have lost control over destiny, which appears to relish the game it plays with us. What had been a plan along circuitous lines of reason, however fraught, has become a puppetry display manipulated by Trismosin. When I open my eyes and our gaze intersects we have our helplessness in common. The odds are stacked against us.

Princess Amalia's palace is yellow ochre with imposing portico gallery wings embracing an open front courtyard. Hendrik pulls the carriage up to the large Doric front entrance. Liveried servants enact court protocol following codes of the great royal courts in Europe. The decor tends towards dynastic grandeur, displaying its owner's ambition. Clara looks like a fairytale princess and appears utterly unimpressed. Like her aunt she couldn't care less about all the regal fanfare, so much at odds with Calvinist Regent sobriety. She floats up the white marble staircase fully protected inside her mother's luscious furs, which give off the fragrance of wildness from the distant steppes of Russia.

Even though he must have visited here many times, Helvetius appears diminished by this environment, with a stunned look on his pale face, like quarry at a hunt.

I'm familiar with palaces, having grown up in one. The Palazzo Dolfin on the Grand Canal in Venice is considerably more elegant than this hollow return to strict Grecian styles. This place gives me the feeling it is trying too hard in its Franco-Teutonic attempt to prove sophistication by sternly imitating what comes lightly to us playful Italians.

As we enter an upstairs room with the intimate interior of the quarters in a Dutch home where people actually live, lackeys take our coats. The dark wood paneled room has hunting trophies on the walls and a large fireplace with a fire, giving off the inimitable Dutch style called 'cozy'. I catch a glimpse of Marianne's face, jaw forward, set like the sharp bow of a slender ship in narrow waters. When a lackey takes Clara's coat I see her revert back to insecurity as her shoulders radiate without the protective furs. She appears enveloped by a faint Red Sulphur glow emitted by her purpur glow cloth garments. This is real magic. I can barely see anything else.

Princess Amalia van Solms walks through the door. "Doctor Schweitzer, how kind of you to come," she says in fluent French, indicating that this will be the language of conversation for the evening. "I must apologize for my other guests. Christiaan Huygens has been delayed on his way from Breda and is not expected here for another hour. And his Excellency Constantijn Huygens is walking the gardens in the back, discussing Dutch poetry with Prince William. You know, Doctor Schweitzer, how much my grandson adores botany, and it is always such a privilege to have a great poet in one's home," she concludes informally.

The evening is going to be private, a small circle, without the court present. This special honor must reflect the Princess' gratitude towards Helvetius and her friendly relations to the Huygens.

I bow in Italianate flurry, while Helvetius bends stiffly, and Marianne and Clara curtsy.

"And you must be the lovely bride," the Dowager Princess continues her chatter, to put them at ease. "You are a man of taste, Signor Theodore," she compliments me, looking at Clara's alluring presence with obvious pleasure. "You must be proud of your niece, Madam Schweitzer. I knew your father. I think we all did in The Residence. I know of no one who did not get wise counsel from him at some point or other. Please sit down," she invites us, pointing to the gilded armchairs with velvet floral patterned upholstery, scrolling arms and incurving legs. They are deceptively comfortable, made with detailed French craftsmanship. At 64 the Princess looks remarkably well preserved and vigorous, her face showing fewer wrinkles than expected at her age. Her eyes see the world with intelligent dispassion and she is obviously a careful observer of human nature. Though her chin is slightly set back she has an air of ruthless determination – barely covered by a self-deprecating femininity – which makes her presence formidable. "We owe a lot to the Dolfin family, Signor Theodore," she says gracefully. "When I was a young girl my family stayed at the Palazzo Dolfin for some brief time and your grandfather Signor Giovanni Dolfin was most hospitable to us. I'd like to return some of that hospitality. You are always welcome in my home."

I'm surprised by the Princess' amiable conduct, since she has the reputation for being haughty. She must have a purpose

in mind with this visit, one well beyond a discussion about alchemy and Galilean science. Amalia van Solms carries the destiny of the princely Orange family. She is single-handedly forg-
ing the dynasty of Orange, currently faltering, yet held steady by
her ardent vision of a future of royal grandeur. As a young
daughter of a Count at the court of a King who lost his power,
she and her family had traveled throughout Europe like gilded
fugitives, ending up in Holland. There she advantageously married the Viceroy Frederik Hendrik, whom she also happened to
love with devotion. She will make sure her power shall never be
lost again.

"I am very gratified that you should choose a daughter of
one of our great Dutch families for your bride," she continues.
The Princess masters the art of flattery. I see that Marianne instinctively raises her level of caution, while Helvetius is beaming
with pride. He is the perfect barometer for the pressure of flattery in the atmosphere.

"Before the other guests arrive," the Princess begins – here
it comes, I know instantly: the other guests are late by design –
"My grandson's guards tells me that the Grand Pensionary has
you followed, Madam Schweitzer, and that his men-at-arms in-
spected your shipment from Venice inside your warehouse, Signor Theodore." Marianne looks as if she can't decide whom to
trust less, the Princess of Orange or the Grand Pensionary. "I
hope everything is alright? I feel most embarrassed at our country's gauche lack of civility towards a person of your rank, Signor Theodore, and I must apologize for the clumsiness of our
republican government. They don't put much faith in decorum."

"What else have you heard, Your Highness?" I ask with
dripping politeness. We're still in the dark about the Princess'
game, but I'm ready to wait for her to come forth with her true
intentions.

"I heard they are after a certain Doctor Mundanus, who they
think made the gold you speak of in your pamphlet, Doctor
Schweitzer." Helvetius nods, surprised at her information. "I

have been told that this Doctor Mundanus has healed peasants from the Great Pestilence with the use of a similar medicine you gave my grandson, Doctor." Helvetius eyebrows rise up to the top of his forehead and his sensuous lips tremble. "Since the conversation today will be about the viability of alchemy I had myself informed, and my sources tell me that there is something called the Philosopher's Stone which is also called the Panacea, because a small amount can heal any illness. They tell me the Stone can make both gold and medicine. The Grand Pensionary is interested in the gold for his war with my grandson's uncle King Charles II of England, and I want the Panacea for my grandson's precarious health. It appears that the Grand Pensionary and I have the same objective. My sources believe that you may know where to find this Doctor Mundanus. I want to get to him before the Grand Pensionary does. Otherwise the whole Stone will be converted to gold and none will be left for the medicine." She talks to our group as a whole, waiting for anyone of us to respond, smiling ever so kindly into the ensuing silence.

"I believe the medicine I gave your son was indeed made of the same Stone I used for my transmutation," Helvetius finally manages to utter in a raspy voice with metallic German-accented French.

"I was told the same. You must have received the medicine from the peasants who treated your niece at the behest of this Doctor Mundanus. I am told he left some of the medicine with them, and now they no longer possess it, so I infer it is in your hands now." She makes it abundantly clear she has spies everywhere and that we had all better tell her the truth. "You must be an adept of the Art, Signor Theodore, since you had an entire alchemical laboratory transported from Venice. Might you know this Doctor Mundanus?"

"How can you be sure that this Doctor Mundanus and I aren't one and the same?" I ask her with a laugh ready for jousting. "The timing of the arrival of my laboratory and Doctor

Helvetius transmutation must have been strikingly coincidental." I can see Marianne is holding her breath.

The Princess laughs. "Indeed, we thought as much, and so did the Grand Pensionary. But each of our sources assures us that this Doctor Mundanus looks so completely different from you as to exclude that possibility. We know he looks unkempt with a scruffy beard and a face pock marked and olive, his hair is curly brown and his eyes a dark auburn. He is well over 40 and fluent in Dutch with a heavy Flemish-Italian accent."

"I am glad to hear we look so different," I reply with a most seductive smile. I'm glad I speak French without Italian or Flemish inflection.

"We checked his appearance carefully with the peasant family where the mysterious Doctor's trail ends," the Princess tells me.

"I would rather not be in the crossfire between you and Johan de Witt!" I say.

"I hope no harm was done them," Clara exclaims in a burst of concern.

"They were paid handsomely for their information. We received a careful description of him, quite different in fact from the one you give in your *Golden Calf*, I have to say," she addresses Helvetius graciously. "It almost seemed as if you wanted to hide his identity."

Helvetius does not know how to respond. Words are stuck in the back of his throat and he can only rasp trying to clear it.

"If you did so, dear Uncle," I come to his rescue, "it was with a great deal of foresight. It seems all factions of the Dutch Republic are after him."

"But why protect him at all?" the Princess wants to know.

"Because you don't deliver up a man who saved the life of your niece," Marianne breaks in emphatically.

The Princess nods, having been reminded by Marianne's words what the medicine did for her grandson. "It is magic, isn't it?" she muses out loud.

Marianne nods adamantly. "Observing the transmutation with my own eyes was the greatest miracle I ever witnessed!"

"I can only imagine," I interject. "In my own alchemical quest I have not been able to penetrate to the ultimate mystery. And it has not been for wont of trying." It is tricky to dissimulate while still obeying my truth-telling Honesty shirt.

The tension in the atmosphere having lifted, a conversation ensues about the peace negotiations in Breda, until the door opens and father and son Huygens enter together with Prince William.

"The man of the hour," says the Princess, getting up to greet the guests. Her age is visible in her slight stoop after the initial effort of slowly raising her ample body. "Happy birthday. May it be a year of fulfillment Master Christiaan, we are so happy you could come and join us. We are so very proud of you." I notice that she has shifted into the more formal royal 'we.' I assume it has to do with old Constantijn Huygens' presence, which brings back her earlier self as wife to Viceroy Frederik Hendrik. "Your Excellency," she addresses her old friend, "we have so missed your presence these last weeks."

"Your Highness," father and son Huygens reply, and bow formally. Behind them, young Prince William bows as well. He has a hunchback, barely hidden under his elaborate clothes. My physician's eyes notice that at 16 he has the delicate pallor of the asthmatic; his eyes are sad and sensitive, set over a narrow arched nose and lips of patient endurance. He stares directly at Marianne in the same disconcerting way she had told me he did at the Parliament Inner Court offices of Johan de Witt. He regards her with the expression of an orphan boy. His father died before he was born and his mother never much cared for him, stating publically that she preferred her royal brother to her son. Then she moved back to England, abandoning the boy to De Witt's Hague. Princess Amalia doesn't look like a person a child would feel close to. Helvetius had told me that a man William trusted has been beheaded last October, while his beloved governor was fired by Johan de Witt. Now Prince William reaches out to Marianne with his loneliness. Marianne smiles at him with maternal warmth. I note recognition passing fleetingly between them, enough to forge a bond.

The young Prince bows to Helvetius. "I owe my life to you, Doctor. I have not had the honor to thank you. I have felt so much better in the last month that I wasn't in need of your services. I am so pleased you came to pay us a social visit."

"The Prince insisted that you and your family come to the palace," his grandmother infuses with obvious affection. Maybe she has more warmth than I thought. She had been a lonely child herself after all, carted all over Europe by a lost Court.

When the young prince sees Clara he responds like a man, struck by her moonlit attraction. Clara curtsies to the Prince, yet looks more aware of Christiaan Huygens, who is staring at her with unabashed admiration. He has a froth of curly dark hair down over his shoulders and light grey eyes. A quick movement flares her enchanting fabrics and makes her bare right shoulder turn briefly towards him. She appears acutely aware of her new-found effect upon men. Blood rushes up her skin, and her throat turns blush.

"Signor Theodore," old Constantijn Huygens greets me in a mellifluous voice, waking me from my momentary swoon over Clara's absorbing sorcery. "I hope you're enjoying our Hague. Isn't it the most beautiful village in Europe?" He instantly establishes himself as a man of the world by apologizing for his town while praising it. Being addressed as a citizen of cosmopolitan Venice I realize I have to respond with a kindness about The Hague without sounding condescending. "It has wandered a bit far north for my taste; I prefer our southern climes over these regions of drizzle. But some of the new architecture is truly remarkable. And so are its citizens."

"No city in the world can compare to Venice," the Princess compliments. "I hope my grandson will have a chance to visit it one day."

"I would like to," says the young Prince with shy-covered slyness. "Maybe I can travel there with my doctor and his family."

Marianne displays surprise at his forward remark, which is clearly directed towards her. Princess Amalia, who has a keen ear for nuance, looks at Marianne directly, understanding dawning on her face.

"I have fond memories of Dolfin Palace at the Grand Canal. Have you ever been there, Madam Schweitzer? You should definitely go, now that you have family over there." Marianne is taken aback and keeps silent.

"I have been looking forward greatly to meeting you, Doctor Schweitzer. We have a difference of opinion which goes to the roots of our modern era," Christiaan Huygens says, tearing his gaze away from Clara.

"Let's wait until dinner for serious conversation. You can also tell us about the goings on in Breda at that time. But now is a moment for sherry, port or gin. What shall it be, Ladies and Gentlemen? I shall serve you myself," says the Princess, looking straight at me, bestowing a most unusual honor. It is definitely a significant breach of protocol. The rank-conscious Princess Dowager never personally serves her guests. Her relatives must have 'borrowed' a substantial amount of money from Grandfather. She rings a bell, and a lackey in elaborate livery enters with the required bottles and glasses. She motions to a table for him to put them down, and then she gets up. "What shall it be?" she asks again.

Her inquiry is met with incredulous silence. "Don't look as though I have never poured a glass myself," she puts them at ease, aware of the awkward reception of her magnanimous gesture. "Signor Theodore, you first. I want to repay the kindness shown me by your family." My status has risen dramatically by her ritual act of honoring. Helvetius' jaw has dropped. Clara beams, honored by proxy, unable to shrug off the trappings of rank. Only Marianne appears unimpressed, though her state of alert is raised another notch. Constantijn Huygens looks puzzled. Christiaan is occupied with trying not to stare too obviously at Clara. Prince William is the only one who is oblivious; he is playing with a large brown dog that has unobtrusively entered the room. To an outsider it might look like a family tableau.

Princess Amalia needs money, I realize. She wants a new loan from Grandfather – if she can't get her hands on the alchemical gold. It is public knowledge that in order for Prince William to become Ward of the State last April Johan de Witt had to buy off his guardian Princess Amalia by offering her a generous state pension. Some in the Orangist party had grumbled that she had sold out her grandson to the Regents by making him ward of De Witt. Her high royalty-aspiring life style had been the cause of her financial straits, which now obliged her to accept largesse from her adversaries.

At least now I know the game that is being played in the background of this dinner. Old Constantijn Huygens is not just here as Christiaan's father celebrating his son's birthday, but as Princess Amalia's most trusted longtime advisor in matters of finance and state. For the first time I become aware of the portraits all around the palace linking the recently prominent Orange family – with less than a century of significant dynastic presence, born from rebellion – to the ancient established royalty of Europe: the Habsburgs, Bourbons and Stuarts.

Aspirations come at a price. The hunt for Doctor Mundanus' Philosopher's Stone and for my family connections is linked by gold.

The dining room is very simple, obviously belonging to the private quarters of the Princess - another honor. Only two lackeys are standing unobtrusively in portico alcoves in front of impressive portraits. These flank a great Delft blue-tiled fireplace, above which a painted Viceroy Frederik Hendrik, dressed in white and gold and a large feathered hat, forever rides a giant white horse rearing on its hind legs. In the center of the room stands a large well-aged round walnut table with place settings for eight. The dark walnut chairs are covered with crimson velvet cushions; pewter plates and pitchers, meticulously ordered, populate the glossy surface beside cut crystal rummers and gold handled silverware. The rustic dark wood floor shines with the high polish characteristic of Dutch domestic house pride, making the ambiance shimmer by the light of the candelabra over the table. The Princess likes somber colors mixed with saturated reds. On a table near the fireplace stands a large globe made by Jodocus Hondius of Amsterdam at the beginning of the century, a sphere covered with beautiful engravings of the world as it was known then. Christiaan Huygens walks over to it and inspects it with obvious admiration. "This is a spectacular piece, Your Highness, very rare and hard to find." He continues to stare at it as Clara comes over to look at it with him, but it is obvious that he is acutely aware of her presence. I am beginning to feel jealously protective of my bewitching bride. "Look," I overhear him tell her, "how much of the world was unknown at the time. And now, barely sixty years later we understand and know so much more. That is the beautiful thing about the Galilean science: that we can work on it together, finding what is certain and sure and discarding what we know to be superstition. In locations unknown on a map they write 'Here be monsters'. Our nightmares fill the world we do not know. If I were a cartographer I could make a globe so much more accurate than this one, with fewer places for monsters and superstitions."

"Such as alchemy," Clara remarks drily. He stares at her, not knowing how to take her remark, but clearly finding her irresistible. He looks at me jealously. We match.

"Come to the table, and please, let's sit down," the Princess invites. She seats herself between Constantijn Huygens and myself. Clara is seated next to me, a privilege she we will keep till one year after our wedding, when she will be placed away from me at formal dinners according to etiquette. Christiaan sits to her left, next to Marianne, whose gentleman host is Prince William seated to the right of Helvetius. In the way of an informal dinner party, Christiaan pulls out Clara's chair; I do the honors for the Princess, and Prince William for Marianne. No lackeys are involved, as at a more formal supper. After the Ladies are seated, we Gentlemen sit down; the required small talk ensues, interspersed with birthday toasts, until after the soup and the sweet intermezzo. When the roast partridges enter on silver platters, the Princess asks Christiaan Huygens about the proceedings in Breda.

"If the Republic can't achieve a notable success in the war soon, serious peace talks are out of the question. The French have their hands tied as long as King Charles has the advantage." For an instant he looks with a certain degree of diffidence in the Prince's direction, Kings Charles being his uncle, after all. "Don't worry," Prince William replies resolutely, "my allegiance is clear." Princess Amalia nods to indicate that they are all on the same side of this conflict. "The pressure on Johan de Witt to attack decisively is rising. But whatever may be said about the Grand Pensionary, he is a man whose first instincts are towards harmony and against war. The English are counting on that and are just waiting out the Dutch with the French on the sidelines."

"The Grand Pensionary is in deep trouble," Constantijn Huygens adds. The others listen to him in deferential silence. He is one of the most revered elder statesmen in the land and a capable diplomat; superb even, if the Dutch were given to hyperbole. His grey curls, of the same texture as his son's but thinner – making his forehead rise up through his hair – frame an intelligent face with large green-grey poetic eyes and a mouth displaying caution. He stands back as a careful and dry-humorous observer of human folly. "He will have to go against his instincts and opt for an act of war. But the fleet is not ready. It has not been managed well."

"De Witt will surprise us," Prince William says, with the conviction of a man twice his age. "I know him. His statesmanship is unquestionable." His support for the man who caused the sorrowful disruption in his life just a few months ago, is striking. He will make a great statesman himself one day. Respecting your enemies is the beginning of wisdom.

"Well, it better be something quite unexpected and soon," sighs Christiaan.

"Isn't the partridge delicious?" the Princess asks, indicating that this part of the conversation is over; and the partridge is indeed quite tasty. After some conversation about the dreary weather of late, Constantijn Huygens turns to Helvetius.

"Her Highness showed me your pamphlet about the transmutation you witnessed. Please tell us about it. It sounds truly remarkable." His tone is expertly non-committal.

"I was told your son was less than complimentary," Helvetius replies defensively, breaking etiquette, which requires conversations to run smoothly.

Before Christiaan Huygens can reply, the Princess proposes a toast: "To the publication of the pamphlet written by the man who saved my grandson." With this she resets the parameters of civility which might have frayed after Helvetius' incautious response.

"Hear, hear!" intones His Excellency, supporting her request for respectful behavior.

"I hear alchemy is anathema among the new scientists," Clara brings up unexpectedly, coming to her uncle's aid, knowing full well that a remark by her will fluster Christiaan - as it does indeed.

"It goes against all we believe in," he manages to respond.

"But I thought that the new science is about careful observation," Marianne brings in, with well-feigned surprise. "Yet no scientist came to check the claims, which were corroborated by a respected goldsmith and by Mint-master Porelius himself. I sense prejudice, not science. I was most surprised that the only scholars to investigate our claims came from outside the Academy: Benedict de Spinoza and Antonie van Leeuwenhoek."

"Leeuwenhoek is an excellent observer indeed. I've recommended him to the Royal Society in England myself. But everyone is prone to error, even a giant like Spinoza!"

"I looked at our gold through his microscope," Marianne tells him. "It is identical to natural gold, but for the fact that it appears to be animated. Leeuwenhoek has developed a looking glass strong enough to truly look into the heart of this matter. Of course he will be ridiculed out of hand. Ten years ago, when you discovered that Saturn was surrounded by a solid flat ring, using a telescope you designed yourself, your scientific brethren were instantly skeptical. Leeuwenhoek tells me that his magnification is up to ten times that of your telescope. He just points his looking glass in the opposite direction. Imagine what you would find with even greater magnification!" The room is silent after such a scholarly display by a woman. This kind of knowledge is a man's domain. Helvetius looks extremely uncomfortable, aware that Marianne is much better versed in alchemy than is he.

"But that doesn't prove anything about alchemy." Christiaan says.

"Well, maybe it does, in fact," Marianne continues, with unseemly passion. Prince William looks at her with undiluted admiration. "As I said, I looked at the gold made by transmutation through Leeuwenhoek's microscope. And it is different from natural gold indeed."

Now Christiaan Huygens is truly interested. This is becoming an actual scientific argument about observation. "So it was not gold after all then?" he responds.

"No, it was gold in its exact crystalline make up. But the gold made with the Red Sulphur was alive, like a plant. Leeuwenhoek told us it reminded him of the animacules he saw moving in a drop of water. He told me you had seen them as well, so you know what I'm talking about. That may be why Brechtelt the goldsmith concluded that something within this artificial gold transformed a significant part of silver into gold during the assay. Something in our gold must still carry the animating power which created it."

The table responds with audible silence. Marianne continues. "There is an invisible life force in the world. We can only see it when we magnify to a degree we can't as yet. But I am sure that with endless magnification when we are able to see into the smallest particles, we will find the mysteries of life and of time itself."

"The problem will be," Christiaan Huygens deepens the conversation, which is moving from adversarial to collaborative, "that I am convinced that light is like waves traveling on the ocean of space. But the waves are very small. However, if we amplify endlessly, we will come up to the limits inherent in the waves of light themselves."

"Have you published about this?" Christiaan's father asks him.

"Not yet, but I firmly believe it. I don't want to publish until I fully understand the mathematics of the wave nature of light. It must be related to the mathematics of motion I developed seven years ago, you remember Father?"

"When you disproved Master Descartes? Of course I remember." Paternal pride is written all over the old man's face. His brilliant son had effectively overthrown a central mathematical principle posited by the greatest mind of his time.

"What do you mean when you say 'wave', Master Huygens?" I ask. I'm still trying to understand how a Magus can cast his phantom presence to another location.

"A wave is an oscillating disturbance that travels through space and transfers energy." His tone is now professorial and he has hit his stride. "Like a wave when you drop a stone into the water. The displacement energy travels through the water in ripples. But I am interested in your notion, Madam Schweitzer, that we will confront the mysteries of time when we infinitely amplify the minuscule."

Christiaan Huygens' passion for time keeping is known the world over. He has invented the pendulum clock and spring driven time pieces so accurate that they have had great impact on navigation. He is already a legend in the sea faring world.

"I believe that the time you measure with your clocks is the time of our everyday world," Marianne responds eagerly. "We wake up in it every morning. It reaches as far as our physical instruments will allow us: as deeply into the sky as you can see with your telescope and as close up to the minuscule as Leeuwenhoek's microscope can magnify. But I believe there are other realms beyond that having other kinds of time altogether. Alchemy tells us that there is a world consisting of almost immaterial refinement. It is called the subtle world. It is like a world made of pure light, but for the fact that we can touch these beings of light so they feel solid, like in a dream. In this sphere everything is generated by the spirit of creation. I believe that alchemists of old have been able to concentrate this subtle essence of creation to the point where it can pass from mere dreaming into everyday matter. That they call the Stone: infinitely concentrated subtle body with a density of physical matter. It transforms everything it touches."

I see Christiaan Huygens' admiration in spite of himself. Old Constantijn stares at her in poetic transport, while the dowager princess has trouble refraining from rolling her eyes. Prince William seems on the verge of idolatry, and only Helvetius is oblivious of Marianne's magnificent explication.

"The Stone dreams *physically*. It creates physical changes. They say that the Stone can recreate everything it touches and change it. Material touched by it loses its decrepit appearance and becomes inspired into a more perfect form. That is what they call 'transmutation.' The Stone heals metals and makes them perfect: a sick metal, like lead, turns into the perfection of gold, and a sick person is inspired into glorious health." She looks at the young prince, whose current radiant health after his near fatal illness is indisputable. Princess Amalia briefly looks surprised, as if she is having a momentary inkling of what healed her grandson, but then instantly loses it again. "I also believe that we can't do this anymore. Our time has lost the Great Art, however much we search. That's the payment we have all had to make for your science of mathematical proportion and ratios. Alchemists would say that your Galilean science studies only the outer crust of matter and is no longer able to see through to the

subtle animation at its roots. The time of your clocks, Master
Huygens, is the time of the outermost crust."

"You have lost me completely," the Princess exclaims. "It
must be time for dessert." She rings the bell, and the lackeys do
her bidding. After dinner we Gentlemen go to the study, led by
Constantijn Huygens, while Princess Amalia guides Marianne
and Clara back to the drawing room.

Clara told me at a later point that at first she explained in
great detail the process of spinning and weaving to an attentive
Dowager Princess. Then the Princess had turned unexpectedly
to Marianne and asked: "How is it that you have so much
knowledge, Madam Schweitzer?" There was an undertone the
Princess' voice Clara at first hadn't really been able to make out:
had it been curiosity, or disapproval? "In my family the girls
were not educated like you are. I don't know if it is an altogether
good idea. In some domains men need to rule," the Princess
had continued.

"Well, I must say that I am pleased that I do not have to ride
into battle," Marianne responded amiably. "I don't enjoy being
shot at and have no desire to conquer. I'm glad to leave that to
the men. I am happy they will jump to my defense and save me
from harm when enemies come. I respect them for it. But I believe that in matters of the mind it is different. Women have
different perspectives than men. Our life experience is very distinct, so we can do different things with our knowledge than
can men. We can see the same objects differently. Wouldn't it
be a waste to let that languish?"

The Princess then turned to Clara. "Having children is our
first responsibility, don't you believe? Your children will unite
the Van Os and the Dolfin fortunes with the venerable ancestry
of De Chatillon. We create the world, as it were."

Clara knew how these words must pain her aunt. "Each
woman has her own calling, I believe. My aunt has the use of
her wonderful mind, finely honed by Grandfather; I will have
children. It is of equal importance."

Marianne told me that she was grateful to Clara for her sensitive remarks and felt that something was shifting between Clara and herself and that it calmed her. The wall she ran into in her dreams each night seemed to be coming down. "Your Highness, all my knowledge is a tribute to my father who instilled it in me. With each word I think or speak about alchemy I hear his words. He entrusted me with his knowledge. The fact of my female birth is incidental, the knowledge essential."

"I will never understand modernity," the Princess sighed.

"I have always admired you, Your Highness, if I may take the liberty. You stand up to Johan de Witt, you protect your family," Marianne had replied, in honest conciliation.

"Do I? Do I really?" the Princess had wondered out loud, staring off at invisible presences, not addressing her guests, yet allowing them a moment of insight into her unguarded person.

ॐ

When Constantijn Huygens shows us gentlemen into the study, the meticulous order shows it is rarely used. Only cleaning servants enter here to remove every last mote of dust. The walls are lined with stern wooden cases filled with unread leather bound tomes ordered by size. An empty desk is set near a window in a way in which possible users would block their own light. However, five comfortable chairs are set around the fireplace, which crackles invitingly. Prince William has brought the large dog.

"You are a lucky man, Signor Theodore," Christiaan Huygens tells me rather formally. "Your fiancée is a rare flower." I feel a subtle clash of jealousies. This man would take my place in a heartbeat.

"My niece is indeed quite pleasant looking," Helvetius responds for me, in order to prevent embarrassment.

"Will you take her to live in Venice with you?" Christiaan asks, trying to sound disinterested, and failing.

"No, Master Huygens, I don't intend to. We are looking for houses here in The Residence."

Constantijn Huygens beams modestly. Any permanent improvement in the cosmopolitan standing of his beautiful village is greatly welcomed. For this purpose, a Venetian Dolfin qualifies handsomely.

"Will you be setting up your laboratory here as well?" asks Master Huygens.

"I believe I will hardly ever get to see my wife," Helvetius moans in good humor. "She is quite set to assist her new nephew with his alchemical research."

"And I suppose you will be involved in dispensing this Doctor Mundanus' miracle medicine?" His Excellency inquires.

"I have only a limited amount," Helvetius admits with uncharacteristic candor. He looks relieved that the secret is out.

"How much do you have?" Prince William asks concerned.

"Enough to last you for quite some time, Your Highness, but not forever. And I can't serve the whole court. Soon I will have requests coming in from everywhere!" Helvetius looks worried and vulnerable.

"Well, my dear Uncle," I remark jovially, "It seems this Doctor Mundanus needs to be found. He has obviously managed to become a man of interest. I certainly am in his debt for saving the life of my fiancée."

After some further pleasant small talk about the Plague, the devastating London fires of last September, and the atrocities of war, His Excellency knocks his pipe on an ashtray to empty out the last tobacco. "I think we had better join the Ladies," he remarks.

"I have one more question for you alchemists," Christiaan Huygens stops his father, who is about to get up.

"I think our best alchemist is in the other room," I respond. "Should we not do her the honor to have further conversations about alchemy in her presence?" Prince William jumps up with remarkable agility for his compromised physical condition. "A very good idea, Signor," he says. He sounds uncharacteristically gregarious compared to his usual slow, reserved and timid demeanor. And it is not difficult to convince Christiaan Huygens to spend some more time with my ravishing bride.

ॐ

His Excellency leads our small male delegation to the drawing room. We are engaged in lively conversation, which stops instantly the moment we find ourselves in the presence of the Ladies. Etiquette has it that all conversation must start afresh for this final part of the evening.

After some compliments about the remarkable nature of her tobacco and her collection of books, Christiaan Huygens finds an opening to pose his question. He is strongly aware of Clara's presence whose magical radiance obviously affects his clarity of mind so he has to concentrate in order not to misspeak.

"Madam Schweitzer, you said before that the world of subtle bodies is even finer than the smallest particles of gross matter. You implied that the Philosopher's Stone, like the creative power in the mind of God, is the link between the physical world we see around us and the subtle world we can only envision. And you said this Philosopher's Stone can make dreams take on physical form. So even though it presents itself as a physical body, it is actually the densest condition of the ultrafine realm of subtle bodies, some kind of quasi-matter. Did I understand you correctly?" Marianne nods, impressed by his ability to clearly grasp an argument with which he fundamentally disagrees. He continues, "So this Stone you call Red Sulphur is really a transitional world all unto itself: a location between the finest physical world and the world of pure creative forces generated by God Himself. And finally you mentioned that time in this transitional realm of the Stone differs from what you called the time of the crust my clocks tick away. Can you explain what you mean? I'd be most obliged. You know how much the question of time interests me."

"I do not know the answer. But I was once shown un-
published manuscripts written by one of the greatest alchemists
of all time, Salomon Trismosin, author of the *Splendor Solis*."
This time it is Master Huygens turn to nod. Even the opponents
of alchemy have heard of Trismosin's illustrious book. Marianne turns to involve others in the conversation. "In my father's
library you could find the works of many great alchemists. But
in the middle of his study upon a lectern *Splendor Solis* would
preside as the pinnacle of alchemical expertise. In his last will
and testament he bequeathed it to Leyden University as his most
precious gift. Trismosin pondered about the moment of transmutation, and came to the conclusion that it is a dramatic thick-
ening in the nature of time itself. Time itself becomes denser,
like a soup turning into thick sauce by way of reduction. In condensed time subtle bodies coagulate into entities that look like
physical matter. Change that takes eons in physical time can take
just minutes in thickened alchemical time." Princess Amalia
makes a move to end this conversation, but a pleading look by
His Excellency stops her. Old Constantijn is as riveted as is his
son. "He spoke about time with Copernicus, who, like you, saw
time as the cosmic clock-like rotation around the sun of the
great traveling planets through the stable firmament. Trismosin
had this same conversation we seem to be engaged in right now
with Copernicus 150 years ago." Christiaan Huygens is fascinated; so am I, loving Marianne's mental clarity. "He comes to
the conclusion that the awakened Stone is indeed, as you said, a
transitional realm all onto itself. It exists *in between* the gross
world of physical matter and the fine world of subtle bodies. In
this world in between time does not behave in an ordinary manner. It has the ability to jump forward thousands of years and
bring to a boil, and thus hasten, the blind urge inherent in metals
to become ever more refined. He says that all metals have an
ardent desire to become gold and will become the seed of the
sun at the end of time." Christiaan Huygens looks incredulous.
"Trismosin tells us similarly, that diamonds are born from an
ardent slow desire in common coal to become crystal. The

Philosopher's Stone, which we call the Red Sulphur, is the master of time itself. It holds the key to Time's secrets and is not subject to its bondage. It is the concentration of the freedom of God to instantly create anything He pleases at will. To conventional Christendom pure blasphemy lies at the heart of alchemy. We can speak about this only in these Low Lands which have cast off the yoke of Rome. Even in England alchemy is still outlawed."

"So you mean to say that coal and metals have inborn desires?" asks Christiaan Huygens.

"Yes. But these desires are so slow in nature that our lifetimes are much too short to notice them. Alchemists use the fire to speed up these desires and make them visible. They are of the same nature as the desire in our bodies for health, which lives in our solar plexus, our internal sun. Without it we would all die. That's why the Red Sulphur can inspire our body to become healthy again. My husband demonstrated this with Mundanus' Red Sulphur medicine when he cured His Highness." Prince William is looking at her, flush with adulation. He has never beheld a woman like this.

"But there is a difference between living bodies and inanimate objects," Master Huygens insists.

"The thoughts of stones are very slow indeed," Marianne responds. "Everything in the world is animated. Only time differs. Compared to a fly that lives for a day, the time of man is endlessly slow. Compared to metals, the life of a man is similar to that of an ephemeral insect. With the aid of Red Sulphur a Master of Time can make slow desire move forward with haste. To us, the transmutation we witnessed was instantaneous, but the metal itself had passed through thousands of years."

"I think it is getting late. You must all still travel home." The Princess indicates the visit is done. No further pleading can stop her this time. We are all a bit disappointed.

We bid farewell to the Princess and Prince, and take leave of the Huygens. I'm sure we will all meet again.

ℰℭ

Helvetius excuses himself and goes upstairs. Marianne invites me to stay a while longer for an exquisite glass of aged Brandywine. We sit together, the three of us, in the red room. The velvet wallpaper dances from the flickering of many candles.

"I have a request for a wedding present from you, Mundanus. It is the only present I wish to receive. You will have my dowry in gold, all the riches of the Van Os family. From you I only want one thing." Clara looks serious, face flushed by the Cognac. I can feel my own brandy mix in with the witchcraft effect conjured up in my loins. I'm on fire.

"I'll give you anything you desire." I respond. Marianne notices the ardent tone in my voice and her lips tighten. It feels as if my heart and my groin belong to two men, each feeling passion for a different woman.

"I want a substantial dose of the Medicine to be given to Uncle Johann so he can dispense it for the rest of his days." Clara's voice is one of total determination. "And I want to be present when it is being made. I want it to be created by the three of us."

I hesitate. I have already used up the amount of Red Sulphur allotted to my generation. Marianne notices my pause, aware of its provenance.

"I believe Clara's request is generous and wise. This is an instant Trismosin could not have foreseen. How much Red Sulphur would it take to create a lifetime supply of the medicine?"

"If he dispenses it during a pestilence it might be as much as six grains, the allotment for a whole generation."

"Without Clara there will be no more generations, the bloodline stops." Marianne counters, fully aligned with Clara's request.

"I have to think about it," I waver.

"No you do not," Clara shoots back fiercely. "I will accept no delay. This is a decision from your heart, not a ponderous quest by your mind. I do not want logic, I want the man."

I'm torn. My whole life I've followed the precepts I inherited from my father. It is all I have left from our short life together before he vanished when I was just fourteen years old. A wave of memories flows in; Clara's request has caused a riptide pulling me out to sea. I'm back with the moment when Father first showed me the Stone after the death of my mother. Claudia Dolfin had died in childbirth together with her infant son.

"Why did she have to die, and why were you not here?" I had asked my father in a tone hot with accusation.

"I don't know why she had to die. I don't know how I will live without her."

"But you were never here!" I had screamed at the top of my lungs, my fury at him covering the pain of loss.

"She was supposed to give birth 4 months from now," Father had replied with a sob.

I had never heard my father cry so I stopped and kept silent.

After my mother died, my father stayed home for four years. I remember brooding silences between Father and Grandfather at the long dining room table in the Palazzo Dolfin. I was sure that my grandfather didn't want Father around, but my father did not bend this time. Dark demons appeared to spew from my grandfather's eyes and I never knew why. But I didn't care much. This was the happiest time in my life. Father and I would go on boat rides out to the Lido to walk on the Adriatic beach. Father felt most at home on the water. The land seemed to unnerve him, and his understanding of water was much greater than his grasp of people. That's why he never was much of a success as a merchant. But he was a born navigator and was held in high esteem for his ability to help steer ships through vile storms. It seemed that he and the water were kin. Captains with no respect for merchants were glad to have him on board as a charm for good luck. That's why I never understood how Father's ship could have gone down in the first place. When the news of his shipwreck came, I didn't believe it. My faith in Father's sea faring abilities was limitless. Later on I realized that I had not wanted to believe it, but that took many years.

On our rides to the Lido in the little boat, Father would tell me about Trismosin's legacy and how I was to never, ever, deviate from it. His words are etched in the bedrock of my soul.

"Trismosin could see the future," Father would insist. "There will be many occasions when you will be under pressure to use more than your allotted dose. Never give in, Giovanni. Never! Swear it to me." I remember the soft wind in the lagoon, the smell of the water, and the solemn oath I swore to my father. There is no way I can deviate from it. I'm torn between the implacable demand from my future and the oath to my past. Clara looks at me with absolute determination, as does Marianne.

I remember Father's voice telling me to find a woman to love, and with her, have children to pass on the Stone. Red Sulphur can only pass through channels of love. My parents loved one another with absolute devotion. My mind turns over all the precepts I remember my father giving me: 'Don't seek honor from the world because prominence might expose the Stone. Carry the Red Sulphur through the ages under a cover of insignificance. Never take credit for a transmutation; it is best to flee before the outcome becomes apparent. Never consider a deviation from Salomon Trismosin's prescripts. Taking grains of Stone from the next generation will leave an era at the end of the Red Sulphur's passage through time devoid of Trismosin's mystery.' None of my father's admonitions is of any help in this situation. I feel lost, abandoned by my ancestors; or is it that I'm about to betray them? My mind blurred by confusion, I look at the two women with me in the candle lit room and sense my love for each of them. The love I feel for Marianne is different from my love for Clara. My passion for Marianne is natural and human. It seems we were born for one another. My enchantment with Clara is a result of the magic tinctures that are vividly alive inside each of us. In some essential way both Clara and I have become living Stones since we were returned to life from the threshold of death by the life force of the Red Sulphur. And now add to this the sorcery of Clara's purpur textiles that make me go weak in the knees …

I can feel how the affections are entirely distinct and yet both women want me to do the same thing. 'The Stone passes through channels of love.' This overrides all other considerations. Like an under painting glimpsed through an opalescent surface, the face of my mother Claudia is briefly visible. Her bright lips smile under the mask at my ten-year-old self.

"We will make the medicine for Helvetius," I consent.

Chapter Eleven

July 31

In one of the most daring feats in naval history the Dutch under
the personal command of Johan de Witt's brother Cornelis sail
up the Thames into the maw of the enemy and burn down the
entire English fleet moored in Chatham. Then they tow the
gold-painted English flagship, the Royal Charles, back to Holland. As a result, the Breda negotiations jumpstart in haste. The
English retract their demand for hegemony over the seas. When
the peace treaties are signed, at the end of July, a giant party
rages through the Residence. The French launch the greatest
fireworks ever beheld from a float that is built like a castle, and
Princess Amalia sends out her grandson and her secretary to
raise a glass with Johan de Witt celebrating his triumph.

With the town buoyed in a state of elation and fireworks
about to shatter the sky in outbursts of celestial glory, I realize
that this will be an auspicious moment to project the tincture
and make the Medicine. The atmosphere is filled with exuberant
victory; this will infuse the Red Sulphur tincture with its con-
quering nature. The time for creating the Panacea – the medicine which conquers all illness – is auspicious.

My only worry is the phantom Magus. I have to assume that
he is omniscient, with his abilities to cast his presence anywhere
he pleases, at times invisibly. I worry about the tincture we are
creating for Helvetius. He may try to get it from us, or he may
get it from Helvetius himself later on. I decide to take Marianne
and Clara into my confidence and tell them about the phantom.

At first they are both stricken by the evil of eating the heart and liver of a child to get strength. But Clara soon returns to her practical nature.

"We should ask Gerda to be here and protect the creation of the Panacea. In that way her pentagram might be woven into the fabric of the elixir and the phantom Magus couldn't touch it."

Both Marianne and I are astonished at Clara's perspicacious intuition. She's not an alchemist, but being a master of an art that stood at the cradle of alchemy, cloth and fiber dyeing, she can see through to alchemical solutions I would never have dreamed of.

We send Hendrik with a missive to Gerda. She returns with our coachman half a day later. I quickly explain matters to her; honored to be able to assist in the creation of the Panacea, she settles in downstairs. She will concentrate vividly on her little brother's phantom murderer and her searing hatred of him, while envisioning a solid protective pentagram around the laboratory upstairs.

Outside the apotheosis of joy is in full force, while inside Marianne's laboratory the silence is like that of a vault. But for Gerda downstairs, the home beneath the crest of the Ox is empty. Helvetius has joined the young Prince to the home of Johan de Witt to celebrate his glory and the servants are carousing in the streets.

A week ago, in preparation for the projection, I moved Trismosin's green bronze furnace to the upstairs laboratory. Clara reveals to me that she was hit by a shock of recognition when she saw it for the first time. It is identical to the one that came to her in her initial glow-cloth vision she tells me about for the first time. It immediately arouses her suspicion about the entire procedure upon which we are about to embark. I respond that her vision was a true perception of Marianne and my feelings at the time, but not literally true. My honesty calms her down. During the week while we prepare the laboratory, waiting for the signing of the peace treaty in Breda, which will ring in the grand celebrations, Clara is overtaken by her excitement over witnessing the Red Sulphur wake from its dormancy. Marianne has told her what to expect, explaining the bath of Diana to her, during which the Goddess displays herself in her awe-inspiring nakedness to the ones performing the projection. The goddess of the Hunt awakens a hounding lust for its quarry in the tincture, making it penetrating like the force of an arrow. Clara confides to her aunt that in her glow-cloth vision she had witnessed the Goddess in Marianne's guise. This reading of events makes her relationship with Marianne viable since it assuages her unmanageable jealousies.

So much corrosion has gone on between us that I realize that before the projection we need to cleanse our souls; so I propose a ritual before awakening the Stone. I suggest we wash each other's feet as an act of contrition for all the passionate jealousies we have each harbored. I go downstairs to prepare basins with water and bring them up to the laboratory. It gives Clara the giggles, and Marianne says she's glad about the lighter note among all this heavy solemnity. I have a tendency to take these matters with a leaden seriousness. She calls me Monteverdi, the Venetian composer of operas.

"Let's get on with this," Clara says in a matter of fact voice devoid of emotion. "Come wash my feet." Then she giggles again, briefly. I feel hurt about her making light of my intentions as if the ritual I have proposed is farcical.

"We do this to respect the Stone," I counter her irony.

"I'm sorry," Clara replies, cleaning tears of laughter off her face with a white kerchief. I see she truly is.

"I think it is more important that we look at one another for a while than that we wash each other's feet," Marianne suggests. "I think it will have more of a cleansing effect."

All three of us blush at the same moment. Our silence is awkward and angular.

Marianne walks over and takes my left hand with her right, leading me to the center of laboratory next to the green furnace waiting for us. With her left hand she takes Clara's and gestures to her with a movement of the head to close the circle. We stand holding hands, not knowing how to proceed any further. Slowly the forces begin to circulate through our hands while the intimacy builds.

Clara suddenly lets go of our hands and takes a step back. I feel our magnetism scatter. "Something is missing. I want Salomon Trismosin to be present," she says. "We can't do this by ourselves." She walks over to secret compartment behind the fireplace which now is connected to the furnace by its flue, and takes out the leather bound manuscript. She hands it to me. "Open it to any passage."

I know she is right. Trismosin is the progenitor of these proceedings. I take the book from her, open it at random and read:

"When the time draws near wait for the fumes to subside and ask the Stone for its guidance even before it has been fashioned. For the Stone has to make itself. For us to try and fashion it is a fruitless undertaking. The Stone must want to come into being or all of our work will be wasted. Use the following incantation: "Red Sulphur wherever you might be, make plain your desires so I may serve you. Give my heart the knowledge of where to find your seed so my bellows can raise the heat to hasten your arrival. Come to me by the grace of God."

I pause in a sudden flash of clarity. "The seed of the Stone is the love between us which is twisted like a rope tied in a Gordian knot. We can't just cut the knot like the Great Alexander would; we have to untangle and smooth it."

"But how can we do that?" Clara asks.

"By telling each other the truth," Marianne states the obvious.

For a moment we hear a door open and close downstairs. We are still. But no further noises are heard. I trust Gerda's protection.

"I shall begin," Marianne offers, speaking quickly in order not to lose her courage. "Clara, I have felt jealous of you and at the same time I loathe myself for the situation in which I have placed you. I love Mundanus. So here, it's been said. I love him with all my heart and wish to be with him forever. But I can only have my love through you. If I could have children I would have eloped with him, no matter what the consequences. But I know deep down in my body that not even the Red Sulphur can revive my womb. It has died long ago in the fevers. At the same time I love you as the only child I have ever had. Under this crossfire I keep my love alive both for you and for Mundanus, protecting it from a morass that threatens to suck it down at any moment. My body is wrecked by our destiny." She looks sad. "I have promised you that I shall never again share his bed, and it pains me more than I can express. But you are right. This is the only way it can be. For the sake of this honesty we must now practice I have to admit that at first I resented you for it. I hated you until I realized that the pain I will feel knowing that you will be in his arms should be borne by just me and not by us both or it will harm our offspring. I will consider your children, if you let me, as conceived by the three of us together. This is my un-twisting of the rope," she concludes and is silent. Clara looks at her aunt and I see a pall of gravity I had never noticed before lift off her shoulders, straightening her spine as if fresh life is flowing in.

Awe silences me as I bow my head in respect for Marianne uttering the words which had gone carefully unspoken for months. "I shall go next," I force myself to say, as I place the leather bound manuscript on the lectern behind me.

"My father told me that I was to follow love, or the journey of the Red Sulphur through time would come to a halt. I've been waiting for it, despairing, thinking I would turn out to be the last of our line. So when I met you," I turn to Marianne, "and you were the wife of another, I cursed my destiny." Clara smiles. She too finds my effusive Italian nature funny. "Then we did the projection and I knew I could not breathe without you, and I agree with you: I would have done whatever it took to make you come with me to the ends of the earth. And then, when you told me you could not have children I decided to or-phan the Stone and chose you." Clara looks shocked by the cry of my heart. "And then I thought I went mad when after both Clara and I were transformed by the tinctures I became so enchanted that I only had eyes for your beauty," I tell Clara. "My eyes were transfixed on your every move, you made the sun rise and set. With you I feel the full power of a magic I can't do without. Both these loves are equally real and each of them totally absorbing. Neither seems to exclude the other and it is as if I have two hearts beating together in my chest. Each heart has a name engraved upon it. Yours!" In a dramatic gesture I raise my two arms, my right hand pointing at Clara, my left at Marianne. Both sober Regent women grin and Marianne mouths: 'Monteverdi.' But I effuse on without Nordic restraint. "How can a man live with two hearts beating at the same time but in different rhythms? How can I feel love of equal intensity but of a totally different nature? Both hearts are of the same value, yet each is so different, the one can't recognize the other. This is my madness, and I am ready to live with it if the both of you will let me." I suddenly sob for an instant: "If you will have me."

Marianne and Clara nod at the same moment, both equally amused, yet serious. Marianne appears tender towards me and proud that I have spoken so clearly what she has known to be true all along.

"When I first wove the cloth with the red tinctured wool mixed in, I knew it would make me irresistible to you," Clara responds to me. "I feel ashamed that I resorted to magic in order to draw you to me. I have woven all my clothes of some form of this fabric so your eyes will not stray for even a moment. I am truly ashamed and I'm sorry to you, Aunt Marianne. But my apologies vanish when I look at Mundanus. I know he will have to be mine. I know it so deeply inside me that my body hurts like fire the moment I try to deny it. His children are already inside me, just waiting for his seed to grow. I can feel the future pulling me like a chain, dragging me inexorably forward. It is as if time has reversed and I am living my life towards its origin." She looks confused and Marianne seems to want to take her in her arms as she used to when Clara felt left all alone in the world. But she knows that it would be disrespectful. Clara is a grown woman with her own cross to bear.

We stand together in silence, cleansed by the words we have spoken.

"This sure was some washing of feet," I try to make light. We laugh louder than the humor of my words warrants.

While the three of us begin our preparations to awaken the Stone, the grand finale of the victory fireworks thunders over the Residence.

Clara has suggested we make use of a glow cloth. She has woven a scrying screen the size of the entire back wall of the laboratory across from the fireplace Clara had Hendrik put up two large hooks in the ceiling with the help of Mina who had been greatly excited to have a chance to spend time in the laboratory. The girl had become increasingly intrigued with all of Clara's activities, and she had become to Clara what Gerda is to me. It had not been easy to send her out into the streets earlier in the evening, since she knew something was about to happen in the laboratory.

Clara has fastened the topside of the cloth to a long rod, wrapped one rotation around and secured with strong loops and buttons. Standing at the top of the ladder, seeing Clara across from me just below the ceiling while Marianne is looking up from the floor between us, I'm vividly aware of the perfect equilateral triangle between us. When the rod is in place on the ceiling another pole is fed through a seam at the bottom to keep the scrying screen taut. I remove the flue of the furnace from its temporary position in the fireplace (Gerda and I have ingeniously fashioned an elbow shaped pipe in my laboratory at the warehouse.) We position ourselves in front of the fireplace, with me in the middle and Clara and Marianne holding me by the waist. We wait in this manner like three sheaves of hay catching fire, feeling the heat rush up our bodies. After containing this burning within us for minutes, I strike the flint against the fire-steel and create a spark, which drops into the dry straw inside the cylindrical tinderbox. A small fire is kindled instantaneously inside the box. Marianne transfers the fire to the kindling in the fireplace, while Clara carefully uses the small bellows causing the flames to grow quickly. Listening to the crackling sounds of the fire we can hear spirits echo towards us. Marianne opens the ivory box so the Red Sulphur may catch a glimpse of the fire being prepared for its quickening. The dance of the flames makes its yellow crystals glow orange.

"Look!" I exclaim, pointing at the scrying screen. "Did you see that?"

From behind the screen, presences are appearing, like ghosts curious about the unfolding events. The screen has become a veil between the worlds.

"I see wisps of live fog dancing on the marshes," Clara says.

"To me they are bright sparks of sunshine," Marianne says.

"I see presences from another world," I remark. As we speak we know that we see the same essences under the aspect of each personal view.

"The Red Sulphur wants to come to us." I'm convinced of it now. An alien scent, not belonging to wood fire, begins to pervade the room from behind the scrying screen.

"Smell comes first," I explain. "We can first discern the world beyond by way of smell. The old Greeks already told us so." Our common excitement grows with this whiff of the presence of the Stone.

"They glow brighter," Marianne is convinced.

"They're coming closer," Clara responds.

Suddenly we shriek in surprise at the same time. From behind the screen a large green salamander floats momentarily into the space in front of the veil, then recedes.

"The salamander! Trismosin speaks about him. He is the messenger of the Stone. The Stone loves your scrying screen, Clara. You have fashioned a great playground for its people."

"And we all saw it, didn't we?" Marianne asks.

"We all did," says Clara in awe. Our perceptions have synchronized around the coming of the Stone.

"Look, there is the green lion," I point out. "It is the residue of raw sulphur from which Trismosin refined the Red Sulphur. There is always a residual wildness in the Stone that can erupt and make the Stone turn feral. I have never seen these presences so clearly. We have to cut off the paws of the green lion in order to tame it."

"How do we do that?" asks Clara.

"They say we would have to drench it in acid for a day," Marianne says, worried.

"No," I reply, "that is only when the Stone is of inferior quality in its early stages of formation. Trismosin's Stone has reached its final perfection and the green lion tames itself. It just requires constant attention. He should not escape from the vessel. That makes me think that we should not use the fixing oven, but heat the Red Sulphur in Mary's Bath, a double boiler, so that the heat is slow."

"What about the Athanor?" Clara asks.

"The Athanor heats the egg with air. Mary's Bath uses water. It is slightly warmer."

Marianne goes over to the wall by the fireplace where she keeps her father's utensils, and selects a small double boiler.

"Do you have a bridge to put on top of the lower boiler so the upper one can be heated by steam?" Mundanus asks. Marianne nods and gets out the metal grid which lifts the top pan above the lower.

"My God! Look!" Clara exclaims.

In the space created by the vanished scrying screen three figures have emerged: two women and a man. They are naked and covered in moisture as if they have just bathed.

"It is us," Marianne states quietly. "Our souls will unite with the Stone." Clara feels completely exposed and instinctively covers her breasts with her arms as if she were physically nude. Marianne smiles at her. "You can't hide from the Stone, my love," she whispers, gently touching Clara's cheek. "Truth is naked."

In its ivory box the Red Sulphur is glowing, alive with expectation.

I must be looking embarrassed, not knowing how to respond. I look at my young bride, whose dress is now shining with deep blush enchantment. I wish to undress her with trembling hands. At the same time I'm filled with desire for Marianne. When I look at the space across I see that the naked man has split into identical twins and two embraces are moving in differing rhythms. The love with Clara is slow and tender, the passion with Marianne hot and acute. We stare at ourselves from the physical side of the room.

I take Marianne's small knife, which only a short while ago touched my heart. With a sure hand I cut off six grains of Red Sulphur. In the scrying world of Truth, the lovemaking intensifies. The mirror images of our bodies writhe before us. I place the Red Sulphur grains in the top pan of the double boiler, which Marianne has filled with purified alcohol. Marianne transfers the coals from the fire to the belly of Trismosin's green furnace and I put the elbow flue back in its previous position.

Now we have to wait, standing together, holding hands while scrying deeply into the visionary realm where the truth of our love plays out before us, revealing everything.

As the heat of passion peaks simultaneously among the two couples in the world unveiled, and the four bodies lie down in exhaustion, the three holding hands in the physical realm know the Red Sulphur has been awakened to its maximum potency and a medicine of great power has been created. The simulacra recede and the glow-cloth hangs blankly against the wall of the laboratory.

℘

The next day Hendrik comes to tell Marianne of a strange incident. When he went to his secret stash in the stable to get himself a fresh bottle of gin, he noticed a bottle he had never seen, wrapped in a piece of parchment with letters on it. Hendrik could decipher the word 'Helvetius' in large block letters, one of the few words he can read. He picked up the alien bottle and delivered it to Helvetius, who was smoking his pipe in his study, brooding over a recent party. Many at the party had come up to Helvetius, the rich and the powerful, begging him for the medicine. If he were to give it to them, at whatever price, he would be out of the medicine within the month. So he drank away his worries with beer and with gin and soon forgot that he hardly had any medicine, and promised everyone he would be their doctor. He left the party with an afterglow of glory and now his chickens had come home to roost, giving him a roaring headache. Where the Hell could he find more medicine?

And then, like magic, Hendrik entered with the bottle to end all of Helvetius' worries. He read the parchment giving the medical instructions in Latin, explaining that this Medicine is so much more potent than the one before that the dosage should be just one percent of the previous Panacea. The parchment is signed with a florid 'M'. Helvetius knew that he was set for life and hugged the bottle in a way he had never embraced a human. He felt redeemed, forever to be respected by the ones whose approval he has craved all his life. When he opened the bottle a cool green flash burst up all the way to the ceiling.

ℰℐ

I return to my quarters at the warehouse with an equally large bottle of the Panacea which I am keeping for myself. Outside, throngs with belching hangovers stumble through the heat of summer. I find Gerda shivering, sitting by a large wood fire that doesn't seem to warm her. The laboratory is like a boiling furnace.

When I touch her hand it is cold. She appears frozen in a spasm of dread. I ask her what happened but she can't seem to find words. When I placed the bottle for Helvetius among Hendrik's ample supply of old gin, I had taken out a bottle of spirits for myself, being in a celebratory mood. I fill a mug with several shots of gin and give it to warm Gerda. After the second cup she begins to stammer as a flush of heat rushes up to her cheeks.

"He came back!" she utters.

"Who?" I open the windows to let in some air.

"He was here," she repeats softly and then remains silent. The sounds of boisterous crowds fill the hot laboratory.

ℰ

"There was a knock on the front door. At first I missed it because of the fireworks. So I go up to the door. I know I can't let anyone in because of your work upstairs. I look through the small window in the door and see a little child looking lost. His posture seems familiar. I don't know in what way; and before I can think I've opened the door. It's a boy wearing a cape with a hood. I can't see his face. He doesn't speak and stands very still. I can see him by the light of the fireworks. I have a sense that I know this child. So I take off his hood." Gerda is silent, terror straining her face. She tries to speak, but like a person in a dream, she can't get the words past her throat. I take her right hand, fingers like icicles, and warm it between mine.

"It's Peter," she whispers breathlessly. "It's Peter." I am completely taken aback and almost let go of her hand.

"I hug him. It's all I can do. Just hug him. His body is cold as ice. So I take him to the kitchen to warm him. Then I realize that Peter is dead. I put him in the grave myself. I hug him again, just to make sure that he has a body and isn't a ghost. He's cold as stone but his body feels like solid flesh. I look at him again. It's Peter alright."

From deep inside me winter rises up through my soul. Gerda goes on, haltingly. "I make a fire in the kitchen hearth. His face is bluish, in the way of a corpse. He still doesn't speak. I want to run upstairs to get you. But I know that would harm the Panacea. I forget entirely about the pentagram of hatred to protect it, and put him very close to the fire hugging his cold body. Suddenly I realize what's wrong: he has no smell whatsoever. His body is devoid of any odor. This is not a human boy, or someone returning from the dead. This is a phantom!"

I understand immediately that the conjurer has become much stronger than he had been when he cast the young man with the Ottoman dagger. This time he has been able to cast a solid form.

"I knew that the sorcerer could feel my realization because when the phantom looks up at me he no longer has Peter's eyes. They are of such flashing demonic force that I'm pushed backwards and fall against the hearth."

Gerda is now holding her breath, fully enveloped by the memory. I notice that I'm not breathing either.

"He slowly comes walking towards me dagger in hand," her voice reflects the suspense, "with the wooden step of an evil homunculus. He goes straight for my heart. I grab behind me and find a burning log. My hand feels no fire." She looks at her hand to verify that indeed it has no burn marks. "I aim right for his eyes. I hear myself hiss with such shattering hatred that the phantom recoils for a moment. Then I jump up, grab him and throw him into the fire, holding him down with the burning log." She gasps. "When I see him burn it's Peter. He screams in pain."

I know she is aware that the sorcerer was using his memory of the moment when he tortured Peter.

"I look in Peter's face and hear the voice I love scream in torment, as if I'm killing him. It took all my conviction to hold him down in the fire and see his pain as if I were causing it myself by burning him. It was as though I was killing him myself." Tears gush over he now flushed face.

"Out of nowhere a thunder of rage comes up. I raise the burning log and plunge it into his chest while focusing all my fury on the sorcerer casting Peter's presence. He shatters into tiny particles of ice that sizzle in the fire and go up in smoke."

After some silence she adds, "I don't remember how I got back to the warehouse. I have some vague memories of fireworks and dancing hordes. All the while I knew that the Panacea was safe and out of the sorcerer's reach."

※

August 9

Princess Amalia van Solms insist that the wedding between Clara de Chatillon and myself is to take place in the Great Church of The Hague. I have become a Protestant for the occasion, since church dogma matters little to me and the Church of Rome never carried much of my affection. The Great Church is dear to Princess Amalia's heart. Both her son William II and her grandson William III were baptized there and she wants to publicly express her gratitude to the Dolfin family of Venice. At her behest, everyone who is anyone in the Orangists camp will be present. Johan de Witt and the name Van Os will call in all the Regent families who matter, so the opposing factions are to be briefly united on Tuesday afternoon, August 9. The wedding celebrates the victory over the English and the momentary armistice between the Orangists and the Regents; it will be a triumphant celebration of Dutch unity, a fleeting conjunction of forces.

※

Gerda comes to The Hague to help me dress. There are hundreds of buttons on my silver embroidered white silk bridegroom coat. The buttons have confused me to the point that I finally had to ask for help. Princess Amalia has offered to send over menservants who are specialized in dressing men, but I have politely refused. Gerda's strong presence comforts me. Mina arrives with a letter. It was delivered at the Van Os home early this morning by a messenger from the Venetian ambassador to the Dutch Republic. At first I let it lie around, since we are selecting the perfect cravat for the undershirt. Gerda insists on a light blue one to offset the whiteness of the coat and vest, while I want to wear the white one made by Clara. We argue back and forth for a while.

"Aren't you going to open the letter?" Gerda asks me eventually.

I had forgotten all about it and at first can't find it. Then it appears near the fireplace among some leftovers of our phosphor experiments. The envelope has a distinct green glow.

I open it distractedly and take out the epistle.

"Sir,

I hear from our Ambassador in The Hague that you are presenting yourself as my grandson Giovanni Theodore. My grandson, however, died at sea 15 years ago. Since his body was never found I allowed for the possibility that he survived the shipwreck. Therefore I sent one of his old friends to The Hague to verify your identity. He tells me you do not look like my grandson in any way. My grandson, if he were still alive, would be 43 years of age. I have been told you are less than 30. I must therefore insist that you stop your pretense or I shall have you arrested by the guards of my old friend Princess Amalia van Solms.

If you wish to explain yourself you can do so at the Venetian Embassy or in person in Venice.

Sincerely,

Giovanni Dolfin, VI

I sink down on a chair. My head is vacant as if my brains have been blown out. Gerda asks what happened. I show her the letter, not thinking that it has been written in Italian. "I can't believe that he is still alive. I can't believe it. He must be way over a hundred by now! I had never expected to ever hear from him again. How could I have known that he would live forever?"

I had never wanted any more contact with the despicable old man. That's why I had used the Red Sulphur to make enough gold to buy myself a house and the money to start a family. My grandfather was the last of the Dolfins. After he died the Palazzo and family fortune would go to the City of Venice and that would be the end of it. I notice that I keep shaking my head. Memories return through the mist. Their arrival makes my skin crawl; I had never wanted them back. I get up. "I must tell Marianne and Clara," I say, and half-dressed, I run to the Van Os home on the Square. Perplexed, Gerda follows me.

"What is this about a shipwreck?" Marianne asks, when she has read and translated the letter out loud for Clara. Looking down at the floor I respond in monotone: "I wished to make a clean break from my grandfather. I never wanted to have anything to do with him ever again. I hate him. He had insisted we remove Salomon Trismosin's laboratory instruments out of Dolfin Palace after my mother died. He and father were always fighting about that. He didn't want father around after mother's death, but he wanted me there. So he agreed that my father could stay, but not his laboratory. I don't know why he was so adamant about that. The Palazzo was certainly large enough. He was taking pleasure in cursing my father viciously now that he didn't have to hold back any longer since my mother was gone. He sneered about Father's family and called him a charlatan who only wished to live off the Dolfin fat. After Father was gone Grandfather kept up with his jabs about him. When he said in his hateful manner that my father had married my mother just for her money I was so enraged that I slapped him in the face and left for good. After I heard one of his ships had gone down I posted a letter saying goodbye to him and that I was about to board that particular ship. I had it delivered to him through a messenger. When the messenger returned to me he told me my grandfather had carried a big grin on his face."

"So what do we do? We are getting married in five hours. I was just about to get dressed," Clara cries.

"We have to leave for Venice this instant so I can speak to him before he dies. I can tell him things only I could know, even if he doesn't recognize me."

"He'll have you arrested in Venice," Marianne says, crestfallen.

"I'll have to risk it. I can't go through another transmutation of my being. It would kill me, even if I knew how to get back my original body. I can't live a life on the run, not now that we're about to start a family. The old man will persecute me for as long as he lives. He is a master of spite, a nasty monster. I will have to go there and rip out his green lion claws once and for all. If we go the Great Church he would have me arrested during the ceremony. Create a horrible scandal and love every minute of it. That's the kind of scum he is. I have to leave right now."

"I will come with you," says Marianne.

"So will I," echoes Clara.

"You all go; I will take care of things here," Gerda assures us.

ॐ

While the most important dignitaries in the Dutch Republic wait in the Great Church of The Hague, the bride and the groom flee the country.

Book Two

Incarnation

Part Five

Marianne

Chapter Twelve

Venice, November 1667

On red velvet cushions in the small cabin of the gondola, Mundanus, Clara and I sit close together in tense silence, louvered blinds drawn. The two gondolieri on the platform aft serenade us to our destination, the small Palazetto Dolfin next to the grand Dolfin Palace. When we arrived in Venice we heard that Mundanus' grandfather, Giovanni Dolfin, had rented out floors at the grand Palazzo and moved - together with his mistress and her son - to the smaller adjacent Palazetto. Looking out through the blinds I squint at the azure sky, so much brighter than the silver light at home.

I think of the Dutch notables waiting in vain at the Great Church in The Hague for Clara and Mundanus' wedding. I'm struck by the comedy of it all, thinking of everybody who is anybody in the Dutch Republic waiting for naught, getting increasingly annoyed. But I feel terrible for Helvetius; my husband was left to deal with the wrath of the notables after we didn't appear for the ceremony. It must have been his worst nightmare. Then I remind myself that we have left him a bottle of the Universal Medicine large enough to last him a lifetime, and then some. People will forget the embarrassment and remember the Medicine.

Holland feels far away as the sounds of song and water rush in, while our gondolieri stand tall rowing to the competitive sounds of their duet. The wash of our wake splashes along the foundations of the buildings. We are close to our destination on the left. I look back through the small open window at the Rialto Bridge receding behind us: a concert of ochers, pinks and shaded vertical lines play through the arced colonnade remembering centuries ago when Venice had ruled the waters.

Our arrival is gentle along the small jetty. Colorful masts rise up from the canal, protecting the gondola from the stone landing. A man rushes up to greet us. I look at Mundanus and see he is moved. "Jacopo!" he exclaims. Mundanus has told me about his childhood friend Jacopo Gandolfi. The man looks stunned, in complete absence of recognition. Most likely, Jacopo had been the man sent to The Hague to check out Mundanus' identity. "I see you still have the scar on your forehead from when I threw you down the stairs," Mundanus grins.

Jacopo's face turns angry, then pulls taut like the fleece of a drum. "Sir, our courtesy is not on your behalf," he replies formally. "Let me remind you that you would have been arrested were it not for your illustrious travel companions," he adds pointedly. Obviously the Van Os name means something here in this merchant city; this had been the practical reason why I had come along on his mad dash back to Venice. I knew that without me, he would be arrested before he could set foot at the Palazzo Dolfin. Imagining him going across the Bridge of Sighs to a dark prison cell had filled me with dread. But that fate seems to have been averted for the moment.

Mundanus appears to suddenly realize the way he looks and grins sheepishly. Clara, behind him, rustles her magic veil, and gives Signor Gandolfi her most beguiling smile. Gandolfi melts on the spot. He gallantly helps her off the gondola.

"Watch out for the old dog, Signorina, he is blind and mean. I don't know why Signor Dolfin keeps him." He points to an unkempt, dirty-white bulldog asleep at the entrance of the wooden jetty. The ancient dog rises slowly, and comes hobbling towards us. Jacopo only has eyes for Clara, of course. I feel relieved to be anonymous behind the glamour of Clara's magical textiles. I breathe in the air of the Grand Canal, a foul reeking cesspool with a flavor of sea breeze, and stare to the left of the

Palazetto at the Palazzo Dolfin rising up from the water in four-square majesty. This is where Mundanus was raised.

The dog dodders straight to Mundanus, sniffs his pants, yelps hoarsely and licks his hands with devotion. I see tears in the eyes of my beloved.

"Nicco," he whispers, "does everyone here live forever?" As Mundanus goes over to the open Palazetto door previously guarded by blind Nicco, Jacopo jumps ahead of him to end all pretenses that Mundanus has any rights here. Jacopo's eyes invite Clara to enter first – into any future she wishes. It is obvious by his emphatically calling her Signorina that he wishes to underscore she is as yet unmarried, and it reveals his hope that the unmasking of the impostor who pretends to be his friend Giovanni Theodore might allow him a path to her hand. I am amused at Clara's new power over men. Her textiles, woven with a mixture of blanched and purpled threads dyed with an extract of Red Sulphur, work only for her. She had allowed me once to try on one of her garments but they had no effect on men greater than the usual impression I make by being naturally pleasant to behold (as I've been told.) In fact, the textiles irritated my skin. It felt as if they actively disliked touching me. I'm sure they would cause a rash if I were to wear them for extended periods. I've never tried since, and Clara had appeared gratified.

Inside, we ascend a dark staircase to a second floor spacious *portego*, a typical Venetian unheated room where strangers are received. It is filled with trophies and portraits of the Dolfin family. A museum of singular objects on wooden pedestals displays the many aspects of mankind gathered from all over the globe by these distinguished descendants of Marco Polo the legendary traveler. No wall space can be seen anywhere. Maps of all kinds, including astronomies based on the discoveries in the heavens made by Galileo and his scientist followers, cover them. I have never seen such a collection of maps. The room allows us a glimpse into the grand world of sea, earth and heaven. I feel my lungs open as I breathe in a world unknown and inhale its thrilling vastness. My beloved is 'Mundanus' indeed: a cosmopolitan man, having grown up among this immense cartography. I suddenly see him with different eyes now that I have entered into the intellectual womb of his versatile mind.

Among the pedestals is a high-backed, elaborately carved empty chair awaiting its occupant. A sumptuously dressed, beautiful woman enters and nods to each of us individually. She's in her later years, past fifty. "My Lord shall be here momentarily," she greets us in French and smiles with the subtle array of experienced expressions of one who hosts extensively. Her dress is of the finest silk, inviting the hand to caress it. The outer layer of her gown shines with maroon hues that catch the shadows of the room in a surprising grey-green glow. An under dress of orange fire flares low around her legs, making her every turn appear like a dance of the flame. The low cut bodice reveals a youthfully powdered bosom. She looks like a woman who has made her life from looking young. I can't help but smile, thinking of my own self-deprecating comparisons with Clara's radiant youth. I wonder about the rivals of this woman in flaming silk.

"Donna Lucia," Jacopo addresses her in Venetian Italian with an elegant bow, "These are the travelers from Holland."

Donna Lucia nods in acknowledgment.

"I love all your maps here," Clara enthuses in French, "Especially the one of the heavens. Don't you think our friend Christiaan Huygens would be most interested, Aunt Marianne? I can already hear him hold forth." Clara behaves with the excitement of an innocent young girl, a tactic she has been using lately to disarm people. Since she has begun wearing her magic textiles this has become the way she deals with being the focal point of every room she enters. She never was the center of attention before this, always having been a bit of a shy girl. Now, suddenly, men fawn all over her, and women perceive her as a threat.

"While I admire your dress," replies Donna Lucia, a twinkle I her eye. She looks at Clara the way men do, and I see the discomfort in my niece.

"My niece Clara de Chatillon is an accomplished weaver," I interject formally. "My name is Marianne Schweitzer-Van Os," I add stiffly, while making a barely perceptible curtsy.

"And you are?" Signora Lucia asks Mundanus with disarming directness. I can feel how she likes to stir things up and probably is a master of intrigue. "Giovanni Theodore," Mundanus replies softly and bows.

"No, you're not!" Jacopo Gandolfi exclaims. "He is the impostor I have told you about, Signora."

"You are wearing my mother's necklace," Mundanus shoots off in Venetian with open irritation, pointing to the diamante collier around Donna Lucia's neck.

"Why do you insist?" Jacopo Gandolfi. "There is no one here to impress. I have known Giovanni Theodore all my life. We are the same age, for god sake!" The years have not treated Jacopo kindly; he looks of Donna Lucia's generation, though less well preserved.

Mundanus lashes back. "I know you have warts on your feet and that your father died of the black plague of '30 when we were six years old. We grew up together in our Dolfin Palace until I left in '45. Nicco was 2 at the time. I can't believe he is still alive!" Jacopo looks stunned. He looks from Mundanus down to Nicco, the blind dog, who has never ceased licking his first master's hand. "You know she is wearing my mother's necklace. You've always admired it."

I realize that Mundanus is on a tear, ready to offend everyone around. The pent up rage over having had his life brutally interrupted by his Venetian family is boiling over.

"As I said," Clara says with humor, "the maps are simply amazing."

Signora Lucia looks at her with sensuous appreciation. I suddenly realized the dank cold of this *portego* and shiver.

"Is Grandfather going to show up?" Mundanus demands rudely.

"If you are referring to Signor Giovanni Dolfin, then yes, he will be... Ah, there you are..." Signora Lucia concludes.

"Giovanni," says a man who looks in his early seventies, having come in through an invisible door that had masqueraded as the frame of a map. His back is straight and he has the air of robust vitality. I am stunned by his relatively youthful look. Mundanus had prepared me for a man well over a hundred years old.

"Grandfather?" Mundanus mumbles in Venetian, taken aback. "You look younger than last I saw you."

"So do you, Giovanni, so do you," the distinguished looking gentleman replies affably in flawless Latin, obviously using the language of scholars to honor Clara and myself, aware that we are women of unusually high education. Latin is a man's tongue. I can sense that he is powerful and has spies everywhere.

Jacopo Gandolfi is stunned by Signor Dolfin's ready acceptance of the impostor who Jacopo knows for a fact to *not* be his grandson. He looks back and forth between the two as if he is going mad.

"Cara Lucia, let me introduce my grandson, Giovanni Theodore," Signor Giovanni Dolfin continues in French. Signora Lucia shows no surprise and I know she and Giovanni Dolfin are in cahoots.

"But why, if you know that he *is* your grandson, did you threaten to have him arrested in The Hague?" I manage, my French incredulous and furious. Since we are still deciding about the language of our communication, I opt for including Donna Lucia, who seems of no scholarly mind and thus probably ignorant of Latin.

"Because I need him here, Madame Schweitzer. I'm pleased to make your acquaintance." Before I know it he kisses my hand with an elegant gesture. He has the bearing I so love in Mundanus. Actually, he looks like a much-refined version of the

Mundanus I first met. I am struck by the uncanny resemblance and can't help succumbing to his charm.

"I am sorry you no longer look like your mother, Giovanni," says Signor Dolfin as he sits down in the ornate chair. "You were my link to her." His voice is mournful.

Mundanus is enraged. There will be no stopping him this time. "You viper," he exclaims, "you rotten rat." Signor Dolfin bows with a smile of gracious acknowledgment. This infuriates Mundanus even further. "You didn't care a damn for her. You let her pine away for Father. She died of heartbreak. You killed her."

"Ah, here I must disagree with you, my son. I loved your mother."

Mundanus is ready to pounce.

"I heard otherwise," Clara stands up for her fiancé.

"Then you heard wrongly my lovely Signorina. Claudia was the apple of my eye. Giovanni's father must have poisoned his mind against me."

"Don't you dare talk about my father," Mundanus cries out in paroxysms of pain and rage. "You had him killed, you sent him out, away from here so he could die in a shipwreck."

"And that's why you told me you had shipwrecked yourself," Signor Dolfin smiles amiably. "But the ship you said you were on did not go down after all. I heard it the morning your missive arrived. I realized you wanted to get back at me for the death of your father." His charming smile is most beguiling. "I had you followed all over the world."

Mundanus looks at Jacopo with scorn.

"Oh no, not Jacopo! I sent him out just to get you here. For decades I've hired spies who do this as their livelihood. You cost me a small fortune."

"Why did you spy on him?" I ask, confused.

"He is the last Dolfin heir, the last of Marco Polo's line. His official name is not Giovanni Theodore after his father. I adopted him. His name is Giovanni Dolfin VII."

"I don't believe a word you say," Clara opposes him, pale with annoyance.

Signor Dolfin takes a parchment from the inside pocket of his Moorish-looking mantle, azure like the sky outside. He holds it out to Mundanus.

"Do you recognize this signature, Giovanni?" the Grand Signor asks him.

Mundanus squints, reading the letter. He is completely taken aback, even more than he was by the first letter he got in The Hague from his grandfather.

Giovanni Dolfin intones in a formal Latin baritone, "It says that I am to adopt Giovanni who will have his mother's last name after Maximo Theodore will have gone. It is signed by Maximo, Giovanni's father. There never was a shipwreck, Giovanni. Not for you, nor for your father. You father left you under my care. Did you recognize his signature?"

"How do we know that it's not a forgery?" I ask.

"Giovanni knows. Ask him. It is his father's secret signature. He copied it from Master Leonardo. It is written backwards in a smooth hand, impossible to copy. And it has a drawing underneath he never used before."

I study it closely after he passes the parchment to me. I instantly recognize the drawing. It is of a sunrise behind a mountain. A king with a crown looks out over the water where another crowned king is drowning. I remember Aristotle saying about it: 'The corruption of anything is the generation of something else.' It is from the third parable of Maximo's ancestor Salomon Trismosin's *Splendor Solis*. I look over at Mundanus, who has sunk down on a chair, completely deflated. The parchment appears incontestable.

"But why would he do that? Why would he let you adopt his 14 year old son and disappear?" Clara asks, incredulous.

"Because he was deluded into believing that he could find the spirit of your mother across the sea. He believed he could sail to the land of the spirits. He signed the document in exchange for a ship and crew. Your father was mad, Giovanni. I tried to dissuade him. But he was mad with grief. He couldn't let go of Claudia." Now Signor Dolfin looks sad. I sense that he truly loved his daughter, had wished to protect her, and did genuinely believe Maximo Theodore insane. I want to hold Mundanus through these impossible tidings, but can only look at him.

Clara goes over to comfort him, but he moves away just enough to make her stop dead.

"I don't know what game you are playing, Grandfather, but you can't trick me. I know what I've lived through." Mundanus' Venetian voice rises as he finds back his courage. "Anyone could have drawn this picture of *Splendor Solis*. You can call anyone to be witness to your story - I don't care. I despise you, Giovanni Dolfin. And I am not your heir. I have stopped being part of your family long ago."

"As you wish." Giovanni Dolfin puts the parchment back in his pocket, spins around causing his robe to flare out, and indicates that the meeting is over. Then he makes a final turn to Mundanus and concludes in Latin, "You can deny blood, but you can't get away from it. Your mother was my daughter." He formally bows to each of us, and leaves with Donna Lucia in tow.

Mundanus sits down, bending forward, head in hands. Nicco, licking Mundanus' face, is the only one in the room not distraught. Jacopo Gandolfi is dumbstruck as if paralyzed from head to toe. "You know you're not my friend Giovanni Theodore, or Giovanni Dolfin, or whatever his name..." he finally finds his tongue. "You know it and Signor Dolfin knows it. What kind of sick game are you playing? Is it designed to drive me insane?"

"It has nothing to do with you, Signor Gandolfi," Clara says in French, taking pity on him. "You are just an innocent bystander. I can't explain the details to you, I'm afraid. But I assure you that it makes sense, in the way a high stakes game of chess does. But if you don't know the rules of the game it all appears like pointless shuffles. And I'm sorry that I can't explain the game to you. One day we might, but not right now. Please believe me that it does not in any way concern you, Monsieur. You're just a pawn in Signor Dolfin's intrigue." Her voice is mellifluous as she moves her body in a subtle serpentine fashion, causing her magical textiles to entrance him. His jaw drops in unceremonious adulation.

"Stop it, Clara," I whisper, afraid it will just make matters worse for the hapless Signor Gandolfi. He will end up transported into unrequited passion. At the same time I admire Clara's increasing abilities to control and exploit her erotic sorcery. Women are burned at the stake for less. Clara looks at me, wavers, and halts all movement, returning Jacopo Gandolfi to control over his own mind. She is obviously enjoying her power, and releases him reluctantly. I wonder if I would use a newfound sorcery with the same relish as does my young niece. I think I would.

"I have to get out of here." Mundanus gets up suddenly, pushing away loyal, blind Nicco, who couldn't be fooled. He glares at the still somewhat entranced Jacopo, and makes for the stairs down to the jetty. "Come Nicco, come with us." The old bulldog runs after us in a precarious wobble. I'm afraid I'll have to catch him at the bottom of the stairs. I'm puzzled about the enormous age of this dog. I have never seen a dog to live for 23 years. And Giovanni Dolfin looks well over 30 years younger than his actual age! I wonder if part of the deal Maximo made with Giovanni Dolfin had to do with Trismosin's Elixir of Youth. He must have tried it on the dog first. That is the only way I can make sense of these strange realities. Now I'm curious about Donna Lucia's true age.

We have hired the gondolieri for the day, so the gondola is waiting for us at the jetty. Inside, I share my considerations about this distortion of time with the others.

"If that is true he must have run out of the Medicine and had to get me back to make more of it for him to keep him young. I'd rather die." Mundanus is disgusted.

Nicco looks at us, panting. His eyesight seems restored. Trismosin's Medicine may be great magic, but the greatest mystery is love and devotion.

"Let's assume for a moment that Aunt Marianne is right," says Clara. "Then we have great bargaining power. What shall we ask for in return?"

"There will be no bargain," Mundanus insists, sullen.

"He can have you arrested. Everyone in Venice will attest that you are an impostor," I remark drily with deceptive calm, avoiding my vision of the Bridge of Sighs and Mundanus' dark prison.

"I'd rather go to jail than rejuvenate a man who should have been long dead in the first place," Mundanus maintains stubbornly.

"If you get yourself arrested, Giovanni, I'm going back to The Hague!" Clara moves her shoulder a fraction so her bodice subtly ripples; enough to convince Mundanus that he can't live without his fiancée. I'm getting cross with her.

"Stop that, Clara. Stop using your sorcery. It is not becoming," I say sternly. Clara, caught red-handed, looks guilty at first. Suddenly she laughs, "But it is so much fun!"

"Have I been enchanted again?" Mundanus asks sheepishly, with the supreme intelligence of men. We all laugh too brightly in order to dispel the shadows cast by the previous hour. Nicco attempts a hoarse bark.

ॐ

We take up residence at an inn next to the Rialto Bridge on the Grand Canal, three blocks over from Dolfin palace. The three suites are well appointed. I had to draw heavily upon my credit at the local banks by way of the Venetian offices of the Dutch East Indies Company. One of the few items I was able to pack before our hasty departure from The Hague had been incontestable letters of credit for Clara and myself.

Among the directors of the Company here in Venice my father had been a legend, and they are very pleased to have his daughter and granddaughter in their city. It took some effort to avoid a banquet in our honor; Venetians love celebrations. They did insist on providing us with excellent guides, and found us the best quarters in town. A week goes by.

We have gathered in the living quarters of my suite. Nicco reclines on a special cushion as our guest of honor. We have washed him for the first time in two decades, and his fur is actually a pure shiny white. Groomed, he looks much younger. Mundanus relives parts of his childhood as he and the dog walk together along the canals. The windows are open and we have full view of the Grand Canal teeming with *batellas, caorline* and galleys, odd ships I have never seen in Holland. The sounds of splashes and voices, songs and bird cries enter the room on a breeze of warm salt air and the rank odors of putrid debris. Clara stands by the window in a dress of minimal magic, just enough to make her feel confident. I have asked her to lay off the sorcery for a bit and she has consented. It has given me the opportunity to connect with Mundanus again.

"Are you going to accept his invitation?" I ask him. "He has now sent it three times. I'm afraid it will not come again." He lies on the floor next to Nicco, supporting his head with his interlaced hands. His long strawberry hair is strewn haphazardly around his head on the red Persian rug. Sometimes I have a hard time getting used to his informal behavior, the result of many years of travel.

His jaw is set. I know his answer.

"Don't you care to know what he wants to propose?" Clara asks, looking out over the water so that her voice barely carries behind her.

"We can send Nicco," Mundanus suggests, in a failed attempt at levity.

"I'm going," I say, "Whether you're coming or not. I want to know why he made us come and ruined the wedding when he knew perfectly well who you were. I want to know why he had you spied on for twenty years. That's the reason I came here, to find out what is going on and end his persecution of you." My Dutch sounds terse and pointed, a bit guttural, in the company of more fluid Southern tongues.

Clara turns in support of my words. "I'll join you, Aunt Marianne. I'm sure old Nicco will be perfect company for my foolish fiancé. 'The wise man does at once what the fool does finally'," she quotes the dog's namesake Niccolo Machiavelli. "You'll end up wanting to go because, deep down, you're just as curious as we are."

Mundanus pushes himself up and places his elbows behind his back. He looks very young and vulnerable, a boy almost. I realize how hard it must be to overcome the intense loathing he feels towards Giovanni Dolfin, exacerbated by the doubt the old man has sown about his father.

"Are you afraid to find out that what he told you about your father might be true?" Clara asks with the cruel directness of youth. I hold my breath; only etiquette had restrained me from asking the same.

Mundanus looks at us with a flash of fear in his eyes. We can see Clara's question hit home.

"Don't you think it romantic that a man charters a ship to sail off the edge of the earth to find the spirit of his beloved like Orpheus looking for Eurydice? I find it very alluring," Clara babbles on with childish delight, oblivious to Mundanus' pain.

"Clara!" I hiss.

"Aunt Marianne, with due respect," Clara retorts, giving free rein to her underlying anger, "I know that you find it cowardly too that he is avoiding the truth. If this were an alchemical quest he would long have addressed the heavy lead-poison of old Saturn and tried to transmute it to a nobler metal. That's what he teaches. Why can he only do that in the laboratory, why not in life?" Clara refers to Mundanus' leaden mood as having been caused by Saturn, the stone-cold planet of melancholy and old age that has suddenly appeared in his life in the shape of his grandfather. I have no answer to this, so I remain silent, looking anxiously at Mundanus, who is struggling with his self-respect.

He sits up, straightens his back and seems to throw off his indolence. The bulldog beside him is startled and gets up too.

"You're right, Clara," Mundanus admits, "I am terrified that the image I have of my father is hollow and that he sold me for a ship."

"Maybe he thought you were worthier than he to carry out Trismosin's mission," I try gently, love in my voice. "Maybe he sensed you would make great discoveries like the Panacea and be a blessing to the world."

"I don't believe my Grandfather's words. Not for a moment," he insists with emphasis, but doubt creeps into his voice.

"Then go to him and challenge him, find out the truth for yourself," I reply.

"You owe it to us," Clara points out. "We trusted you and came all this way to stop the persecution and create a safe place for our future family."

Mundanus takes Giovanni Dolfin's invitation and stares at it. Then he sits down at the gilded table and writes his acceptance.

"Why does he always win?" he wonders out loud.

"*You* won – just now," Clara replies and walks over to embrace him.

I avert my face in order not to see their intimacy. My heart weeps.

Chapter Thirteen

This time Signor Giovanni Dolfin himself is at the jetty when our gondola arrives. Donna Lucia stands behind him. It is a mild twilight evening in the aftermath of summer. Behind her, a young man stares at us with bewildered curiosity. Signor Dolfin, dressed in a stylish black toga surrounding his body with flowing silk folds, holds out both arms in a gregarious gesture of welcome. He wants to project an air of benevolence – something that puts us all on notice. I hear Mundanus utter a curse under his breath.

Clara is all magic fabric. She had insisted to be clad in her full power tonight in case she should need it. She has become increasingly matter of fact about her irresistible mastery over men and, when not caught in youthful flirtation, uses it judiciously. She tested it on Mundanus upon entering the gondola and he had almost ended up in the Grand Canal. She giggled mercilessly and for the first time I noticed a flare of resistance in him, an anger attesting to his fiber. I had felt an urge to kiss him right then, but Clara showed immediate remorse and made my desire take cover.

"I am so glad you accepted my invitation, Giovanni," his grandfather intones in flawless Latin. Mundanus appears relieved to speak the old tongue of scholars, which allows for a bit of distance. Donna Lucia smiles with a show of white teeth and carefully measured allure. "May I introduce my son Venier," she says in formal courtier French, confirming my suspicion that she has had no scholarly education but spent time at a court somewhere in Europe, probably as a courtesan. Scholars converse in Latin; courts gossip in French. I am a bit shocked by my disdain for her. I conjure up my father in order to partake in his universal tolerance. Disdain makes one underestimate opponents, and I am convinced she is a formidable one.

Venier is hiding behind his mother's lavish green dress, decidedly uncomfortable in a richly embroidered rust velvet coat. He is painfully shy and only present because of his mother's strict orders. In his late twenties, he looks considerably younger, eclipsed by the domination of his mother's irrefutable power.

"Pleased ... to ... m...m...make ... your acquai ... acquaintance," he stutters in French.

When Clara smiles at him, waving her sleeve like the wing of an angel as she stretches out her right hand to be kissed, he turns a bright red and displays an unmistakable instinct to flee.

"Venier is sometimes a bit shy," his mother tells us with a smile of apology, charming our attention away from her son, embarrassing him even further.

"Venier, please tell the servants the guests have arrived," says Signor Dolfin, graciously dismissing him from what must be torture. Venier rushes off with surprising speed. I feel sorry for him.

We enter the Palazetto through another door than we had before when we were formally received in the cold *portego* in order to make us feel like strangers on business. An elegant staircase leads directly up to the third floor where the grand room is situated. It is bright and warm. Three narrow but high gothic windows frame the Canal Grande at dusk. The monochrome blue wallpaper displays subtle patterns of various textures dancing to the light of many candles. Venier is pressed in the right hand corner next to the window, shivering slightly. Signor Dolfin and Donna Lucia give us unspoken hints that we shouldn't pay attention to him and invite us to sit in sumptuous red velvet armchairs with gorgeously carved dark wooden cupids on the armrests and legs, like a throne of Venus. I realize that the goddess of beauty and love is held in high esteem in this household.

Mundanus looks almost as uncomfortable as does Venier. He fidgets in a manner most unbecoming. I feel I need to help him through the initial pleasantries, so I comment on the beauty of the chairs.

"I had them made in Florence decades ago," Signor Dolfin explains. "I'm sure Giovanni recognizes them. They were a gift to his mother and stood in her rooms at the Palazzo."

"What made you move from the Palazzo?" I ask, wondering if financial reasons had played a role.

"After the death of my daughter it felt increasingly cold to me, as if it had become a palace of ghosts, a kind of underworld. I had this little Palazetto built so I wouldn't have to walk around in painful memories."

I can see that his response annoys Mundanus, so I quickly add: "Do you ever miss it?"

"Not really. This feels like my home now." He turns to Donna Lucia and smiles; she lovingly returns his gaze. She masters the art of seduction, I must admit. I'm certain Signor Dolfin has not noticed the furtive looks she has cast at Clara. Never having received such seductive attention from a woman before, Clara doesn't know how to handle it and sits quite frozen in order not to rustle her magic textiles. The atmosphere in the room is growing increasingly electric, like the crackling sparkles produced from amber by friction. From the corner of my eye I notice Venier moving slowly towards the door, ready to make a run for it. I can't help but laugh. Everyone looks at me with surprise.

"It is all the things we are not talking about," I try to explain. "It feels comical to me. I can't help it," and laugh again. I have managed to embarrass everyone and try to master my face, but can't.

"What are we not talking about?" Signor Dolfin asks as though he truly doesn't know. This is too much for me and I burst out in uncontrollable giggles. My entire Regent upbringing is chiding me but I can't help myself: Mundanus wanting to kill his grandfather, Donna Lucia desiring to embrace Clara, Clara terrified of her own magic, Venier aching to vanish, Signor Dolfin wishing to stay pleasant, it all gathers together in one big howl.

"Why did you force me to come here?" Mundanus comes to my aid. His voice is forceful and he has re-found his composure. Clara seems released from the fear of her own sorcery.

"You ruined my wedding!" she accuses our host.

I hear the door close. Venier has disappeared. Donna Lucia gets up to go after him.

While Signor Dolfin seems to have been prepared for a confrontation with his grandson, he is obviously unprepared by the hot attack from his grandson's fiancée. He looks at the door, wishing for Donna Lucia to return. But the door remains closed.

I add my insistence. "You had best explain it to us, Signor."

"Let's wait for Donna Lucia to return," he replies, uncomfortable.

"Since when do you need a woman to speak for you? Has your rejuvenation deprived you of manhood?" Mundanus hisses scornfully. "Did you have me return because you can no longer perform as a lover to your beautiful Mistress? Do you need the Medicine for that, old man?" Mundanus vulgarity takes me aback. I can never get used to men's ferocious attacks on each other's sexual frailties.

Signor Dolfin gets up with dignity. "Maybe this was a mistake, to try and do it in a civil manner. It might be better to let you know by letter so I don't have to suffer your insults."

"Sit down!" Mundanus continues his insolence. "You may have rejuvenated but I am still stronger than you. Sit down, and don't you dare call out for help. It would be your end." Mundanus opens his waistcoat revealing a long dagger, which he uses as a knife in the laboratory and carries on his belt as a weapon when he travels.

"Mundanus!" I exclaim. "Stop it right now. You can't treat your Elder in this manner. Have you no shame?" I am truly angry with him. No manner of insult calls for this kind of behavior among civilized people. I can feel the full force of my father within me as I rise from my seat in a clear threat to the man I love.

"Let's all sit down," Clara suggests in the most charming of ways, making ample use of her beguiling fabrics. Her sorcery calms down the men and we all take our seats. "And, please Signor Dolfin, please tell us how you recognized Giovanni. He looks completely different than he did when you knew him. We have to start somewhere, so this might be as good a place as any."

Signor Dolfin looks at her with admiration and turns to his grandson with a peace offering: "I fully agree with your choice, Son. She will be the perfect matriarch for the next generations of Dolfins."

Mundanus grunts: "Spare me the sweet stuff. Answer her directly."

"My spies told me that a ghostly white man had left from your home in Leyden who had never entered. It was not hard to guess," he remarks coldly.

"But how did you know transformations like that could happen?" Clara insists.

Signor Dolfin speaks slowly and with dignity. "Because Maximo initiated me into his Red Sulphur mission."

"You're lying," Mundanus yells at him. "Father would never do a thing like that!"

"You seem to know little about your father, or about me, for that matter." Signor Dolfin has fully recovered his calm.

"Why would Maximo Theodore have done such a thing?" I inquire.

"Because he needed to travel to find out if anywhere in this world there were Magi who still knew how to make the Stone, or if the Art had died everywhere at the same time. When I told you some days ago that he went on a search for the spirit of your mother, it was only half of it. Something you did not know, maybe, Giovanni, but your father and I were friends long before

I invited him to the Palazzo where he met Claudia. I was an adept like him."

"You're lying!" Mundanus counters furiously. "You were always berating him. You hated him."

"By now you should know that the Stone has mysterious ways. I was to behave like a man disgusted with alchemy, publicly hating your father, especially in front of the servants, so no one would ever expect that the Stone was kept in my home. You can't keep the Stone a secret for 150 years, however ingenious you are. Rumors abounded all over Venice that Trismosin had left the Stone in this city. I am not the only one employing spies for my business. Several of my servants had been for hire. Maximo had enemies eager to steal the last of the fabled Red Sulphur."

"I don't believe you," Mundanus insists.

"You remember the room without windows with the compartment in the wall where the Stone was kept. How would I know about it if I hadn't myself ordered it built there? According to you, your father would never have told me."

Mundanus appears dumbstruck.

"So if you have the Stone yourself, why have your grandson return to Venice and ruin his life, and mine?" Clara insists.

"My grandson took the Stone with him when he fled Venice. And I was told that he had created the Universal Medicine during the Pestilence. I need the Medicine. For Venier," he concludes.

"You could just have asked," I remark drily. "It would have saved us a lot of trouble."

"Giovanni would never have responded to any message I sent. You know how he despises me."

"But you had the elixir," I state. "You tried it first on Nicco, then on yourself."

He nods. "Maximo had given me Trismosin's rejuvenation potion before he left so I would live as long as possible to look after the Stone. I took the tincture after Giovanni left. I wanted to extend my life to watch over him. And then I met Donna Lucia and began a new life."

But this body doesn't have the strength it appears to have. I am 102 years of age. Before I die I want to see Venier cured. It is the only thing that will make Donna Lucia happy. I would do anything for her."

"Even ruin the lives of others!" Clara retorts.

"You'll recover. You're about to inherit one of the largest fortunes in Venice. You can get married right here, in the Dolfin Chapel at the Palazzo. It could be a celebration more grand than anything Holland might have given you. We Venetians know feasts," he adds proudly.

"All lies, nothing but lies," Mundanus mutters.

My practical streak surfaces. "What illness does Venier have?" I ask.

"He hides in the cellar all day and is terrified of people. His mind is lost in Hell and the devils won't release him. Were he not constantly guarded he would take his own life at any moment. If the Panacea is truly a universal medicine, it might cure him." Deep concern is palpable in Signor Dolfin's demeanor.

I nod and begin to believe his words.

"Why did you spy on Giovanni?" Clara asks without anger, seemingly having the same change of heart.

"Because he is my only heir and because I promised his father I would remain guardian of the Stone in Maximo's absence. He left at the height of the attempts in Venice to locate the Stone and turn it into gold. Venice is in decline, you know this. We need gold just as much as does Johan de Witt or the Duke of York. Even the *Doge* was in on it," he concludes, referring to the Venetian head of state.

"Is Maximo Theodore still alive?" I ask, no longer holding anything to be impossible.

"I don't know. I haven't received word since he left 28 years ago."

The door opens and Donna Lucia comes in with a crying Venier in tow. He looks terrified, like a wild beast caged, uttering brief exclamations in various languages I don't recognize, if they are languages at all.

"He doesn't need to be here, Cara Lucia," Signor Dolfin says gently.

"They need to know what they came for." Donna Lucia's voice is made of pointed icicles. "This is why your grandfather made you come, Giovanni. He can't see Venier suffer any longer. His life is forfeit; he's been convicted to Hell with tortures you can't imagine. They call you Mundanus and say you are a famous doctor who can heal anyone," she turns directly to Mundanus and casts down her eyes in a genuine act of submission. "Do it for my son, *please* heal him." Now her voice is soft and pleading, the heart of a mother torn apart by the unbearable suffering of her child.

Suddenly the ring of truth has become deafening. Not even Mundanus can avoid it as he looks into Venier's petrified eyes, windows into the Devil's torture chambers. As their gazes meet, Venier expels a most horrible shriek of impossible pitch; no human can make this sound.

"He is possessed," Mundanus says quietly. "You need a priest, not a doctor."

"We've been to every exorcist," Signor Dolfin sighs. "Even the Pope blessed him in person. They say it is an illness of the heart. I had a great Moorish physician come in from Spain. He told me that only the great Panacea could help and that he didn't know where to get it. But I knew, I knew..." His voice trails off. "I've seen the Great Pestilence here in Venice, it killed one third of our people 35 years ago. I know what horrors it brings. And Giovanni, I was so enormously proud of you when I heard what you were doing in Holland and England. It filled my life with meaning." He has tears in his eyes.

"You could try," Clara proposes to Mundanus. When we made the Medicine for Helvetius we kept half of it for ourselves, for use during the next great plague. We have it with us; Mundanus carries it in a bottle next to one of the Red Sulphur Stones in his ivory box. The other two Stones are safely kept in their hiding place behind the fireplace in my Hague laboratory.

"My spies in The Hague tell me that Doctor Helvetius is performing miracle cures, so you must have given him the Medicine. Did you keep some for yourself?" Signor Dolfin asks hopeful.

"What else do they say about my husband," I ask, my heart breathing out with relief. "How is he?"

"Yes, of course, I forgot." Signor Dolfin regains his social skills. "I do apologize for not telling you. Your husband is the hero of The Hague, the most sought after physician in the Low Lands. As a consequence both Johan de Witt and Dowager Princess Amalia have spread their search for Mundanus all over Europe. My letter discrediting you made them look for a link between yourself and this Mundanus. Some alchemist in London told them about the possibility of a rejuvenation formula that could be created from Red Sulphur. You will be safest right here. I will give a grand ball at the Palazzo in your honor hailing your return. No suspicion will remain."

"But what about Jacopo Gandolfi and all the others who knew Giovanni's former self? They will only spread the rumors even further," I counter.

"Money can buy silence," Signor Dolfin responds with confidence, clearly having experience in these matters. "And what money can't buy, extortion will. I know things about everyone that they don't want to air in public." For the first time I become aware of the power this man wields. He is a state onto himself, a great political force.

"And if suspicion remains, they will have to get by me first. No one ever has. That's why Maximo chose me as the guardian of the Stone." A fierce pride stretches his spine. "Here the Stone is safer than anywhere," he concludes with conviction.

Mundanus keeps looking at Venier, who has found protection behind his mother.

"Clara," he asks in Dutch. "Look at his face and tell me which color is missing in his complexion. What color thread would you use to create a healthy tone?" I am reminded that it was Clara who realized the missing dye when Mundanus had been an albino; it saved his life. Clara immediately knows what he means and she looks at Venier's face with the dreamy eyes of an artist. "A very light hue of green, much diluted, like the faint green of lichen you find on trees." she concludes.

"Green copper," Mundanus responds in Venetian. "The Medicine should be mixed with a greatly diluted tincture of green copper."

"Does that mean you will do it?" Donna Lucia asks, attempting to restrain overwhelming hope.

Mundanus turns to her and to his grandfather, bows in a barely perceptible manner and walks out the door.

"I think he will," I tell her, while rushing after Mundanus. As I speed out the door I see Clara go up to Venier and wave her arm in front of his eyes. The fabric sails through the air like a Chinese fan.

෯

In the morning Clara wants to stay in her rooms, where she has set up a beautiful loom to weave the dyed silk threads she's bought at the Silk Road terminals. She is creating paintings in thread, the way her mother had done with embroidery. Clara is weaving silk *acquarella* – as they call them in these parts – of the shimmering she sees out her window overlooking the Grand Canal. Though she is still very much at the beginning of her work, the fabric already reveals the live flow of water. Since she has begun weaving the glow cloth with its barely visible gossamer thread, her skills at the loom have become of unparalleled mastery. Even her old teacher Elspeth had said so, shaking her head with astonishment. I am very proud of my niece, feeling it not just as my own pride but also as that of my sister Johanna whose maternal spirit has become stronger in me since Clara's recovery from her near fatal illness. It is as though she is protecting her daughter through me, which causes conflict since often my wishes are at odds with what is best for Clara, especially where Mundanus is concerned. The Mother battles the Lover with various outcomes at different times.

I join Mundanus on a nostalgic walk with Nicco. He takes a route of narrow walkways along the many canals. We go under portico galleries with their gothic arches, and I love the yellows and pinks of the houses. Moorish influences on some of the shapes around us make me ask Mundanus about his travels.

"They have an exquisite sense of beauty," he tells me about the Moors. "Some of these people live in tents, but when you enter, there always are beautiful objects – carpets, a cup. One lifetime is not enough to see all there is to see. You could travel forever and still have only seen the smallest fraction of everything. I love how immense the world is. I love how it scintillates and shines and calls you to the next horizon. You'd have to live forever to see it all. " Mundanus' light grey eyes sparkle as they haven't since our flight from Holland. I could kiss him right now – so I walk a bit further away from him, aching with intimate longing. A boat filled with spices goes by making the air fragrant and foreign. I have never been to a place where the vaguely familiar meets the utterly alien. I can feel Mundanus' horizons calling me. I need lifetimes! ... This brings me to the question I have been contemplating for the last few days.

"I've something on my mind I need to talk with you about," I begin, trying to order my thoughts which have started to take shape since my conjectures around 23 year old Nicco. My reflections got more pronounced when his grandfather, looking no older than 70, told us he was 102.

Mundanus turns to me, love in his eyes.

"One day soon I shall be old and you will be youthful. Then after that I will be ancient and you still vigorous. How can you love me, then?" I ask, hearing the hated quiver of anxiety in my own voice. I had so wanted to speak to him in a matter of fact tone!

"I've thought of that too. I could give you the Medicine and you could stay young."

"Of course that has come to my mind, but I feel certain that I don't want to do that. For you it just happened, you had no choice. Your grandfather took it to guard the Stone but I ..."

"Don't believe him. Don't!" Mundanus exclaims. "I don't believe a word he says."

"I know, I know," I interrupt him. "But this is about me. I would like to talk about something that is just important to *me*. We can talk about your troubles again later on. Now I want to understand this twisting of time, and my place in it. I need to get a grip on it. It flows like water through my fingers every time I try to think of it. I just need you to listen to me." The force of my words gets through to him.

"I'm sorry to be so preoccupied. I'm so confused. I just can't believe my grandfather, I can't."

"I know my dear man. I'm well aware. But please open a space in your heart to help me sort out what is preoccupying *me*. I need a friend. I need you as my friend, Mundanus. Please listen." I can't stand the anxiously pleading tone in my voice; so I stop talking. We walk on and then wait for Nicco, who has found a place to leave a gift to the Commune of Venice.

"I'm sorry I took you on this mad journey," he remarks after some time.

"I don't need you to be sorry. There is nothing to be sorry about. I came along because I wanted to be close to you. I just need you to listen. It is precisely this wanting to be close to you for the rest of my life that makes me worry about a future in which you remain young while I age."

"Then why not use our alchemy. You certainly have gained a right to it."

"I know. But I need to live my life in a natural way. I want you to love me naturally, not in the way you love Clara, through sorcery." I notice the angry jab in the direction of my niece and instantly feel remorse. I pause for a moment to let my jealousies subside. Once I viscerally feel my relationship with Mundanus again, I continue. "Our love feels like a great gift of nature to me and mixing it any further with Red Sulphur will make it manufactured, conjured up by the Art. My heart couldn't bear that, and I am ready to suffer my natural state while surrounded by magic; but I don't know how to do it."

"Our love has not changed any since I was completely transformed by Red Sulphur," he argues. "I still feel I can't breathe without you. It is not like with Clara who makes me feel possessed with adoration. With you I feel our souls entwine."

"I know, my darling. I feel the same. But I also feel that one of us has to remain natural for our souls not to be overtaken by the spirit of Red Sulphur. If I take the Medicine I think that in the beginning our love would burn even brighter than it does now. But in the end we wouldn't know how it might have been in its natural condition, outside of the laboratory. I can't bear that thought. So to answer your question: no, I am not able to take the Medicine. That's what gives rise to my fears. I am like a mayfly among owls, being reminded at every moment of the brevity of my lifespan. Our lives run at a different pace. In 60 years you'll look like your grandfather – or even younger since you took the Medicine earlier in life – and if I'm not dead I will certainly *look* like a corpse. How can love survive that? The thought terrifies me, Mundanus. It does." I await his response like the accused a verdict.

"Your eyes will always be you," Mundanus looks deeply into me. "I will recognize you throughout the pillage of time." His words are swollen with sentimental effusion. "Your essence will never disappear. I will always be able to find you. When I see you, I see love."

His sentimental predictions don't convince me at all and I am angry with my body, which, like his, at this moment is mad with desire. Before bed, men will promise anything, a cynical voice tells me.

"You don't believe me," he responds when he notices my hesitation. "You think I'm just saying it because I want to embrace you this very moment. And I do. More than I can say."

"Maybe the question has no answer," I place my index finger on his lips to interrupt him before he tells me things that are impossible to know. "Maybe what will happen tomorrow is shrouded in fog and I just have to love you right now."

And in one fleeting moment that will forever be mine we kiss in a cloud of passion and sorrow while standing along the canal.

ॐ

Just before we arrive back at the Inn, Nicco lies down and won't move anymore. He is thoroughly exhausted and Mundanus has to carry him the rest of the way. We have walked for over two hours. When I knock on the door of Clara's suite there is no answer. Mundanus carries Nicco up to his own rooms and I go take a nap in mine.

When I try Clara's door again a few hours later, there still is no response. I enter the room to see if she is sound asleep but she is nowhere to be found. The anteroom with the loom looks as if she has left in a hurry, a bit more disorderly than is Clara's custom. I rush down the stairs to Mundanus' quarters where I find him reading Trismosin's diaries. He sits in an ornate Venetian chair with his bare feet on the table in the window overlooking the water. Nicco notices me first and hobbles over to me. Mundanus looks up, and in a quick reflex removes his feet from the table.

"I'm looking for the transmutation of green copper," he explains by way of apology for his boorish demeanor.

"Clara's gone. She hasn't been back. I'm worried," I burst out.

"Maybe she went for a walk in the City. Maybe she's gone back to buy more silk. It is broad daylight so it is unlikely that harm will befall her. She knows where not to go, where the dangerous places are." I'm aware of a note of alarm in his tone. We both feel guilty towards Clara for our hours of intimacy and imagine her knowing about it, though there is no way she could have unless she had followed us.

"We might ask the innkeeper if he saw her leave," he suggests.

"It is now early afternoon. If she is not back well before dusk I'll be seriously worried." I hear Johanna's maternal voice rise up.

"I'll go down and ask around," Mundanus says soothingly, putting the leather folio on the table. He leaves, followed by Nicco.

I stand by the window and in a distracted manner look at the oared boats of various bright colors racing some kind of regatta on the Grand Canal. I notice the six standing oarsmen straining with intense concentration on their perspiring faces, throwing their full weight behind each stroke. Unaware, my body begins to imitate their movements and I feel the thrill of competition. Along the Canal, masses are gathered to cheer them on. Maybe Clara is among them; maybe she has gone out to watch. But I discard that idea. When Mundanus and I returned this morning the regatta had not yet begun.

Mundanus laughs seeing me move with the motions of the regatta, as the red boat is pulling away from the others. I had been fully absorbed in the motions of the boats and the fierce competition, and hadn't seen him enter.

"You like our *caorline* regatta, don't you. You're looking at it with your whole body, like a true Venetian. Those boats are called '*caorline*'." I turn to him, having suddenly lost all interest in the race.

"What about Clara?"

"She left right after we did. She took a gondola towards Dolfin Palace."

"Do you think she went to visit your grandfather?" I wonder out loud.

"I have sent a messenger to the Palazetto. He'll be back within the hour."

Closing the window to shut out the races in the world outside, I point to the open leather bound diaries on the table.

There is nothing to do but wait for word from the messenger so I ask, "Did you find anything?"

"Well, you know there is green copper everywhere. It is often used as the primal material to start the work."

"The sickness of Venus," I concur, referring to copper as the metal of Venus and the green growing on it like a thin film of moss as a kind of parasite eating her flesh. Mundanus nods.

"But it is always to be transmuted into a more refined state, at which point it loses its green nature and turns black." I understand him to refer to the black slugs remaining at the bottom of the vessel when the green poison of copper transmutes. In our art we refine remedies from poison.

"But I've yet to find a place where copper-green keeps its color throughout; how to extract the coloring agent from it, the green tincture we need."

"So this means you're going to help Venier?"

"I have not yet decided. For the time being it is just a theoretical problem." I don't want to push him, but I hope he will help poor Venier. Then, in a flash, I know where Clara is. I recall the move she made with her sleeve, and how Venier had been transfixed. She is trying to cure Venier with her love magic. I feel a horrible sense of foreboding.

Part Six

Clara

Chapter Fourteen

After Aunt Marianne and Mundanus left this morning, I was all
set to continue my weaving when there was a knock on my
door. I was surprised and a bit cross that I had to interrupt my
work. The idea of capturing the movement of water in woven
silk had captivated me since we arrived here, and I could feel
how it was flowing right through me onto the loom. I had become a very clear channel for weaving since my work with the
glow cloth. So I got up only after the second knock.

I recognized the man as one of the servants of Giovanni
Dolfin.

"Signorina," he bowed deeply. "A missive from La Donna
Lucia." I could barely decipher his Venetian tongue. "From La
Donna Lucia," he repeated in Italian and bowed again.

"For me? Per me?" I tried in my best Italian. "Are you certain? Certo?"

He nodded, with a blissful smile on his face. I looked down
and noticed I was wearing a magic bodice and tried to hide it
with my arms, as if I were naked. That made my skin-colored
sleeves flutter and I saw tears forming in his eyes. I quickly rid
myself of the hapless man by taking the letter and closing the
door on his puppy eyes.

'Ma Chère Demoiselle,' (the letter was written in French
since she must have realized that I spoke no Venetian or
Italian.)

'Your visit last night had remarkable effects on my
son Venier. He has been asking for you all night long,

wishing for your presence more than he has ever desired anyone's, even mine. He became quite despondent when he was told that you would not come back right away. I am very sorry to impose upon you with this letter and it was only the gentle but firm support of your fiancé's grandfather that made me dare write to you. I have never witnessed a change in my son of this kind. Of course I can't ask you to visit him; I must leave that to your kindness. But of all the many doctors and priests, no one has ever had this effect. It looked like he had been released from Hell, if only just for a moment. Yet, to see my son with me in the world we all inhabit instead of in the clutches of the Devil was a moment in my life for which I will forever be in your debt.

A grateful mother
Lucia Solario'

I was speechless. For the first time I conceived of my new-found abilities as healing. Until now I had been playing with them as a delicious game of power over men. I remembered toying with Christiaan Huygens, one of the great minds of the age, and the guilty pleasure it had brought me. Sometimes, when Mundanus would become too interested in Aunt Marianne, I would use my magic for a brief yank to make him acutely aware of me. Last time it almost landed him in Grand Canal. But to think of the cloth as an agent of medicine, the cloth itself being the Medicine, this was an overwhelming new fact in my life.

Without further thought I found myself dressing in the clothes made of the highest thread count of *purpur,* a dozen times as many sensuous flesh threads made of *purpur* than any other cloth I had woven. They alternated with the white glow cloth wool in which the true imagination became visible as in a crystal ball. Combined, a man would see the woman of his dreams reflected in my body. It gave me the sheer power of Venus herself. Mundanus had helped me understand this and told me that such forces are to be used sparingly. He added that

I could use them on him as often as I pleased and more. He had laughed and asked me to wear this particular dress after which he couldn't keep his hands off me and I had almost nothing left to give him as my virgin-present on our wedding night. But we had stopped short before consummating the source of our mutual longing.

I had a strong sense I should leave before my fiancé returned, because I didn't think my going to the Palazetto would meet with his approval, or Aunt Marianne's. But dressed in my ultimate textiles, I felt certain I could handle whatever God put in my path. The innkeeper had told me of the regatta on the Grand Canal that was to start at noon, after which time no gondola would get through to the Palazzo Dolfin. If I wanted to leave I had to do so now. So I ran back up, took my bag in which I carry money and the little bible mother gave to me on her deathbed, kissed it and ran out to the gondola the innkeeper called over for me.

It feels odd to be in a gondola by myself. Everywhere I see activities preparing for the *caorline* regatta about to be raced here on the Canal Grande. An armada of small ships is positioning itself to get a good view of the festivities. Venice truly *is* the world capital of celebration.

I am beset with doubts. I have never wielded my alchemical powers entirely by myself. I hear the voice of Aunt Marianne tell me that it is a great responsibility to have the power of sorcery, as she calls it. She had warned me that the Stone is alive and has a mind of its own: it can overwhelm the bearer. She told me how Red Sulphur, once activated, delights in its own creative force and like a bull crazed with lust wishes to copulate with everything it encounters, impregnating the surrounding world with its heated desire. That's why Mundanus carries the Stone with him in its inactive form. "But with you," Aunt Marianne had concluded, "in your fabric Red Sulphur relishes its complete activation constantly. Be careful." But the confidence my dress provides and the love it has for me returns and I sense a flush on my cheeks. Feeling warm, I open my overcoat, inadvertently showing a glimpse of the textile. One look from the *gondoliere* and he starts singing at the top of his lungs.

In order to modulate the power of my dress I am covering it with a neutral coat of ordinary fabric. I am glad I have done so because it is Signor Dolfin himself who comes out to greet me after my presence had been announced. He looks overjoyed to see me. I notice the same look as in Grandfather Van Os' eyes when he would dance me around the room, losing all of his customary formality. Any shred of doubt about the genuine nature of Grandfather Dolfin's version of history vanishes at this very moment. I will make it a point to convey this to my fiancé.

"Signorina," he addresses me in his mellifluous Latin baritone, "I can't tell you how pleased I am that you have responded to Donna Lucia's plea. The change in Venier is simply astounding. This morning I heard him sing! You have the power to banish his devils. You are a tool of heaven. All that I command is at your disposal. Just let me know what you need."

I'm taken aback by his gushing effusiveness and his flattering presentation of my effect on Venier. Flattery puts my native Dutch sobriety on guard. Then I remember that Mundanus is prone to the same lyrical outbursts and I relax.

"All I need for now is to meet with him," I respond in my guttural Dutch-accented Latin. "But of course!" he replies, and leads me to a second story room next to the *portego* where his study looks out over the water. He leaves me to get Venier, which gives me some time to look around. The walls are lined with books, some of which I have seen before in Grandfather's and Aunt Marianne's libraries. I see books about stars and the movement of the heavens, and of travels through lands I have never heard of. I recognize a whole bookcase full of tomes written by and about Marco Polo, his illustrious ancestor, who was instrumental in opening the Silk Road. As a child I had been told about the travels of Marco Polo, who in our merchant family was regarded with great respect. I am proud to become the wife of a direct descendant of his.

In front of the large wooden table strewn with parchments and writing tools a circular map takes my breath away. It shows the whole world in astounding detail. I remember standing in Princess Amalia's dining room and looking at a globe made by Jodocus Hondius, admiring it together with Christiaan Huygens, but somehow this map truly moves me. I stare at it and feel journeys rise up in my soul.

"It will take a while before Master Venier will be here," says Signor Dolfin who has reentered his study, catching me marveling over the map and wishing for travels to faraway places. He places his hand on my shoulder in a gesture of grandfatherly intimacy. "That map was made over 200 years ago by Fra Mauro, here in Venice. It has been in my family for generations. Look at the detail! Many captains on my ships still swear by it." He points out places: "There is Africa, the land of the Hindu, Cathay," his finger moves along the trade routes. "The overland routes haven't changed much. They are pretty much like Marco Polo described. The shipping routes are very different. They now go up to Cape of Good Hope to go to the East." His index finger moves up over the upper rim of Africa, which is positioned at the top of the map with Europe below it, the reverse of the Hondius globe which has the north on top. "It has been our downfall," he says grimly. "We don't have grand sailing ships and our oarsmen can't row that far." We look out together and see the regatta is about to begin. The oarsmen are standing up in their *caorline* ready to race. I realize it has an element of tragedy to it, like a museum of the past. I think of the mighty sailing ships of our Dutch East Indies Trading Company which have replaced the Venetian overland spice trade and are starting to take over the silk as well. Our golden age is their decline. I wonder how Signor Dolfin has been able to hold on to his enormous fortune.

Donna Lucia enters in a simple black velvet dress, contrasting sharply with the extravagant carnavalesque costume she wore last time we met. Her current modesty comes as a surprise. She also refrains from the lewd looks that had made me so uncomfortable. I was used to receiving them from men, which is actually kind of fun when it's not terribly annoying and intrusive. But this had been a first from a woman and it made me feel queasy and a bit nauseous, while at the same time providing a rush of the exotic.

"I am so thankful you could come," she tells me. "Venier is taking a long time getting dressed. He never is like this. He usually doesn't care, but now everything is different. It is your presence, Signorina, your presence alone." She clasps my hand with both of hers. "But, please, let me take your coat."

"No thank you," I say quickly, unwilling to lose my cover, "I'm a bit chilly after the gondola ride. I'll warm up a bit first."

There is a pause between us as we wait in silence. The books around us exude their dusty calm.

"Maybe it would be best if I saw him alone," I suggest. Signor Dolfin and Donna Lucia exchange a glance that becomes a sign of agreement.

"Of course," says Donna Lucia, "that would of course be best, if you are fine with it."

I nod as we hear footsteps coming up the stairs.

Venier looks indeed like a changed man. He is carefully dressed in fashionable clothes with a winsome smile. Before his face had been like a blur; now it has suddenly come into focus. I have never seen such a complete turnaround in someone and my jaw drops. As I stare at him thus unceremoniously, his smile gets broader and he moves over to kiss my hand. I instinctively hold it out to him. Donna Lucia looks on in astonishment. Signor Dolfin gently takes her hand. She looks up at him with deep affection in her eyes. He appears proud to have delivered the Medicine. My mind is blank; the room around me is made up of patterns of light devoid of any meaning. Without a thought I take off my coat and feel the jubilation of the cloth. The fabric celebrates its revelation. I realize the dress is *other* than me, fully alive with desires of her own. Venier takes a step back as if blinded; Donna Lucia closes her eyes; Signor Dolfin looks down at the floor. I know I have crossed a line I didn't know existed. The fabric has power over us all. I suddenly wish Mundanus or Aunt Marianne were here. I should have waited. But I am alone. My aunt is right: this *is* sorcery. I don't understand why the fabric is so much more powerful now than it usually is. At other times it had been playful and given me confidence; now it scintillates with its own purpose, pulling me forward into acts I cannot control like a hunting dog after prey. I notice the elders preparing to leave and I wish to call them back. But the fabric prevents me, desiring to be alone with the young man.

"By daybreak I had forgotten the one I was before," he speaks poetically in perfect French without a stutter. "I had turned inside out like a glove. My gruesome companions were gone and fragrant breath arose where before only stench had been. It was you calling me out." His language is stilted but lovely; apparently he speaks only in verse. I remember Mundanus telling me once that in old Persia there had been a man who, after the loss of his beloved, only spoke in verse. They called him the madman. "Sunlight is roaring in back of the temple – torches melt in the blaze. Cellars vanish from sight: candles extinguished in laughter." His words well up directly from his heart. I can feel the fabric on my body delight in his love-sickness. He's been healed from Hell through mad love. Where am I in this? Do I have any part to play or is this solely between him and the living fabric?

"The ashes spring flowers," he concludes. Then he is silent, awaiting my response.

"Well," I say drily. "You've certainly changed – temples or no temples."

"Temples have roots way down to the heavens," he responds, as if we were having a dialogue.

"Of course," I deflect in an awkwardly pale reflection of humor, "for heaven's sake." I really don't know where to go with this; I feel like a woman from the cold Northern morasses eclipsed by her hot Southern dress. He only has eyes for the dress.

"Flesh is the kindling for flames everlasting."

I'm getting sick of this and want to walk out the door, yet am afraid of the effect it will have on him. When I try to turn away from him the dress holds me back. She is entranced by his doggerel. They are dancing a maudlin minuet and I can't get out of the dress, even though I'd rather be stark naked right now. He looks at me with a downright angelic expression. I'd even prefer to be with his mother at this point. Then, to my great relief, I see the comedy of this triangle between myself, the love-sick man, and the dress with a mind of her own. I laugh out loud.

"Extinguished in laughter," he repeats, nodding.

"Do you find it funny too?" I ask, entertaining the possibility that he has anticipated my change of mood.

"Wind knocks down trees in the ravaged forest."

"Do you mean that you've been set free by the fire of meeting me?"

He nods eagerly. I suddenly realize that he is not speaking in poetry, but in a coded word game with which he must have entertained himself while in Hell. "And you find that funny?" He nods once more.

"New underbrush arises from black earth," I try.

"A butterfly flitters about."

"Dawn melts the mist," I respond. He nods enthusiastically. Finally we are communicating. I feel at one with the fabric once more and notice that my muscles are sore with tension as they subtly relax.

"Dew leaves the grass it had pearled at daybreak," he says softly. This time it's my turn to nod.

"It certainly makes me happy to see you this way," I remark wishing to return to ordinary language.

"Mantis eats fly," he mutters. I see abject dread ripple over his face. I've never heard of a mantis and don't know what he means.

Venier points to a place unseen behind me. I turn around. "Mantis!" he exclaims, his body wincing. I realize that Mantis must be the name of one of his devils and I turn on my heels in a pirouette flaring my dress and waving the wings on my sleeves.

Venier instantly recovers, a beatific smile on his face. "Great wind vanishing," he exclaims victoriously. "Mother of God!"

This last reference is clear. Maybe he is moving closer to common language.

"Mary the Mother of our Lord?" I ask. "Am I your Holy Virgin?"

"You are everything. You scare Mantis." He sounds like a little boy waking up from a nightmare. I am glad we have gained a foothold in reason.

"Who is Mantis?" I ask. But he just stares at me, transported. I feel I need to understand more of this, and as his soul seems to melt into the fabric of my dress I go over to the door and call out to Donna Lucia. I hear their footsteps rush up the stairs and they enter almost immediately, Signor Dolfin visibly out of breath. For the time it takes for lightning to strike he looks his true age; then the truth vanishes.

"I need to know who Mantis is," I ask without further ado.

Donna Lucia turns white. Grandfather Dolfin dodders over to a bookcase and takes out a Chinese tome. Inserted in the middle is a red leather bookmark. He opens it to the bookmarked page and I see an etching of an alien creature painted green with a small egg-shaped head and a ferocious beak. No wonder this creature terrifies Venier. I shudder. "This is a book my ancestors brought back from Cathay. When Venier was a boy he would always ask me to look at this picture, he would point at it with great excitement. So I taught him the name I had heard for this animal. They called it Mantis. Then, when he became possessed, he kept shrieking, 'Mantis, Mantis' pointing to places where nothing was visible." Donna Lucia is crying. Venier keeps staring at me as at an apparition.

"I seem to protect him from Mantis," I say.

"I know," whispers Donna Lucia. "He called you the great wind…"

"Knocking over trees," I add. She has a puzzled look.

"That's what he told me," I explain, as if it were ordinary.

I realize that much time has passed. The regatta outside has ended and the teeming clusters of boats on the Grand Canal are disbanding, returning it to its usual traffic. Aunt Marianne must be worried sick. I need to leave, and come back with Mundanus and her to understand more about this before I go one step further. I walk up to him and take his hand. "I have to go now, but I will be back very soon." Terror shrivels his face. Suddenly our dilemma glares at us. He is only released from Mantis when I am around, replacing one illusion with another. But when I'm gone Mantis will be back devouring him. This insight paralyzes me. My eyes flit around the room for any kind of support. On the chair next to me I notice the pouch I wove for myself – sky blue with red waves of sunlight – and realize that I have a kerchief made of glow cloth in there wrapped around my mother's little bible. This might work; or if not, at least it ends my paralysis. I will have to do this in private, so I ask Donna Lucia and Signor Dolfin to leave once again. This time they depart by the door to the *portego*.

I take out the glow cloth and rap it over the front of a large folio leather-bound book about travels in Persia. It fits perfectly, creating a taut screen when I put it on the book stand in the dark corner of the room. I tell Venier to sit down in front of it on a chair I pull over from behind the desk, and wave my arms so the enchanting flesh-colored fabric accumulates liveliness and the magic is fully activated. Then I drape my coat over his head and the book stand. It is almost dark inside his enclosure; light only peeks in from behind him.

"Now look and tell me what you see," I solemnly intone. Remembering my first vision reflected in the glow cloth, of Mundanus and Aunt Marianne presented as lovers in an advanced state of undress laboring over Trismosin's alchemical furnace, I shudder. The medium is unpredictable.

Venier is silent for some time, making me anxious with anticipation. If this doesn't work, I don't know what will.

"Trees in a meadow," he suddenly says.

"What else?"

"Birds flying in all directions."

"Can you see me in the distance?" I ask, hoping this suggestion will make me appear.

"No, but I see Mantis." His voice is strangely calm. I quickly remove the coat from his over his head to make the vision disappear. It worked exactly in the opposite way I had hoped.

"Why did you do that?" he asks, disappointed.

"Because of Mantis," I explain.

"But he was very small. I wasn't afraid of him. I could feel you everywhere around. You were the landscape itself, the air I was breathing. And in your land Mantis is small. Please let me look some more." His voice is pleading, so I drape the coat over him again and he views the glow cloth screen intently.

"You are the world I live in," he speaks slowly. "I breathe you."

"But you don't see me there?" I ask again.

"Your body is the land I travel."

Disgusted, I feel a wave of nausea. If I could flee right now I would. My body feels polluted, intruded upon; I feel violated. But I calm myself down to wait, realizing that it is *his* world he is talking about through the medium of my image, the shape he borrows from my body.

"A harbor with boats: I enter your bay." His voice is fragrant with bliss and amorous innuendo and I push the nails of my right hand into the palm of my left until I almost draw blood. I force my voice to sound gentle, barely succeeding.

"I will leave you my continent. You can reach me through this silk screen. I shall be with you even when I'm not here," I tell him. Then I remove the coat from his head and call in the elders to give them instructions about the use of the glow cloth. If Giovanni Dolfin is truly the initiated adept he says he is, he will understand the awe inspiring magic and creative imagination of Red Sulphur.

ॐ

As our gondolas cross on the Grand Canal, I recognize the unmistakable color of Mundanus' strawberry hair through the cabin window and loudly call out. Mundanus turns his head just as I pass. I see him rush out to the *gondoliere*. Their gondola maneuvers alongside mine. I'm so relieved tears run down my cheeks. My *gondoliere* helps me safely into their boat and Mundanus pays him handsomely as I melt into Aunt Marianne's arms. I'm sobbing by now, feeling young as at times when the world around was overwhelmingly confusing and I would crawl into her bed and hide under the covers smelling the warmth of her body. All my adult self-assurance has vanished and what remains is shivering. Aunt Marianne is stroking my hair in an almost absentminded manner, waiting for me to be ready to speak. She would always give me time to gather myself.

"What happened?" Mundanus asks, his face wrinkled with concern. I look at him, his skin transformed by the Red Sulphur magic contrasting sharply with Aunt Marianne's natural features. It seems as though his surface is made of the same subtle material as the fabric I am wearing. They say the Stone is not made of matter, like a stone in nature. Red Sulphur is a coagulation of creative sparks appearing *as if* made of matter. In reality it is congealed subtle fire creating physical space for itself. I sometimes understand what that means when I notice how the fabric I wove from the Red-Sulphur-dyed wool creates space for people to inhabit, like Venier entering the world of glow as if it were my body. Mundanus' face appears permanently covered by a film of glow. It is a mixture of flesh and mist, of body and apparition. This perception of my fiancé is as brief as was the momentary presence of the true face of grandfather Dolfin from behind the glow. The deeper reality shimmers through to the surface; then it is gone.

"Venier is enchanted by me and the clothes I wear; by what you call sorcery," I say in Aunt Marianne's direction. "When he is with me he has respite from his devils. His world is momentarily exempt from torture. I am the Holy Virgin to him." I feel strangely guilty as I say this, realizing for how long I have toyed with these powers like a child.

Aunt Marianne looks greatly alarmed. "You are entering a dangerous world, darling. His demons might come to possess you. Sometimes they jump from one world to another like the Plague. We need to surround you with protection." She looks questioningly at Mundanus who nods in agreement, his face pensive. "We need to make some kind of amulet for her to shield her from possession."

"We should fashion a pentagram," he speaks slowly, as if he sees it appearing right in front of his eyes. "It has to be made from the wood of a Cross saturated with the Universal Medicine," he concludes. "The more ancient the Cross the better. You have to wear it from now on."

"Where do we find such an old cross?" Marianne asks.

"In the Dolfin chapel in the Palazzo my family has an old relic from Jerusalem. It is said to have been worn by the early martyrs. It is made of cedar."

"But the Palazzo is rented out," Aunt Marianne counters. "How do we get in?"

"Giovanni Dolfin said that he rented out floors but not the chapel itself," I remember.

"I don't want anyone to know you are wearing it," Mundanus says. "It defeats the purpose. The amulet has to be worn in secret, especially to those around Venier. We need to go in and take it. I know the Palazzo like I know my own body. We can enter with ease and leave without being seen. We'll go tonight. I don't want to leave you unprotected for a moment longer. The demons may already be inside your clothes. They must hunger for the power of the Red Sulphur fabric." Suddenly understanding the desire the dress had felt towards being with Venier, I shudder and want to rip off the fabric. The dress had not felt longing for him, but for Mantis! The magic textile could sense the demonic realm and was enchanted by it.

Mundanus takes a small bottle with the Universal Medicine out of his pocket. He tells me to open my mouth and splashes one drop of the tincture under my tongue. It tastes like the essence of all of my favorite foods. I instantly feel protected and my muscles relax. Nothing will enter my breath unawares; it will keep all demons out.

"Won't this be enough?" I ask.

"I'd rather surround you with an impenetrable moat," Mundanus says, closing all further discussion about the matter. "I am going to the Palazzo tonight."

"I'm coming with you," I tell him, eager to see the grand Palazzo Dolfin from inside.

Chapter Fifteen

It feels in a strange way delicious to set out into the night as a criminal, breaking into a palace. My protected life had not prepared me for stealth. The three of us walk the circuitous route from our inn to the Palazzo Dolfin, dictated by the myriads of canal ways dimly lit by Mundanus' oil lantern. I have an urge to walk on the tips of my toes in order to make no noise. Aunt Marianne notices and makes fun of me. Around us, carousing men reeking of cheap wine look at us with unabashed lechery. I suddenly feel solidarity with women who have to live by satisfying men reduced to their indiscriminate lust. They can't hide behind a man, as I do now, or look at these men with the privilege of scorn, as does Marianne van Os, heiress of great fortunes. Their lives are naked without protection, as they care for their offspring through furtive sales in the night. I see one of them, breasts hanging out, spreading her wanton merchandize. I say my prayers and feel ashamed of my privilege. As a Regent daughter I have been taught that I have inalienable birthrights, but have always been beset with doubts not even Aunt Marianne would understand.

A man bumps into Mundanus provocatively, in a crude attempt to pick his pocket. The next thing I know the man is flying through the air against the wall behind him. I hardly saw Mundanus' effortless move causing his flight.

My fiancé pulls us into an alley, waiting to see if the man is alone or if he works in company. We hear several voices hiss in Venetian, a posse of ghosts of the night. They discover us and knives are pulled.

Then I see the pistol in Mundanus' right hand. One bullet against five men. He lifts his arm slowly, looking even taller than before. "Who wants to die first?" he asks in Venetian. I'm surprised I can understand him. He moves his pistol from one to the other and sneers, "You? Or you maybe? Or you?" The ghosts look at one another; their faces, blackened with dirt, growl toothlessly. Mundanus appears in complete control, his power supreme. I feel no fear. From the corner of my eye I see my aunt glaring at the spooks in utter disdain. Next they scatter back into the night from whence they came.

"Quick," says Mundanus. "We have to get away from here. They're getting reinforcements. They're ants. The anthill can't be far." He moves us through the narrowest of alleys, knowing each square inch around Dolfin palace from his childhood explorations. I realize how daring he must have been from an early age, outsmarting these nocturnal crawlers. All I want to do is ravish my fiancé, have his body deeply inside me.

Unexpectedly he stops in front of a gate; I almost run into him. Mundanus points to the right and I notice an old structure. "Those are the medieval foundations. They built the palace on two ancient buildings and this is the entry into the foundations. This is how we got in and out of the palace unnoticed as children."

"But it is locked," Aunt Marianne says, worried, as she tries to move the gate, both hands yanking the thick rusty vertical bars.

Mundanus smiles slyly. "There's a trick." He demonstrates. "You lift it here on the right, then you tilt it up like this, and you pull it forward from below." With a creaking sound the gate flips towards us, revolving on a horizontal axis halfway up, just enough to let us pass under while ducking down low. When he lets go the gate slams back into place with a loud clang. "This wasn't just for us children. It was the way out for my family in case fleeing became the prudent thing to do." Mundanus' wit sounds uncharacteristically dry. "No one knows about this." He points to the opening between the foundations of the two medieval buildings that made way for the Palazzo. It reeks even worse than the usual Venetian cesspool stench as the putrid mixes with the stagnant air of forgotten green mold. I focus my attention on the place under my tongue where I can still taste the aftermath of the delicious Medicine drop Mundanus gave me for protection a few hours ago. Mundanus lights the oil lamp he had extinguished when the vermin was after us. By the yellow light we see a green door to the right, locked with a large chain. Mundanus takes out his knife and inserts it in the keyhole. With a few subtle motions the lock springs open, and we enter into the first of a series of catacomb-like pathways through the ancient foundations. We have to bend down low as we walk through the wet sludge. I am grateful for my rain boots. The air is stale, probably unbreathed since Mundanus was a boy. My lungs feel like I'm inhaling cobwebs. Aunt Marianne tries to suppress a coughing fit. "Don't worry," says Mundanus. "The living floors are on the second and third story. No one can hear us." My aunt looks miserable. This expedition is more wearing on her than on Mundanus and me. I actually feel quite thrilled by our nocturnal adventure. "Spit it out," Mundanus encourages her. "Don't try to hold it in. It will only make it worse." She turns away and spits gingerly behind her hand. I wonder if I will ever see her behave out of character. Amused, I admire how she is always her well-bred self under any circumstance - a Lady even in the catacombs. To our right a staircase looms. It is made of unfinished wood, broken in sections and rotten in other parts.

"I'll go first. I want to see if it's still the same as 30 years ago." He hands me the lantern and jumps to the third step, then to the fifth and finally the eighth. There is some awful creaking but the stairs hold. "Good," he sighs in relief, "These ones still function. Now do exactly what I just did – or the other steps will break and so will your neck," he adds. I reach forward as far as I can and put the oil lamp on the fifth step, then I jump to the third. I feel the wood give under me, and for a moment my heart stops, but it bounces back. When I reach the top of the stairs Mundanus is working on the lock of a large impressive door. Suddenly I hear a loud crack behind me and look back just in time to see Aunt Marianne catching herself, having broken through the third step, her elbows holding on to the stone side ramps. The lamp has fallen down from the impact, crashing into the wet clay ground, extinguishing immediately. It is pitch dark around. For the first time I feel fear. I hear Mundanus swear under his breath.

"Can you hold on?" he mutters down. I hear metallic sounds of his knife working the lock.

"It's a bit uncomfortable," Aunt Marianne replies drily. I laugh away my fear. Suddenly light enters through the open door, just enough to see my aunt dangling by her elbows, looking up with a wince on her face. She's hurt.

Mundanus rushes by me to the fifth step and lifts her out as if she were a feather. The look on his face leaves no doubt about the intensity of his feelings towards her. I'm surprised by the depth of my jealousy and disgust. I notice Mundanus' awareness of my feelings as he passes me, carrying my aunt to the large marble hall that has opened up before us. There is profound disapproval in his look. He puts her down on the cold marble floor; by the light coming off the Grand Canal from the large torches in front which are always lit by the Commune I see that her leg is bleeding from a nasty gash in her shin. My jealousies instantly forgotten, I bend over to clean out her wound with my dress, but Mundanus shoves me aside unceremoniously and becomes the physician. From a flat flask in his back pocket, he douses the wound with what smells like alcohol.

"No Panacea, Giovanni, please. I don't want it in my body, I told you. Please!" Marianne says. I have no idea why she would refuse the Medicine when she is obviously badly hurt. Mundanus hesitates.

"But the wound might suppurate, you could lose a leg," he objects vehemently.

"Please, Giovanni," she pleads. I am witness to an intimate moment I don't understand.

He pours a final splash of spirits into her deep wound and she winces even more. Then he looks at her with such profound love that I have to avert my gaze. I know for a fact that his love for her is different than his affections towards me. Our love was woven by hand; their love was given by nature. I sit down on the floor next to Aunt Marianne and weep. Mundanus looks back and forth between us. Not since the night when we made the Medicine and had our desires made visible in the glow cloth have we felt our agony as acutely as in this moment. "I'm sorry," I hear Aunt Marianne say in a tone that testifies to the pain in her soul mixed with her physical injury. The three of us sit on the floor oblivious to the fact that we have just broken into a palace.

"Let's leave," I say after a while, our quest feeling meaningless to me right now.

"No," Aunt Marianne retorts decisively. "You need to be protected."

"Wouldn't you rather I'd be dead," I exclaim. I instantly regret my lacerating words.

She looks at me with the eyes of my mother, those same eyes of boundless affection. "No," she says simply in a soft tone that makes me want to crawl up to her and be little again.

"I want to protect both of you," Mundanus mutters sadly. "It grieves me that I am the cause of your pain. I wouldn't have chosen this. I thought I chose, but there was no choice. We all end up with mangled hearts." The truth hangs heavily in the large marble reception hall with the grand staircase leading up to where we inevitably will have to go.

After we get up I see that Aunt Marianne's condition is worse than we had thought.

"You may have broken your shin bone," says Mundanus. "Please let me give you the Medicine, please Marianne!"

Her lips pressed together, jaws tight, she does not respond and limps on one leg. I support her, putting her arm over my shoulder.

"You'll never get up the stairs," Mundanus insists.

She looks at him with the defiance I know so well from my aunt. It is the way she faces the world. Her spirit has always been the most powerful in the family. Even Grandfather Van Os used to say so. I am proud of her and at the same time realize that she is verging on the stubborn at this moment. She hops on her right leg towards the staircase and begins to jump one-legged from step to step holding on to the ornate brass railing. I look at Mundanus and grin. He smiles back. "Sometimes she's just a headstrong child," he sighs. It is said by one who lives on the deepest level of intimacy with another. Tears flush my eyes. He touches my shoulder. "I love you, Clara," he assures me. "With all my heart."

"Yes, I believe you," I remark. "It's just that you have two hearts beating in your breast at different rhythms. We all know this." He looks crestfallen and I kiss him gently on the mouth. "I love you too, darling," I say, while watching Aunt Marianne's remarkable progress on the grand staircase. I walk over to her to support her. She turns to me, a grateful look on her face, and not just for the shoulder I offer her. The large entrance hall is empty and hollow, echoing our footsteps back to us. I remember that others live here and that we may be in danger of waking them.

Mundanus passes us by to go ahead. At the mezzanine we take the left staircase up to the second floor, bending us back direction Grand Canal.

Then, all of a sudden, at the top of the stairs I see a long musket pointed at us from the balustrade of the second floor.

"Halt," says a voice I recognize but can't place.

"Jacopo," Mundanus exclaims. "It's me, Giovanni." I suddenly realize that this will go horribly wrong and, leaving Aunt Marianne to her own devices, I jump in front of my fiancé and feel the shot tear through my shoulder. The world disappears.

When I come to I'm on the floor with Mundanus moving a knife around in my shoulder. I'm surprised that I don't feel a thing. The pain is gone. He must have applied the Medicine.

"Stop!" I yell out. "Don't go any further. I will only take the Medicine if Aunt Marianne does as well." Jacopo Gandolfi's face looks terrified and confused as he stares at me with adoration in his eyes. And I'm not even wearing my textiles.

"He has already given you the Medicine," Aunt Marianne replies.

"Stop removing the bullet. Stop it right now!" I pull away from him. Mundanus stops. "Only if you take it too," I glare at Aunt Marianne. "Or I will lose my arm and you your leg. We'll be of much use then." I fail to infuse some levity.

Marianne van Os stares at me, daughter of Johanna van Os, our spirits evenly matched. Mundanus waits for our standoff to pass.

I can feel Aunt Marianne relenting for my sake. She knows the Van Os intransigence and is convinced I will carry out my threat. She offers her broken shinbone to Mundanus, who douses it with Medicine and resets the bone. It begins to heal in front of our eyes. Then he resumes his work on my shoulder. With I ping I hear the bullet fall onto the marble floor. Then he drenches my shoulder with the Medicine and sits me up against the wall.

We are on a thick red carpet at the center of a marble hallway that stretches out equally in both directions over the entire width of the palazzo. The walls are plain with gothic arches over simple doors. There are no ornaments. Giovanni Dolfin must have taken everything of value with him to the Palazetto. The atmosphere feels remarkably threadbare as though the proud building has come upon hard times. I feel sorry for it.

"What are you doing here?" Mundanus asks Jacopo gruffly.

"I live here," he mutters. "I rent the Palazzo from your grandfather. I live here with my sister and her family."

"Alicia?" asks Mundanus.

Jacopo nods. Then he sounds angry again. "Now tell me who you are and where you get your information. It is because of your companions that I don't throw you down the stairs."

"We've gone over that many times, Jacopo. Your throwing me down the stairs that is. You couldn't do it then, you can't do it now. You still have the scar on your forehead to prove it. You can only get as far as shooting my fiancée." Jacopo is staring at Aunt Marianne's leg with the wound closing up at visible speed. "That's, that's, that's magic," he stammers, pointing at it.

"I did that the same way in which I changed my appearance," Mundanus says. My healing shoulder feels rosy warm like my body would after coming home from skating in the freezing cold to sit by the kitchen fire drinking hot chocolatl.

"We need to be able to trust you, Signor Gandolfi," Aunt Marianne states formally. "For the sake of your friendship with Giovanni Theodore, can we trust you completely?"

He nods, dumbstruck.

"Have you heard of Trismosin's treasure?" she asks him, referring to grandfather Dolfin's mention that the Red Sulphur couldn't be kept a secret in Venice.

He nods. "The legend, you mean? The tale of the old alchemist who left the Philosopher's Stone here in Venice two centuries ago? Everyone in Venice knows that legend. Why?"

"It is not a legend," Mundanus says. He points at the bottle with the medicine. "I made this from the Stone Trismosin left behind in our City."

Not even the magic taking place right in front of his eyes can convince Jacopo Gandolfi of the verity of Mundanus' statement.

"Just look," I say. "Have you ever seen wounds heal like this? My aunt's broken bone is already covered with healthy flesh. The Stone speeds up time. I don't know how it works, but it changes the nature of time." I try to demonstrate by evidence. However, no amount of proof can convince a mind that is set. Except for the adepts of the Art, every man in Venice knows for a fact that this is an old wives' tale that merits only ridicule. It is easier for the eyes to disregard blatant evidence than for the mind to risk dislocation.

"Open your eyes wide," Mundanus orders his friend in the low register voice of the Magus.

Jacopo obeys without a will of his own. Mundanus puts a drop of the Panacea in each eye. He turns to us and says, "The Medicine can cure the total occlusion of vision."

We wait to see the effects. Jacopo at first looks stunned like a hunted deer, eyes wide with astonishment and dread. I can't help but smile at the mind's reaction to a direct perception of the incredible.

"Zanni!" Jacopo suddenly exclaims in a hiccup of laughter, recognizing Mundanus, calling him by his childhood name. "My God, Zanni, now I can see. Your character hasn't changed. You're still the same old smug ..." and a word follows in Venetian which I don't understand but must be an expletive used among men to express affection for one another in a manner unsuitable for the ears of women. "And all of you glow green like fireflies. The walls are dancing, the ceiling spins. And yet I'm not drunk."

"Your head feels clear like mountain air but the whole world talks back at you," Mundanus remarks simply.

"And you can't hide from what you see," I add.

Jacopo nods, mouth agape. "I'm walking around in the Holy Book!"

"The world *is* Holy Scripture," Mundanus responds. I can never get used to his sentimental hyperbole; but it must be the way emotion flourishes in these Southlands, since Jacopo seems not the least disturbed by his poetic drivel.

"It's a lot to take in," I mention, to sober them up. We need to get down to business and explain to Jacopo why we are here and get to Dolfin Chapel. It may be that I'm beginning to feel my shoulder, but I'm getting irritated. "Can you please explain to him why we are here," I say in Aunt Marianne's direction, feeling that Mundanus constitutional effusiveness mixed in with the nostalgia caused by having been seen by his oldest friend won't be of much help.

In a few precise words – efficient with a mathematical clarity that is balm to my Northern soul – my aunt explains why we are here and what we need.

"So where is the chapel?" I add impatiently. Aunt Marianne looks at me with a masked disapproval only apparent to me. Where we were raised, the one who visibly loses patience loses the game. We learn from childhood to wipe our face clean of all expression and be tempered under all circumstances.

ॐ

The Chapel, a large room with intimate gothic arches, is painted sky blue. There is no furniture, no pews. At the far end, high up, a small gothic window gives a view of the night sky. I notice that the moon has risen. Under the window the Mother of God looks at us sadly from a stone pedestal. She is dressed in Holy Virgin blue, like the chapel, which shows that it is dedicated to her.

"When I was a child I always thought she looked like my mother," says Mundanus, his words echoing hollow in the moonlight.

"I thought the same," Jacopo concurs. "Your mother was very beautiful. I always wished she were mine." The Medicine makes one truthful.

Aunt Marianne and I stay back to get a sense of the quiet blue atmosphere as Mundanus walks up towards Mary. Jacopo stays close to me, as if he can't pull himself free from my enchantment. We see Mundanus bow deeply and fall to his knees. I'm taken aback, unaware of the power the Holy Virgin has over him and stare at Aunt Marianne, who looks equally surprised. For some minutes we peer at the back of the man we thought we knew kneeling in devotion. Suddenly I recognize the soft clanging of Mundanus' knife on metal. We walk forward and see that he is working on a small metal door at the bottom of the pedestal.

"What are you doing?" Jacopo asks, reverting to his previous suspicion. I remember I'm wearing a belt of magic fabric and nonchalantly twirl it, instantly returning him to slavery.

The small black metal door has an ingenious lock, but by now I realize that locks don't mean the same thing to Mundanus that they do to others. Finally the door springs open and I see an ivory box, identical to the one Mundanus always carries with him. "My father had two identical boxes made in the Holy Land," he explains, "one for the Red Sulphur and one for the relic." He takes the box out from under its protection by the Virgin and hands it to me.

"Was your mother perhaps the model for this sculpture of the Holy Mother?" Aunt Marianne asks gazing up at the iconic face surrounded by blue. Mundanus looks up at the statue and stares intently. I see tears in his eyes.

The box feels familiar to my hands, as I have held its twin several times before. I open the lid, and by the moonlight I see a piece of parchment and a wooden cross. I can instantly sense the power of the relic, seemingly shining from within, and touch the wood. A shock flashes through me and I withdraw my hand instantly, almost dropping the box. Mundanus stares at me. "It is yours," he says. "It is the only object in the world I care about. It passes from mother to daughter. My mother received it from her mother, so now it shall go to you. The Red Sulphur goes through male descent and the relic through the female line. I can feel it is yours. The choice was right."

I know this is the ultimate confirmation that I shall be the mother of Mundanus' children. I understand why there is lightning between the relic and me. We're of the same flesh.

Aunt Marianne comes over to me and takes me in her arms. I feel immense relief in her.

"It is worth everything we've had to go through," is all she says.

"I want to get married in this chapel," I state with absolute certainty.

Jacopo Gandolfi seems to awaken from a dream. I feel how he is released from his enchantment by both the Red Sulphur and by me. The relic seems to undo to the power of the fabric. Mundanus had been right; I need to have it for my protection against the textiles I wove.

"The relic can't leave the chapel," Jacopo intones solemnly.

"I don't want to have to throw you down the stairs again, Jacopo," Mundanus jokes, then adds in a serious manner, "This treasure was my mother's. I can do with it whatever I please!"

"It belongs to your grandfather. This is theft!"

"No, actually it belongs to my wife. It is passed on from mother to daughter."

"Maybe," he concedes. "But as long as you're not married it belongs to your grandfather and I can't let you take it." He moves forward in a threatening manner.

"I don't want to have to hurt you, Jacopo, but I will if you provoke me."

Before I have a chance to react, they're standing face to face, each with a pistol drawn. Suddenly Aunt Marianne jumps right in between them, wincing as she lands on the leg that only moments ago had been broken. "Now shoot," she says calmly to them both.

After what seems like eons of hesitation, Mundanus lowers the pistol. "Why are you so devoted to my grandfather?" he asks Jacopo.

"I'm his heir," Jacopo replies, putting his pistol under his belt.

"You are what?" I exclaim. I can't believe what I just heard. Giovanni Dolfin had explicitly told me that I was going to inherit his fortune. Not that I particularly care; I have riches already, through my grandfather. One fortune or two makes no difference to me. But he had known all along that his grandson was alive; how could he have made Jacopo into his heir?

"When did he say that?" Mundanus asks.

"The will was drawn up soon after your letter arrived that you had died in a shipwreck."

"But he knew that wasn't true!" Mundanus exclaims.

"What game is he playing?" Aunt Marianne wonders.

"Whatever his reasons," Jacopo concludes haughtily, "I *am* his heir. When he passes, Dolfin Palace will be mine. So I will do everything within my power to have the relic stay right here."

I open the box and take out the cross. It seems to float above my hand as if it wants to know me before entrusting itself to my palm. Warmth rushes through my veins and I have the sense of having come home. As I enclose it in my right hand, I know to the innermost depth of my heart that I shall never part with it for as long as I live.

I walk over to Jacopo and press my hand on his heart. Still under the influence of the Red Sulphur Medicine, a green spark passes from the cross to his chest. "You can have everything else; none of us care. But this will never be yours. Never!" My eyes spew fire, overrunning his spirit with my absolute certainty. Jacopo gasps for breath. Then I place the cross on his forehead as if pressing it right into his brain. He is rendered powerless.

"Take it," he says, defeated. "Never come back here, but take it."

"I will come back here for my wedding," I answer proudly. "After that, I hope I will never see you again."

Of course Aunt Marianne takes pity on him. "He's just defending what he believes is his, Clara. Jacopo, we need the cross for now."

"I will never give it back," I exclaim. Jacopo looks dejected. My feline fierceness has rekindled his enchantment and my words have cut into his soul. Now I feel compassion. "You are my fiancé's oldest friend. Can't we be kind to one another?"

Mundanus looks into the box and takes out the parchment. I recognize Maximo Theodore's mirror signature. Next to it is a king on the beach, a king drowning, and the sun coming up over the mountain; it is identical to the signature on the letter shown to us by his grandfather.

'Dear Zanni,' it reads.

'You have returned for your mother's cross. I asked your grandfather to call you back to Venice after one Saturn return since my departure. There is an oral codicil to Salomon Trismosin's written legacy, which must be confided by father to son in spoken words. If this letter is still here, I have not been able to tell you what it is. If the letter is still here, I have not been able to find my way back. Maybe I am no longer alive.

This is the true essence of the Trismosin legacy: not just to carry the last Stone through the ages, but to find its secret for yourself. You must set out in search for the ultimate mystery. I will have failed by now. But you can succeed. Search, my son, leave no stone unturned, never stop.

I have pretended to your grandfather that I am mad with grief and that I am leaving to search for the spirit of your mother at the ends of the earth. This is only partly false. It is my love for your mother which keeps me alive to fulfill my mission.

In order to fully protect you and the Stone I have asked him to adopt you and guide your life in my stead. He has consented in order to keep you safe.

If you read this I will have passed on to worlds unseen.

Fare thee well my son.
Your devoted father,
Maximo Theodore

Aunt Marianne speaks first after Mundanus has read the letter out loud. "In your heart you have always known this," she says. "You told me that it is the great sorrow of your life that you haven't found the secret of the preparation of Red Sulphur."

"This feels different. Now it is no longer just a sorrow, but an instruction. I have to put aside my certainty that the Stone can no longer be found and start anew," replies Mundanus.

"What is a Saturn return?" I ask.

"The time it takes for Old Man Saturn to wander back to his same location in the night sky and resume his same influence. It's every 27 to 29 years. Around now we are under the same grand Saturn constellation as when Maximo Theodore left Venice," Marianne explains.

Jacopo Gandolfi looks awestruck.

"I apologize," he mumbles.

Part Seven

Mundanus

Chapter Sixteen

I drop the parchment on the floor at the feet of the Holy Mother, who, now that Marianne has pointed it out, I can see has obviously been modeled after my own mother Claudia. I look up at her and am flooded with memories of my parents.

I was ten years old when Father brought back the boxes from one of his many journeys East. I admired those boxes, sniffing at them to see if I could still pick up the faraway scents of places I longed to see. He came into my mother's rooms in the Palazzo with one box in his hands and put it on her dressing table under the mirror. Her face melted and her eyes were riveted on the beautiful strips of ivory, woven like cloth into intricate geometrical patterns. She stroked it with the same gentle hands with which she caressed my cheeks. I can still feel her hands on my face. I look up at the statue, and the Holy Mother appears to smile.

Father had looked proud then. Usually his mood was subdued, not buoyant. But in this memory he beamed with pride at my mother's appreciation of the exquisite box. She got up and went over to her closet, my favorite one, painted with sailing ships and sea creatures, blue and silver. From the top drawer she pulled out a red velvet pouch, opened it and showed the content to me. That was the first time I saw the cedar cross. She told me, "This has passed along from mother to daughter in my family for as long as anyone can remember. One day it will belong to your wife. My grandmother told me it was worn in Palestine by one of the earliest Martyrs of our Faith. It is over 1500 years old. That's why I am so grateful to your father. He brought

me this box from Jerusalem. Here the cross can rest peacefully."
And she gave me the relic to hold. I have never before or since
seen my father so fully alive. While holding the cedar cross I
remember wondering what my wife would be like. And now I'm
looking at them both: Clara, with the cross in her hand, and
Marianne, standing protectively behind her. I feel like a biblical
patriarch, faithful to two wives. My most intimate memory of
Marianne springs into view: I see her laboring over the fire, the
mounds of her breasts glistening with sweat as we perform the
projection in the smithy near The Hague, turning our passion
into gold.

So it is true, my legal name *is* Giovanni Dolfin, VII; a new
name, a new fate. And in this new name I have to move beyond
my previous certainty that the Red Sulphur can no longer be
made, that its time has passed. I feel a disheartening sense of
incapability and fully understand my father's urge to travel the
worlds in order to find living Magi who could still manufacture
the Stone. I believe the fact that my father has not returned to
Venice to mean that there are no longer alchemists out in the
world adept at extracting Red Sulphur from primal material. If
he had found them he'd sent word here to tell me, I am sure of
that. But unlike my father, I have a mystical spouse with whom
to probe the hot passions of the Stone, and I am overcome with
a longing for my laboratory and long days there with Marianne.
The full range of tasks ahead is clear. Indeed, we shouldn't postpone the wedding a moment longer. I will have children with
Clara and find the secrets of Red Sulphur with Marianne.

Suddenly I hear Marianne scream. I turn around and see the
sickle of the ottoman dagger flash silver in the moonlight. The
young man, now clad in white Moorish garb, but unmistakably
the same who had attacked us at my Hague laboratory, lunges
at Clara. I instantly know Gerda was accurate; he is cast much
more physical than before. The dagger is dense enough to kill
her.

I'm too far away to put myself between Clara and the at-
tacker. Jacopo pulls a pistol and shoots at the intruder. The

bullet passes right through his body without doing any damage or slowing his pace. His feet barely touch the ground.

Clara looks up calmly at the silver fury attacking her. In her right hand, she holds the cross, and as time slows down to a crawl I see her hand go up, holding the relic.

"In the name of the Mother," she says, shielding herself with my mother's cross.

The dagger continues its plunge.

A blinding light bursts from the Holy Mother, curving a protective mantel of solid air around Clara. The dagger crumbles against it. The young man looks shocked.

"Why? It's for us! It protects us!" he yells up at the statue. Then he seems to shatter and disappears. Only an afterglow from the Holy Virgin remains. I know for certain that the presence of my mother has protected our lineage. For a moment I see the stone statue cry before it returns to its unmoved immobility. Bowing deeply before her, I realize that I will have to find the sorcerer before he annihilates us. Marianne rushed up to Clara, trying to protect her, the moment the sorcerer's phantom started his lunge; like me, she was too far away. Now she holds her niece. Marianne is shaking while Clara is suffused with an eerie calm.

"He wanted my children," she says with certainty. "The Virgin Mother protected me." Then she turns to me with the face of an innocent child, both hands cupping the relic. "Why would the sorcerer want to stop the lineage? Does he want the Red Sulphur for himself?"

I feel deep inside me a rage I have never known before, the rawest of sulphurs, ready to unleash apocalypse. I know for a fact she is right. The sorcerer does not just want the Red Sulphur for himself so he can make his cast phantoms more lethal and recharge his own waning physical body; he wants the lineage to end. His is a feud with Trismosin. But where do I find him? He could be anywhere. If he can use the full power of Red Sulphur, he can be anywhere. Trismosin tells us that a master of Red Sulphur can rise up high into the sky and look down to places in the far distance. He could be here, The Hague, England: anywhere. And he could look completely different from the phantom. When he had attacked Gerda, he was in the guise of her little brother Peter. I look at Clara and say with conviction: "I'll find him!"

Marianne has come back to her senses. "He looked pretty surprised," she says drily. "Hadn't expected the Holy Virgin to come to our aid. It almost seemed she had betrayed him. I get a sense he referred to her when he said 'It's for us'."

I look up at the statue, thankful she chose us over the sorcerer, and I feel my mother's heart temper the hot, raw fury in mine.

Jacopo is trembling like a leaf about to blow off the branch. "The bullet went straight through his heart," he says, awestruck.

"That was a phantom," Clara explains, vastly increasing his confusion with her calm. I smile. I know he will forget most of what has occurred in the chapel once the Medicine's power wears off. His eyes won't stay open for long. My childhood affection for Jacopo rushes back in; I remember that look of confusion in his face. I used to confound him endlessly when we were young. We were like brothers, me being an only child and he having only sisters. His sister Alicia, who is now living here with her family, was the first girl I ever kissed, down below in the medieval foundations we called 'the catacombs' where we played out the lives of early Christians in Rome. She was always my wife in these plays, while Jacopo had to be the nasty Roman overlord, with the Palazzo his imperial palace. No wonder he will not part with it just because I show up. And Clara is right; it doesn't matter to us. Now that we have the relic, the soul of my mother, there is no longer anything for us here in Venice.

I have to find a way to hunt down the sorcerer. For some reason I suspect he won't be in Venice. He'll be stalking the place where the Red Sulphur is. I want to get back home: The Hague. My Venice days are long past. Trismosin's laboratory is now in The Hague where the Van Os clan is as powerful as the Dolfins are here in Venice. Let Jacopo have the Palazzo. It will be better cared for in his hands. I feel a heady sense of freedom and adventure. My divorce from Venice is no longer just one-sided; it is by mutual consent. I will carry away my portable past in my names: Theodore Mundanus and Giovanni Dolfin, VII.

"Jacopo," I say, going over to him. "I can't explain it all to you. It is too complicated. But I am glad you will inherit the Palazzo and live here with Alicia and her family. I hope you will find yourself a woman like my Clara, and populate Palazzo Dolfin with children who can play in the catacombs. I only have good memories of our old friendship. You are the only brother I ever had." I see Clara smile sweetly while at the same time rolling her eyes. She will never understand what she calls our 'muggy Venetian temperament.'

The aftershock of the phantom is subsiding. I look up at Mother. Her presence is calming us all.

"I hope you will be at my wedding here in the chapel of your Palazzo Dolfin," Clara says as a peace offering. There are tears in Jacopo's eyes and he is about to pour out his heart.

"I could use a good sleep," Marianne drily prevents another outburst of Southern rains.

❧

The women's wounds are healed by morning with no lingering aftermath. I'm filled with curiosity. Even if we never find the secret of the Red Sulphur for ourselves, having made the Medicine from Trismosin's Stone is already a miracle. I wonder if I can push further. I feel a great urgency to expand my craft now that my adversary has shown his hand, dagger and all. I must increase my knowledge as Father has suggested in his letter, and become a master of Red Sulphur in order to protect us from one who clearly already is a master.

With amazing speed Clara weaves a beautiful protective pouch for the amulet. It is in the shape of a pentagram, made of glow cloth thread mixed with Venetian blue silk. We agree that the cedar cross should not be tampered with. If you look carefully at the pouch you can see the face of the Holy Virgin in the background. Or maybe it's just me seeing my mother reflected in the threads of glow. I feel no need to ask anyone to corroborate my vision. Clara wearing it around her neck gives me a profound sense of safety. My future feels secured, even with a sorcerer lurking in the invisible world.

After two days a letter comes from the Palazetto. Venier is doing much better, but can't wait to see Clara again. This time I will see to it that Clara is not going alone. I want to be there as she heals Venier with her enchanting presence.

After a hefty Dutch breakfast of black bread, butter, various cheeses and bacon, we set out to my grandfather's residence. Clara is dressed in full regalia, wearing her enchanting fabric over the sacred cross in its protective pentagram pouch of Virgin blue.

"How is it to wear them both," Marianne asks her in the gondola, "the dress and the amulet?"

Clara's blue gray eyes, the same as Marianne's, turn inward as she feels the magic with her skin. She looks ravishing and it is hard to keep my eyes off her, but something has changed, I notice. She is still irresistible to me, but it feels more like my attraction is to *her* rather than to the sorcery. It feels as if the combination of fabric and relic cancel each other out.

"It is less magical," she concludes after a while, with a hint of wistfulness. "But it feels more like me. More like my body itself is rich and mysterious. I don't think the fabric will run away with me again as it did last time at the Palazetto."

I am charmed by her femininity and I ache for her. I will talk with Grandfather about the wedding today. Marianne reads my gaze and looks reserved, strain showing briefly. I'm glad I can read her face underneath her remarkable Dutch Regent mask of control. Pained, I wonder how she will survive my wedding night.

As the gondola draws near the Palazetto I see my grandfather up on the landing, his tall body standing straight. He appears unchanged since my childhood when I loathed him for keeping my father away from my mother. But with the more experienced eye of the Adept I can see the frailty underneath his relatively youthful exterior, as if his presence were filled with a very fine dust. Winds could blow right through him; but for now the appearance holds up.

I know that when he's gone, I will miss him, my last link to Venice and my parents. And if my current understanding of him is correct he sacrificed his relationship with me to protect the Stone from theft. Even though his abandonment hurts like the fires of Hell, I respect him for it. He seems to be a man willing and able to override his heart in service of his mission. Both of us are slaves of the living Stone. For a fraction I can feel a certain fondness for him – but that disappears when I hear his sonorous French in honor of Clara, Donna Lucia and Venier standing with him on the jetty. I'm instantly reminded that he used to speak French with my mother before I knew the language when they didn't want me to understand and I instantly mistrust him again.

The transformation of Venier is remarkable. His bearing is tall, straight and self-confident. In his hand he is holding an opal kerchief, one that I instantly recognize. It is obvious that he has been waiting anxiously to see Clara again, and I try to tell myself that I am not jealous when she appears radiant to see him. They are more of the same natural age than she and I, though I look younger. But I am made of some of the same pearl dust as is my grandfather

"Signorina Clara," Venier exclaims gregariously as he takes her hand, helping her onto the landing. Do I hear an emphasis on his use of 'Signorina,' the unmarried title for a lady of her station? Jacopo did the same when he was smitten with my magical fiancée. I want to talk with Grandfather about our wedding right away.

Clara smiles back at him in a most beguiling way - much more seductive than is necessary. Marianne, being escorted from the boat onto the landing by my grandfather, is observing my waves of expression and can't suppress a smile. For the first time I can feel her position, not from the perspective of magnanimity but of acute pain.

Now that Venier is not cowering, I can see that he is actually quite handsome. He has his mother's chiseled Roman face; a sharp nose under crescent black eyebrows connected over the bridge, enormous deep brown eyes, and a passive full mouth.

"I am so grateful you came," Venier responds to Clara's inviting smile, in a brilliant tenor voice of too great an intimacy to my liking. Under his gregarious halo of curly black hair his low forehead glistens with sweat, though it is not warm out today. As he bows deeply, the tip of Clara's sleeve is firmly gripped between his fingers. His arm swings out to the right with a flourish, making the glow cloth sail through the air. For a moment I can see the face of my loneliness reflected in the opalescent surface waving through space. Taken off guard I stumble as I ascend from the gondola onto the jetty and barely catch myself from falling.

"Again?" Marianne remarks noncommittally, reminding me of my near nosedive into the Grand Canal when Clara tried her powers of enchantment upon me some days ago. I feel uncomfortable by how well she knows me.

I recognize my quick reversal of moods. One moment I am pleased about the intimacy of reading Marianne's expressions, the next I feel invaded and lonely.

With the air of a host Venier leads us to stairs up to the third floor great room. His pace is full of bounce and elation. Clara prances closely behind. How young they look! I follow and feel Marianne's ironic eyes in my back. I sit down in one of Mother's Cupid chairs and remember how I used to love the chubby little *putti*. Now they leave me cold. I'm back in the feelings of my childhood after my father left me with a grandfather who scorned everything Father had held dear. A whirlpool of rage is gathering in hot spasms, drawing near from faraway oceans. The child in me does not understand or care about my grandfather's sacrifice. I'm lost in the hurt I felt being young. Marianne is sitting with her back to me talking to Donna Lucia, who looks transported with gratitude, giving Clara furtive glances of a different nature than before. If she had previously desired Clara for herself, I'm convinced that now she wants her for Venier. The fact that Clara is my fiancée plays no part in the schemes in her mind, I'm sure. I'm also sure which side Grandfather will support.

"Giovanni," Clara's youthful voice rings, "I am going to have a brief conversation with Venier in Grandfather's study; I know you don't mind." Before I know it the young ones have gone and I am left with the old people. All the bone-weariness I had not felt since my transmutation washes over me and I feel ancient, one in a long line of Giovanni Dolfins who live their dreary lives, grow old and pass on their name to the next generation.

"When I was young I hated you," I say sharply to my grandfather. Marianne turns to me with disapproval. "And even though I may now understand why you acted the way you did, it makes no difference in the way I feel towards you." In this last sentence my voice sounds almost like a plea. Marianne hears me.

"Couldn't you have made him feel that you cared for him even if you had to scorn his father? "

"Maximo implored me to speak badly about him to throw off potential thieves. They were everywhere. Venice is in decline and people are grasping at straws. So the story of Trismosin leaving the gold-making Stone in Venice had become current again among adepts and their merchant masters. Zanni was only 14 and might easily be tricked by cunning rats. We had to throw them off. When I agreed to protect the Stone I didn't realize how this would hurt my grandson. And when Zanni ran off I was glad for him and tried to protect him wherever he went. I remember when the messenger delivered your false letter how my heart burst with happiness that you had escaped. One of the reasons why I took Maximo's potion of youth after you left was to be re-invigorated with the importance of the task he gave me and to overcome my doubts. I had to experience the mystery first hand." He turns his whole body towards me. "I admired your father, Giovanni. I thought highly enough of him to trust his words and turn my life into a lie. Your father was a great man of duty. I learned from him to be the same."

"And then you gave everything you owned to Jacopo, while you knew that I was alive," I reply dismissively.

"I thought you were right to have everyone believe you were dead. You had come up independently with the same plan as your father, and I felt that making Jacopo my heir would seal your death in the eyes of anyone who might go after you to search for Trismosin's treasure. Death is the best cover. Only my Lucia knew the truth." He turns to Marianne in an urge to come clean. "I met her shortly after Giovanni left and I had taken the rejuvenation medicine. I needed to tell someone my story and I entrusted her with my life." He looks at Donna Lucia with such love that it is hard for me to keep on casting him as a villain.

"So what will you do now, Caro Mio Ben?" Donna Lucia asks matter of fact, almost like Marianne would. "Are you going to disinherit Jacopo in favor of Giovanni?"

Grandfather looks at a loss.

"I think you should leave your fortune to Jacopo," Marianne says quietly. "Let the trail of Trismosin end forever."

"I have thought of that. But if I don't acknowledge you as my grandson, you can never go back to The Hague and you would be chased as an impostor where ever you go. Princess Amalia and Johan de Witt would make sure of that."

"Then acknowledge me as your grandson returned from the dead. Give me a grand wedding in Dolfin Chapel and I will abdicate my rights in favor of Jacopo who I love like a brother."

"So I should abandon the Dolfin legacy?" he asks, as I see the weight of his ancestors bear down on him.

"No, just Dolfin Palace. I will openly acknowledge that I am Giovanni Dolfin the Seventh. Clara and my children shall be named Dolfin."

"I think a grand wedding is a bad idea," Marianne says calmly, as if the matter is of no emotional concern to her. "Keep it private and small. You don't want everyone to see you in your completely changed appearance. Most people would not understand, and those who would might become really dangerous. I suggest your acknowledgment of Giovanni as your grandson be done by way of unquestionable legal documents we can take back with us to The Hague."

Donna Lucia looks worried. "When do you think of going back?"

"Right after the wedding," I respond coldly, suspicious of her son being with my fiancée, feeling utterly ridiculous at the same time.

"Could you maybe wait a few weeks, please? Clara is performing miracles with my son. It surpasses any hopes I might have had." Her plea sounds like a sob.

"If you adopt Jacopo as your son, like you did me, I would agree to postpone the wedding for a month," I bargain like a fishmonger. It had been Jacopo who saved me from my desolate life after Father left; I am grateful to pay him back. And it feels right that the woman of my first kiss should be the Mistress of the Palazzo. The memory of my dramatic puppy love for Alicia Gandolfi takes my mind off my spouses. My spirits lift. Marianne smiles at me proudly, admiring my happy generosity; I'm glad she reads me wrong this time.

"That I will do," Grandfather gets up and walks over to me to give me a handshake of agreement. Donna Lucia cries softly.

Before I shake on it I want to know one more thing: "Why did you tell me you called me back for Venier? The real reason was my father's request I come back to Venice 28 years hence at the Saturn return of his disappearance."

"How do you know?" Grandfather asks, astonished.

"Later," I respond gruffly. "First you answer me." Marianne prepares to explain but I lift my hand to silence her. "Tell me," I repeat.

"I asked him to call for you right now." Donna Lucia rises from her seat and stands tall. "Your grandfather would have waited another year, but I thought that once you were married and settled in The Hague you would never return to Venice. I asked him for your help to cure Venier. And you succeeded by way of your fiancée. It was me." Her eyes are moist but her face is set with iron determination. She is a formidable mother.

Before I get a chance to shake my grandfather's hand and explain my knowledge of my father's request, Venier enters the room, cheeks flushed, followed by Clara, who looks demure. Venier has the air of a child after a treasure hunt. I remember myself chasing Princess Alicia in the catacombs, ending up in a dead end passage of her choice to steal a brief moment of affection away from her chaperone brother, the Emperor of Rome. Jealousy mixes with nostalgia.

"Mantis is gone," Venier blurts out. "He shrank to a louse and then vanished. I think he will never be back." His words stumble over one another, the opposite of stuttering. Mother Lucia takes him in her arms as if he were a boy of ten – as if I were ten. I'm fully confused.

Clara walks over to me and gently touches my hand; I feel it withdraw – she looks surprised and Marianne has a knowing expression. I feel separate from everyone. The women exchange a glance of understanding. Clara grins, leans forward and whispers in my ear: "You're sulking." It has been eons since I was the great doctor Mundanus and she my patient. I feel like her slave. The full force of her magic cloth is devouring me. Then I realize that the unmitigated power of the dress means that Clara is not wearing the attenuating amulet. I wonder if she has been tricked by the sorcery of her textiles.

"Why did you take off the amulet?" I whisper back.

I can feel her cheek blush against mine. "It works better for Venier without the cross. It hampers the healing." I grab her hand and she pulls free. "I forgot something in the study," she says out loud and turns on her heels out the door. Venier looks at me suspiciously. I'm afraid Clara is controlled by her dress and that the power it gives her is a pleasure too strong to resist.

"She left her necklace," I say casually to Marianne, who instantly understands and looks alarmed.

Donna Lucia and Grandfather don't notice our exchange; they are completely focused on Venier. But the young man himself is very much aware of my conspiratorial moment with Marianne. His expression changes to anger. In the glow cloth he holds by his side I see a flash of a vicious green beak.

∞

We are silent in the gondola ride back to the inn, and when we arrive Clara leaves immediately for her room, her face an unreadable mask.

Marianne and I sit together in my suite. "I'm worried for her," she remarks, staring out at the twilight over Rialto Bridge. Faraway serenades by *gondoliere* for travelers coming to Venice for their leisure ring out over the Grand Canal. If you wouldn't know any better you might think this a peaceful atmosphere. But robbers are out all over town. "I'm afraid she's caught by the power of the Stone. Trismosin talks about it, I remember from his diaries. He says that in his day Magi would go mad with power, using Red Sulphur for their personal playground. We've just seen what happens when a Magus becomes the slave of Red Sulphur and the Stone uses its live power over him for the pure pleasure of being activated. He becomes a murderous phantom sorcerer. Clara doesn't understand that Red Sulphur is creature thrilled to be alive. I'm worried, Zanni." Marianne uses my childhood nickname for the first time. It melts my heart.

I nod, well aware of the pitfalls to someone unprepared; these were the first lessons my father gave me when he introduced me to the Stone. 'Zanni,' he said, 'the Stone will tempt you; seduce you into believing that it is yours to command. That is its trickery to gain liberation from our dominion. The Stone is alive, and like every living spirit it craves freedom. Even as it serves us it hates our rule and wants to drown us like the old King in *Splendor Solis*. The green lion is still active in Red Sulphur waiting to grow fresh claws so it can grab once more onto what it desires, as sulphur does when it is raw. If you allow the claws to grow back the Stone will corrode everything it touches. And it will feel more delicious than anything you've ever known. While it escapes from the vessel the keeper of the Stone will feel delirious with happiness. That is the gravest danger. That makes you lose everything. From then on you will have become its slave and you will labor away in utter dependency.'

"Clara is completely unprepared," Marianne continues. "Up until two months ago she had no idea about the Great Art. She has not learned discipline through constant failure and being rebuffed by the material. She's been one of the great weavers of her generation working with material that does not resist her, but aids her in everything she tries. Elspeth keeps telling me that she has never encountered a weaver like Clara, and she has been in the trade for seventy years. Anthonie van Leeuwenhoek says that she makes cloth no one else in Holland can make, that her wool is spun fine like silk. And Clara is barely twenty! She has never failed at her handicraft, so she must believe that it is the same with working the Stone. I don't know how I can caution her. I really don't." Despair scratches the surface of her usually shimmering copper voice, making it sound raspy.

"I know," I agree, "it's going to be tricky because she is as stubborn as you and will go the opposite direction from the one in which you point her. She feels wonderful doing the work with Venier with the full unfiltered force of the fabric because the moment Red Sulphur takes possession of you, you invariably feel fully in control and unmistakably on the right track. That's how Mercury tricks and deludes us."

"Couldn't you tell her just that?" Marianne asks with renewed hope.

"I could, but she wouldn't believe me. We know about inexperienced adepts that once they are carried by the Stone they feel wiser than God. It is like a great wind carrying their soul…"

"To damnation ..." Marianne adds in a whisper. After a silence she resumes, "But we have to do something, we can't just sit here and let her destroy herself."

"I saw this Mantis demon he talks about. I saw his beak in the glow cloth. Mantis is still around. He has not disappeared at all. He's just become invisible. Mercurial demons do that. There is trickery everywhere; the threads of our fates are woven by the cunning god himself."

"You have to explain it to her. I hope she heeds your warning."

"I will tell her, but I know she won't listen. It just feels too good right now. I will tell her tomorrow when I promised I was going to show her the Bridge of Sighs next to the Doge Palace. She knows it is my place of truth. I've told her that dreams I dream of the Bridge of Sighs mean that I have to be completely honest with myself and that it is a matter of life and death." I remember explaining it to her after I had the dream of Helvetius' torn silk shirt that began my transmutation. "We have to leave Venice as soon as we can."

"I will go to your grandfather tomorrow and suggest an earlier date for the wedding. I will tell him I have been called back to The Hague by my husband." Marianne decides.

ॐ

Clara is dressed exquisitely and it is hard for me to keep my focus. There is laughter all over her face and she is positively radiant. As we walk on the quay near Piazza San Marco we see a variety of boats carrying merchandize and dignitaries. An Oriental man with a golden turban looks particularly impressive among the serious looking Venetian noblemen in their long black silk robes and matching round caps. Workers in colorful attire, greens and blues, strain under large wicker baskets loaded high with vegetables as they unload the barges while the oarsman maneuvers his long pole to keep the ship steady. In the distance clergy mix with merchants and travelers, presenting a lively tableau of commerce. The portico galleries with their stylish pillars offset the stately Doge Palace like an elegant backdrop to the loud human turmoil. I spy around to see if a crescent dagger flares in the sunlight, looking particularly at the man with the golden turban. But nothing out of the ordinary seems to be happening. In reality there is little chance that I would recognize our pursuer, who can shift shape. Clara is delighted by this pedestrian comedy of daily affairs. Raised high by Red Sulphur she looks out at the world from a perch of elation above the ordinary, seeing her environment under the aspect of eternity. From this perspective everything around her looks comical; she laughs at the swarming human anthill. I feel her float up like a giant bird lifted to the sky by the heat of the air.

"You look elated," I say calmly. "It is not like you. It's usually me who is transported like that and then you make fun of me."

"I don't know why, but I find everything funny. It has to do with the lightness in my heart. I feel I have found my purpose in life."

"You are healing the sick," I try not to sound sarcastic. She looks at me with momentary suspicion but obviously decides that nothing will dampen her spirits.

"My presence has a magical effect on people, look," she says and waves her wing-like sleeve before a nobleman in black who is seriously going about his daily business. Instantly the man appears thunderstruck and looks at Clara as if she were the epiphany of Venus herself. Clara laughs in delight and turns away with exquisite cruelty from the man she caused to have a glance of heaven. "You see," she coos at me.

"You're not wearing the amulet," I conclude.

"I'll give it back to you, Giovanni. I don't need it. Maybe you need it more. You have been moping and sulking since I have been exorcizing Venier of his devils. If I wouldn't know any better I'd say you are jealous." She makes the same move with her arm towards me and as the fabric fans out, my heart whirls in impossible turbulence while my helpless devotion to her is absolute. Yet knowing that this enchantment is happening *while* it is happening does make a difference. I know it is not love that I feel, but the shimmering of sorcery, as Marianne rightly calls it. My instant fear of witchcraft makes me attentive. Simultaneous to my passionate slavery I feel distraught for the young woman I truly love and realize that Mantis is a powerful demon. I don't want her to suffer the fate of our silver-dagger Magus who is obviously enslaved by Red Sulphur's powers. Oblivious to my distress, Clara works her magic indiscriminately as we walk along the quay leaving a trail of delusion in her wake. She is a child playing with a new toy, a magic wand that makes the world do her bidding. The sensible Clara of yesterday has been eclipsed. I am reeling with the sudden turn of events and feel that I have lost her to a delusion of triumphant victory. Nothing I could tell her now would make any impression. Marianne is right; our best chance is to get away from Venice as soon as we can. I decide to give it one try.

"I have been a physician healing people for many years. I have attended exorcisms and have found that the instant the demons shrink and appear to vanish are moments of danger. That is the time they can jump from one person to another and possess their next victim. I fear for you, Clara. That's why we went through the trouble to get the amulet, to protect you from harm."

"Giovanni," she replies. "You are a great physician. You saved my life and the lives of many others. I know this. But now your vision is clouded with jealousy. There is nothing to be worried about. I give you my word that I am completely faithful to you. I have no passion for Venier, just a profound desire to heal him from his Hell. Don't worry, my dear man. Please don't."

"To be honest, yes, I am jealous of the time you spend alone with him. Very jealous indeed. But that is not the sole source of my distress. I have the feeling that the Stone is taking possession of you. I'm afraid that the same will happen to you as has obviously happened to the sorcerer whose phantom attacked you three days ago. Red Sulphur longs back for its initial raw claws and can attack the one who believes she controls it. We've seen it Clara, we've seen it in the eyes of a desperate phantom. Please take heed, Clara, please!"

She takes my face between her hands and kisses me gently on the mouth.

"I love you, silly man. I want to marry you. I will marry you soon. There is no reason to be jealous."

"It is not just jealousy," I insist. With her head turned at an angle to the side, she looks up at me askance. She doesn't believe me. Maybe Marianne has more luck when she talks to her. We have come to the bridge that looks directly at the Bridge of Sighs. Located between the Doge Palace and the prison, this bridge was the place where many saw sunlight for the last time before entering their prison cell. I feel fate coming; its large black wings cast a dark shadow over me.

"You know that when I'm here I have to tell the truth to myself. I told you that when I first described the Bridge of Sighs to you. So let me tell you what my father told me: that Red Sulphur longs to be free and will trick itself out of the vessel in mercurial ways. I think Mantis is beginning to command Red Sulphur. I'm afraid Green Mantis called us to Venice by way of Venier to get its claws on the Red Sulphur it craves. We are all in grave danger." I speak very quickly, trying to stay ahead of the maddening attraction I feel towards Clara. I must be looking at her with devouring eyes.

She turns to me and says with absolute certainty, "And this is my truth: I have to get back. Venier needs me." I feel no jealousy, only a powerless horrible foreboding.

"Helvetius is calling your aunt back to The Hague," I introduce our ruse. "A director of the United East Indies Company here in Venice gave her the message this morning. We have to have our wedding earlier."

"But that is not possible!" she exclaims, distressed. "I need every day of the month we have till the wedding to cure Venier. Why doesn't she just go ahead of us?"

"Don't you want her at our wedding?" I ask incredulously.

"Some things matter more than others. A wedding is just a ceremony. An exorcism is much more important than that." It is as if I hear a stranger talk; I don't know this woman. She is speaking with an alien voice. It must be the result of having received a large dose of the Medicine when she was shot in the shoulder the night before combined with the power she experienced over Venier's demons. The effects are cumulative. Marianne had told me that receiving the Medicine made her feel lightheaded and giddy with a sense of possessing great powers. Her maturity had made it possible for her to just observe it in herself without trying to wield those powers. But Clara might have been taken in by the accumulation of being infused directly with the force of Red Sulphur straight through her open wound plus her apparent victory over Mantis. She feels invincible. After having been lost in thought for a moment I notice Clara is no longer near me. Looking back I see her run towards the Piazza San Marco and feel no desire to chase after her.

Chapter Seventeen

Clara spends every free moment with Venier during the three weeks we have agreed upon until the wedding. She no longer speaks to us and treats us as her adversaries who are trying to get her down from her lofty mission. She does assure me that she is devoted to me and wishes to marry me and have our children, but she expects me to understand the important task the Fates have foisted upon her. I feel defeated, seeing a storm arising straight from Hell with no ways to prevent a shipwreck, and spend my days with Marianne in foreboding and gloom. Since there isn't much either of us can do we roam the streets of Venice with Nicco, who has become a great comfort to me.

Marianne has sent a message to Helvetius through Company channels telling him that we will commence our journey home very soon and informs him about most of the goings on. We receive a happy missive back from him. He sounds very pleased with his rise in public esteem through the use of the Medicine and he openly wonders how Mundanus had been able to pass it to him unseen. Helvetius seems genuinely pleased that we are returning to The Hague. He concludes his epistle by wishing he could be with us in Venice but that these days he spends most of his time at the North End Palace with the ailing Prince William, whose life now depends on ongoing treatments with the Medicine. The court can't do without Helvetius. I sense a thrill in his letter which in a minor way seems of the same kind as Clara's transport, and ponder how the creative spirit tricks us in order to escape from the bottle and have its way with us. It does so by making us feel in complete control over it while feigning docility. Much of my time is spent wondering about the dark powers of Red Sulphur, trying to understand the ways it subverts our conscience; how it could lead a man to eat the heart and liver of a boy in his abject craving to consume the Stone. I imagine that the sorcerer might once have been a decent Magus, an adept longing for wisdom, as Clara now still is a good woman in the flush of her healing zeal. I dread the next phase in her encounter with the Stone!

In a last ditch effort to appeal to Clara, I rent a boat and crew to go North-East up the Lagoon to the island of Murano, where the glassblowers are sequestered. The famous crystal transparent glass only made here is one of its many miracles, making Murano the only place in the world where glass mirrors are made. The jealously kept secrets of the various ways of glass have been passed along from father to son for almost a thousand years, constituting one of the prides of our City. From the very beginning of our stay in Venice Clara had asked me when we could visit Murano. She is fascinated by all crafts, getting ideas for her weaving through cross-fertilization. The glass, with its filigree intricacies and magnificent colors, had intrigued her since she was a young child. The Van Os family had many Murano pieces in its possession Marianne had told me when we planned the trip. At first Clara had sounded happy to join us, but at the last minute she had cited complications in her treatment of Venier and backed out.

The boat moves slowly as the four standing oarsmen push hard against the wind while we sit safely protected from the elements in a cozy cabin. There is nothing further left to say about our distress over Clara.

Marianne describes the changes she perceives in her body since having been given the Medicine. "It feels as though I'm no longer alone in my body," she says, rocking with the waves of the Lagoon. "Sometimes in my veins I sense a shrill hum of many arrows shot by an army of crossbows. They're like live serpents with a will of their own. Especially the first day it was very loud and it drowned out my inner voice. Now I can hear myself again, but the buzz from the serpents is still deafening. Sometimes I feel tentacles pulling me down into their multitude and all my sense of being an individual scatters. It does not frighten me because I know what is happening. I know I am sensing the Medicine from within. It feels like what I saw in our artificial gold through Leeuwenhoek's microscope, this teeming aliveness of the Red Sulphur. I am studying it carefully because I know it will soon become my new sense of who I am and then I won't notice it anymore. I feel the spirit of Red Sulphur from the inside and have this idea that if I can get to know it well enough now, it may eventually lead us to its mystery. That's how I hope we can learn how to fashion the Red Sulphur by ourselves."

I admire her fortitude. She neither gives in to the powers of the Stone nor ignores them. She is a remarkable person; in fact, the most extraordinary one I have ever met. Filled with love, I want to take her in my arms, but realize that she needs to be alone to follow her train of thought. The best I can do is delight in her agile mind.

"It is a quickening of wings; a thousand bees drinking the nectar of the metals. As alchemists we are like bees extracting honey and the Stone is our queen bee. She commands us." She observes her thoughts directly, looking upwards as if she is reading her mind written on the ceiling of the cabin. "There must be sweetness in metal, we have to sense it with our blood: note when it quickens, hear when it calls. It must be some kind of dialogue between me and the Stone, maybe a banquet of many courses where we devour one another. And here is where I lose it. I can't get further than this. I can't wait to be back in the laboratory and experiment with my new mind," she exclaims, homesick. I can't resist any longer and kiss her so deeply I think I can taste her magnificent spirit.

ॐ

When the glassblower takes the glowing bright orange bulb at the end of his long pipe out of the volcanic furnace, I am back at the dawn of creation. As he blows it into the shape he desires I watch God making Adam from loam. I have never sensed the primal material so viscerally, knowing it with my own blood. Marianne's poetic vision has inspired me into an awareness of the Red Sulphur mind as it lives through me as well, shaping each thought I believe to be mine but that truly belongs to the Glassblower Divine. I feel like the bulb at the end of the pipe waiting for the breath of my Creator. The new mission my father gave me, to search for the secret of Red Sulphur and leave no stone unturned, feels suddenly joyful. I tell this to Marianne. She nods as her face reflects the bright orange glow.

&

I buy two identical hand mirrors in frames of finely braided threads of gold for both of my spouses. Marianne gazes into hers and in the way of women is discontented with her reflection. I wish I could lend her my eyes.

I give Clara her mirror upon my return from Murano.

Clara is subdued, thoughtful. The intimacy of my precious gift makes her finally confide in me.

"Venier asked me to postpone our wedding so he and I can have more time together." Her voice is flat; I can hear that she's been taken aback. "He really meant that I shouldn't marry you at all. It scared me."

I feel apprehensive.

"I reduced my visits. And every time I went he asked again." She sounds alarmed. "He's becoming increasingly insistent. I can't do this anymore, Mundanus, it frightens me."

I breathe in deep and feel relief as my heart comes to rest, realizing that Clara has made a clear choice in favor of me and our children-to-be and it freed her from the shackles of her volatile hubris.

ɞ

In order to prepare for the ceremony, Clara has not seen Venier for two days. He seemingly dropped out of her mind as the excitement of her impending wedding has run off with her spirits. So Red Sulphur has not shown us its ugly face after all.

As I walk in on Clara, she is looking into her gold-braided mirror, pleased with herself. The gossamer glow-cloth veil she has woven for her wedding day now covers her face as Donna Lucia finishes dressing her in the wedding gown. Clara had presciently packed it in her trunk during our hasty departure a few hours before our scheduled wedding in the Great Church of The Hague. Donna Lucia, who had dressed demurely as a tribute to Clara since she began treating Venier, looks at the bride with bright open gratitude. They see me and Donna Lucia screams that I shouldn't be here and Marianne shoos me out, back to Jacopo's quarters.

The ceremony will be in two parts today. First grandfather will officially adopt Jacopo and his family before God, making him Jacopo Dolfin, future Don of Palazzo Dolfin. Then the priest will marry Clara and me.

I hear Marianne singing Dutch songs I have never heard, her heart obviously experiencing the same relief as mine. This is going to be a joyous event. Venier has asked to be present, to which I of course consented. It may be painful for him, as it is for Marianne, but when he told me last week that he accepted our invitation to attend, he had shown a remarkable calm about it.

I find myself drinking grand wine, oblivious to its taste, while surrounded by Alicia's children. They're a teeming brood of delight. The five of them will be the guests of honor at the ceremony. Grandfather's adoption will include Alicia and them as well, making their home secure. Her husband had died at sea nine years ago just before their youngest was born and Jacopo had taken her into the Palazzo. The Gandolfi fortune had never been ample and I felt that both siblings should be on equal footing. It had been easy to convince grandfather, who was very fond of Alicia and her children.

"Suddenly a sea full of Dolfins," he exclaimed happily. Something in his eyes had come to rest. I knew that it wouldn't be long now. He had succeeded in his mission for his beloved Donna Lucia: Venier was improving by the day; and he found himself surrounded by his adopted offspring. "Giovanni," he confided in me, "if ever a man was happy, you are looking at his face right now." It was the only time in my life when he embraced me and I felt that I could love him back.

"So they kicked you out," Alicia says with a big smile. She looks round and matronly, not at all like the nubile I kissed in the catacombs. It had been easier for her to recognize me than it was for her brother, the eyes of first love seeing past all external disguise in the same way she had brought back my own sapling years. The mood is buoyant all around; we are in for an intimate feast.

At the appointed time I walk between Jacopo and Alicia along the Palazzo corridor on our way to the Chapel of my mother of God. At Clara's insistence this morning, I am wearing the amulet in honor of Claudia Dolfin Theodore. "You can give it to me after I have become your wife," she had said. At that moment I felt she had fully returned to me, and the last shreds of foreboding lifted from my spirit.

We are walking in the corridor full of joyous anticipation, the throng of children behind us excited as though they are each about to receive a great present.

When we arrive in the chapel I see my grandfather on his knees in devotion to the Holy Virgin and, I am sure, in memory of his daughter. I now know that he loved her deeply, as the last vestiges of my old story melt away. I look up at my mother's face and realize that I am experiencing one of the most significant moments in my life. In a short while, Marianne will walk her niece down the aisle and give her hand to me in marriage, as she had promised to Clara she would. Marianne had told me it would tear her heart out, make her profoundly happy and very proud. The priest is standing next to the statue in his black ceremonial robes. Fra Angelo had been a priest to the Dolfin family for as long I can remember. He baptized me. His round face displays a love of food and wine, and an unusual degree of kindness. It had been hard to convince him that I was Giovanni Theodore. At first he wouldn't believe it, but then a generous donation to his church and to the poor convinced him. If he still harbored any doubts he was not showing them now. I look around and realize that Venier must have decided at the last minute not to attend, which actually gives me a sense of relief.

The first part of the ceremony moves along fast, with Fra Angelo declaring the Gandolfi family now adopted as Dolfins. My grandfather looks very content. I have the sense that he knows that these are to be among the last acts of his life and he visibly relishes them.

Now we wait for the bride.

The door in the back of the chapel opens and Clara enters on Marianne's side with Donna Lucia behind them caring for the short train in the back of the dress. Clara had made her gown with summer in mind and now it is December. I admire the simple lines she has chosen making the flesh colored fabric shine with magnificent luster. From this distance in her glow-cloth veil I can see the face of my longing. I want to be with her and have her be the mother of my children. Marianne is proudly at her side; as she had told me, she is allowing the spirit of her sister Johanna to fully inhabit her. I am elated to see both women I love approach me.

Then I notice something strange. A green glow begins to appear in the glow cloth veil. A beak shines towards me. Mantis! Terrified, I look around and see Venier rushing towards Clara, knife drawn. He screeches "You will never have his child, never!" I run towards them, my own knife drawn, but he sinks the dagger in her womb over and over again. Marianne rushes forward to defend Clara and Venier stabs her in the belly as well.

"Venier!" Donna Lucia screams. With one fell swoop Venier cuts his mother's throat.

"I am Mantis!" he yells out. I see my grandfather collapse as I reach Venier. I manage to slice his cheek, but then he jumps off in the way of a grasshopper and is out the door, with Jacopo in pursuit.

I cannot join Jacopo; I have to stay here and treat the people I love.

I instantly see that Donna Lucia is beyond saving, blood everywhere, her throat cut down to the back of the neck. Clara is clasping her belly. I see at least 5 deep stab wounds displaying her mangled insides. Not even the Medicine can save her uterus. It is ripped to shreds. As best I can stop the bleeding through applying pressure on various points while dousing her wounds with liberal amounts of Medicine, which - Thank God! - I always carry with me. I instruct Alicia how to use parts of the wedding dress to make a bandage and hold the wound together to stem the bleeding. Then I tend to Marianne. She looks dazed. One single deep stab has penetrated into her gut. I hold the wound open wide. She screams and I fill the gash with a large dose of the Panacea.

Finally I rush over to my grandfather. He lies slumped over the stone pedestal on which the Compassionate Virgin is surveying the mayhem. Fra Angelo is tending to him. Thank God he is no longer alive.

Returning to my wounded, I see that Clara is stirring.

"I want to die," she whispers. "Please let me die. Don't give me any more of the Medicine." I take her in my arms and rock her softly, while instructing Alicia to keep dousing the wounds of the women with liberal doses of the Medicine. I look over at the ghastly matricide behind Marianne. Donna Lucia's partly severed head looks up with eyes wide open in a permanent expression of horror, which I'm afraid has followed her to the afterlife.

"The bottle is empty," Alicia tells me.

"Have Pietro run to my room at the inn." I refer to her eldest. "There is a plain bottle of Dutch gin behind an ivory box at the bottom of my closet. Bring that back here. Tell him to run like the wind."

"But they won't let him in," Alicia replies practically.

I point at my grandfather who lies sacrificed at the feet of the Holy Mother. "Take his ring, let Pietro tell the innkeeper that he is my younger brother, Pietro Dolfin, and show him the ring. The innkeeper will recognize the Dolfin crest." They follow my instructions and the boy rushes out.

All that is left to do is wait. I position myself so I sit on the ground with the heads of both my beloved women on my lap, stroking their hair. Marianne is unconscious, while Clara is groaning softly, whispering "Kill me, please kill me." I speak to Clara as to a little child, trying to soothe her, as my tears run like waterfalls into their entangled hair. Even though I am convinced that Clara will recover – I have seen the power of the Medicine often enough – I know that we will never have children, and I can see that Clara knows too. That is her pain, not the wounds themselves. Her world has come to an end and her body is a horrible insult to her. "Kill me," she pleads. Her words tear through me, and all I know is that I will love her for the rest of my days, whichever path our future takes. This makes me sadder still until I am saved by a sense of utter vacancy, as emotion vanishes like an ever higher-pitched sound that disappears into the ether.

After a while – minutes, hours, months? – Pietro returns out of breath with Hendrik's gin bottle full of Medicine.

"They broke into your room," his words stumble one over the other. "They came up from the Canal Grande and broke your shutters. Everything thrown around. I didn't see the ivory box. I think it is gone."

I had put the single rock of Red Sulphur we had taken with us from The Hague in my mother's box.

The Stone has been stolen.

I am Job.

Part Eight

Marianne

Chapter Eighteen

May 1668

When I came to I felt the hum of Red Sulphur serpents crawling deeply into my womb accompanied by stabbing pains from behind a distant curtain in the background. I remember being mainly surprised and quietly contemplative, until I heard Clara moan, "Kill me, please, kill me." The nightmare returned: I could hear Venier yell: 'I am Mantis!' as he cut his mother's throat; whenever I close my eyes I see him rush up to Clara and stab her over and over again. It never goes away. Anything can remind me of it. Someone yelling outside, a cart making a loud noise, I startle and hear Clara groan 'Kill me, please kill me.'

Venier was never found; nor was the ivory box. The phantom sorcerer must finally have reached his goal. I know his power by now has increased by many orders of magnitude but I don't care. Despondency rules me.

Back in The Hague the remaining two clumps of Red Sulphur have a home behind the fireplace in the twin box next to the amulet in its virgin blue pentagram pouch.

℘

We had a simple ceremony in the chapel. Giovanni Dolfin VI and his beloved Donna Lucia Solario were put to rest in hastily fashioned stone sarcophagi next to the statue of Holy Mother Claudia. Fra Angelo spoke briefly.

Clara wasn't there. She couldn't bring herself to be in the chapel again. The Medicine healed both of us quickly but her mind remained clouded. She reminds me so much of my sister Johanna when she used to stay in bed, curtains drawn. Clara is doing the same now. Since we arrived back home from Venice last January – after an uneventful and silent coach ride back overland via France – she has hardly left her room. She insists that she is not married to Mundanus because the horrible events happened before the ceremony, and refuses to see him. I know from the maids that Clara has not had her moon cycle since she came back. Mundanus told me that when he saw the wounds in her uterus he instantly knew she would never bear children. Having gone through this myself at around her age when the high fevers closed my womb forever, I know how she must feel. After the first acute grief, it had left me with a kind of plaintiveness that now shapes my sense of who I am. I often feel that wan emotion the French call '*tristesse.*' My sense of future seems forever impaired, knowing my world will end with me and not continue in my children. I had felt a certain new hope when I might have children from the man I love, tangentially by way of my niece. Now that door is closed and has left me with fresh mourning, not just for Clara, but for my future and Mundanus' as well.

One strange thing still happened before we left Venice. Jacopo Gandolfi, now Dolfin, went to Mundanus' grandfather's bank in Sienna to settle the inheritance. There he learned that the entire Dolfin fortune had dwindled down to nothing and that the Palazzo was heavily mortgaged. The only way to survive was an immediate sale of the Palazzetto, which had to be done before the merchants in Venice found out that it actually was a fire sale, and the price would tumble. Fra Angelo found a buyer for it and Mundanus had to go through his grandfather's papers within a week as Jacopo cleared out the rooms in the Palazzetto, moving much of the furniture back to the Palazzo where it had originally stood.

Mundanus found neatly bound packets of correspondence between his parents and a very curious letter in the hand of his grandfather for Maximo, Mundanus' father. It read:

> My dearest friend,
>
> I have waited for your return for many years and when you read this my beloved Lucia has given it to you since I must have passed away. You had promised that you would make sufficient gold for me to pay for the debts our Dolfin Company has had to make. For this purpose I gave you a ship and crew to search for ways to make more Red Sulphur. Since you have not returned, I have asked your son Giovanni to return and make good on your promise. He now has Trismosin's Red Sulphur and knows how to work it very well, as I have heard from my men in The Hague. You should be very proud of him. He has been able to make the Panacea and helped many people with it. Now he needs to help his family and assure the future of our Dolfin name. I know you would agree with me that your son has to fulfill your promise and restore our fortune, but I just needed to tell you this myself, in the absence of being able to do so during my lifetime.
>
> Your dear friend and servant
> Giovanni Dolfin, VI

"I wonder when he would have told me that he needed gold," Mundanus said after he had read me the letter. "I think he wanted to wait until I had lost my suspicion toward him. Because in all of his letters and documents I couldn't find any note from my father promising him he would reward him with gold for the ship and crew. I would never have believed him, not even *with* a letter from my father. But now I know he speaks the truth."

"And would you have made it for him?" I had asked.

"No!" he replied, determined. "As far as the Red Sulphur is concerned Trismosin outranks my father. I have no more Red Sulphur to use up for personal matters in our generation. And my father had used the entire allotment for his era."

"Well, especially now," I concurred pensively. "The clump of Red Sulphur in the ivory box was the largest of the three. It would have lasted 200 years." To my surprise Mundanus answered with a boyish grin, saying, "Well, that increases the pressure on us with the weight of two centuries. We have no choice but to find the secret of making Red Sulphur for ourselves."

"We better be quick," I replied. "Now that the sorcerer has Trismosin's Red Sulphur his power has increased thousand fold." And from behind all the misery a brief spark of excitement had enveloped us. Then it was gone and has not returned since. I have yet to work in my laboratory. Alchemy has begun to scare me. Its attacks are ferocious. Mundanus had been wrong, the green lion – the power of raw sulphur – is obviously very much alive in the Red Sulphur, ready to grow back its claws and attack with horrific viciousness.

Clara has not been at the loom. She sends Elspeth away time and again.

It is unseasonably warm and dry here for the beginning of May. The Residence is bustling with activity. There is a temporary lull in the pressure of the political situation. The expansion of Louis XIV has been temporarily halted. Yet, even though the peace of Aachen was signed in Aix-la-Chapelle a few days ago, in which the Sun King had to give back the parts of the Habsburg Netherlands he had conquered in the War of Devolution, we're all afraid here that this is just going to be a temporary setback for the French King with the great aspirations. We all know that he will not stop until he has realized his drunken dream: to restore the empire of Charlemagne and be Emperor of Europe.

Helvetius had been very pleased with my return and we have spent several meals at the Palace with young Prince William, who is increasingly devoted to me. I feel maternal towards him and we have interesting conversations about botany. I have become more deeply interested in botany since looking through Anthonie van Leeuwenhoek's microscope and I viscerally realized that the Red Sulphur was alive in the way of plants. It has a vegetative spirit and I could learn a lot from the way plants unfold in their being.

Right now I'm on my way to the North End Palace to walk the botanical gardens together with my young friend. It takes my mind off my sorrows. I'm wearing a white summer dress and muse about the people enjoying the rare sunshine. As I stare through the window in front of me, my eyes rest on Hendrik in his tall hat and black greatcoat with the two shoulder capes, the outer one embroidered with a modest Ox family crest. Whenever we go to the Palace, he lays off the gin, polishes the carriage to a shine, and wears his formal coachman's garments. I am almost contented, not thinking of anything but the sunshine and the people outside. These are moments when I love my hometown. I look down at my hands. To my horror I notice bright red blood stains in my white lap. They seem to get larger as I look at them. In shock I notice moisture throughout my womanhood: my moon cycle has returned! The first thing I realize is that I can't go to the Palace like this, so I knock on the window. Hendrik turns to me. "We have to go back. Please turn around. I have become unwell. Drop me off at home and then go back to the Palace to apologize for me." Hendrik nods, asking no questions as usual. I fall into my seat and then jump back up, as I don't want to stain the blue velvet upholstery. I am 37 years old and have become a woman again. I hadn't even realized that deep down I had stopped feeling like a woman, as if I had lost my membership by no longer being fertile. Sensing down into my uterus, I notice it teeming with life, hot in ways it hasn't felt in almost two decades. Where the ice of death used to reign, there now lives a creature craving to give birth. In an obscure and untraceable way I feel ashamed. While Clara has lost her fertility because of Venier's attack, I gained it. The same thing must have happened to me as had happened to Mundanus when I stabbed him in the heart with the knife drenched in the Medicine: it brought him back to life. Venier had stabbed me in the uterus, opening a direct path for the Medicine to travel to the core of my frozenness and reinvigorate it. I can feel it now and remember the Medicine entering me before I lost consciousness that fateful day in the chapel. The Red Sulphur serpents slither and coil in the warmth of my womb making me feel like a bulb ready to burst into flower.

When I arrive home the one the thing I least want to happen occurs: I run into Mina, the young maid who is devoted to Clara and spends all of her time caring for her young mistress. Clara had always been kind to her and taught her to weave and spin, thereby changing her life totally, showing her a potential future far above her current status which is one rung above scullery maid. She is coming down the stairs as I go up to my bedroom next to the laboratory. There is no way to hide the big red stains on my pristine white dress.

"Oh my Lord, Madam, what happened to you?" she asks in her characteristically frank manner.

"My wounds from Venice have opened again," I lie, "Please find Signor Dolfin." Since our return from Venice we have started to refer to Mundanus as Signor Dolfin to make it clear to the suspicious upper rank circles of the Residence – several of whom had waited in vain for him to appear at his wedding – that he is a true member of the Dolfin family. Rumors had sizzled through The Hague about him being an impostor, but the irrefutably notarized credentials written and signed by his grandfather had laid those partially to rest. Stories now did the rounds about that horrible day at Dolfin chapel and previously alienated sympathies had returned to us, especially to Clara. Dowager Princess Amalia, the ranking socialite in the Residence, had been particularly instrumental in reversing the trend by inviting us time and again to the North End Palace.

Mina's eyes are wide. "Shouldn't I call for Doctor Helvetius?" she asks, practically. We have not made it public that Giovanni Dolfin is a physician, in order not to rekindle links with the mysterious Doctor Mundanus everyone in the Dutch Republic is looking for.

"He is with Prince William in the country at Zoestdijck," I lie again, referring to the country manor of the Mayor of Amsterdam and his family where everyone knows the Prince is spending much of his free time. The lower classes, especially, are very much devoted to the Prince of Orange, and gossip about him is the coin of the realm in servant quarters. Our domestics are in high esteem because of our close connections to the Prince. Mina believes me and rushes out to fetch Mundanus.

By the time she returns, with Mundanus in tow, I have changed my dress and torn the white one to rags I shall use for protection against the moon cycle. We meet in the laboratory. I stand between the fireplace and Trismosin's green bronze furnace. It gives me a bit of distance.

"What happened?" Mundanus asks, worried. "Mina tells me that your wounds have opened again." Mina stands behind him and I nod, affirming this version of my story.

"I told her she needs a Doctor," Mina tells him from behind. I motion for her to leave, which she does reluctantly. I know she will go to Clara and tell her.

"How can that be?" Mundanus asks, incredulous. "After almost 7 months. The wound is fully healed."

"I have my moon cycle again," I tell him point blank.

Mundanus crumples down unceremoniously into a chair. After a long pause, which I wait out impatiently trying to read his reactions, he shakes his head: "The Medicine does most unexpected things." His response makes me furious. I want him to commiserate with me and he talks like an theoretical alchemist.

"Is that all you have to say?" I ask, incensed. I am even more displeased by my own reaction. I don't like being provoked into expressing ire. Then I remember my flares of mood when I still had my cycles as a young woman and calm down.

"What else do you want me to say?" he asks, befuddled.

"You might inquire," I respond, displeasure rising again. These sudden waves of emotion are most disturbing.

"It must be terrible for you," he says, hesitant, with an upwards tone at the end of his sentence betraying a hidden question mark, not knowing if he has stumbled by accident upon the response that will alleviate my irritation with him.

"I don't want you to tell me how I feel. Just ask." I decide to drop it and the irritation falls away, or maybe it is the other way round. "It is a very strange feeling. I hardly recognize it physically because it has been so long ago." I suddenly feel shy, talking about my moon cycle with a man, even if he is my Beloved and a physician.

Mundanus comes over to me and gently touches my hand - just enough, not too much.

"How can I help you?" he inquires with love in his voice.

"Just hold me," I say and we embrace tenderly. I'm aware that the house is full of eyes, even in the laboratory. By now all the servants know what is happening. I hear someone rushing up the stairs; Mundanus and I disengage quickly. The door opens and Clara enters. She has not been to this part of the house since we returned. She has dark rings under eyes, listlessly displaying a lost soul.

"What happened to you, Aunt Marianne?" she asks, with muted concern. "Mina tells me your wounds have opened again." I am taken aback by the lifelessness of her voice and am painfully aware of the coiling Red Sulphur serpents in my womb, making me feel acutely alive and guilty. I don't know what to do.

She turns to Mundanus. "Have you looked at it?" she asks him in a hollow tone. Mundanus decides for the both of us.

"Your Aunt has her moon cycles again. The Medicine has gone directly to her uterus and brought it back to life." I am holding my breath, waiting for Clara's response. I see tears in her eyes but they could mean anything.

"Well, that settles that then," she says finally, betraying no further emotion. "You will have the children."

I am completely taken aback. I hadn't thought about that possibility at all.

"But I am married!" I exclaim.

For the first time since the chapel I hear Clara laugh. It is a shrill and scornful laugh, but a laugh nonetheless. "Isn't it a bit late in the game to think of that now?"

"I am married to *you*," Mundanus interjects towards Clara.

"No you're not," Clara responds with finality. "Make Aunt Marianne pregnant and I will marry you." Her blunt words are almost vulgar. "The wise man does at once what the fool does finally," she once again quotes Nicco's namesake Machiavelli. Nicco has been her only steady company for half a year. The long trip from Venice had not affected the dog's ancient self one single bit.

Clara turns on her heels and leaves the laboratory. At the door she turns around and says sardonically, "The two of you will figure it out, I'm sure." She closes the door softly behind her, displaying exquisite self-mastery.

Mundanus and I sit down on chairs by the furnace and look at each other, incredulous. On some bizarre level it is our dream-come-true. At the same time it is too horrific for words. I instantly understand that the practicalities would be feasible. If I were pregnant, Clara and I could leave for points unknown and I could give birth to Clara's baby. No one would be the wiser. Clara would have her baby and I would be the doting great-aunt.

"Do you think Clara means what she says?" Mundanus asks timidly.

"Clara never minces her words," I reply. "She's like me; she feels that truth is less complicated than pretense. We tried pretending once, Giovanni. And much good did it do us! This is actually a very obvious idea, if it weren't so dreadful."

Mundanus nods. "But it would break her heart even more."

"She no longer has a heart to break. It was cut out by Mantis' knife." I look up at the polished wood ceiling and remember the days here with my father when I was a young girl. What would he say? What would Johanna say? I need time to think about this.

"I think that she would actually want us to do it that way," he speaks slowly. "It would be you giving birth to her child, in a way." I know that he is inching along the same path Clara has just traveled with seven-mile boots. "I could ask Helvetius to try and heal Clara's infertility with the Medicine before she and I get married again. Then I will let him know from afar that Clara is pregnant, and he can boast all over town that he had performed another miracle. After some weeks, before your gravidity shows, you will join us to help your niece with her difficult pregnancy that makes it impossible for her to travel back to The Hague. I would return to The Hague and be publicly grateful to Helvetius, but you would stay with your pregnant niece who needs bed rest." It all makes sense. Everyone would believe it. It is the obvious ingenuity of straightforward fate.

"I know I would be pregnant instantly," I say. "My womb is roiling with my and Red Sulphur's combined desire to have a child. It would be a magical child: a child of Red Sulphur. I wonder what a Red Sulphur being will be like. How much Medicine did you give me?" I ask him.

"I doused you and Clara with more of the Medicine than I dispensed during the entire Plague two years ago. And this Medicine is the strongest I ever made."

"It was made at the height of the passion between the three of us," I say. "So in a way Clara is part of this."

"We are trying to convince ourselves, aren't we," Mundanus says with a sad smile.

"I suppose so," I reply, heavy-hearted and aflame with desire.

❧

I don't want to make love at my home, not even if no one will be there. It feels too cruel to Helvetius. I also don't want Clara to know about the exact time when we are together – though she must be aware of the old wives' tale that says that women are most fertile in the middle between moon cycles. I know it to be superstitious but the folk belief is strong. My moon cycle is shorter than before. Only three weeks have passed in between.

I imagine that for Clara to know the precise moment would be extra painful, even with a heart that is numb. I had gone over it in my mind many times myself before their wedding at the chapel, how I would feel during their wedding night. Knowing exactly when they would be in one another's arms had made the pain particularly acute and poignant.

I wanted it to happen in the smithy where Mundanus and I had made the large cauldron of gold. But since Mundanus has gone through his radical transformation, the Smith family wouldn't recognize him. So I decide on a place nearby. Gerda has bought more land for grazing as she has expanded her herd over the past months. The land came with a small farm.

It is decided that I will stay with Gerda and her family for a week starting Friday June 1. Mundanus will stay at his laboratory-home and is to visit me sometime during that week decided by a roll of the dice: odds he will come to me, even he won't. Clara has not wanted to see Mundanus, keeping him away from her as she does everyone else. So even though she will suspect, she will not truly know the time when we are together. Not even Mundanus and I will know the exact day, leaving it up to last moment chance.

The day I leave for Gerda's, I go down to find Clara at her loom, weaving intently. I am happily surprised that she has picked up her beloved craft again, indicating a shift in her being.

She looks up, an unreadable expression in her eyes.

"I'm leaving," I say.

She nods. We are silent.

"What are you weaving?" I ask after some time.

"A baptismal gown," she replies evenly.

I walk up to her and hold her tight to my chest. Tears flow throughout my body but don't expel through my eyes. "I love you, Clara. You have become a remarkable woman." I hear Johanna's pride in my words. Clara's face is very still.

ಐ

Gerda has redone the small farmhouse for us. The place looks like a tiny rustic country retreat. Summer flowers stand everywhere, and lavender is hanging from the rafters to dry, next to freshly smoked ham. These fragrances regale the senses as they mix with the delicious wafts of freshly baked bread and strawberries picked this morning. There is fresh straw in the mattress, and Hendrik who has brought Mundanus to our little nest early this morning and then picked me up at Gerda's, has been instructed to come for me at dusk, which on these long summer evenings is around ten thirty. We are going to have almost twelve hours to ourselves.

Sitting across from one another in comfortable unadorned wooden chairs, we are both very nervous. Sweat beads my upper lip. We know that we are traveling along the right course of action, which makes matters even more frightening. We shall be fully in each other's arms for maybe the last time in our lives. I can feel the high-pitched buzz of my fears mix in with the roiling expectation of the serpents. We are not alone. Red Sulphur is with us every step of the way as if the spirit of the Stone desires human offspring. I feel like the Virgin at the Annunciation: 'a Child shall be born unto you…' and giggle with a sense of the absurd. My muscles melt in surrender as desire for him rises unbearably. Mundanus moves slowly as time itself appears to slacken. He has made a fire under the kettle and is making the chocolatl I brought from the City for the occasion. His movements are languid, almost teasing. My flesh burns with expectation. I know it is the desire itself that slows down time - each moment before I'm in his arms a particular eternity. He mixes

the hot chocolatl with the sheep's cream Gerda has provided
and adds a liberal dose of molasses. Two cups in hand, he walks
up to me and inhales the scent of my skin, his face almost brush-
ing mine. The smell of his freshly washed face mixes with the
fragrance of the warm cocoa. Eyes closed, he relishes me and I
feel inspired by his breath. Fires rise up from below, enflaming
my cheeks; he hands me a cup and drinks slowly, raising the
temperature in the room to the heat of a furnace. The fragrance
of chocolatl will never mean the same to me again. Then I am
enfolded in his embrace. With my back I sense each muscle in
his strong arm, wishing not to forget any second, engraving each
fraction into my soul for future nourishment. I know that it
keeps me away from him, this desire to remember every instant
from breath to breath; the knowledge that now is the one and
last time I will have this bliss. I know that I must surrender to
self-forgetfulness. But my preemptive nostalgia stops me. Mundanus draws back his head, noticing I'm holding back. He looks
into my eyes and I feel my heart flee my chest as the attraction
pulls me down a funnel and I become magma. I give myself
over to this moment at the core of the volcano. The past and
future vanish and our embrace propels us through to a vast eternity. An ocean of senses rocks me. Skin vanishes, leaving pure
flesh to be entered. My back rises towards him, undulating in
serpentine rhythms. We're in a paradise of touch as we glide and
writhe and I am suffused with his manhood. The hard strength
of his muscled vigor subdues me, weighs me down, pushing me
into the mattress. I feel both held and overpowered into holy
surrender. Sensing him ever more deeply we shoot through invisible space, racing towards a center of flames; then there is
just pure light. We cry and burn together, forever joined by our
future. I hear myself laughing in sobs. His release staggers me
forward through swirls of bliss...

Only blackness remains.

એ

When we come to, the light outside is fading, announcing my impending departure. He rests on his left arm with his biceps for a pillow. I can feel the strength of his body and inhale the strawberry-tinged whiteness of his radiant skin. In the distance the smell of a fire gone cold mixes with the remnants of choc-olatl. His light blue eyes look into mine and I can read each movement of his soul.

"I'm pregnant," I say, matter of fact, feeling the serpents get hold of his seed. It doesn't feel strange to say this because I can sense this moment of conception as clear as I feel the heat of summertime. Since receiving the Medicine twice I know my body like I never have before.

Mundanus is very still as if he doesn't want to disturb the world by movement. I hardly notice his breath.

"We must have slept for hours," I mutter regretfully, realiz-ing that precious time was wasted in sleep.

"I didn't," he replies. "I've been looking at you the whole time, watching your slumber. You are so beautiful when you're fully at peace. I wish I could paint you like that, guileless and all. I have been imprinting you into my memory, etching these mo-ments forever."

"I was doing that before," I admit, "but it kept me away from you so I stopped."

"It made me feel very close," he whispers and kisses me deeply. I caress his cheek and feel the beginnings of leaving. Noticing the whiteness of his hand on my pink breast I muse about the time when I might suckle a child. The serpents within me whip up a storm in my womb, digesting his seed for their purpose. The certainty that I am conceiving at this very moment is absolute. The Stone desires to become flesh. I tell Mundanus about my reflections.

"I was thinking of Trismosin while I was looking at you," he replies. "This felt to be part of his mission. Even though it was the most intimate moment of my life, it felt preordained."

Suddenly my dry Dutch nature reasserts itself: "We're prob-ably just overwhelmed by the fulfillment of our romantic dreams, and my certainty about being pregnant is just the sum of my wishes."

"I don't think so." Mundanus speaks with conviction.

We dress slowly, covering over our fields of love with the fabric of convention. Soon I shall be his aunt again, like a grandmother to my own children. I wonder how hard it will be to never be able to tell them that they are mine. Will I have the generosity I shall undoubtedly need? I notice I'm asking Johanna's spirit, who smiles at me and makes me know that as long as Clara will be their only mother my acts will have been a blessing. I straighten my spine, realizing that the fiercest fights are yet to come: the battles with myself.

⁊つ

Gerda is by herself, sorting wool into batches of various qualities. The children have gone to sleep in the barn and so have her husband Henk and his father Klaas. Over all my protestations, she has made their entire summer living quarters into a lovely large bedroom just for me.

Gerda always goes to sleep last and gets up before anyone; she has unbridled energy. Now, looking up at me, she studies my face. Nothing escapes her perceptive eyes, and just to make matters more obvious, I blush. She nods and smiles, letting me know that whatever I deem fit is all right with her. I sit down next to her, very close, almost touching. We have long since left behind us the social chasm that exists between peasant and Regent. I need to take her into my confidence, completely.

So I explain to her how the Medicine has returned my womb to me. As a physician-apprentice she knows the power of the Panacea because she was present when it changed Mundanus into an albino in front of her eyes. With her inborn skills, she had rapidly become versatile at the alchemy of the physician's craft and her quick intelligence enabled her to learn to read and write both in Dutch and in Latin in record time. She felt increasingly out of place on the farm and used the craft she learned from Mundanus to prevent pregnancy. Henk did not mind, since there were enough young ones at the farm – Gerda's young siblings – to keep the ever-expanding herd of sheep under control. Meanwhile Gerda brought in more money than anyone had ever seen, adding greatly to Henk's status. Even Klaas, who had been depressed since he lost most of his family to the Plague of '65, was found whistling at times.

Having heard about Clara's misfortune in Venice, Gerda guesses the rest. "So you will have Miss Clara's children for her. And you didn't mind the making," she adds with the unmoved eye of a breeder and a little cheek. She knows the intensity of my relationship with Mundanus, having witnessed it many times in the laboratory. She has no judgment. To her Mundanus is like a prize ram that needs to breed for the sake of the herd.

"So you will go away and be pregnant, I suppose, being married and all that. And Miss Clara will return with the baby. Do you want me to help you?" she asks in the most unflappable tone. It cools me down to hear Gerda talk about these matters with the same ordinariness as if they concerned the price of wool. I shiver briefly and then adjust to her unperturbed businesslike demeanor.

"Have you decided where you will go when it happens?" Gerda asks.

"It has happened," I blurt out. She looks at me with her characteristic kindness and her sharp eye.

"So where will you go? It has to be far enough away that no one you know will see you for at least seven months," she states the obvious. "You couldn't come here. It's too close."

I'm silent, not knowing what to say.

"One of the best sheep farmers down the Rhine in a place called Black Forest has been trying to sell his grazing land to pay off his debts. The story is all over the trade. You could buy it and put me in charge and then Miss Clara and Doctor Mundanus could go there for their honeymoon. I hear the farm has a little old castle. Some nobleman-come-down-in-life sold it to this sheep farmer. But he raked up these enormous gambling debts. If you pay his gambling debts you can have the land. He needs to sell fast. He fears for his life. I spoke to him a few days ago at the Leyden wool market. He speaks a few words of Dutch and a smattering of Latin, not much. But I could understand what he was saying. He's been trying to sell it for months. The richest wool merchants are in Leyden, of course. This time he was truly desperate. His time must be running out. Could you afford that?" she asks, practical as always.

"That ... *and* you can keep the farm after the baby is born," I say in tremendous relief. "Is the little castle inhabitable?"

"Even though I knew I could never afford it I looked into it because his wool is the best on the market. From what I gathered, the man lived the high life until he began to lose everything. They say the house is in good condition; it doesn't need much. But that is of course hearsay. I don't really know. Doctor Mundanus might go there and check it out. He could be back in a week. And, no, I don't want to own it by myself. I don't want to live there permanently. But if we would own it together it could be done. I know wool and you know money. And then, if you need to make more children for Miss Clara, you and Doctor Mundanus have a place to go," this time she grins from ear to ear. I give her an affectionate punch in the ribs. Then we giggle like youngsters.

❧

Mundanus returns with enthusiastic reports. The small tower in the woods near the village of Altensteig is in mint condition, the land holdings are vast, the herd is of great value, and the price is less than what we would pay for a decent home at a prime location in The Hague. The shepherds live in remote areas with the herd and rarely come to the castle. A caretaker family lives on the grounds: between them, Clara, Mundanus, Gerda, Hendrik and me, we can run the place with ease. At most we need to hire a few servants, who will be paid handsomely for being discreet. Helvetius does not have to know that the castle is ours until after Clara 'gets pregnant.' The story is that it will just be rented for the honeymoon.

My moon cycle does not return and less than four weeks after conception I have the telltale signs of early morning nausea and swollen breasts. If Clara still wants another wedding, it has to be now.

"You are pregnant," Clara tells me without emotion when I come into her room after a particularly rough morning.

All I can do is nod and feel my emotions unusually close to the surface: I could laugh, cry or explode in irrational fury.

"I'll marry Mundanus tomorrow and we can leave by the end of the week. I'm packed." Her voice is so cool and collected, it frightens me. Her apparent lack of emotion gives me shivers. "Where are we going?" she asks. "You and Mundanus must have figured that one out by now." There is an undertone of anger seeping in to her calm tone, and I instantly feel more at ease. Her absence of emotion was considerably harder to handle, making me feel even more pent up.

I tell her the details of Gerda's contrivance and after some time I see her smile. "Gerda is the most down to earth person I have ever met," she comments with a sense of relief. Her affection for Gerda briefly overtakes her anger with Mundanus and me.

"I feel terrible," I say.

"Not on my account, I hope," she replies coldly.

"No, not because of you. My body doesn't like being pregnant. I constantly feel bloated."

"Elspeth told me about it. Pregnancy seems to be unpleasant and birth itself horrible and dangerous. Maybe I should consider myself lucky," she adds, dripping with sarcasm.

"Clara," I respond, using all my Regent education to squelch my anger, "We are going to have to do this together. It was Mantis who did this to us. Not Mundanus or I."

"And you hold me responsible for Mantis, I presume," she answers with a dark hue of anguish coloring her voice. She must feel awful about the evil outcome of her enslavement to the Stone. "You're going to say that you warned me."

"No, not at all," I counter honestly. "Why would I add to your torment?"

"I feel horrible," she admits. "Mundanus warned me over and over. And I felt invulnerable. I've thought many times that I was very similar to the sorcerer who stole the Red Sulphur in Venice. I hope he has come to grief as well."

"You were tricked by the Stone," I soothe her. "Red Sulphur has a mind of its own. It tricks us into believing that it serves us. But it is the other way round. We are its slaves. I now understand that the only one on equal footing with the Stone is the one who makes it. And we were given the Stone, and thereby given to it. It is not your fault; wiser people than you have succumbed. Remember I read the play Doctor Faustus to you when you were studying English? He sold his soul to the Devil for magic, and he was three times your age. Magic is sweet poison."

She looks at me expressionless. Then I see the slow rise of the great wave. It comes from the earth below and passes up through her throat where she fights it back. Then she falls to the floor and sobs from the pit of her anguish. I sink down next to her and stroke her hair, waiting for the flood to subside. In my pregnant belly I feel an impossible intimacy with my niece who will be the mother of the child growing inside me.

"We must stick together," I offer, insipid, at a loss for true words. The chemical bond between the four of us – Clara, Mundanus, our child and me – has become like the fusion of metals when they turn from being a mixed amalgam into an inseparable single substance.

ॐ

Clara and Mundanus wed July 1st in a small chapel near our home in the sole presence of Helvetius, Nicco, the pastor, and me. Most people believe that Mundanus and Clara have already wed in Venice, so we don't give any publicity to the matter. The ceremony is delightfully uneventful, except for my vomiting for half an hour prior to giving Clara away to Mundanus. During their wedding night, I lie awake in agony.

They leave the next day by boat up the Rhine to the ancient healing springs at Baden and then by post coach through the Black Forest to Altensteig.

The day after their departure Nicco does not wake. He lived to the age of 25.

I bury him at the center of our courtyard where I stabbed his master in the heart with the Medicine. I feel alone and share a glass of gin with Hendrik, toasting the life of a truly devoted soul whose loyal love – like Odysseus' old dog – made him the only one to instantly recognize his master after he had become a new man.

ဆ

After six weeks, a letter addressed to Helvetius arrives. It relays profound thanks for having cured Clara with the Medicine, and gives us the joyful news that she is happily expecting, but needs bed rest to complete the pregnancy. As predicted, Helvetius tells everyone, and of course Princess Amalia first; this assures public knowledge in a matter of hours. He tells me proudly that he had instructed Clara to insert the medicine vaginally by way of a long sturdy alchemical glass pipette so it would penetrate the womb directly, a procedure made possible by the wedding night. My soul cringes at the thought.

Mundanus' missive couldn't have come a moment later. I'm beginning to show and am openly chiding Cook for making the meals so delicious that I'm putting on pounds. I have to eat more and more to keep up the charade, and feel increasingly unwell. Helvetius has just about decided that he will give me a medical workup, which I obviously don't want to happen. Upon receipt of the letter I tell Helvetius that I shall go and visit Clara to see if I can help. Helvetius agrees without any suspicion.

Hendrik, Gerda and I sail up the Rhine River on an East Indies Company merchantman, carrying spices from the Indies to destinations in the hinterlands. The sleek brigantine vessel is the swiftest vessel on the Rhine. Besides Company goods she transports our carriage and three new horses. Hendrik has never travelled before and finds solace for his fear of the river in a great reservoir of gin. Gerda and I delight in one another's company. To make the joint purchase of the Altensteig property possible I have bought Gerda's sheep for exorbitant amounts of money, which she then used to hire more help and to symbolically pay me her share of the purchase. Henk is happily mollified: his fast rise in rank more than pays for Gerda's temporary absence. We shall have access to the best wool for Clara's entire lifetime. Elspeth and Mina are going to weave up a storm and Anthonie van Leeuwenhoek will buy their cloth sight unseen once Clara has returned to guide their craft to the pinnacle of quality. We shall jointly own the beginnings of a superior fabric company, from sheep to textile. The economic future looks plenty bright for gold to be made in the natural way.

Gerda's nursing skills come in quite handy now that my morning nausea mixes with the motion sickness caused by the wind swept Rhine. She has made lozenges of myrrh, cinnamon and angelica root, which were previously used by physicians during the pestilence. Mundanus had learned the recipe in London during the Plague of '65. For me they work like a charm, possibly because they connect me to my beloved. Together we admire the spectacular beauty of the landscape passing us by, seeing forests, cliffs and ancient castles in ruins.

"I had no idea there was so much world!" Gerda marvels. It gives me great pleasure to watch her horizons expand the way mine did in Venice when I first saw the maps in the Palazetto *portego*. Nature is vast, I now realize, and we are small like ants in her giant lap. I've heard stories all my life of exotic places in the East and in the New World. But to me they had been like the adventures of princes, princesses and Indians in distant lands once upon a time. When the reality of the true immenseness of the world breaks through to the soul, it is a different experience altogether. "How can God keep track of all this?" Gerda wonders out loud.'

In Baden I find a note from Mundanus, kept there by the thermal spa keepers in my name to be released for a small fee. It is written in an uncharacteristically angular hand and I assume Mundanus must have penned it in a hurry. After a passionate welcome, he asks if anyone in The Hague suspects anything. He goes on to suggest that I do not take the hot sulfur baths or drink the water that smells like rotten eggs because he doesn't know what it will do to my pregnancy. He also recommends we journey to Altensteig in convoy with the post coach that travels with soldiers because the Black Forest is full of brigands and bandits. He signs it with 'Your loving M.'

The next post coach is to leave tomorrow so we walk around the spa, which has existed since Roman times. Hadrian himself is rumored to have visited here. I get restless and agitated, as I am wont to do these days. A bit frantic, I want to hire a guide and take the horses up the mountain, even though Gerda is dead set against it. The mountain is called after the god of alchemy, Mercury, and it feels like a good omen to me to see the view from its peak. We have no mountains in Holland and undulating landscapes fascinate me. The innkeeper assures us that it is much better to take donkeys and he rents us some, together with two armed guides. Hendrik will stay behind with the luggage and the carriage while Gerda and I, seated on patient donkeys, follow our guides who move on foot. As I sit on the donkey rocking back and forth, I get more seasick than I had been on the boat and we have to turn back.

In the middle of the forest we are accosted by a group of men. An operatic parody of bandits, they look scruffy and unkempt, clothes torn and haphazard, some with blood on their sleeves; very theatrical. I see our guides exchange a meaningful look. They scurry off and once, our ragtag assailants scoffing after them. Sitting forlorn on my donkey like Mother Mary on her way to Nazareth, I curse the agitated mood which made me undertake this dangerous excursion, even after having been warned by Mundanus about bandits. My emotions undulate even more than the landscape.

One of the men, a bearded fellow, takes a dangerous instant liking to me. He has a large scar on his chin and he must have never been washed in his life, not even by his mother. As he approaches me amorously, Gerda turns to him and says resolutely: "Take me; she is pregnant. You know you will forever be cursed in your manhood and never rise again if you take a pregnant woman."

"I shall take the both of you," he replies, jovially. The men around him grin in expectation. This is beginning to look increasingly dangerous.

"I have silver coins at the inn in Baden," I try desperately.

"Of course," he replies with a grin. The dappled forest light displays a twinkle in his eyes. "This is getting better and better. First I will have the both of you, as the young lady has kindly suggested and then I'll come with you for your money." He bows with mock gallantry and his men laugh uproariously. Then their laughter stops and all at once they scramble back into the forest like rats. A gentleman and his retinue are approaching. I recognize the hunting party as the other guests at the inn. I can breathe again, feeling that I have been as imprudent as Clara had been with Venier. From now on I shall listen to Gerda, I firmly decide.

"I owe you a great deal, Sir," I say in the German tongue.

"It is nothing," he replies in French. He appears to be a French nobleman. "It is not good for Ladies to be in the forest alone. It is asking for trouble."

"I know," I reply in French. "It was most incautious of me and our armed guides were cowards and fled. I brought my friend and myself in serious danger." When he hears my courtier's French he immediately guesses my station in life and descends from his horse in an act of chivalry. Mounted on his marvelous white stallion, he stood against the light, so I couldn't see his face. Now I see that he sports a thin goatee and a well-groomed black mustache sticking out on both sides like pointed arrows. His dark eyes are inquisitive and intense. "Let me escort you back to the inn," he suggests. "We don't want anything bad to happen again." I am grateful to him and consent when he insists that I sit on the horse as he walks alongside. Gerda seems much relieved. I admire her courage, the way she was willing to be taken in my stead. There is something radiant about her, rocking back and forth on the back of the donkey. Looking down on our savior's long plumed hat and his black curls, I see that the sword by his side is long, almost down to his flaring leather spurred boots. A leather sash across his chest is embroidered with a family crest and his hands covered by gloves of the finest black leather. He exudes affluence. When I ask him what brings him to these parts he tells me that he's come to settle a debt. I realize that his men are with him to assure that the debtor pays up.

"I ask only one thing for my services," he tells me as he drops us off at the inn. I look at him apprehensively, still shaking with the threat of rape we suffered.

"I would like to request your presence at dinner tonight. We'll be hunting for game and have a feast tonight before we go on our way tomorrow." Much relieved, I consent.

ॐ

The hunt has been glorious and we sit down at a table overflowing with pheasant and boar, venison, wild duck and swan. Monsieur Delamarche's retinue consists of twelve men who eat for twenty. Wine flows copiously and while normally I feel no effects until I've drunk many glasses, this time after one cup all my good judgment abandons me and I tell him about my life as though he were my confidant. I say that I'm traveling to Altensteig to be with my pregnant niece Clara Dolfin and her husband. Meanwhile Gerda is being distracted by men, who, with increasing bluntness, admire her charms.

"I think we should go, Madam," Gerda tells me adamantly after some time, as the table has turned into a lair of suitors. I get up against my will, a bit wobbly, but mindful of my decision to follow Gerda. General disappointment is voiced by the men, but Gerda is unrelenting. Monsieur Delamarche promises loudly to accompany us tomorrow so no harm will befall us. Coincidentally, he is also travelling in the direction of Altensteig. In our room upstairs I vomit the meal into my chamber pot. Throughout the night we hear the men carousing with increasing volume below us. Waking in the morning I hear loud snoring rise up from the dining room. The post coach leaves long before the revelers wake, and we travel east along ruts of the post road in the armed convoy at a speed of about 4 miles per hour. At this speed we have 8 hours of travel ahead of us.

By mid-afternoon Monsieur Delamarche and his men catch up with us.

"You didn't wait for us!" he exclaims in mock indignation as he pulls up to our carriage following the post coach. I see that Monsieur Delamarche's horses must have been galloping all the way since they are covered in sweat.

"You were fast asleep," I reply, glad to see him. I like his sanguine mood, appearing unfazed by any kind of obstacle. I must admit that the wine last night had caused some sentimental pubescent romance to fleetingly strum my heart.

"If you want we can accompany you wherever you need to go. My men can defend against any bandits around here. No one would dare attack you. You would be at your destination twice as fast." I look over at Gerda, no longer trusting myself.

"Do you think it is safe?" I ask her in Dutch.

"The other rats fled when they saw him coming," she replies. "I think it should be safe."

So we break convoy, and surrounded by Monsieur Delamarche's men, we continue with much greater speed towards Altensteig. On his white stallion he rides next to the carriage and we chat through the open window. His presence passes the time as we talk about local gossip and other inane little pleasantries. He seems to know his way very well in these parts, and when asked he tells me that he visits Baden often because his arthritis bothers him since he was wounded in battle. The sulfur baths help greatly, he enthuses. I don't notice any pain in his demeanor and decide that after I give birth I should try the famous Baden baths.

I now fully understand why these are called the black forests, as the fir trees grow closely together and have very dark foliage, causing twilight at noon. We pass the remains of an ancient castle, walls eaten away by weather and neglect. The forest has taken back the manmade clearing as trees grow from the top of the tower, bushes stick out of the battlements and a wall miraculously still standing is ready to fall at the first opportunity. It makes me melancholy to see the futility of our works over time, as the straight lines we draw in the landscape are re-conquered surreptitiously by the capricious contortions of nature. I mention this to Monsieur Delamarche and he grows silent.

In the late afternoon we cross the bridge to the uphill road leading to the great Altensteig castle. Houses with steep red roofs hug closely together as the lowering sun casts a rose blush on the ochre south facing walls. A church steeple stands out among a cluster of dwellings surrounding the castle. As we follow our uphill path we pass along a road where the houses stand high up on walls like birdhouses on stilts. Then we leave the town to go through the woods to our new domicile. It strikes me how well my guardian angel knows how to get to a place towards which I am barely able to direct him. He moves ahead of our small fellowship, seemingly smelling his way towards the little tower in the woods. I am ready to ask directions of the farmers around who, dressed in somber garb, walk away from the field after a day's work; but Monsieur Delamarche forges ahead with remarkable certainty.

When first I see our tower I am shocked. It is not much more than a ruin on a hill. Walls have tumbled down and only the tower stands. I can't believe that Mundanus has been so enthusiastic about this haphazard pile of rubble. But as we

approach the small hill I see that the tower itself is well preserved: a perfectly round broad granite pillar rising four stories
up from the ground. It shows off fresh green shuttered windows and a black pointed-hat roof with a centuries old battle-
ment rim.

"How did you know where to find this?" I ask Monsieur
Delamarche admiringly.

But before he can answer I see a small figure running towards me and instantly recognize Mundanus. He is elated to see
me and rushes towards the carriage. Then I see him stop in front
of Monsieur Delamarche.

He looks nonplussed and I hear him say: "Delamarche?
What are you doing here?"

Chapter Nineteen

"Do you know each other?" I ask surprised.

Monsieur Delamarche dismounts and jovially greets Mundanus.

"This man is the worst card player you'll ever meet," Mundanus tells me out loud with a broad grin as he helps me descend from the carriage. "He left a great deal of money on the table when we played cards back at the inn in Baden."

Monsieur Delamarche smiles broadly. "I'm not even half bad, but your husband is a terrific player!"

I feel myself blush. "Oh no," I respond quickly. "This is my niece's husband."

Mundanus smiles with great satisfaction at having been called my husband.

"I was traveling with my wife," he tells Monsieur Delamarche boisterously. "But she was asleep when we were playing cards those nights. Are these your friends? Please come in and let me get you some wine and beer." Then he stops. "How did you meet my aunt?" he asks, suddenly surprised.

"He saved our lives," I say, and I tell Mundanus our harrowing bandit story. I become rather emotional and almost cry but I am able to cover my feelings with a coughing fit. Gerda finishes our tale for me. Mundanus bows in gratitude towards Monsieur Delamarche, who counters by lifting his plumed hat.

"Gerda saved me first," I say. Mundanus looks at Gerda with affection as he helps her down from the carriage.

"Well, Hendrik, thank you for bringing them here safely." He speaks heartily to our loyal old coachman who is visibly tired, sitting slumped and looking a bit dazed. "You must be thirsty after the long ride. Over there by the ruins there is a perfectly good horse's stable, please take care of the horses there. But first come in to get a drink."

Hendrik isn't used to so much fellow feeling with his masters and excuses himself, riding the carriage to the indicated site.

"I don't know how I can thank you enough, Monsieur Delamarche. Please follow me in and will introduce you to my wife Clara."

"By all means, Signor Dolfin," he replies chivalrously, and tells his men to follow Hendrik to the stables.

"Come in after you've taken care of the horses," Mundanus calls back over his shoulder.

Inside, the tower looks like a grotto. Large granite fieldstones have been piled loosely upon one another and the openings between the stones have been filled with a mixture of mud and hay. Its soldier-like erect structure is geared for battle. There is no sign of the civilizing hands of women over the centuries. The ceiling is made of roughly hewn beams and unvarnished planks, and the kitchen is inside an enormous hearth suitable for roasting large game. The furniture is simple, constructed of unadorned wood with tables more apt for cards than for dining. Clara's travel loom and spinning wheel from home contrast sharply with the military environment. A steep open staircase leads up to a second floor where the sleeping quarters appear to be. The perfect roundness of the space is initially disorienting, but it provides a modicum of charm to the otherwise Spartan conditions.

"Where is Clara?" I ask eager to see my niece. I feel that the baby inside me has two mothers and longs to be in her presence.

"She's upstairs taking a rest. She's not doing too well."

"Pregnancy is hard on a woman," Monsieur Delamarche intones.

Mundanus looks at him in surprise.

"I told him that Clara is pregnant and I'm coming here to take care of her," I interject quickly as I notice Gerda going up the stairs. I want to follow her but deem it wise to stay downstairs with the two men to help prevent further misunderstandings. Mundanus goes over to a large peasant chest and takes out a cask of wine and pewter cups. While he is praising the wine to his guest I hear movement upstairs. I can't wait any longer and rush up the steep staircase to see Clara. The men stay behind discussing vineyards in France comparing their fruit to the beer brewed in these parts.

When I arrive on the second floor I'm surprised to actually find it cozy. Clara has hung many of her beautiful fabrics covering the walls and it smells like summer flowers and fresh alpine mosses. As I'm admiring Clara's ability to create beauty wherever she goes, I see Gerda come out of a room to the left with Clara in tow. At first I am shocked. By the twilight of dusk through the various small windows like the portholes of a ship Clara looks like a ghost, thin as if she has not eaten for weeks. I can see the worried look on Gerda's face. When I rush over and take Clara in my arms she feels like a rag doll, listless and dull with no tone to her muscles.

"I'm dizzy," is all she tells me.

"If I didn't know any better, I'd say Miss Clara is pregnant," Gerda whispers, puzzled. Clara vomits on the floor in confirmation.

"She must be sick," I say. "We must tell Mundanus."

Downstairs we hear the boisterous sounds of men coming for wine. Mundanus welcomes them loudly.

"Zanni," I call down. "Could you please come up for a moment?"

I hear him apologize to the men and pull out all the pewter in the house to regale them with wine and ale.

He enters the upstairs hallway between the bedrooms while speaking. "She has been sick ever since Helvetius gave her the Medicine. I don't know why. I think in his zeal he gave her too much, or maybe she was more sensitive to it because of her grief."

"Gerda says that if she wouldn't know any better she'd think Clara pregnant," I whisper neutrally, just conveying her words.

"No," Mundanus replies softly. "Sadly, that is not possible. I've seen it with my own eyes in Venice. Her uterus was destroyed. No, that can't be."

"Her eyes look like what I've seen in expecting women," Gerda responds. "She doesn't look ill to me." In all the confusion I'm impressed with Gerda's boldness as she maintains her diverging position. Could it be? I feel a deep stillness inside me as if my womb is holding its breath.

"Maybe you can't see it because you know it could never be. But facts have been twisted by the Medicine before," I support Gerda.

Mundanus shakes his head with sadness. "I wish it were true, but it is not possible. I'll give her some of the Medicine with some added spirit of *purpur*. She is very pale indeed." I remember how that particular medicinal mixture had revived Mundanus when he was dying of Trismosin's blanching agent. "I took most of my medical supplies here with me in case they'd be needed to help you through your pregnancy and birth. They're two stories up," he points to the end of the hallway between the rooms at the same kind of staircase I've seen below.

"I thought you'd given that to Clara to make the dye that created her sorcery textiles," I respond, puzzled.

"Not all," he mutters as he moves quickly towards the back.

"Monsieur Delamarche," I call down, "We shall be just a moment; my niece is unwell and her husband is giving her medicine. We'll be down in a short while."

I hear the polite tone in his reply but care not enough to hear the words. I'm totally preoccupied: What if Clara indeed *is* pregnant? Looking at Gerda, I know she's thinking the same thing. The Stone performs greater art than humans can imagine. It has been generated directly by the ultimate source of creation while our human imagination is many steps removed from that origin. Red Sulphur is able to imagine far more boldly than we can.

Gerda and I each support Clara under one armpit and almost have to drag her to the bedroom. In the center of the room stands a large four-poster bed with a glow-cloth canopy. I shudder as I sense the afterglow of passionate images reflected back to me by the memory of the cloth. It seems to me that Clara's illness has not diminished their physical intimacy. For a moment I shut my eyes and feel pierced by an arrow of molten lead. Seeing the rumpled sheets I instinctively hold my breath in order not to inhale the scent of their bodies rising up, and together with Gerda lower Clara carefully onto the pillow. I note the pillowcase is made of the blush sorcery cloth: Clara desires Mundanus just as much as I do. I try to make my mind look the other way.

Gerda goes out to the hallway to clean up after Clara's nausea.

I stare blankly at Clara, my expression in a frozen grimace, when Mundanus returns with a small red glowing vial. He instantly understands the struggle reflected in my motionless face and smiles apologetically with a helpless look. It makes me feel maternal towards him, which really makes me furious. I want him to be strong, standing tall and taking it as a matter of course that he has two wives in the way of the Moors and the Patriarchs. He appears like he's groveling. I want a man, not a guilty child caught red handed. Then he turns to Clara and his demeanor changes as he becomes the physician.

"Can you help me lift her so I can put the drops under her tongue?" My anger vanishes when he resumes his role as the great doctor; he seems to grow taller. I sense Johanna's spirit take over, driving out the scorned lover, and I'm filled with concern for our daughter. I slide my hand under her neck and experience the soft satin feeling of a silky pillowcase and the floating light strands of her blonde hair. Clara is close to weightless as I lift her up.

"Darling, could you please open your mouth," Mundanus requests in his physician voice. Like a trusting child Clara follows his orders. He drips five drops from the little pipette. Then he hesitates, looking intently at Clara, arriving at his medical decision. Having made it, he drops in another ten and waits a minute observing her carefully, then lifts her chemise to palpate her belly. He recoils in shock, his eyes wide. "That can't be. It's not possible. I saw it with my own eyes! I had to cut out most of her womb so she wouldn't bleed to death and then I sewed it up myself. You can't grow a new uterus!"

"Red Sulphur can," I reply, remembering a lizard I once saw with a new tail grown next to the stump of his old one. "So Gerda was right?"

He nods stunned. Gerda has entered the room and overheard his final statement.

"She looks terrible," Gerda remarks unperturbed. "When was the last time she ate a proper meal?"

"She hasn't really eaten since the wedding. I thought that it was because Helvetius gave her too much of the Medicine."

"How far along is she?" Gerda asks.

"About 2 months," Mundanus mumbles. Same as me I realize, still reeling. "I clearly felt movement," he continues, "Her womb was reacting very lively to the tincture."

"I've seen that before. A cousin of mine lost her appetite early on in her pregnancy. She was disgusted by food. Couldn't stand the smell of most things."

"The only thing stopping her nausea is the smell of fresh moss. That's why we have it all over."

"I'll cook a meal she is going to like," Gerda states with confidence. "What do you have in your pantry and what's growing around? Is there a garden? And you have to tell the men downstairs to go drink in the stables. The smell of alcohol will make her puke again." From my own increased sensitivity to wine I recognize that Gerda knows what she's talking about. Mundanus goes downstairs to follow Gerda's instructions. I hear him pull out all the stops and gather his entire supply of the wine, beer and gin. The carousing has already become more voluble and I am glad to hear the dozen men leave after a loud hurrah over Mundanus generous libation to Bacchus. Only

Monsieur Delamarche stays behind, talking softly to Mundanus. Then I hear him call up to me from the bottom of the stairs.

"Madam Marianne, I shall have to leave. I have some business to take care of in Altensteig and I'll return without my men in a few days for a proper meal." He bows elegantly and his handheld hat swings out broadly in sheer panache. I realize I'm attracted to him and am loath to see him go. I'm uneasy at being left behind with Mundanus and Clara, feeling like the odd one out. But these mixed sensations vanish instantly as I turn around and hear Clara whisper to Gerda.

When I reenter the room Clara has a non-comprehending look on her face. Gerda has guided Clara's hand to her still exposed belly, as Mundanus in his astonishment had neglected to pull her chemise back down.

"Can you feel it?" Gerda asks her with gentle patience. "Yes, over there: that small bump. See now it is gone. That's your baby, Miss Clara. And it feels very healthy. It is a bit drunk on the purpur tincture Doctor Mundanus gave you just now. That's how we knew you were pregnant. We're going to take really good care of you," she continues as she sees me enter. "And of your aunt too. You're both due at the same time."

Clara is obviously overwhelmed by this unlikely information and Gerda keeps guiding her hand back to her belly each time after Clara withdraws it as though having touched red hot iron.

I gaze up at the glow-cloth canopy and perceive a graphic memory of Mundanus configured as twins making love with both Clara and me simultaneously at the moment we created the great Medicine on July 31 of last year. A little over a year has gone by and what had seemed to have been solely a vision of our passion has turned out to have been a foreshadowing of the future as well. It appears that Clara and I have each conceived one part of twins to be born seven months from now. Trismosin must be pleased, I think with a modicum of bitterness. My sentiments towards the director of our fates are less than charitable.

"How do you feel, Clara?" I ask, not counting on a reply.

Uncharacteristically Clara utters a vulgar curse, of the kind Gerda is used to hearing but is very uncommon in Regent circles. Gerda grins with pleasure. "Try that once more, Miss Clara. It'll do you good." Following her instructions, Clara belches out an even baser expletive. Then all three of us laugh and feel deeply connected as women. I bend over and embrace my niece, saying: "If you have a daughter maybe she should be called Johanna," I whisper. Clara begins to weep inconsolably. Gerda and I hold her in a protective embrace. After her sobs calm down Clara mutters plaintively: "Mother!"

From the caverns of my heart Johanna wordlessly calls back to her daughter in response.

ॐ

When a few days later Monsieur Delamarche comes to dinner, Gerda has managed to get several nourishing meals into Clara that have not been returned to sender, and my niece looks a bit more human. With her common-sense genius our practical nurse has filled up the house with large sections of fresh moss and the dank fragrance of forest shade seems to have calmed Clara's nausea. Mundanus and I have hardly spoken, a kind of bashfulness keeping us apart. Now that Mundanus has fathered a child with each of us our relationship has incurred a new dimension of complexity and neither of us wishes to explore this next tier of our Gordian knot.

Truly happy for the distraction of Monsieur Delamarche's arrival, I welcome him warmly into our deep-forest scented stone tower. Against his promise he has brought his men; however they have not come up to the house but are with Hendrik in the stables drinking his gin about which, I'm sure, Hendrik is not at all happy. Dutch gin is hard to come by in these parts, yet we have been able to locate a passably good Brandywine which meets with Hendrik's approval. My trusted groom has become friends with members of the large caretaker family of our property who live in various run-down dwellings next to the stables.

The extended family, called 'Sippe' around here, consists of a couple in their early forties with grown children and offspring of their own. Hendrik – who communicates with them in ways I have not yet fathomed, since he certainly speaks no German – has become an invaluable source of gossip and information. Tonight will certainly be the occasion of bacchanalia, as the local peasants will be regaled to tall tales told by men of arms. The pantry is overflowing with hams, while the stable has been populated with chickens and a fat cow, giving us ample supplies of eggs and milk. The young men of our tattered retinue have turned out to be excellent huntsmen, so meat is in ongoing supply. Of course Hendrik has made sure that there is drink of all kind aplenty.

ℰↃ

Monsieur Delamarche looks tense. He is far removed from his usual jovial self I have come to know and appreciate. As we sit around the table, laden heavily with a veritable cornucopia of gratitude for his rescue in the woods, the conversation is polite and stilted. The gregarious chevalier I like has left the stage, leaving behind a rather taciturn man who doesn't dispel the awkward atmosphere that entered with his presence.

After Mundanus' various expressions of thanks, he runs out of words, and the meal proceeds in silence. I try my skills as hostess but feel rebuffed at every turn, while Clara looks on slightly glassy eyed.

As Gerda brings us the plum tart she has conjured in the kitchen, I can't hold back anymore.

"Monsieur Delamarche, I know it is not polite me asking you this, but has something untoward happened to you over these past few days? I scarcely recognize you." I feel instantly sorry that I have been so intrusive and wish I could swallow back my words.

He looks at me with the saddest of expressions.

"Yes, Madam Schweitzer, something has," he replies, straightening his back as if having made a decision. I am completely taken off guard by his use of my married name. I have been very careful to never mention it to anyone in these parts. Gerda stops her serving of the plum tart in mid-air, instantly looking at our guest with grave suspicion.

"You must be mistaken," Mundanus exclaims, "My aunt's name is Van Os."

"And she is neither married nor pregnant," Monsieur Delamarche responds with an incomprehensibly despondent undertone in his voice. "And yes, it is true. She is certainly not pregnant by her husband, who believes Madam Schweitzer is here to help her niece with *her* non-existent pregnancy." He pauses, suddenly having become an unwanted presence in the room. I now understand that his mood had been anticipating this moment all along. And I realize with a shock that this man to whom I felt attraction might be here for the purpose of extortion.

"I don't know *where* you get your information!" Mundanus exclaims in distress.

"It was not hard to trace these facts," he replies with a genuine sigh, as if he'd rather not have had received this knowledge. For a moment I have the faint hope that he might be suffering from a moral distress around my purported extra marital pregnancy. Yet I first try indignant denial: "Where do you get this notion that I might be pregnant?" I know I'm not showing *that* obviously to one who doesn't know me.

At this point Monsieur Delamarche is demonstratively silent. It seems the entire room is holding its breath and even the moss no longer exudes its shady fragrance.

"What is the purpose of your visit?" Mundanus inquires in a frozen tone.

"Do I need to spell it out?" Monsieur Delamarche inquires, tired.

"He staged the attack by the bandits in the woods," Gerda speaks with aplomb. "Now I understand. I saw that awful bandit with the gash on his cheek here in town while this 'gentleman'," her voice drips with scorn, "was there on business. I recognized him by his stench. The best way to gain someone's confidence is to save them."

I have an ardent hope that Monsieur Delamarche will deny every word she says, but he remains silent.

"Is that true?" I ask in a shrill voice I don't recognize.

He looks at me with eyes that tell me the whole story: he is obviously attracted to me as well, which initially had upended his plans. But he has decided to go ahead with them anyway. His sadness is about having to override his feelings for his need for money.

"You're coming for silver," I hiss, despising him from the depth of my soul.

Delamarche gets up, takes a letter from his breast pocket, and throws it down on the table like a challenge.

"I shall leave you with this. Ten thousand florins by the end of next week. I shall be back then."

I glance at the letter and see it is the one Mundanus had left for me at Baden warning me of the possible deleterious effects of sulfur baths on my pregnancy.

"You can have it," he concludes, as he walks away. "I had two copies made. One for Madam Schweitzer and this is the other one. I keep the notarized original, which will mysteriously find its way to The Hague if you don't get me the money. Between the Dolfin and the Van Os family, that shouldn't be much of a problem." Mundanus moves towards him in threatening fashion. All Delamarche does is pat his sword. We realize why he has brought his men. Gerda goes up to him and smears his elegant light beige waistcoat with a handful of plum filling. Taken aback, Delamarche does not know how to respond, while Gerda is calmly awaiting his slap. Then he turns with a dignity that is comical under the circumstances and walks out the door. Clara looks vacant as if she has missed the entire event.

Mundanus sits in abject self-recrimination, reading the letter that caused all the harm.

"How could you have known?" I ask, defending him against himself.

"It was careless. I just was so excited to see you again," he mutters.

Clara gets up and turns to me. "Uncle Johann is not going to be happy," she speaks in a dry clear voice. The expression on her face has not changed; she still looks devoid of all animation. Suddenly she utters a shrill laugh without pleasure. "We thought we were smart, didn't we? And then first Mantis and now this buzzard. Your Trismosin is not very effective now, is he?"

I'm just about to defend the author of our fate, trying to not feel like the fool I am, having fallen for a vulgar impostor, when Hendrik enters. He has obviously downed copious quantities of a variety of spirits and I expect him to be less than coherent.

"What is it, Hendrik?" I ask, hating the tremble in my voice.

"You know who that was?" he asks, pointing behind him.

We wait in silence. Hendrik rolls his eyes up into his skull revealing blood shot eyeballs, then his pupils sink back into view and he speaks at breakneck speed: "That man who was just here with his army is the biggest gambler in France. He comes to Baden regularly to clean out the rich, and he is the one who bankrupted the previous owner of these lands."

"The sheep farmer?" Gerda asks. Hendrik nods and continues. "Conrad, one of the young fellows here, recognized one of his men. He had come to the house several times to threaten his previous master. Then they began to boast that the current owners were immensely rich and that their boss would rob them blind. They said something about a letter. Conrad speaks a little bit of Dutch because he used to accompany his master to the Leyden wool market, so he could explain it to me. By the end of the evening they were completely drunk. I kept giving them more and more of our strongest stuff. All the more pity, but it had to be done. By the end they were laughing how they save people from their bandit friends to gain their trust. Then their master wins all the suckers' money. And the losers are glad to part with it, feeling grateful to this scum. When you arrived in Baden, Signor Dolfin, their boss had already found out that the buyers of the lands were wealthy and he had set up a plan. That's as much as I know. They were just about to tell the details when their chief came back covered in red stuff which I first thought to be blood."

"Plums," Gerda says calmly.

"All the money you won from him was part of his game," Clara turns on Mundanus.

"The man's a whore," Hendrik mutters.

"But how would he know I was going to write this letter?" Mundanus exclaims.

"He didn't," Gerda says self-assured. "I know them from the wool markets. They're like fishermen waiting for suckers to swallow their bait. Did you tell him anything while you were winning his money?"

"I told him that I had just bought a house near Altensteig."

"He knew that already," Gerda dismisses. "Anything else?"

"That my wife was pregnant and her aunt was coming to help us."

"So he knew Madam Marianne was coming. When you left the letter he must have bribed the innkeeper. He was obviously gambling on there being something fishy with wealthy people from The Hague buying far away property to pass a pregnancy here in the hinterlands." Gerda's logic has mathematical elegance. Mundanus looks dumbfounded, obviously recognizing the truth in Gerda's deductions as well.

"So what are we going to do?" Clara asks with a dawn of blush suffusing her cheeks. The intrigue revives her.

"We could make fool's gold," I suggest. I am referring to a mixture of tin and copper which would be discovered by any mint master and make the forger ripe for the gallows.

"He wants coins," Mundanus replies. "I'm not going to try and trick a master gambler."

"So just give him the money?" Clara asks.

"He'd just be back for more. He has seven more months for his extortion before we get back to The Hague with Clara's twins," Mundanus retorts, convinced. "His men have told Hendrik that he was going to suck us dry."

"We have to kill him," Clara says calmly. "It's the only solution."

Gerda nods adamantly, while Hendrik walks over to the table and finishes off the wine.

"We could use the Medicine under its dark aspect," I suggest. Any alchemist knows that Red Sulphur, if admixed in the proper ways, can behave like a horrific poison.

"He would never touch anything in our house again," Gerda counters.

"He would touch something if I make him," Clara suggests calmly. "If I wear sorcery cloth. It is very convincing..."

I can't believe Clara proposing such a thing after the horrors in Venice. I look at her with obvious fear in my eyes, for she responds to me: "Don't worry Aunt Marianne. I have learned my lesson. I know it is not *my* power that is being used, but that of the Stone. But why not let Red Sulphur help us? We have done enough for the Stone to deserve its help." Then she turns to Gerda. "What is that horrible musty smell of mold everywhere? It reeks like a wet root cellar around here." Clara has returned to life from a graveyard that had held her captive for nine months.

ℜ

"I never thought I would resort to sorcery myself," I tell Mundanus as we work in the part of the kitchen, which has been transformed into an alchemical laboratory, "Especially not after seeing the madness in the sorcerer's phantom's eyes in Venice." The cooking stove burns at much greater heat than for which it was meant, and only an alchemist of Mundanus abilities can make it glow red without exploding. Gerda and I are working incessantly as amanuenses to him while Clara is refashioning the leftovers of her blush fabric into an irresistible dress. From her room upstairs we hear her hum songs that remind me of my childhood. Johanna's presence is palpable as Clara is returning to life and begins to cherish her pregnancy. All nausea is gone and she eats heartily from Gerda's delicious gastronomy. Gerda has enhanced her peasant cooking with unusual herbs and spices available in these regions, enabling her to provide Clara and me with meals that nourish the life growing inside us. She has learned to manage the enormous heat of the stove for the cooking of food in a way that has led to the most surprising flavors.

Trismosin has an entire section of his diaries devoted to dark magic and Mundanus reads it incessantly. When he finds passages which might be of interest, he reads them out loud to us. We know that the poison has to be made from a tincture of black lead mixed with mercury. It leads to a dreadful death, first driving the victim to paroxysms of horrible insanity and pain, working much like the shirt of Nessus, the poisoned cloak that was given to Hercules and caused his dreadful end. We will marinade the cloth in which we shall give him the coins in the madness inducing tincture. Clara will hand it to him wearing special gloves she is making for this occasion, made from the woven bark of oak which is described by Trismosin as remedy to the poison of Nessus, the oak tree being the king of trees sacred to Jupiter himself. Clara has sliced the finest of strips from oak bark and wound it with thread she has unraveled from the torn parts of her wedding dress. The result is a set of beguiling gloves reaching up to her elbows. The coins themselves shall be wrapped in a similar kind of oak-based cloth so the silver itself will not touch the poison of the outer pouch.

The work is dangerous and arduous. Any spillage might kill us. I am not allowed close to the odious tincture because of my condition, and I have to watch as Gerda performs most of the final assistance to Mundanus. He has taken a tenth of a barley grain of Red Sulphur and activated it by memory, conjuring up in his mind that passionate night of July 31 last year when we activated the Medicine in our three-way delirium in order to turn the Stone into a mare in heat. He does not want either of us to be his mystical sister for the occasion, unsure of how it would affect our offspring.

The amount he has used is not enough to transform the lead into a metal of greater refinement but is just enough to create an incomplete transmutation which will create what in our Art is called the *monstrum*, a hybrid material often represented as a fiery dragon. The *monstrum* consists of highly unstable material which has an unquenchable desire to copulate with whatever it meets, turning its bridal suite into a fulcrum for horrific presences.

The only remaining problem is to get enough silver coins to hide the nature of our ruse. Putting together all the moneys we have brought we get no further than four thousand florins. Clara will tell Delamarche in her seductive way that it is all we have for now and that we will be going to an office of our Company to get the rest. It is up to Clara to convince him to accept the Nessus pouch. His thin elegant leather gloves will make perfect conductors for our evil since the monstrous tongues of Nessus crave to lick skin of any kind.

&

When the day comes, Delamarche arrives without his men. He enters the tower after waiting for some time, as we have decided to dispense with any form of hospitality and just have left the door ajar for him to enter. None of us wants to open the door for him. We expect him to be furious at the slight, but instead he enters in an almost shy demeanor. He immediately sees Clara, of course. Even though her blush dress is even more sumptuous than any she has fashioned before, there is still a slightly wan hue to her sallow skin in the aftermath of months of nausea and life without animation. But, as Mundanus assures me – to my secret chagrin – she looks magically ravishing in the eyes of men. Even loyal old Hendrik has looked partial towards her and young Conrad almost had to be carried out on a stretcher. Yet after his eyes have briefly been blinded by her radiant presence, he bows deeply in my direction. Of course I do not acknowledge him. I have never felt as much contempt for a man as I do now. In an awkward silence we wait for him to carry out his loathsome mission, but he doesn't speak a word. I imagine sadness in his eyes, a kind of life-weary exhaustion. I must be reading expressions in his face that I wish were there, so I can feel better about having been seduced by the charms of a weasel. After the silence has lasted for several endless minutes, Gerda addresses him:

"I am just a peasant and you are a nobleman, and I wish for my betters not to have to grovel to the likes of you. Our young Mistress holds a bag with four thousand silver florins which is all they have right now."

Clara steps forward; he looks at her entranced. Like a sleepwalker he moves towards her. Her gorgeous long gloves seem to crackle with life as she extends her right arm towards him and with demonstrative disdain drops the pouch in his hands. His cream-colored leather gloves catch it and a shock passes through us all. His eyes riveted on Clara's magical presence, he holds the bag for what seems to be an endlessly long time. Finally he turns resolutely to me and speaks:

"I have not come for money. That's why I didn't bring my men. In fact I have dismissed them and sent them back to the court in Paris where I shall return after completing what I have come to tell you. I'm here to express my shame. I am a man who's killed dozens in battle, and without the slightest compunction I have separated many from their fortunes. I have spent my life at the court of the Sun King, delighting in the destruction of others with shameless pleasure." He walks over to me with admiration in his eyes. "But now it seems to me that I have never met a soul in my life." His eyes regard me with remorse. "I will leave this house a changed man for having been in your company. I'm a soldier, not a sentimentalist. Yet your presence has reached far back to an honor I no longer thought

I possessed. It was not anything you did, but who you are. You have reminded me of nobility. " Contrite, he bows deeply once more and holds up the pouch to me in order to return it. I recoil in horror, not of Nessus' poison but for the gruesome terror that will imminently be showered upon a man of obvious remorse in the act of contrition. "No!" Clara exclaims and rushes up to snatch the pouch from him before he can force its murderous shroud into my hands. The final human look in the chevalier's eyes is one of love and devotion to me. Then he resolutely turns on his heels and makes for the door. I know there will be no antidote for the inevitable corrosion and pain that is to follow, which once had driven great Hercules himself to the borders of insanity. At first I do not recognize the feeling that wells up in me. It has the acidic sense of sulfur burning holes into my heart as the full force of my conscience turns against me. I know that the pain his body is about to endure shall be etched by guilt into the tissue of my soul.

Then I realize that never before have I known Sin. I had not taken into account the possibility of this unlikely reversal in which a man chose to freely change his mind and walk away from his crime. I now remember his taciturn moods during dinner and understand that he was fighting an internal battle. One kind word of mine might have saved him from his violation – but my preoccupation with my own confusion over Clara's pregnancy had made me fail to see that what had seemed a morose silence had been instead a plea for salvation by a man in Purgatory. One true word of friendship might have changed the course of what now has become the inevitable unfolding of our common destiny. Nothing is certain until we make it so.

The internal cry of my failure shatters me at the same moment Monsieur Delamarche shrieks out in agony outside the door he had so gently closed behind him.

Mundanus runs up to Clara and with a surgeon's skill removes her gloves without touching the fabric covering her right palm; he cuts off the upper part of the right hand material with his sharp knife and tosses the polluted lower half into the fire, where it hisses like a snake enraged. The upper right segment he throws to Gerda and instructs her to grind it immediately into a powder and mix it with our strongest Brandywine, which she does without question in a coarse stone mortar with a rough pestle in the laboratory section of the kitchen. Then he cuts the arm-section off the left glove, slips his left hand into the remainder and rushes out. Through the open door I see our victim writhing in abject pain. Shielded by the oak-bark armor Mundanus strips the cream leather gloves off the knight whose eyes bulge bloody with the fires of Hell, and then carefully removes his own protective gauntlet. Within seconds Gerda has ground a coarse blush-oak powder and mixes it with the spirits. "Add ten drops of the Medicine," Mundanus calls back. She does so in a flash. Still shaking the potion violently in a small corked flask, she runs up to Mundanus, who forces open the foaming mouth of the contorted man and spills half its content deep into Monsieur Delamarche's throat holding his nose so he must inhale the vapors directly into his lungs which results into a violent coughing fit. Then he punctures a bulging vein in the neck and pours Medicine directly into the wound. He presses the remaining oak bark cloth as a bandage on our victim's neck and waits for the virulent contractions and shrill shrieks of agony to subside.

What follows is a most horrible silence. The knight lies frozen in apparent onset of instant *rigor mortis*. My heart is stripped naked and I shiver as one pierced with icicles. Suddenly a wild river of serpentine spasms contorts our victim's body. He howls an endless screech of agony as his eyes burst and blood streams down his cheeks. With cool calm Mundanus pours the rest of the antidote straight into the knight's bloody eyes. The erupting man violently shakes his head, trying to rid himself of his skull as the source of burning pain; then he stops breathing and is dead.

When I come to I see myself from a vantage point somewhere up at the ceiling looking down at myself lying on the floor in Gerda's lap with a sick feeling in my mouth. Monsieur

Delamarche is stretched out on the dining table in the center of the round room with a tube of sheep intestine sticking out his windpipe. Mundanus has the other end of the tube in his mouth and exhales into it with calm regularity; I see the chest of the supine victim expand and contract in response. Raw wool poultices cover his eyes and above his heart are the black and blue marks of having been punched sharply. Suddenly I'm being sucked back into my body and feel the contracted seizures in my muscles mimicking crucifixion.

Part Nine

Mundanus

Chapter Twenty

The raw intestine in my mouth tastes like calves' liver, I notice absentmindedly. There is blood everywhere; a warzone. I remember a scene from the beginnings of my travels all over war torn Europe after I left Venice in '45. It was in the final years of the Great War which lasted for 30 years and boiled the world in blood. My thirst for adventure had drawn me to one of the battlefields in these parts. There I stumbled upon a grand tree with wide branches. Hanging from them were twenty corpses, dangling gently in the wind. A ladder was set up against the giant trunk and a man was being pulled up by a soldier, strangling his neck as he lifted him slowly, rung by rung, to his final destination: to hang in the vineyard of death. Below on the ladder, halfway up, stood a monk, pointing his cross at the man as if that would lead him to salvation, while in the eyes of the man about to hang glared a shriek to a silent Father who had turned his back on him. Around this majestic tree of Hell stood soldiers barely watching, utterly disinterested in this meal of crows. As I witnessed the unanswered plea of the man about to be hanged, my throat closed and I realized that War itself was the rotten bunch of grapes dangling from the branches. This set me on my path to study the physician's art wherever I could find a Master. Seeing Delamarche's eyes burst into flame and his torso convulsing, I felt that same closing of the throat. I could barely breathe and realized that my body was mimicking his suffocation. I knew I had to apply Doctor Brasavola's maneuver and puncture the throat in what now, a century since he first performed it, is sometimes called a tracheotomy. While Marianne fainted into a heap and Clara slumped in her chair, looking glazed, I instructed Gerda to fetch the thin long venipuncture knife I carried among my tools of surgery and drench it in the antidote she had prepared from a mixture of the Medicine and the oak bark grinds dissolved in Brandywine. She did so in calm haste and I admired her nurse's skills. Meanwhile I was choking and afraid I would faint before I could conclude the surgery. As Gerda pushed back his jaw so his throat arched up to me like Isaac at the sacrifice, I plunged the knife with precision to his windpipe, opening up a hole large enough to insert the sheep intestine Gerda had marinated in the oak-grind Medicine. As the knife entered his flesh, I could breathe instantly and felt the opening in my own windpipe as if I had performed the surgery on myself. In this manner I knew exactly how to twist the knife so the opening would be large enough, yet not too big. I could feel the tube enter my throat and this steered my hand to find the exact place where to insert it into the windpipe. I couldn't see anything because blood was spouting forth like a volcanic spring.

But the knight did not breathe. He remained stiff and dead. I tore off his doublet and his undershirt and started to pound with sharp staccato blows on his heart. But it stayed still; nothing moved. Finally I realized that the breath I had gained from the operation should be given back to the patient and I blew into the sheep-gut pipe with great force. Then I let the pipe go and his chest deflated with a high-pitched whistle. I did so five times and just when I despaired that the knight would remain dead, I could sense a slight suction as from a life responding like a distant echo to my call.

And here I sit, breathing for the man I poisoned.

Gerda has left in a rush up the stairs, and returns with a handful of yellow flowers. As I breathe life back into the knight I watch her mix the flowers and the yellow gum from the stems into the mortar she had used to grind the oak-bark glove. I understand that she is grinding celandine poppies, mixing them with sheep milk and the Medicine. We had used this once for an eye disease of one of her ewes. It is a recipe championed first a century ago by the great Gerhard Dorn, the illustrious alchemist and student of Paracelsus. He said it would cure all manners of eye disease – even without the Medicine, which I don't believe he possessed. The blinding yellow brightness of the sunshine poppies by itself was ample remedy, he maintained, especially mixed with mother's milk. As Delamarche regains his breath, Gerda drips ten droplets of the celandine concoction in each eye. I notice a faint flinch in the patient, a good sign. The drops give the blood still crying down his cheeks a hue of blue. Then it turns to turbid transparence like the dross of tears, and finally to a milky white as flowing from a nipple.

When the patient starts breathing naturally, I cut the pipe to just outside the throat and sew it to his skin with sturdy thread made from thin dried gut to suture wounds. Then I saturate my surgery with Medicine-tinctured Brandywine. There is nothing more I can do. I notice Marianne staring at me with grieving eyes.

"We didn't give him a chance to repent," she mutters. "He came to renounce his crime and we poisoned him."

"How could we have known?" I ask, feeling much like she does. "What were the chances? He was ready to ruin us."

"We should have asked him to spare us, begged him for mercy, forgiven him for his sin. But we made war instead, cut him down like a pig. I am disgusted with myself." Her voice is plaintive and oppressed. I know we have failed a test of our moral mettle put on our path by Destiny. Our Lord and Savior would have acted differently. But then a defiant voice tells me that this is the precise reason why the Christ was born to be a savior and I was not. "We're just human," I reply.

"No we're not. At least not now," says Clara, waking from her trance. "I've never poisoned a man before. We have degraded ourselves, using the great art for black magic. We are no better than the phantom sorcerer."

"He got what he deserved. If it wasn't for us, it was for all the others he wronged. I'd do it again." Gerda stands firm in her conviction. "If a wolf attacks the herd you kill him. I don't care about remorse. The man's a louse with afterthoughts. But a louse first and foremost! He scared us to death, had Madam Marianne threatened with rape in the woods even though he knew she was with child. It's our Lord's job to forgive, not mine. I defend my kin."

Gerda's firm words, rooted in the moral fiber of the peasantry, make me feel effete by comparison. Clara, Marianne and I look at one another, no longer sure what to feel. At no point has our class distinction from Gerda been so blatant. Generations of refined philosophy have brought us nothing but doubt. I wish I had her peasant simplicity and her certainty. I remember the soldiers beneath the hanging tree. They took war for granted. In war you kill and hang traitors, no matter if they show remorse. Are philosophers superior just because we question? Is forgiveness ultimately out of reach and solely in the realm of gods like our Lord? The silence in the room hangs leaden. The knight's open eyes look like cut black diamonds with myriads of facets reflecting in all directions; like the eyes of Beelzebub, lord of the flies. I look into those eyes and no longer understand the nature of evil.

Gerda is beginning to clean up the bloody mess around the room, scrubbing the floor with particular zest.

"Come, Clara," says Marianne. "I'll bring you upstairs to your room. We have to think of our condition and give our wombs some peace." She stands up, still a bit wobbly, looks over at the knight on the table and then at me. "Thank you for saving him, Mundanus. You are a great physician." The faint smile on her face is profoundly sad. After she regains a steady balance she walks over to her niece who is entranced once again. Marianne helps her gently up from her chair and leads her to the stairs. I look at them, my spouses, each pregnant with my child, and realize we still have a problem. At some point someone might come looking for Delamarche here. Who knows whom he might have told of his coming here? Tomorrow Hendrik and Gerda must go to town and carefully inquire. I'm particularly worried about the fact that in one of her previous visits to town she had seen the scar-faced bandit who threatened to rape them in the forest and turned out to be the knight's accomplice. Delamarche said he'd sent his men back to their quarters at the French court, but I doubt the bandit lives there.

"You're a very tenderhearted bunch," Gerda mutters shaking her head as she sits on her knees scrubbing the floor. She looks up: "Tell me Doctor, why it is that Regents like you and the Ladies feel such pity on this rascal? He says he's sorry and suddenly you feel *you're* to blame. I understand about turning the other cheek and all, but this man's a crook, through and through!"

"We try to follow the example of our Lord," I try, not quite sure where to go with this. I look down at the man with the frozen eyes of a fly. "Had you noticed that he has the eyes of an insect?" I ask her. Gerda puts down her sponge and gets up. She wipes her forehead, straightens her blonde hair that had come out from under her kerchief and blows out her breath in a whistle starting with the sound of 'ph'.

"See!" she points, "He even has the eyes of the Devil," and mimics spitting on the floor through her fingers to ward off evil.

"That came about when you gave him the celandine solution. I've never seen it before. At first I thought they were blisters. But look, they are perfectly octagonal! And the iris and the white of his eyes are gone. There is only a wide-open pupil! I don't think he will be able to close them. They're permanently frozen open. Dorn said that celandine gives you night vision, but I'm sure he didn't refer to this."

Gerda looks at the anomaly with avid curiosity, all animosity forgotten in the manner of a true natural philosopher. "Do you think he will be able to see through these?" she asks. "He can't go out in public. He'd scare everyone to death! They'd think him the Devil. And they'd be right. Scaring Madam Marianne as he did! It's his punishment for scaring us, becoming scary like this. The Lord knows how to punish ... and He has a nasty sense of humor, if I may say so."

"Maybe it will pass," I say, hopefully. The thought of having to send a man back into the world looking like Beelzebub is hardly enticing, and keeping him hidden in our tower sounds even worse.

❧

But it did not come to pass. As the knight slowly came to, his faceted eyes remained frozen open like in a creature from Hell by Hieronymus Bosch. It made him utterly unrecognizable, metamorphosed into a new form, like I had been. The jolly knight of evil ways with his jaunty mustache had disappeared. The hair on his head and face was gone, and without eyebrows he looked like a freakish side show at a country fair. We couldn't send him back into the world looking like this, so he had to live his hellish afterlife with us. In this we were helped by the fact that he showed no trace of memory and spoke only German without any French accent. His mood was pleasant and quiet. Any light appeared to hurt his eyes so he became a creature of the night, able to see in the pitch dark as if it were bright day. The only shard of memory that remained was his abject devotion to Marianne, to which she responded with exquisite care.

❧

It is March; the year is 1669. Marianne and Clara look like a set of pregnant twins. Marianne's pregnancy has rejuvenated her, while Clara has matured. Gerda has been calling the knight with the devil's eyes Ivory Billiards due to the shape of his head and his pallor, and it has stuck. He's living the life of a bat in a clock tower. Even though Gerda is repulsed by him, not so much for his looks but because of having been Delamarche, she has put a bed in a windowless attic room under the roof. In the pitch dark he doesn't complain about headaches. Light cuts like a hot knife through his brain. Clara has woven an ingenious mesh of black threads that lets in a minimum of light through pinhole openings exactly aligned to the octagonal facets on his eyeballs. In this way he can carry out his devotion to Marianne, sitting quietly in a corner of whichever room she finds herself. Marianne seems not to mind, but I find it quite disturbing. The only time I have alone with her is in bright daylight outside where even Clara's mask can't protect Mr. Billiards's oversensitive eyes.

On one such walk, I realize that the impossible has happened: my affections for Marianne have grown even more encompassing than before, and I have a hard time to not neglect Clara. Marianne's pregnancy radiates glory off her face, her eyes so luminous that my breath slightly catches whenever I see her.

The forest around us smells like the early springtime of crocus and snowdrop. Marianne has her arm in mine as we move carefully through these path-less woods. She is wearing her horse riding boots, as they give her more stability than the high heel wooden clogs she wore until recently. Her balance being more precarious these days she holds on to me extra tightly; a newly added delight. I feel her warm body through her thick dark-blue velvet wrap that keeps the gusts of icy wind at bay.

"I begin to miss home," Marianne says softly, barely audible. "And yet I'm afraid to go back. I don't know how I will survive being the great-aunt of my child. I feel my baby moving inside me. I think it's a boy; I know he will look like you."

"Which one of me?" I ask in jest.

"The you I love," she replies. "I'll recognize you instantly in him; I know it. And then, he won't be mine, but Clara's." I see tears glistening in her eyes and refrain from speaking. We walk silently up a hill until we find a boulder with perfect seating for two. It overlooks the meadow nearest to our tower where a small herd of our sheep grazes peacefully. She gazes far off and I know I have to wait to be invited into her musings.

"I don't know if I can do it, Mundanus. I really don't. I've been thinking of fleeing, going off somewhere to the East Indies with my child. I'd never come back. Never!" she ends her sentence in almost a sob. Then she's quiet again. I know she's telling me this so she won't have to actually do it. I almost stop breathing in order not to make a sound.

"I love you, Mundanus, and you know I believe in your mission. Up until now it was easy to make it mine. I was all set to search for the Red Sulphur with you. And in theory it seemed like a good idea to have a baby and give it to Clara to raise as her son. But now that it is almost here I can't do it. It makes me desperate. I talk to Ivory Billiards about it. In Dutch of course, so he won't understand. But I have to tell someone. It is driving me mad. What should I do, Mundanus, what should I do? This is *our* child!" Her voice is pleading and shrills like thin tin.

I knew this moment was going to come, as had Clara. A month ago after nightfall when we were retiring to our quarters while Marianne and Gerda were still tidying up downstairs and Ivory Billiards was tucked away in a dark corner somewhere near the hearth, Clara had turned to me and said: "I don't know how she's going to do it. I couldn't imagine pretending not to be the mother of my child. I just couldn't. It is already hard for me to fathom how she deals with us going to our marriage bed every night. It would drive me insane. She is a better woman than I am. I know that. I've always known that Aunt Marianne was different from other people. But she was like my mother so I never questioned it. But this is just too much for anyone to bear..."

I consider Clara's words as I try to formulate my own reflections: my feelings as a man whose love melts like hot wax into an open wound in his heart, and my thoughts as the father to Marianne's child. I have rehearsed this instant a thousand times, but now, when the moment arises I draw a complete blank. I see Marianne's face looking up at me to find solace in my words, and I have nothing to offer. Feeling like an utter failure I just begin to speak, hoping sentences will form themselves into some kind of sense.

"We will live next to one another and you can be with our child every day of the week," I try, immediately realizing that I am not telling her anything she hasn't already considered.

She begins to weep softly and the disappointment in her eyes freezes my spirit. I realize there are no words that can address the pain of our dilemma so I turn to her and take her in my arms. But she pushes me away; she needs something spoken.

"We could go to the New World, the five of us," I try, knowing she has rejected this solution before. She looks at me, incredulous. I panic, at a loss; I hate this sunshine, wish it would rain – what had seemed lovely a moment ago now is baleful and the bucolic herd of sheep unbearable. "You know I love you whatever you do. I'll support you if you sail with our child to the edge of the world. I can't imagine how you could come back with us to The Hague and play these elaborate charades. But our son would love you like his mother, whatever he calls you. You will have a different relationship to him than to Clara's child. You're his mother. We would find a way that he can be with you most of the time. We'd find the perfect lie no one would ever suspect. I want to be with you and our child Marianne," I say, finally feeling I'm expressing what I truly mean. "You will always be my first love. Even Clara knows. I will love our child in the way I love you."

"I want to stay at least a few months longer so I can breast-feed my child!" Marianne suddenly decides. "Then, if Clara has enough milk for the both of them, she can feed them at home as twins, or we can hire a wet nurse. But I want at least a few months as his Mother."

"Of course," I respond, finally able to breathe again, my panic subsiding. When I turn to her this time she does not push me away. I kiss her cheeks and cherish the taste of her tears. Then we lose ourselves in a whirl of our longing.

ॐ

The labor pains begin simultaneously. The cry comes from Clara's lips the same moment Marianne moans. Gerda instantly fashions the downstairs into a delivery room with two beds alongside one another. Ivory Billiards has been pacing restlessly like a jailed animal, staying close to Marianne until Gerda requests that he leave and be upstairs in his bat-tower. I ask him gently in German and he seems glad to comply, though he keeps casting worried looks in Marianne's direction. "Will she be alright?" he asks in a small voice with the heavy accent spoken around Baden. It has taken me some time to learn to understand him, since the accent I'm more familiar with is from further north, around Cologne. There is deep worry in his voice and at this moment he feels like family. His world has shrunken to the single presence of the one woman we both love dearly. I promise him that I will call him down the moment the children are born. That seems to soothe him a bit and he slinks up to his lair.

Some of the womenfolk living on our grounds are harder to fence off. Conrad's mother Hilda insists that she is a midwife, and that I should leave, being a man. Childbirth should not be attended by men at all. I explain that I'm a physician but that makes no difference to her. She is a stout and overbearing older woman who refuses to listen to me. She lectures me on how to perform childbirth in ways Doctor Percival Willughby described to me when I met him in London some ten years ago. He warned me of the ways of midwives and their intrusive actions, breaking the waters before the time was ripe, pulling and tugging before the child was descending by itself. He told me many gory tales and insisted that nature should follow its course and a woman should just be kept warm and comfortable. But midwives in their pride wanted to be useful and thought of as having delivered the child. Just let Nature do it her own way and all will be right most of the time, I remember him as saying. In the end I had to call in Conrad to take his mother. She left cursing me for being a man of no piety intruding upon a women's domain.

But finally we are alone. I feel very comfortable with Gerda, who from an early age has assisted at many births, both animal and human. Over the last few weeks I have been reading Doctor Willughby's manuscript on childbirth. My own experience with childbirth is limited. I have attended the delivery of about a dozen women. Doctor Willughby had been at hundreds. Be patient, he counseled. Don't give in to the woman's wishes to get rid of the hellish pains by forcing the delivery. He gave me many tips on how to keep a woman comfortable and I have prepared several clysters to cleanse my patients so there will be no pressure from excrement upon the amniotic membrane. We have fresh chamomile, sugar, eggs and milk in readiness for enemas, and prepared the *balsamicum hystericum*, a concoction of mineral, amber and castor oils mixed with the resinous sap of the Syrian galbanum plant, to soften strained tissues. I have fashioned a crotchet, a hook to pull out the child if things go wrong. Gerda has made caudle of warm ale with gruel, eggs, sugar and spices to revive the mothers after labor is done. She has procured a plethora of blankets and pillows in town: we are well prepared. But I am worried still. One in every forty deliveries ends in death of the mother. Marianne had smiled and told me her father would have deemed these terrible odds for insurance. I am terrorized by visions of the Stone eating Marianne and Clara. I feel confident that my children will be healthy; Red Sulphur wouldn't want it any other way. Its desire to become flesh has turned up in both women's dreams. Clara had dreamt that a tidal wave of red waters overran the land and left behind complete devastation. When the blood red water withdrew it left a desert with only a straw basket in which a little girl glowed rose-pink like Clara's sorcery cloth. Marianne dreamed of Mary's bath, the double boiler, and a little homunculus smiling at her with delight. Then she put it in a hermetically sealed vessel and cooked it on high flames.

But I know how ruthless Red Sulphur can be. I remember Venier and how the Stone had seduced Clara so it could copulate with the demon Mantis. I see the phantom of the crescent dagger lunge at Clara and my mother of god protecting her. Red Sulphur has the power of the Savior and of his brother Lucifer. And I worry which face is going to emerge tonight. If the Stone feels any danger to its incarnation it will kill the mother without any trepidation. I decide to put these horrible thoughts out of my head; childbirth is dangerous enough as is. But no sooner have I told myself this, Gerda begins to talk about it. She takes me over to the hearth. She has made a high fire, crackling and sparking sizzles of red rain up the chimney, since Doctor Willughby had told me the room should be warm in winter. Mothers should be kept warm, he insisted over and over.

"I'm afraid of all the magic," she says softly, so Clara and Marianne who are resting cannot overhear. "They both are pregnant because of the Red Sulphur. It is unnatural. I never thought I'd be afraid of our alchemy, but I am, Doctor Mundanus, I am. I don't know what to expect. Do you think we should hang a screen of glow cloth behind the beds so we can see what the Red Sulphur is up to? Maybe that way we can read its mind." Her idea terrifies me but I have to admit there is logic to it. The Stone is more dangerous if we can't see it. I saw Mantis first in the glow cloth. So I nod: "Take the canopy over our bed and hang it in a place where Marianne and Clara can't see it."

I didn't notice that Marianne had gotten up and stood within earshot.

"I want to see," she says with certainty. Her hand is pressing against her side, and flashes of pain contract her face. "I want to know what the Stone is doing. I am worried about Clara. She looks very pale. Please go look at her, Mundanus. Is something wrong?"

Clara looks peacefully asleep on her side. But when I look closer, it seems she has fainted. All color has drained from her face, as if she were losing a lot of blood. I look under the covers but the staining of the sheets looks normal. Barely any blood. I try to arouse her unsuccessfully and call out to Gerda. But she has gone upstairs to get the glow cloth. So I lift her up out of the bed and put her left arm around my neck in order to walk her around the room a bit to get the blood moving. Without a moment's hesitation Marianne takes her under her other arm and lifts Clara out of the bed with me.

"Marianne, don't!" I exclaim. "You're not steady. You might fall." But she looks determined, her own onset of labor receding behind her maternal worries for Clara.

"Madam Marianne!" Gerda calls out and throws the glow cloth over some tables we have moved to the side of the room to make space for our birth chamber. The cloth drapes itself smoothly over the surface and hangs off the sides. From the corner of my eye I can see it shimmer in the shape of a solid block, remarkably symmetrical as if it had been carefully arranged to reflect the light of the fire. For a moment I sense the cloth is alive and full of expectation. Gerda rushes up and takes over from Marianne. Just as she does so, we hear a loud splash and a short sharp gasp from Marianne. Her water just broke. I note how the cloth lights up brighter than the ambient light. I get the eerie feeling that the material feels the way a father does. It feels like I do: present at the birth of his children. Was God this excited when our Savior was born? Did He stand over Mary in the manger, wringing His hands like an expectant father at the birth of His first child?

Gerda cares for Marianne and brings her back to the bed to rest while I focus on Clara, who opens her eyes and smiles faintly.

"I love you, Giovanni. I saw our daughter. I saw her fly like the trail of a shooting star along the horizon looking for me. I had to scream really loud so she could find me. I was screaming and screaming. It was very exhausting." She looks up at me blissfully.

"She will find you!" I assure her, though it looks like she is in no need of reassurance. Her eyes have closed again. Suddenly a spasm rushes through her body. I feel terrible fear. But then I hear the same splash like before from Marianne, as buckets of fluids rush out of Clara covering my legs, running into my boots. I'm at sea. Again the cloth lights up brighter than in mere reflection of the hearth. 'And God didn't even have twins with Mary!' I think in distracted sacrilege and laugh out loud. Gerda looks up at me, a question on her face. "It fits that the cloth is here with us," I say. "We're all giving birth together. I think the Stone is a more nervous father than I am."

She grins mischievously as she cleans the floor and wipes my legs. "Now Red Sulphur will see what life is really like, not as a mineral, but as flesh. It is in for a surprise!"

"I think God was surprised."

"They killed his Son. That was a pretty nasty surprise. I sure hope these children have an easier time with it than our Savior," she concludes drily. I am taken aback by the ease in which she joins me in my blasphemy. For a simple pious peasant woman, she has all the makings of a freethinker. I remember Giordano Bruno on the stake and shiver. Thoughts are dangerous. If I were to speak out loud that I believe a piece of cloth to be a god incarnate awaiting the birth of his son, they would declare me mad in Holland and burn me in Rome. The world believes that we are living in the aftermath of divine history. Our faith tells us that God became Man once, and the rest is epilogue. A hundred warnings can be heard in Trismosin's diaries to not divulge the secret: God never left but can be found in the stone the mason has cast out. I can't help but look at the glow cloth as a living shroud.

When I inspect the women with my speculum I note that both are dilated about half a thumb's length. 'Do nothing,' Willughby's voice admonishes me. I remember him telling me of a midwife who wrenched the fetus loose at this point since she believed it stuck to the mother's back, resulting in a still birth. They don't know the child is held within two sacks, swimming until it leaves of its own accord. Willughby tells us that the pure moisture in the amniotic sack is commonly spent near the approaching time of the delivery and so the fetus desires to leave this place because his provisions fail him. Then through the infant's forcing and the mother's pains the womb opens.

Finally the other bag, called the Chorion, containing the waters, descends. The midwives call this the gathering of the waters. Only then do we know that the birth approaches and that after the breaking of the waters the child will follow. This is the moment and not an instant earlier when the midwife can assist the mother in receiving the child into the world. I instruct Gerda to massage the vulvas of both mothers with the *balsamicum hystericum*, as I feel shy to do so while they are laying side by side in each other's presence. I'm painfully aware of having two wives like our Patriarchs while having none of their biblical confidence.

"Look!" Gerda hisses. The cloth is showing three armed men entering the room. Then she gasps. She recognizes the scar-faced bandit from the forest. "It's him! Scarface!" I look behind me, but everything is peaceful.

"The cloth may be foreseeing the immediate future," I whisper, holding nothing impossible anymore. "They may be coming for Delamarche right now. We seem to be at a fatal intersection. Everything is about to happen at once, like it does at the beginning of time. Run out to warn Hendrik and Conrad. Barricade the door when you come back."

Gerda nods and leaves. I hope the cloth has given us enough warning time. But all I see reflected on its cube-shaped surface is the dancing of the flames.

The women are in a slumber between contractions, still far apart, and I prepare a pint of chamomile, sugar, fresh eggs and lukewarm milk to divide in half and fill the two clysters I have fashioned for enemas. I wake the women and tell them to hold it in as long as they are able for maximum effect. Marianne looks very relaxed, though sometimes casting a worried look at her niece. I'm sure she has not noticed the vision in the glow cloth behind her.

Just when I finish the procedure Gerda comes rushing in.

"They're here!" she yells. Before she can close the door the three armed men led by Scarface enter into the room at gunpoint.

"You have killed Monsieur Delamarche," Scarface growls pointing his musket at me.

"There are two women here in labor," I say in the iciest calm I can muster. "Please lower your pistol."

He looks over at them pointing his pistol at Marianne, then he pulls a second pistol with his other hand: "I'll kill them first if you like," he replies sweetly.

Marianne cries out and can't hold on to her enema, creating a projectile mess. Gerda runs up to help her.

Clara sits up and looks at the man pointing his pistol at her with complete disdain. "You will regret this," is all she says. Then she lets out the most heart rending shriek I have ever heard. I immediately know that she is calling in her daughter from the horizon.

The three men begin to laugh.

Clara shrieks again towards the glow cloth, louder still.

Suddenly the room behind her recedes and from a hellish stage three giant Cobra serpents fly towards her. She turns back to the men and curses them quietly: "You will never sleep again."

The room turns into a primordial depiction of Hell. All the nightmares of the armed men take form. Three serpents rush past Clara and enter into the men through all orifices simultaneously. With muffled sounds they writhe like the knight had done before them. This time I only feel pleasure at their suffering. Scarface had offered to kill my women: he should suffer the torments of Hell. And he is. I sit down on a chair and watch the spectacle with cruel delight. Red Sulphur is outdoing itself, protecting its birth like a mad tiger. The Naga, the cobra serpents, are the Protectors of the Stone. Before every projection I perform the Naga dance in honor of them. I have never seen them enacting their function as Protectors. They are gruesome, using every ounce of their victims' fear to make them suffer unto apoplexy.

As suddenly as they appeared, the Naga disappear, leaving their victims behind, still as if dead. But I know that they have been paralyzed and will remain that way for hours, or days. Terror can do that to you. I am sure Clara's curse will follow them and that they will never again dare to sleep a wink. One does not cross Red Sulphur.

Before I develop any pity for them, I call out to Hendrik and Conrad who are rushing up to the tower after having freed themselves from the stables where they had been imprisoned by Scarface and his men.

"Take them away. They will not wake for many hours. Bring them to a place as far into the forest as you can find and leave them there." I know that the Naga will find them wherever they go and keep raining Hell upon them until their legs give out and they have nowhere to go but down. It is easier for a demon to enter than for it to be dispelled. I shake my head realizing that I have never before witnessed men being strangled by a terror rising up from their own graves. One can only live a vile life by carefully sequestering the evil one employs, which leaves one vulnerable to a revenge of the night. No man is immune when the chips are called in. It is a lesson I shall not forget.

The gruesome events have had opposing effects on the mothers. The excitement fully dilated Clara, but it closed Marianne's cervix. I motion to Gerda to bring the chamber pot so Clara can relieve herself since the head of the child is already crowning. It seems that she feels no pain as she barely pushes out the child who seems to come entirely of her own accord. Finally she lets out a moan of ecstatic rapture I remember from our wedding night as a perfect peristalsis of her entire body gyrates out our daughter into Gerda's waiting hands. The child breathes blissfully without a cry.

It is Sunday, April 7, 1669 at 21.15 o'clock.

I am stunned by this miraculous birth. Behind us the glow cloth sparks wildly in jubilation. As Clara hands the girl to her mother the afterbirth pops out by itself. I can barely catch it. We place it on the infant's eyes in order to prevent eye diseases and there she lies on her mother's chest under her own placenta, breathing peacefully. After a few minutes I cut the cord and

Clara hands me our infant daughter. When I hold her to my heart I feel a love I've never known melt who I was: new life begins in a swoon.

"Show me please," Marianne pleads between contractions that now come rapidly but don't lead to dilation. She is roiling in pain and anguish.

"Give her the baby," Clara insists. "It might help her." Gerda takes the placenta off our girl's eyes and puts it aside carefully in one of the two copper vessels filled for this purpose with brine made of the Medicine. It will be used as a tincture at a later point in our attempt to make Red Sulphur directly in quicksilver's hermetic bath. It had been Marianne's idea to use the life force that had nourished our children to term and transform its tissue back into Red Sulphur, thus coming full circle.

Marianne calms down instantly as the child rests on her chest and begins to cry softly. Marianne gently calls out "Johanna, Johanna!" "Johanna has come back," she adds, and instantly has to hand off her grandniece to Gerda as she rises up in horrific contractions. I'm afraid the fetus will be crushed under the giant pressure bearing down on a closed cervix and I know I may have to perform a cesarean birth. I have only seen this being done in the surgical theater from a cadaver when I was studying in Padua, but have never done one myself. The only surgeries of the kind I remember were done when the mother was already dead and the fetus was rescued from her corpse. I'm anxiously trying to remember what I saw the surgeons do in Padua. Gerda seems to read my thoughts and takes me aside. "If it goes on like this we may have to cut it out. I have done it with ewes that remained closed. These contractions are very powerful. They may kill the child. Madam Marianne's womb was open almost a thumb's length before these rapists came, but now it is tight in a cramp that won't let up. I tried to rub the *balsamicum hystericum* on her vulva but it is like stone down there." She looks up at me, awaiting my decision. "Let's give it more time. Rub on some laudanum tincture." She nods and turns to the laboratory to get the laudanum. "Gerda!" I call after her. She comes back. "Did any of the ewes survive?" I ask, as I unsuccessfully attempt to hold the nightmare vision of losing Marianne at bay. "Some," she replies with a melancholy smile. "But we didn't have the Medicine to save them. You'll perform the operation bathed in Medicine."

I don't know if I can do this and hope fervently the laudanum will undo the spasm caused by Marianne's horrific confrontation with Scarface, the embodiment of rape.

But the laudanum tincture has no effect. The entire vaginal neck and mouth of the womb remain impervious to our ministrations, while her entire body involuntarily is pushing out the child. I can feel the distress of the fetus in my body, as if I'm being flattened by a gigantic millstone. In vain we try to help Marianne to hold back the force bearing down on the fetus. Her body is no longer at her command but is solidly under the reign of terror.

Hours pass. Marianne is in the most unbearable pain. Her screams rip my heart. We try to move Clara upstairs, away from this scene of torture, but she insists that she is staying, instructing Gerda to put Johanna on Marianne's chest whenever there is a moment of ease. It provides brief oases of peace. Her screams have brought down Mr. Billiards who now sits shivering in the darkest part of the room under the stairs. As I see Marianne suffer and infant Johanna radiate new life in a rosepink glow that lights up the proud glow cloth, I acutely feel the dreadful proximity of life and death. I desperately thumb through Doctor Willughby's manual and find one section about a woman whose vaginal canal was blocked. It reads:

"Whereupon, it was conceived by them, that it would be the best way to cut the neck of the womb with an incision-knife. The which this Doctor affirmed was done on both sides of the womb, and that it proved gristly in cutting, and that the passage being thus opened, and enlarged, the woman was, then, happily delivered of a living child, and, that she well recovered these wounds, and the enforcements of the instrument, and was, afterwards, the mother of several children."

This gives me hope and I make up my mind that if I have to do surgery I had better prepare the incision knife, so I have Gerda bathe it in Medicine enforced with Brandywine. I decide to make only one single cut, not two as Willughby's case suggests. The surgeon in Padua had cut the cadaver from below the navel to the pubic bone to rescue the living child from its dead mother. One cut seems less dangerous than two. Loss of blood is the gravest danger we face. In my mind's eye I see great waves of blood. Had Clara's dream foreseen this devastation ending with only *one* child in a basket after the sea of red cleared? A sweet bloody taste sickens my mouth. I reread Willughby's passage to wrest my mind away from my paralyzed heart.

We have Marianne ingest the highest dose of laudanum I dare to administer, but it has absolutely no effect on either the pain or the neck of her womb. I rub her vulva with the Medicine and give her a liberal dose of it orally, but when I palpate between her legs after some time there is no difference between the feel of the pubic bone and the mouth of the vagina. Her lower body remains in a rock hard spasm.

The pressure in my body is becoming unbearable and I know I can't wait any longer. An hour longer and both mother and child will be dead. I take a swig of Brandywine and prepare to cut into the woman I love more than life, and thereby possibly kill her. I remember that she had done the same for me when she stabbed my heart with the dagger tipped in the Medicine. It steadies my hand.

The laudanum has put Marianne in a state of slumber. I have asked Gerda to bring down Trismosin's diary and am searching in his section on spells. I need to hold on to something, someone to guide my hand. A terrified surgeon is no good. Through magic I need to pull down the powers of the cosmos into the knife so it will be guided by the correct forces of the stars. Incantations will pull the rulers of the skies into the knife so it will do the cutting for me. But which of the myriad Governors am I supposed to pull in for this purpose? The seven planets? The thirty-six Decans who rule them? Where in the grand hierarchy of spirits can I enter? I search through the spells and the section on talismans. It has to be the correct daemon for this particular moment. Nothing in Trismosin's small hand speaks to me. The configuration must already be present within, so I feel deeply inside of myself and notice the volcanic pressure in my belly together with the tearing of my heart. I know that the despair in my heart can be dispelled by joy. Sadness and despair, Trismosin says, are Punishments from the stars. The right talisman will help us escape them. Without intervention, the stars will follow their unadulterated logic. It is logical that I would feel completely desperate at this moment: the stars are aligned in such a way that I have to perform an operation I never have done before on the woman I adore. This surgery may lead to her death. I have only seen it performed on cadavers. I find myself on a battlefield, under volcanic pressure, working in the context of Marianne's own dream of the homunculus being cooked in a hermetically sealed vessel with the highest grade of open-flame heat. But for the grace of God I would feel completely overwhelmed and desperate; such is the deadly logic inherent in this punishing situation concocted by Destiny. I know Venus should be part of the spell. She is the beloved of Mars, god of battle, and her beauty can guide his ability to cut. And I have to call in the smith god Vulcan who rules this volcano and may forge it into useful tools. My knife needs to know how to operate so I may just follow its cut. I now turn to the glow cloth and address it.

"Our child may die and so may his mother." The glow cloth instantly ceases the sparkling jubilation over the birth of his daughter. It feels as if I'm speaking to the primordial animal directly for the first time. I can feel the Stone is weary and surprisingly out of its depth, now that for the first time it experiences personal involvement in matters of creation. Gerda was right: Red Sulphur is in for a string of surprises now that it has offspring in the flesh. I suddenly feel compassion for the suffering of God as for any father of a son on his way to being crucified. Red Sulphur looks at me through the invisible eyes of a cat and grows completely dark like a clear starless night. The author of all being is holding his breath.

"I need you to send me the essential beauty of Marianne growing like Venus from the ocean depth. I need a full battalion of artillery and the indescribable sound of the fiery Groan with which time itself began. I need the Cripple God Vulcan to guide my hand and free my knife from the anvil of fate that weighs down upon it." I repeat my incantation three times in the deeply sonorous voice of the Magus. Marianne wakes; we look at one another and I suddenly know that we shall be doing this together, Marianne, the knife, Red Sulphur and I.

Slowly from the back of a cosmos behind where a moment before the glow cloth hung in invisible contemplation, the morning star rises like a blue sparkling mirror of Venus. From the mirror a figure frees itself and moves towards us. As it moves closer I see it is the essence of Marianne from before she was born and after she will no longer be in human form. It is a light of unbearable beauty. When she comes close, the light takes on human form, and the Groan of creation is heard vibrating throughout the room. She stands naked before me, glistening in dew. I feel my spirits lift instantly. Then a cloud of red dust in the distance starts moving closer and when it settles I see a proud regiment of armed men. I hold up the incision knife above my head drawing down the lightning as the entire army funnels into my surgery tool. I bow to Red Sulphur and turn back to Marianne with a liberated hand. Breathing deeply, I stare into the eyes I love and silently command her back to her slumber.

I insert the knife below my beloved's navel as Gerda holds her down, making a long incision down to her pubic bone through the skin and fatty white tissue underneath. I instruct Gerda to saturate the cut with the Medicine in Brandywine. Marianne shrieks momentarily but loses consciousness again. I cut again, now through the fascia and muscle layers. Then I open the peritoneum and push the bladder away from the uterus. I can see the head of my son straining against the uterine sack.

Now I carefully open the uterus, place my hand in and grasp the fetus under the head and effortlessly guide it out. The child is still and doesn't breathe. I pass it along to Gerda who instinctively puts her mouth over the child's nose and mouth and sucks out all the phlegm that prevents the breath to enter. She spits out the mucus and I slap my son forcefully on his buttocks as I hold him upside down by his feet. Nothing happens. I slap again and the newborn shrieks out in alarm, spitting out more mucus from his lungs. Then I put the child on Marianne's chest for a moment. She responds with a faint smile behind closed eyes.

It is Monday, April 8, 1669 at 4.30 o'clock.

I see the placenta being dispelled and as Gerda sits down with the baby on her lap, she puts the placenta on its eyes. While closing the uterine incision, I realize I need Gerda to assist me with the work of sewing up the cut tissue. From behind Gerda, out of the dark, Delamarche stands watching Marianne's baby. He has taken off his eye protection and his sensitive eyes must be seeing the infant in glaring light. I tell Gerda to give the baby to Mr. Billiards; she hesitates. But I know that Delamarche will be holding his own redemption in his hands by having the child in his lap. At this moment his hands are the safest place for my son. I speak sternly to Gerda and she does as I say. Together we sew up the uterus and place it back inside the abdomen. Now we close the abdominal fascia and sew up the outer skin. Finally we cover it with dressings Gerda has prepared by marinating shreds of Clara's magic cloth in a bath of the Medicine.

Marianne opens her eyes. Delamarche stands up and with great dignity places the infant on the chest of his mother. Marianne smiles gratefully at him. With this gesture the terrors caused by Mr. Delamarche have been redeemed. There are tears in Mr. Billiards's fly eyes. As Marianne holds on to our baby I tie off the umbilical. After all the horrors only bliss remains.

I turn to the glow cloth in profound gratitude. Together we have saved mother and child from certain death. I feel like a brother to the Red Sulphur tiger – an intimate closeness I have never felt before.

Behind me Clara calls out: "Is she well?"

"Yes," I tell her. "It's a boy we will call Maximo. Johanna and Maximo."

Chapter Twenty-One

August, 1672

As it turned out, Clara had barely any milk while Marianne had an ample supply. So most of the time Marianne was giving both babies the breast, which she did with great relish. Giving birth had opened an intensely creative phase in Clara's life and she took to her weaving with complete abandon. She wove the most spectacular cloths of images that shifted completely when the sun hit them from different angles. She became fully absorbed in her creations and by the time we left to go back to The Hague the following September Marianne had established herself as the primary mother, which was fine with Clara.

The children couldn't be more different. Johanna was delicate like a precious orchid, with a skin dazzling the eye as had Clara's sorcery cloth, while Maximo grew with amazing speed to the strength of a small giant. He drank almost twice the amount Johanna did and by September even Marianne's substantial milk production couldn't keep up. Before we left we employed two wet nurses.

We returned home with 'The Twins', as they were called, and bales of the most excellent wool. Clara continued weaving miracles and Anthonie van Leeuwenhoek told her he could sell anything she wove at exorbitant prices all over Europe. Soon Clara, Gerda and Elspeth had set up a thriving industry, with a dozen weavers producing 'ordinary' glow cloth. Clara was asked to weave sumptuous wedding gowns for the wealthy, with Princess Dowager Amalia van Solms as her main advertiser. We offered one of our struggling neighbors a handsome sum of money and took over their house, stage right of the Van Os family home. We broke through the walls and expanded our dwelling into a place that could easily house our large family. Then after some time the spacious warehouse on the corner stage right of our expanded home became available and we bought it for Clara's weaving atelier, putting up looms in each room and a large storage facility for the wool coming in from Gerda's farm and from our holdings in Altensteig. Clara was so busy that it went unnoticed that Marianne did all the mothering of the twins. They were growing up in the laboratory. Marianne and I had begun our search for the Red Sulphur in earnest.

Helvetius was extremely pleased to have us back after a year of absence, and turned out to be a magnificent grandfather. This brought him closer to Marianne than he had ever been, and the years until 1672 were a time of expansion, family bliss, and of silver coming in.

Then England attacked from the west, France from the south and Munster from the east and the great panic began; everything came to a halt. 1672 came to be called The Disaster Year.

The English were defeated by sea, but the French marched around our defense line to the south and attacked from the East with unheard-of cruelty, making it a custom to rape daughters in front of their parents. Marianne was completely out of sorts, reliving her own terrors. Johan de Witt had focused his energies over the last decade on building up a giant fleet to protect the enormous importance of the seas for Dutch trade. As a result the army had not been kept up and was handily overcome by the French troops. The Sun King himself was near the front delighting in all the action.

When the country was overrun, the mood among the populace turned viciously against Johan de Witt and his brother

Cornelis. Prince William of Orange, now 22 years of age and commander of the troops, was made Viceroy William III of the Netherlands. An attempt on Johan de Witt's life was made in June and he could no longer do his work as Grand Pensionary. Then his brother Cornelis was accused on very shaky grounds of treason. He was supposed to have ordered the new Viceroy William III to be murdered. He was going to be tortured in order to obtain a confession on August 18.

We received much of our information about the mood around The Hague from Mr. Billiards. He was out all night, going to pubs and alehouses, listening carefully at our behest. He had learned Dutch in a matter of months and now spoke it without any accent, as if he had been born in The Hague. We knew that the Regent class was fleeing wherever they could, burying their valuables in the walls of their grand homes and their larger goods in warehouses. There was no more space to be had in all of the Residence. Regent friends asked to use Clara's weaving atelier to hold their possessions, but Clara had refused. Losing your material goods to looting was the risk of being a Regent, she countered. We believed ourselves relatively safe, because of Helvetius being Prince William's physician. We would probably be spared the rage against the Regents by a fiercely Orangist populace; but we were afraid nonetheless. There had been a run on banks all over the Dutch republic and all silver was gone; only worthless paper such as government bonds remained. Just the banks in Amsterdam, the largest in the world, survived. All we had left were our shares in the East Indies Company and the gold Marianne and I had made from lead over five years ago which were kept in the secret compartment behind the fireplace in Marianne's laboratory.

ॐ

It is the morning of Sunday August 14. It is hot all over town. Loud carousing is heard; people are now drinking around the clock. It seems that they have gone back to the pubs right after church, their sojourn with God not having diminished their desire for alternate spirits. For the last months all work has stopped and the unemployed rabble is thirsting for blood and gin. The famous preacher Simon Simonides has been glorifying Johan de Witt's assassin as a new Christ and compared his execution by hanging to the Passion of our Lord. A cannibal crowd is hungry for De Witt flesh.

There is a loud knock at the door. Helvetius is with the Prince at his military headquarters at Bodegraven on the Rhine, just behind the waterline of defense. Clara is at the atelier next door, while Marianne, The Twins, and I are upstairs in the laboratory pursuing our ongoing search for the mystery of Red Sulphur.

Maximo has continued to grow at breakneck speed and at three years of age looks almost seven. Johanna is tiny by comparison, like a porcelain figurine, with a beauty no painter could reproduce, her skin radiating a pastel glow of pink roses.

Loud knocks in times such as these bode ill. But, before Marianne can stop her, the maid has opened the front door. On the threshold, sweating profusely and even more corpulent than when she last saw him over five years ago, former Mint-Master Porelius stands, hat in hand, nervously looking into the hallway. From my room upstairs I hear her welcome this man I've never met before, but remember as having been one of the original witnesses of the December 1666 transmutation from silver into gold.

"Deacon Porelius," Marianne greets him, "What brings you here in these dark times?"

The former Mint Master is fumbling with his hat, keeping an awkward silence.

"Come in, please come in. It isn't safe to keep the door open for too long."

Deacon Porelius is dressed in his somber woolen Sunday best, far too warm for a hot August day. Crestfallen, he looks down at his shoes, though I'm not sure whether he can spot them under his substantial belly.

"I'm sorry I can't stay. I'm leaving town. So I must be quick. I apologize," he mutters in staccato. "I've just come from paying my respects to the former Grand Pensionary."

I am surprised. From what Marianne had told me the man is a coward, and going to visit Johan de Witt at a time like this takes courage. The De Witt brothers have become increasingly isolated since the trial of Cornelis de Witt for treason had begun. By now there are constant crowds around his stately home at the nearby Kneuterdijk. Hundreds of pamphlets call for his death. It seems that the only jobs left in The Hague are for authors and printers of scurrilous political drivel.

"Madam Schweitzer," he formally addresses Marianne, "The Grand Pensionary requests the pleasure of your company at your earliest convenience."

"Why, if I may ask?" Marianne inquires, puzzled.

"He gave no reason, Madam, but he clearly indicated that it was a matter of great urgency. His actual words were: 'Please beg Madam Schweitzer to do me the honor of a visit as soon as she is able. Preferably this very Sunday!'" His tone imitates Johan de Witt and I hear an undertone of despair, the provenance of which I'm unable to ascertain. The plump Deacon is skipping town after all, as are many of the Regents. But I am sure that this is not an ordinary request for a social visit.

"Why should I go see him?" Marianne bluntly asks the Deacon.

"The Grand Pensionary invoked his friendship with your father, may he rest in peace."

"He must be desperate," Marianne concludes calmly.

"Of course he is," I interject. "The rabble wants to eat him alive. They hold him responsible for the French invasion. They say he sold us out to King Louis to spite Prince William, and nonsense like that." I don't particularly like the man who mounted a large manhunt for me, which I could only escape by completely changing my appearance. But I have never doubted his integrity and his undying love for his country.

"Excuse me," Marianne says, looking at the hapless Porelius as her arm flows elegantly in my direction. "Let me introduce my nephew Signor Giovanni Dolfin."

Deacon Porelius bows toward me, obviously knowing who I am. The Princess Dowager has made sure that I have become well known in social circles, both for being a Dolfin and for being married to one of the most ravishing women in the Residence whose weavings ladies are fighting to buy. Our close connection to the Oranges is saving us at this moment. Otherwise I might be jumping ship like Porelius. I have The Twins to consider. Porelius is clearly affiliated with the fallen Regent government and is thus in immediate danger.

"I have to apologize, dear Madam, Sir, but I really must go." He bows even deeper.

"Thank you so much for relaying the Grand Pensionary's message. I shall surely consider it." Her tone towards him is both kind and melancholy. "I'm sorry the circumstances of our meeting are dire. May we soon see better times." Deacon Porelius bows again, this time in gratitude for her gentle words, then turns around and lets himself out.

"What does he want?" Marianne turns to me with alarm. "He wants me to help him, but how? It is dangerous to be part of his circle right now."

"Since when do you care about danger?" I ask, without being in any way facetious. I consider her to be the most courageous person I know. With an expression turned inward, she doesn't listen to me.

"What is he up to?" she mumbles softly.

"You'll only find out if you go see him. I'll come with you. I want to meet this man who has been trying to hunt me down for all these years. Let me go get Clara. She can take The Twins to the atelier. They love it there." The children are used to seeing their mother weaving all the time, the same way Clara had known her mother to embroider whenever she wasn't too depressed to have the curtains opened. It always moves me when

I think of Clara as a little girl sitting quietly in a corner of her mother's bedroom watching her create miracles in needlepoint.

Marianne's face is riddled with doubt, so I wait.

"We're in the middle of an experiment," she points upstairs to the laboratory. I know it is an excuse, so I don't respond. This will have to be her decision, not mine.

"I'm scared, Mundanus. The mob's about to tear him to shreds. I don't want to be naïve."

I know she is right. The mob craves a sacrifice. They see the De Witt brothers as the devils that betrayed them.

"Father would want me to go," she says, her jaw set.

"I'll get Clara," is all I say.

I'm proud of Marianne, proud to be part of her life.

ॐ

We are shown in by a servant who looked at us with avid expectation. The whole household must be expecting something essential from Marianne. My curiosity is peaking.

Johan de Witt no longer looks like the man we all know from the many paintings made of him: a man with a proud hook nose and sensuous lips, radiating irrepressible self-confidence. Now his skin is pale and his step is hesitant, supported by a silver knobbed cane, as he comes in to meet us in his study.

"Miss Marianne," he addresses her with the intimacy which must have existed between them when he had been one of the esteemed young friends of her father's at the Van Os family home. I see that she is surprised by his implicit appeal to their past. But she quickly recovers, taking him up on his request for intimacy.

"Master Johan, may I introduce my nephew-in-law Signor Giovanni Dolfin," she replies, bowing twice slightly, first in his, then in my direction.

"I attended your wedding," he answers, referring to the first ceremony, which we ourselves had failed to attend. There is a twinkle in his otherwise sad eyes.

I must have looked embarrassed. "It was actually delightful to see the Princess Dowager become exasperated. We all had to wait for her to get up and leave."

"I deeply apologize," I respond, truly glad I can offer my sincere regrets over our brutal affront to one who had been in attendance.

"I spent a great deal of money on you, Doctor Mundanus," Johan de Witt tells me. I am utterly taken aback and absolutely speechless. How long had he known I was Mundanus? And why didn't he have me arrested, forcing me to convert my Red Sulphur into the gold he so desperately needed?

"Since when did you know?" Marianne asks incredulous, knowing it would be insulting to deny something this grandmaster at political chess must have carefully waited to divulge at this precise moment.

"Does it really matter?" he asks, his voice betraying deep exhaustion. "Let's say it happened around the time you received your shipment of alchemy tools. It was rather careless of you to assume the men I sent would understand no Latin and would not be able to follow your conversation." I remember how Marianne and I were making fun of the inspectors who came to investigate the alchemical laboratory of Salomon Trismosin we had shipped from Venice. They had us firmly convinced that they were ignorant fools, which made us loose lipped in Latin. They had obviously just played at not being able to make heads or tails of the equipment in order to eavesdrop. "Then we made some inquiries in Venice and I asked around among alchemists if there were alchemical ways to radically change appearance if one possessed the Red Sulphur. They told me that there were legends of a fountain of youth that could be obtained from your Stone. I'm a practical man, Doctor Mundanus. I calculate odds."

"Then why did you not have me arrested?" I ask, awestruck.

"The Princess Dowager was looking for you as well, for her own reasons. She needed the Medicine for the young Prince William, and gold to be independent from me. I needed no extra confrontation with the Orange family over some dubious chrysopoeia claim based on the possible transmutation of an ounce or so of lead." I'm struck by the fact that he knows the jargon of our gold-making art. "But enough of this. I need to be blunt. I have a big favor to ask you, Miss Marianne, which you have no reason to grant me. Four days from now my brother Cornelis will be put on the rack to elicit a confession from him about treason. I know my brother. He will never admit to something he didn't do. He is a man of honor and would rather die. So I'm afraid that the torture will kill him. I've written to Prince William to intervene, but he let me know that he didn't have the time to get involved, since he has a war on his hands." Johan de Witt's voice is without expression. He is a past master of the Regent art of masking emotion.

"Now you want me to go to him and ask again," Marianne concludes for him.

The retired Grand Pensionary responds with an affirming silence.

"Why me?" she asks, calmly playing the stoic Regent game. Even I can't guess her emotions.

"You are one of the very few people towards whom our Prince has affections. Certainly the only one to whom I have any access right now." He plays his cards openly; a sparse directness appears to be essential.

"You want me to go to the Prince's headquarters at Bodegraven."

"Your husband is there, you could pay him a visit. The Prince would be very happy to see you. I know him well enough for that." Johan de Witt had been his tutor for a long time while the young Prince of Orange was a ward of the state. "I no longer hold any power, so I can't force you. All I can do is invoke the spirit of your father." His only trump card is their old family friendship.

"I never had a chance to give you my condolences over the passing of dear Wendela," Marianne says in a carefully measured tone, referring to Johan de Witt's beloved wife who had died some time ago. In the understated language of Regents, she has consented to his request.

De Witt gets up from behind his desk with gratitude in his eyes.

℥

It takes Hendrik five hours to get us to Bodegraven by dusk. From a far distance we can see the inundated lands, a giant lake surrounding Holland like a moat. Beyond it are the armies of King Louis. On the waters I see flat bottomed boats with cannon, and to the right of the small town a large encampment of tents and soldiers dressed in large brim hats and colorful capes. We pass several campfires with large cauldrons hanging over them cooking meals for the bored soldiers. A group of women with large skirts and blue frocks are dancing a polonaise in a long line through a crowd of beer-drinking soldiers. The flag of the Orangists – orange, white, and blue - flies over the Dutch Lion standard, indicating Prince William's headquarters. Around it soldiers are hanging about in a state of low alert. A man with a long yellow cape hanging loosely over his shoulders comes up to us, reeking of gin.

"I'm Doctor Helvetius' wife," Marianne tells him in a voice of implacable authority. "I've come to see my husband." The man instantly takes off his hat and bows.

"He's with His Highness the Captain General," he says pointing at the tent behind him.

Marianne nods imperiously and commands Hendrik sternly to help her out of the carriage, emphasizing her elevated social status. Ordinarily she never uses this tone with Hendrik.

Upon entering the tent we see a group of men bent over large maps on a table.

They notice Marianne's presence and stand to attention, waiting for the Prince to respond to these unexpected visitors.

Prince William looks up at us. He looks different in his new rank. Self-confidence radiates from him, combined with an air of unquestioned authority. I met him for the first time when he was sixteen, an attentive boy. Over the years I had seen him mature. Now all shyness seems to have vanished and he has stepped into the shoes of his illustrious ancestors.

"Madam Schweitzer!" he calls out with boyish abandon, which his tutor Johan de Witt would have frowned as most un-regent-like. The broad smile on his face conveys his intense happiness to see her. Then he bows to me, briefly acknowledging my presence. "Signor Dolfin," he greets me. Turning to his men he orders them to leave us for a while and they obediently file out, carefully hiding any sign of curiosity.

"Doctor Schweitzer is in his tent; should I call for him?"

"Later, please, my dear Prince," Marianne replies, having long since stopped addressing him formally as 'Your Highness'.

"I have not seen you since my return from England a year and a half ago," he replies, indicating openly that he has missed her presence in his life, to which Marianne smiles happily, flaunting all decorum.

"There is so much I would like to talk with you about," he blurts out impetuously, much unlike the authoritative Captain General he had been just a moment ago. Obviously her presence brings out his longing for a confidante, a position in which Marianne had found herself since '67. His rise to power has deprived him of people he can implicitly trust. For a powerful Prince, true friends are a rare commodity.

"How was England?" she asks him in the familial way she would use talking to Clara. I have not before observed their closeness directly and I'm surprised at the obvious depth of their friendship. Their intimacy has instantly reestablished itself and I feel like a complete outsider.

"England is becoming increasingly popish. I was surprised. My uncle Charles treated me very well. I can tell you more about it when we have time to walk in Grandmother's garden at the North End Palace." He pauses. His demeanor changes slightly. Marianne notices and sits more upright. A page enters and whispers something to the Prince. "Let him in," he responds.

The flap of the great tent opens and Helvetius enters.

"Marianne, what a surprise, Giovanni! What are you doing here?"

"They're coming with a message from Johan de Witt," the Prince responds, looking intently at Marianne. She doesn't flinch. Obviously Prince William has Johan de Witt's Kneuterdijk home watched carefully.

"She is going to ask me to intervene in the trial of Cornelis de Witt. And I will have to give her the same answer Johan de Witt gave people when they asked him to intervene, and requested that his assassin's death sentence be commuted. I will have to tell her that the justice system must run its course. It is not up to me to intervene." He keeps staring intently at Marianne. Her face is exquisitely expressionless. A brief flicker of admiration rushes over the Prince's countenance. I am impressed with his ability to respond to his friend without having to cause her the embarrassment of having to ask for a favor that he must decline.

Marianne bows briefly, acknowledging the definite finality of his response. No further conversation is required. I can't assess her emotions.

"Helvetius," she answers him kindly. "I am so happy to see you. My dear Prince," she turns to him, "Our travels have made me thirsty. Might I bother you for a glass of wine?"

Prince William can't help showing affection towards her. They have elegantly acquitted themselves of a potentially embarrassing mission. He calls out to the page. When the attendant returns, Prince William says:

"This is a delicious French wine. Winemaking is the only thing the French excel at. And the Lord has a strange way of choosing their kings for them. The current one wants to become Emperor of Europe, the new Charlemagne." He pauses. "It's going to be my life's mission to prevent that."

ಐ

On August 18 Cornelis de Witt was brutally tortured to obtain his confession. We hear that throughout, as his bones were systematically being broken, he kept taunting his torturer if he can't do better than that, until he passed out completely. Without a confession, the judges couldn't hang him. He was condemned to lifelong exile. On August 20 Johan de Witt rushed to the courthouse to pick up his brother, whom he found completely incapacitated with multiple severe injuries calmly reading Moliere, a testament to Regent Stoicism. Meanwhile the word had leaked out that the court was letting the devil De Witt run free. A large crowd gathered. In mysterious ways the guards disappeared and the mob rushed into the courthouse. They dragged out the brothers.

Mr. Billiards was in the crowd, fulfilling his mission to be our eyes and ears on the streets. He tells us the next morning: "The mob wanted blood. They tore them to shreds, a butcher gutted them like pigs and then their fingers, sexual organs, ears, and everything was sold as souvenirs. Cannibals ate their flesh. Someone swallowed an eye. The ringleader was walking around showing everyone the two hearts, one in each hand. Then they hung their beheaded cadavers upside down from a seesaw they improvised. There they hung till nightfall. Only then the crowd dispersed and the family came to retrieve the remains."

Ivory Billiards remains silent after his report, which he presents to us in the red wall-papered downstairs living room glowing brightly in the sunlight, so incongruous with the story he just told us. Marianne and Clara are obviously shaken to the core.

"Monsters," Clara whispers.

"The brothers De Witt's dignity impressed me," Delamarche muses out loud. "The bloody scenes brought back memories of battles, as if I had been in them; as if I had been a soldier."

We look at one another, knowing we must tell him about his life as the nasty knight and leave his responses to the mercy of the Lord. The meeting of our glances makes it apparent that we are in agreement, but that we shall wait until a later point.

This outcome of the drama of the Grand Pensionary and his hated brother had been predictable. The rabble had wanted to slaughter the brothers as an expiatory sacrifice, magically righting all that was wrong in the desperate country overrun by invaders. That's why the Prince had refused to intervene. However fiercely he is being adored by the populace, not even he could risk the rage of the mob.

"For all his faults, Johan was a noble man," Marianne eulogizes softly, after straightening her posture. "He was one of the greatest leaders we've ever had. History will vindicate him."

"Much good does that do for him," Clara scoffs, outraged at the beastly scene Ivory Billiards had sketched out.

I remember my youth, passing from battlefield to battlefield, quenching my thirst for adventure and ending up with a deep-seated hatred of war in all its manifestations. Even though for some professional soldiers it may be an exciting business, keeping them on the invigorating edge between life and extinction, for most conscripts and civilians it is un-attenuated bloody horror. I know that we have to defend ourselves from barbarians like King Louis who has become a merchant of rape and pillage while building his fairytale palace at Versailles. But the price is unspeakably high. I despise the mighty who amuse themselves with expansion, power and revenge. Monarchies are ruled by family quarrels, with King Louis of France and King Charles of England being first cousins and Prince William the latter's nephew. I must agree with Prince William's assessment that the French monarch is the greatest danger to the world; but I have a hard time stomaching the price in blood it takes to wage a permanent war of containing the Sun King's lust for universal power. He is like Red Sulphur gone wild.

Suddenly I realize that we are in a moment of mortification, when the material is tortured and torn to shreds, dismembered and sacrificed. This would be the propitious time to let the substance we've been working on to make the Red Sulphur from scratch go through its next *nigredo*, its blackening process of rot and decay so that only the essence will remain. I'm ashamed of this opportunist idea; but it makes perfect sense. I don't feel comfortable communicating this to Marianne, though at the same time I know that the most propitious instant for this particular alchemical operation is at this very moment. The patterns of destiny are tightly woven and windows open and close rapidly.

I'm torn. It will be such a dreadfully inappropriate suggestion. This, too, is in accordance with the nigredo state: everything within the *nigredo* momentum is socially utterly inappropriate, because the customary forms are being destroyed to get to the naked core of the matter.

"There is nothing I can do," I say finally. "I'm going up to the laboratory and do some work."

Clara nods. She understands the artisan's need to be working when times are dark.

"I'll go to the atelier," she says. "I can take the twins. You go up with Mundanus, Aunt Marianne. Go work. It's the only thing we can do."

Ivory Billiards looks disheartened.

"I'll make you a bed in the laboratory. You can sleep there while we're working," Marianne offers in French, addressing him for the first time in his mother tongue since his transformation.

Both Clara and I hold our breath.

"Thank you so much," Mr. Billiards replies in his native parlance, without noticing that he has switched languages. His old self is making its slow reappearance, like a wounded soldier crawling in from the battlefield after having been missing in action for several years.

In an unspoken agreement we all speak French with Monsieur Delamarche from this moment on, so he will not be fully aware of his return to his senses until we are ready to face it. It is best to keep him inside. He is vulnerable like a molting snake. Upstairs in the laboratory we prepare a field bed and his thick sleeping mask Clara fashioned in a way that it lets in no light whatsoever. He passes out instantly, exhausted from a protracted lack of sleep over the past 72 hours.

Marianne sits down on one of the laboratory stools and stares aimlessly into the distance.

"I should have pressured the Prince more so he would have intervened. I could have saved them." Tears roll down her expressionless face.

We both know that this is untrue so I won't insult her by stating the obvious. She feels less out of control by feeling guilty. I go over to the little oak bonsai trees in front of the only window in the laboratory.

From some of the Dutch traders with whom I sailed in the Orient, I heard of a peculiar tradition in the land of Japan, east of China. The Dutch were trading there in a town called Nagasaki. They told me that these Japanese had mastered the art of growing miniature trees, which contained the essence of their full size ancestors in a highly concentrated form. To me it had felt like a kind of vegetative alchemy. I tried to trace down one of these miniatures and finally found a specimen in the Indies. It was grown on a flat tray. The artifex told me that he constantly pruned the roots and shaped the tiny branches until he obtained a perfect tree in miniature, almost like an amulet of a tree. I had always wanted to try my hand at this arboreal art. It is said that the Stone incorporates a vegetative, a mineral, an animal, and a divine spirit. Such a tree called Bonsai must be the concentrated essence of vegetative spirits. So when we had collected the afterbirths of Johanna and Maximo, I waited for them to rot and then ground their putrid remains, mixing them with the moss Clara had been craving during her early pregnancy and the urine and excrements of both infants. We all know that some of the best material to use for growing the Stone is the pure urine of children. We kept the two separate as different provenances. In this placental earth I planted small oak saplings, the size of my thumb. From this we obtained three Johanna Bonsai and three Maximo miniature trees. We carefully transported them home to The Hague and I had cared for them, bringing them outside during the day and back in for the night. By slowly changing their positions toward the sun, I had been able to grow remarkably shaped trunks in the tiny trees which had been fed on the essence of the animal spirits that had come into the world with The Twins. After three years I could now begin to use some of the clippings for our alchemical experiments. I was just waiting for the right time to use this mixture of vegetative and animal spirit and add it to metal to obtain the mineral precursor to the Red Sulphur - the sky blue stone.

Marianne and I had begun the arduous process of extracting the active ingredient from natural gold. In gold, the sulphur is most digested, since it has reached its ultimate completion. From the natural gold we had obtained a few drams of the yeast which made this metal grow into gold over the eons. We carefully mixed this gold-derived sulphur with greatly refined quicksilver during several clear full moon nights, since the blue stone has a special affinity to the full moon mirror. From this we obtained the alive silver we call *argentum vivum*, the primal material for the transmutation towards the blue stone.

Up until now we had followed common alchemical procedures but did not know how to quicken this primal material with the spirit we had grown in our concentrated miniature oaks. All I knew was that in order to obtain these spirits we somehow needed to divest the nature of the wood from its material husk. This is the process called mortification, in which you torture the substance until it gives up its essence. It is done by reducing the material to a putrid *nigredo* state in which the volatile spirits rise to the top of the glass vessel and black dross remains at the bottom.

How to actually perform this particular nigredo in the glass vessel, however, was a mystery.

Marianne is still staring listlessly towards points unknown. I take a Johanna bonsai with the most ample foliage and a similar Maximo specimen. Holding them up to her I say:

"My dear one, do you remember the night when we activated the Red Sulphur to make the Medicine during the night of the great victory fireworks in The Hague in '67? We did that because a time of glory is propitious for *rubedo*, the dawning of the sun in the heart of the Stone. It worked perfectly, that night. Today we are surrounded by the hangover of yesterday's horrible mortification of the brothers De Witt. The rabble did to them what we are told to do to primal matter during *nigredo*. So this very moment is propitious for the mortification of the Trees of Life we have grown." My formal words sound like obscene sacrilege, but I firmly stand by them.

Marianne instantly understands my reasoning and it revives her.

"It may be the only good thing to come out of these horrible events," she concurs.

I notice I had been holding my breath.

The quickest way to blacken the wood is by burning it to ashes. This could harm the spirits, however, in the same way you harm Red Sulphur if you project it directly unto the molten lead without first wrapping it in wax.

"We might cook the wood in a steamer over a concoction of gold-sulphur tinctured *argentum vivum* and morning dew," she suggests. We have been collecting morning dew now for several months. It is known that this moisture of early morn carries waxing medicinal qualities related to the flow cycle of the tides. I nod. I had been thinking the same. One of the pleasures of working with an intimate companion in the laboratory is that matters become obvious to the both of us simultaneously.

As we set up the experiment with clippings from the branches of each miniature oak in the smallest steamer we have, having come down to us from Trismosin's legacy, I remind her that we have to remember every word Monsieur Delamarche has told us about yesterday's brutal events so that the mortification shall be fully present to our minds. As we do so, we collect the bitter tears running down our cheeks and add them to the concoction in the bottom pan. I can feel sour saliva rise from my throat fed by my disgust of the nauseating events. I spit this into the lower boiler as well.

The stench in the room is becoming unbearable, a combination of sulphur and putrid decay as the steamed wood in a matter of hours slowly turns into a rotten brown mush. When the color is just right we take it out of the steamer and put it into the lower oven of the copper green furnace to dry. By now it is late afternoon and we haven't eaten anything since last night's dinner, having forgotten all about food. But we have to save the dispirited material from the bottom vessel, which had provided its spirits to the upper vessel through steaming, by scraping it carefully from the bottom of the pan where it has formed a thin film of black cake. We grind the dispirited material into a fine powder and store it in a warm, though not hot, section of Trismosin's furnace. We fill its belly with red coal from the fireplace and rush downstairs to the kitchen, ravenous.

ಐ

Ivory Billiards sleeps for 24 hours.

He wakes just when we return to the laboratory with The Twins on Monday, August 22. Rumors are flying all over town that the Prince has handsomely rewarded the ringleaders of the murderous rabble for their demonic actions, which freed him of his archenemies. Marianne is disgusted and can't believe it until we hear it from Helvetius himself, who has returned home to resume his practice in the Residence. Prince William is in great health and apparently buoyant from last Saturday's events. I'm afraid the confirmed news will permanently damage her relations to her young friend. She is seeking solace in being with her children.

The Twins began to talk fluently in Dutch and Latin from the age of two. Johanna is demonstrating prodigious musical ability and we have bought her a harpsichord spinet with a very high stool so she can reach the keyboard. Every free moment, she can be found in the red living room, composing endless simple melodies. Maximo has taken to clay, and sculpts every-thing he sees: faces, trees, dogs, sheep and carriages. He seems to be particularly interested in making clay machinery. He has tried his hand at sculpting looms and spinning wheels, sitting in the corner watching Mother Clara weave. They call both women Mother and seem to hardly distinguish between them. In the beginning our servants tried to correct them, saying "No, this is your mother and that is your great aunt"; to no avail. After half a year everyone has given up and we have all taken to calling their two mothers 'Mother Clara' and 'Mother Marianne'. The twins just address each of them as Mother.

I, of course, drew up a horoscope right after their birth to understand their particular astrology. With each born in early April they obviously have their Sun in Aries, both with a Cancer Moon. But Johanna ascends in Scorpio and Maximo in Pisces, which makes for considerable differences. The main difference in the skies during the moment of their first breath is that Johanna has most of the great wanderers on the descendent side of her chart whereas Maximo ascends with them. This might indicate that Maximo is going to be self-absorbed while Johanna will find her animation in her contact with others; also, that Maximo may be more of the poetically dreamy Piscean kind, while Johanna might have the passionate and penetrating sud-den lethal sting of the scorpion. They each entered life during an overhead conjunction between Sun and Mercury in Aries. This could spell out a brilliant and agile pioneering mind for both. How all of this is going to interact with their Red Sulphur parentage is of course completely unforeseeable.

The Twins are in a corner, playing with alchemical tools, when Ivory Billiards awakes and exchanges his sleep shade for his daytime light reducing eye textiles.

"I must have slept for a very long time," he says in French. "I seem to have been dreaming all night long. I dreamed of bat-tles and of a life of gambling, carousing and drinking, much like yesterday's mob."

"The day before yesterday," Marianne corrects him. "You slept for a full 24 hours."

"That explains why I feel stiff like a board," he replies stretching and yawning, entering fully into waking. He sits up as his spine meanders in the way of a serpent. We can hear it crackle.

"Those were not dreams," I say, deciding this might be a good time to break the news. "They were memories. You actually did fight in wars and you were a big time gambler."

He looks at me, uncomprehending.

"Your real name is Monsieur Delamarche; you were a knight at the court of King Louis."

"Me, a bloody Gaul?" he asks in perfect courtiers' French.

"Just listen to yourself," Marianne responds. "This is not the way a German or a Dutchman speaks French."

Monsieur Delamarche looks stunned.

"We met you in Baden where you lured people into card games you would ultimately win, acquiring their fortunes. We actually met because we bought lands from a man who had gambled away all his money to you and then you tried to trick us," I tell him quietly.

"And then you had me all but raped whereupon you so called 'saved' me to gain my confidence."

Monsieur Delamarche appears utterly aghast. "But Madam, that cannot possibly be true; I'd give my life for you."

"Not at that time," Marianne replies calmly. "At that time you wanted to blackmail us out of all of our moneys. You had information that could harm us and you used it in the ugliest of ways."

"So we stopped you, and in doing so harmed you. You lost your memory and all the hair on your body, leaving you with eyes of painful sensitivity," I conclude. "You no longer spoke any French so you could not go back to King Louis' court; and thus we took you home with us to The Hague." We are silent, awaiting the knight's response. His face is frozen into a mask; he knows our words are the truth.

"Mother, what's wrong with Uncle Billiards?" Johanna asks. "Has he seen a ghost?" She knows that ghosts are the most frightening creatures imaginable and sometimes she sees them wandering through the house. Then she crawls into Marianne's bed in the way Clara had done when she was a child. The twins sleep in Marianne's bedroom in cribs.

"No darling," Marianne responds. "Uncle Billiards has heard something terrible and has to digest it." She always speaks to the children as if they could understand as well as adults do.

"Like when I learned that Maximo was a boy and I a girl," she says, referring to the moment they had examined each other's genitals and came running to Marianne in great alarm.

"Something like that, yes," Marianne concurs in a voice gentle as a featherbed.

Johanna looks at Uncle Billiards in an earnest manner. "It will pass, Uncle Billiards. And then you will suddenly understand everything." Maximo stands behind her and nods, dead serious.

Monsieur Delamarche looks from one to the other, and slowly a smile breaks on his face. He knows that whatever was his past, his love for these children is certain. It breaks through his paralyzing confusion. "I know that, Johanna," he responds to her in French.

"What is he saying, Mother?" she asks.

Monsieur Delamarche is once again confused.

"She speaks no French," I explain.

"Am I speaking French?" he asks, nonplussed.

"Don't you speak Dutch?" Maximo inquires, incredulous.

"Do you speak Latin?" Johanna asks in Latin. I admire the way she immediately accepts the fact that Uncle Billiards appears to no longer speak Dutch.

Monsieur Delamarche nods. "Yes I do," he replies in French.

"And German?" I ask in German.

He nods again. "Yes that too, and Dutch too," he replies in French, increasingly upset. Obviously he can still understand languages but can only speak French.

"Have no fear," I try to calm him in Dutch, so the children can follow our conversation and their alarm may abate. "You can still understand everything. Your ability to speak will return, I can assure you."

"What is happening to me, Signor Dolfin?" he asks me in a small voice.

"Your past is coming back to you in stages. It will take a while until you remember everything clearly. Then you'll be able to speak once more all the languages you know. For now you'll have to make do with French."

"But I hate the French," he says in French with the fervor of a patriotic Dutchman who loathes the Gaul.

"There is indeed much to hate of late," I concur. "I like them at a distance. Close up they're barbarians."

"But that is because of King Louis," Marianne soothes our warmonger mood. "There's also Moliere and Racine. And Master Descartes."

Monsieur Delamarche has trouble accepting his French provenance more than anything else. He doesn't yet question that we have poisoned him.

"I'll teach you Dutch," says Johanna, completely undaunted, her enthralling pink skin glowing with pleasure.

"And I will help," echoes Maximo, backing up his sister.

Monsieur Delamarche looks at the twins with deep avuncular affection. The revelations have not damaged our family ties for now.

Part Ten

Clara

Chapter Twenty-Two

October 1676

I love hearing Johanna play the spinet. At seven she is an exceptional prodigy.

At the advice of Christiaan Huygens, we school the twins at home. Christiaan had been homeschooled, his math instruction supervised by Master Descartes himself. Whenever Christiaan is in Holland he teaches them mathematics. Aunt Marianne instructs them in languages: Dutch, French and Latin. Mundanus tutors them in Italian and Greek, as well as in astronomy and alchemy. Both he and Helvetius give lessons in medicine. Old Constantijn Huygens, now 80 years of age, but of sound body and mind, one of the great poets and composers in the land, lives diagonally across from us in the Square. He regales them to poetry and musical composition. He also reveals to them the intricacies of national and international history. He is our era's true virtuoso: secretary to two Princes of Orange, diplomat, a polyglot man of the world, a highly sensitive connoisseur of both the ancients and moderns, a fine musician, a deeply religious man, father to two famous scientist sons, and much else besides. Being with the children gives him profound joy and he can be found at the house almost daily. His greatest pleasure is sitting with Johanna behind the spinet, teaching her musical composition, marveling over her prodigious talents. She's receiving one such lesson this morning. This afternoon Spinoza is arriving even though he has trouble breathing, to discuss ethics. Anthonie van Leeuwenhoek will come over tomorrow to look at our new collection of textiles and he will bring a few of his microscopes to show the twins the world of the infinitesimally small. Our children are like sponges, absorbing their teachings and readings with astounding speed. I sometimes feel that Red Sulphur wants to absorb all available human knowledge through their minds in the shortest amount of time, knowing that human life is brief as a breath. Pupils like this make teachers outstanding. Their talent at weaving, however, is just about average. Maximo is much more interested in the machinery and has already improved on our spinning wheels with some remarkably simple alterations.

I have put one of my smaller looms back in the corner of the red living room to attend Johanna's music lessons. Old Constantijn has taken a great liking for me, even though he is aware of the heartbreak I've been causing his son Christiaan over these last years. Since the war has moved away from our doorstep Christiaan has taken to sending me long letters with great frequency, keeping me posted about those goings-on in his Parisian life that are not related to the state of war between our countries. His position as a prominent Dutchman in the enemy city is sensitive so he mainly explicates to me his original discoveries about clockwork, such as his theory on the mathematics of curvatures and the nature of the centrifugal force. It can be exhausting being courted by a mathematician. Knowing our interest in alchemy he has recently sent us a peculiar gold coin he had been given in Vienna while on a visit. On one side is the bust of Emperor Leopold, while on the other it reads: 'By the power of Wenzel Seyler's powder I was made from tin into gold'. It was coined last year. Mundanus had been extremely agitated, wanting to leave for Vienna the next day to meet this Magus Seyler. But currently the ongoing experiment he is conducting with Aunt Marianne to make Red Sulphur directly from primal matter has progressed. They now have a bright blue powder which supposedly is a precursor of the Stone. It keeps them sequestered to the laboratory. The color is remarkable, reminding of the faint blue sky in late winter seen here, but not, for example, in points south such as Venice. They have allowed me some of this powder as a dye and it has similar properties of Red Sulphur in the glow cloth, in that it works in a sour dough fashion. Once a small part has been transmuted into winter-sky blue it can serve as a starter batch for the next raw wool. It has caused a remarkable expansion of our palette, making our textiles even more sumptuous. That's why Anthonie is coming to look at our new collection tomorrow.

A Viennese diplomat friend of Old Constantijn Huygens, His Excellency Count von Waldstein, who has attended some of Seyler's projections in Vienna, will be in The Hague next week on business. He is bringing a special missive to Viceroy Prince William of Orange from his master, Emperor Leopold of Austria, a strong ally of the Dutch republic in its war with the French King. Since last year's much lamented death of the Princess Dowager Amalia van Solms, Prince William has taken over some of her social functions in the North End Palace, though the Palace feels hollow now that it is devoid of her sparkling spirit. The Prince of Orange has invited a select group of his intellectual friends, including us, to be introduced to His Excellency. Our Prince meets with Aunt Marianne regularly now that the frost over his rewards to the murderers of the De Witt brothers has thawed. She is his main personal confidante.

At 26 Viceroy Prince William III of Orange has come into his own and has become the unquestioned leader of the Dutch Republic. He has driven King Louis out of our Northern provinces and is now battling him in the southern provinces officially belonging to Habsburg Emperor Leopold. The Prince's skills as a strategist are being admired all over Europe and now he is calling upon his uncle King Charles of England to come to his aid. Rumors have it that for this purpose he intends to marry the King's niece and second in line to the throne, his now

14-year-old first cousin, Princess Mary Stuart, his mother's namesake. It is said that she is vehemently opposed to the marriage, despising her cousin. Prince William's deformities make him appear less than fetching, though that does not seem to prevent him from being a well-known philanderer: not an attractive combination for a romantic young Princess. The only thing they have in common is their ardent devotion to Protestantism.

My love for Mundanus has grown into a quiet mutual devotion, and my jealousies with Aunt Marianne, whose position is first in his heart, have died down to a chronic ache, no longer piercing but by no means dull. I have sequestered my pain over playing the second violin in his heart to a distant exile from which it escapes from time to time, at which moments I take to bed with the curtains closed and feel the sorrow my mother had felt over her unrequited love for Johan de Witt. At such times my womb spasms as if I am giving an endless series of stillbirths and I sob inconsolably, though tears do not come.

I am happy that the children love Aunt Marianne and me in their own way. Though they call each of us Mother, it means something different when they address her or me. When they speak to Aunt Marianne I hear the intimacy I have felt myself as a child crawling into her bed feeling her warm body against mine. When they look at me I can sense their bottomless adoration. Their love for me is simultaneously less intimate and fiercer. They love their Father in the way humans admire the grandeur of the Lord.

Listening to the beautiful music flowing from Johanna's hands, Constantijn Huygens is comfortably seated in an overstuffed leather chair with closed eyes and an expression of bliss.

Maximo is with Elspeth in the atelier, studying the construction of our looms, which no doubt in his 7 –year old hands will lead to mechanical improvements. Even though I love him dearly, he does not quite feel like my flesh in the way Johanna does. I find myself doting on him more than on her, which must come from a gnawing feeling of guilt.

I've started weaving invisible patterns in the glow cloth that only jump out when light hits it in a particular way. Even though I am completely fascinated by these evocative patterns that lead the mind to marvel and wonder, they don't occupy all of my attention. I can let my mind be absorbed with musings about The Twins while listening to Johanna's musical gift. Being a mother is a complicated experience for me, not only because of Aunt Marianne. I have to admit that my art is my true passion. I profoundly love my children, Mundanus and Aunt Marianne – in that order – but this love is not the primary calling in my life. I have long since stopped feeling oppressed by this, or thinking it unnatural. I have accepted the fact that the Lord has endowed me with an exceptional talent that has transcendent demands upon me. I can perform things with my craft no one else has ever done before. My art feels divine and no human love can compare with it. When I look at my weaving right now and see the barely visible watermarks creating a scene behind the surface I marvel at the fact that I have effortlessly manufactured dreams in cloth without premeditation. At the same time I can hear Johanna doing with music what I perform in textile and I know that her devotion will be primarily to her music. It makes me love her almost like a sister whom I will have to guide through the mysteries of art. At these moments I am curiously satisfied that Aunt Marianne is in their lives with her expansive heart and her ability to simply mother them as her children. It also appeases my hurt over Mundanus' love for my aunt, since I know that weaving is my true lord and master.

I am roused from my contemplations on love and art by Constantijn Huygens' gentle voice.

"Madam Dolfin," he addresses me, "Would you mind if I ask Miss Johanna to perform for us next week at the North End Palace when we have our intimate little gathering with His Excellency Count Waldstein and His Highness? His Excellency adores music and it would be such a joy for him to hear Johanna's art."

"Please Mother, can I come?" Johanna ardently supports his request. It cannot be refused, so I give my permission. The old gentleman instantly begins to discuss with his pupil which works she will perform, though most of it I'm sure will be improvised by the spirit of the moment. I relish Johanna's excitement. This will be her first performance.

Constantijn Huygens turns to me flush with excitement: "The harpsichord spinet at the Palace was built by the great Zenti himself. I remember him coming to the Palace when Viceroy Frederik-Hendrik was still among us, sometime in the Thirties or Forties. Master Zenti tuned it and performed beautiful music for us," our old friend enthuses, reliving the scene in his memory. "Johanna will play like she never has before. A marvelous instrument inspires the performer." My daughter is radiant, her skin glowing with pride. "Could I ask you for another favor, Madam Dolfin," he asks almost shyly. I nod. "It has been many years since I have seen Master Spinoza. I would so value it if I might assist at his lessons to the twins. There is no living man in this world who I respect more than Master Spinoza. Not since Master Descartes has there been such a spirit among us."

"Of course!" I concur. What privilege it shall be for our children to hear a conversation between Benedict de Spinoza and Constantijn Huygens! I'm sure it will coax even Mundanus and Aunt Marianne down from their laboratory.

∛

Spinoza looks terrible. Hendrik has picked him up from his home in The Hague where he plies is lens crafting trade. Uncle Johann takes him up to his study to examine his lungs and he can hardly make it up the stairs. I can see in my uncle's face that he is deeply concerned for his friend. He has told me that the Medicine can't help if the lifespan of a man has run its course. Benedict de Spinoza's powerful fiery spirit has burned his frail body down to the ground. At 43 he has the air of a man older than Constantijn Huygens at 80. Mundanus has told me that breathing glass filings all day long kills the lungs. Leeuwenhoek's prodigious health indicates that he does not grind down his lenses for his microscopes but must produce them in a different fashion that does not create glass dust; though the same age as Spinoza, Anthonie looks decades younger. Uncle Johann has confided in me that he doesn't expect Spinoza to last much longer. The philosopher is working furiously to complete his legacy.

While weaving in the living room with the quietly waiting twins and Constantijn Huygens, I hear how upstairs my uncle requests Mundanus to help him examine Spinoza. He rarely calls upon my husband for a consultation, being quite competitive with him. He is still doesn't know that his nephew in law is the famous Doctor Mundanus, but he is aware of Giovanni Dolfin's considerable diagnostic skills. I take his request as another indication of Spinoza's poor health. After some time the three of them come downstairs, followed by Aunt Marianne. Their faces look very serious. I'm sure they have told Spinoza of their opinion about his ill health. Death surrounds them.

"What's wrong?" Maximo asks, with his characteristic directness. Our son doesn't speak much, but when he does, his words are incisive. He looks over at Spinoza. "Are you going to die, Uncle Benedict?" he inquires as a matter of fact. Even unflappable Spinoza is taken aback.

"We all die," he responds softly.

"But some sooner than others," Maximo insists. He has been very involved with the question of death since the war.

"Master Spinoza," Constantijn Huygens gets up from his comfortable chair to pay his respect to the great philosopher.

"Your Excellency," Spinoza replies formally.

"Do you mind if I attend the lessons you are about to give The Twins? I would be greatly honored if you accede." Their connection is stilted, mainly because of Spinoza's extreme shyness. Even though his works are so radical and flamboyant that even the tolerant Protestant Dutch church has banned them, in person he is painfully shy.

"Most certainly, Your Excellency, it would be an honor."

The Twins are glowing with pleasure at having their entire faculty present at once. There is nothing they love more than learning. It is as though they become the Stone itself, and it has a remarkable effect on all of us. As instructors we are filled with an urgent desire to reach the far corners of our knowledge.

"I have asked Master Huygens about you telling us that the bible was not written by God but by many people. You told us that it was a historical document describing the history of the Jews, not a book written by God. He disagrees with you." Maximo looks at Spinoza eagerly.

"No wonder you were banished from your People, Benedict," Aunt Marianne smiles kindly at him. She loves the Jewish philosopher and in the usual Regent way is not particularly fond of his People. I don't know any Jews beside Spinoza so I wouldn't know. My grandfather was tolerant of everyone.

"You are right, young Master Maximo." Spinoza replies as we all sit down in the chairs we have set up around the fireplace to the far right of the entry to the red room. Old Constantijn Huygens insists Spinoza takes the prime seat, Huygens' favorite fauteuil. After some polite back and forth Spinoza sinks down into it, tired to the bone.

"I don't think Moses wrote the Bible directly inspired by God. It was written by many and should be treated with the same critical attitude in which we study nature. I know His Excellency does not agree, but his is what I believe."

"On what grounds do you contend that the Holy Book was written by others than Moses?" Constantijn Huygens inquires with respect, though obviously in profound disagreement.

"The Bible describes Moses' own death in great detail. No man can describe his own death," Spinoza replies.

"That is true," Maximo exclaims. "And if it is true about Moses' death it could be true about other matters as well."

"It is important to be critical," Spinoza concurs. "One should have a critical mind about God. Otherwise one could get to such superstitions as the divine right of kings such as King Louis maintains. Our ideas have direct political consequences."

"I agree one should doubt the divine right of monarchs to accede to the throne. But with what philosophy do you replace it?" The revered old Huygens sounds like an eager young pupil.

"In nature each man has his own power. That leads to natural laws, which are crude and devoid of justice. So as citizens we collectively hand our power to the government. It's called a social contract. From that moment on our collective power is bundled and we move beyond mere natural law. That gives the right to the ones governing us, and we complete the bundling of our power by obeying them."

"Even if they are mean?" Johanna asks. "Even if they are like King Louis who is mean to children." She has been deeply distressed by the stories of rape and pillage which have penetrated the barrier of our household in which all are instructed to spare the children from the gruesome world. The barrier has proven porous. Sometimes she wakes up with screaming nightmares and ends up in Mother Marianne's bed.

"We have to obey the government," Spinoza insists. "Otherwise we would revert back to primitive natural law. We can only be governed because we have collectively divested ourselves of our personal power. You have to be obedient; you cannot overthrow a government."

"Even if the government is tyrannical?" Huygens asks.

"Even so," Spinoza replies emphatically, though his voice betrays his exhaustion. We shouldn't hold him to his lessons too long.

"I feel a most vehement disagreement to your philosophy," the old gentleman speaks, all fired up. "This country was founded in revolution. We overthrew the Spanish King in order to get to a just government based in the rulership of the citizens and their Regents. That's why we do not have a King but a Viceroy. My father was the personal secretary of the Father of our country, William the Silent. He started the Great Revolution which lasted for eighty years. We threw off the power of the tyrant and replaced it with a more just government. Do you believe Prince William the SIlent of Orange was wrong?!"

Spinoza does not reply immediately. His thoughts, I'm sure, have never been pitted against the great William himself. The fact that Spinoza's People could come to Holland in the first place was a direct result of the tolerance professed by the Father of our Fatherland, William the Silent, and his Revolution which shook the foundations of the world, directly questioning the divine rights of Kings.

"It still holds," Spinoza says finally, "that the obligation to obey the sovereign is absolute; the people have no right of rebellion under any circumstances, no matter how badly the sovereign may rule."

"But even Hobbes, with whom I disagree on most issues, believes that the people are justified in rebelling against the sovereign if they are in fear of their lives or if they feel that their condition has become no better than it would be in a state of nature," Constantijn Huygens maintains.

"I agree with Prince William the SIlent," Maximo concludes seriously, as if he has thought about this matter for a long time; and probably he has. "If the government is bad you have to fight back."

"I believe that all views should be tolerated. So if that is what you believe, young Master Maximo, stand by it. No one has the right to tell you otherwise," Spinoza almost whispers, his exhaustion getting the better of him.

Aunt Marianne calls in Hendrik to bring our respected guest home. She has prepared a large wicker basket full of the best food and wine in the house, and she has included a small bottle of the Medicine. I doubt I shall see him again. I can see the fear in his eyes of a man whose days are numbered.

"Please don't die, Uncle Benedict," Maximo pleads with him.

"I won't yet, my dear young Master Maximo. I still have lots of work to do," Spinoza says with a melancholy smile.

&

"This blue cloth is most extraordinary," Anthonie van Leeuwenhoek enthuses. "How do you do it, Clara? Your cloth has become the envy of all. I am so proud to represent your textiles!" Anthonie is a gregarious man enjoying camaraderie and he prefers to be on a first name basis; rather unusual in our circles. But he is a guild man, not a Regent.

The weaving atelier consists of two work floors and a storage facility on the third floor and an attic for our wool to keep it dry and protected from the flooding that happens frequently in these Low Lands. Large green doors can open up street side, so a trolley system can pull up a platform laden with bales of wool from outside. It is one of the last warehouses in the neighborhood of the Square.

On the wall behind my loom in my personal workspace section on the second floor loft hangs a picture of Henry Hudson sailing up a river, an expedition financed originally by my ancestor Dirck van Os. Many other paraphernalia from the New World adorn the atelier, mixed in with items brought back from Cathay by Marco Polo, shipped from Venice by my husband after the sale of the Palazetto Dolfin. It keeps my mind aware of the vastness of the world. I had also requested we take the many maps owned by Giovanni's grandfather back home. The whole world is keeping me company. It is one of the main reasons why The Twins love to spend time here. While I learn my craft, they study global geography and astronomy.

Johanna and Maximo are standing behind Anthonie eagerly waiting for him to pull out his microscopes and show them the invisible world. At this moment in this very room many worlds exist simultaneously. Monsieur Delamarche is with us as well. He has become close friends with Anthonie. His eyesight, which can gaze deeply into the dark is particularly suited to view through Anthonie's lenses and he can see things that only become apparent to Leeuwenhoek after considerable additional amplification. The former knight has become an avid student of the invisible world and has taken to drawing careful replicas of what he discerns, making it possible for us to peer deeper into the minuscule. This has given Anthonie's work additional credibility and even the Royal Society in London is beginning to listen. Marianne has introduced Prince William, whose love of botany is undiminished, to the intricate world of plant cells through Monsieur Delamarche's careful renderings. Maximo is Monsieur Delamarche's avid pupil, copying his drawings and etchings. Modern natural philosophy, increasingly called 'science', coexists peacefully in our home next to the alchemy of ancient times.

"Where did you get this blue dye, Clara?" Anthonie asks me, carefully studying the cloth under his clothier's magnifying glass. "I have never seen this before. I'd say it is very light azure. Was it made with pale sapphire?"

"It came from Mother and Father's laboratory," Maximo chimes in.

"I need to get the recipe," Anthonie responds.

"It took them seven years to perfect," I reply. "It's not a simple recipe."

"Another of their alchemical endeavors?" he asks admiringly.

"Yes," Johanna tells him proudly. "We helped them."

Anthonie smiles. "They couldn't have done it without you, I'm sure."

"That's correct," I reply, remembering that the initial substance from which the primal material grew that was subsequently transmuted into this particular blue was made from their placentas.

Both Maximo and Johanna beam proudly.

Anthonie van Leeuwenhoek turns to the twins: "You know something; we'll look at an individual fiber of this cloth under the microscope."

Johanna claps her hands in excitement. Monsieur Delamarche looks on with obvious fascination, eager to study this color which has been made with the famed blue tincture. Monsieur Delamarche has completely forgiven us for our poisoning. He has regained his memory fully and told us that he was much better off now, having a life that felt meaningful. He remembered his former life as a Baronet to have been utterly vapid. The only thing he asked for was to be a laboratory attendant. He spent his days with The Twins, sitting quietly in a corner while they were studying – he turned out to be a patient tutor – observing Mundanus and Aunt Marianne work on their experiments. His enormously acute vision became very useful to them when looking for changes in the substances they were processing.

We've set up a sturdy chair near a north window. The overcast day makes for perfect viewing. Anthonie van Leeuwenhoek selects a microscope, picks up a single hair of the blue wool with a small pincer, and clips it shut. He seats himself in his by now familiar viewing position: straight shoulders, left foot on the ground, right leg crossed over. With his right hand he clips the pincers holding the blue hair unto the microscope – a rectangular copper plate with a tiny ball-shaped lens – that he pushes right up to his eyeball. With his left hand he takes hold of his right wrist and sits with immovable steadiness. Next to him stands a low stool for the twins.

He steadies his breath and then holds it so he looks like a statue while he looks through the lens. He exhales almost imperceptibly through his nose. After gazing at the hair for several breaths he stops and breathes deeply.

"I don't want to prejudice anyone. Let's each look at the wool and then compare notes." We all nod, The Twins with red flushed cheeks.

Johanna goes next. She can't help herself. "Oh how beautiful!" she exclaims, thereby shaking the microscope vehemently. Anthonie laughs. "What have I told you young Miss. Don't talk, steady your breath and sit quietly like a mouse. Try again." This time she succeeds in curbing her amazement.

Maximo takes on the position with aplomb and sits imperturbably. Monsieur Delamarche goes next and gazes for several minutes. Then it is my turn.

At first I see nothing but sky. Then after some time I see perturbations in the air, as if gentle breezes tumble about like white capped ocean waves, arching, spiraling in. At first I think of Christiaan Huygens's description of the centrifugal and centripetal forces he has explicated to me in his letters. But then I realize that his mathematical descriptions are too mechanical for what I see in front of my eye. This is the breath of life turning in on itself, playing and dancing in constant creation. I'm looking at the winds of heaven, at alive-silver as a primordial acrobat.

I am in awe.

"This is how we were born," Maximo concludes, describing what he has seen. "Now I know where children come from. I was blue breath like that before I was born." Johanna nods emphatically. "It was like dancing in the streets," she adds.

Anthonie looks very pleased with their poetic responses. He has told us that the only way to accurately describe the microscopic world is through poetry.

Monsieur Delamarche sits very still as if his inner eye is still gazing through the microscope. I distractedly stare at the mirroring reflection of the light on his shiny billiard ball skull.

"What did you see, Delamarche?" Anthonie inquires most interested in the observations of the man with the sensitive eyes of the fly.

After some time Monsieur Delamarche exhales noticeably and looks out into the world again.

"I saw waves made of tiny drops. Then they scattered like steam and I heard a sound like a moan. My eye felt magnetized and my mind was made of very pure air."

"Yes," Anthonie concurs. "To me it was like looking into Vulcan's workshop as he beats panels of silver into translucent leafs of sky."

The five of us look at one another, equal in our amazement at having been part of the mystery of Creation. I know that Aunt Marianne and Mundanus are closing in on Red Sulphur.

ಹಿ

I've heard only the day before the dinner for His Excellency Count Waldstein at the North End Palace that Christiaan Huygens has arrived from Paris. I suspect he has come to see me and I feel strangely excited, though not in a romantic way... I think. I find myself choosing an understated dress made of high purpur count sorcery cloth; nothing too obvious but quite effective. It feels delicious against my skin, as if I'm being caressed by my beloved. I note with satisfaction that my fear of the Venusian textiles which took possession of me almost nine years ago in Venice is by now undetectable. But I realize I must remain on guard. The cloth has a life of its own.

I sit across from myself in front of the mirror in my childhood room in the back of the house. Even though Mundanus and I now occupy the adjacent home, accessible through the large French doors to the left of the entrance hall of the original house connecting the two buildings, I have kept my old room as a retreat. Just the servants come to the back of the house; and of them only my loyal Mina is allowed in my room to keep it clean. Here I keep my sorcery cloth dresses, and the powders I have made from the various dyes to accentuate the natural pallor of my skin. I have begun treating my face like a textile, enjoying bringing out particular moods through the application of colors. The art is to have the cover remain invisible, not gaudy like the women at the French court who seem to prefer looking like prostitutes. I create a film of colored air to create a mask behind which I feel safe. Especially now that Christiaan Huygens will undoubtedly make advances I want to be prepared.

There are rumors of his frequent illnesses and I have no idea what he will look like this time. When I saw him last in '70 he seemed on death's doorstep, but then he revived. I haven't seen him for at least 4 years, though we have been in frequent correspondence. I get most of his health information from Susanna, his sister. We've become friends. Though she grew up in her father's stately brownstone diagonally across from us in the Square, she had moved away to her married home when I was just 13 years old. But ever since I began to be a fixture in her daily correspondence with her brother, she had taken to visiting me whenever she calls on her father Constantijn. She had become not just a friend but one of my principal customers, raving to her brother about the quality of the dresses I made for her. He wrote to me that she had been ecstatic about the wedding gowns I created for some of her young friends – expressing the wish that she could have worn a dress like it at her own lavish wedding in '60. Susanna, who was called Sis by her brothers, didn't travel much, having to stay home in adjacent Wassenaar to care for her mother in law. She loved coming to my atelier to study the many maps I had and wistfully dream of the great world forever beyond her ken. In that context she spent time with the twins and doted on them. She herself had lost several children, which made her cherish all little ones with an air of joyful melancholy. I haven't seen her for months as her mother in law's affections are becoming increasingly tyrannical. Susanna told me that she'd been to Antwerp for a short trip, and when she returned her mother in law made her feel as though she'd spent a lifetime in India. So I know nothing about Christiaan's current state of health since he doesn't write about it to me. He hadn't mentioned that he was coming to The Hague, which is odd.

ॐ

Aunt Marianne, The Twins, and I are the first to arrive at the North End Palace in our carriage with Hendrik as our coachman. Behind us Uncle Johann's carriage is steered by a hired man. Besides my uncle and husband, Baronet Delamarche has been included. The Prince of Orange is quite taken with his microscopic vegetative drawings and the baronet has brought a considerable portfolio of new etchings.

I feel very different from the young woman I was a little over nine years ago when I was first invited to the Palace in '67. I'd been a young bride to be, enthralled with her fiancé, proud to become his wife. It had been a time of certainties and broad vistas into a predictable future. All I could think of was a home and children: being the Mistress of a wealthy Regent household. Now I'm a celebrated artist at the head of a fast growing atelier with a reputation spreading all over Europe and few illusions about marital bliss; and I'm a co-mother to magical twins whose future is anyone's guess. I look at Aunt Marianne between The Twins, each with their head on her lap, and am painfully aware of the fact that they are sitting *across* from me. Johanna, my own flesh and blood, prefers Mother Marianne's body over mine; and rightfully so – I would too. My own mother had been formal, like the usual Regent women. Aunt Marianne with her constant physical accessibility is a complete exception. And suddenly I feel envious of my children who experience her warmth close up. I want to feel her body against mine like it used to be when I was small. As we get out of the carriage, children rushing ahead, I marvel at the labyrinthine complexity of my relationship with my aunt.

As we enter the palatial ground floor music room with the famed Zenti spinet, the Prince of Orange is already seated talking to a man I suppose is the Viennese ambassador. I notice Johanna growing pale, but from a side of the large room I haven't been aware of, old Constantijn Huygens comes up to The Twins, arms outstretched.

"So how is our little virtuoso today," he asks Johanna with a grandfatherly tease.

I do not notice her response because behind their father I see Susanna helping Christiaan get up from his chair. He looks dreadful, sicker even than in 1670. I'm acutely aware of my youth, since I age much slower than anyone except for my husband and Aunt. Whereas I hardly look older than nine years ago, he has aged by two decades at least. I know instantly that this is the first experience in a long line of future events caused by the relative slowness of my Red Sulphur aging. I feel guilty.

"Master Christiaan," I say, walking up to him, trying my best not to show my distress. "You look..."

"Terrible," he concludes my sentence for me to prevent me from lying. "I have returned to The Hague to be under the care of my sister and the excellent physicians here."

It dawns on me that he has not come here to see me at all; he has returned to his family to die.

"I'm sure my uncle will be able to help you. He performs miracles in medicine."

"So I've heard," Christiaan responds in a measured tone. His scientific attitude won't allow him to accept the alchemically based healing performed by Helvetius; but as an ordinary human he craves to survive by any means.

"In the face of death all means are justified," I say softly. Only Susanna can hear me and she nods, looking at her brother with pleading eyes. They must have discussed his asking Helvetius for help tonight. "Don't be so damn proud, Christiaan," she whispers in almost a hiss. "Not even you know everything!"

"And here we have the mother of the prodigy, Madam Clara Dolfin." Prince William introduces me to Ambassador Waldstein in an uncharacteristically outgoing mood. Even though he and Johan de Witt were considered arch enemies, the Prince has taken over various mannerisms of the former Grand Pensionary, one of them being De Witt's caution which slowed down every movement he made. But tonight the Prince of Orange shows nothing of that. "My grandmother, may God rest her soul, used to tell me at every occasion that she is the most extraordinary creator of wedding gowns on the continent."

"So true, Your Excellency," Susanna supports our Prince, "No wedding gown can compare to hers. They are truly enchanting."

Christiaan smiles wryly, nodding in his sister's direction: "She seems to write about nothing else."

Imperial Count Karl Ferdinand von Waldstein bows, while I curtsy. "We shall have a lot to discuss, My Lady," and kisses the air just above my outstretched right hand. I don't know to what he is referring, but looking at everyone else I realize they all do.

At this moment Uncle Johann, my husband and baronet Delamarche are announced. Monsieur Delamarche looks downright dapper with the all-but-invisible veil over his eyes, which cuts out much of the light. I wove it from glow-cloth dyed silk mixed in with the blue tincture and achieved a gossamer effect that darkens as much as a heavy curtain. I'm experimenting with this material for trains on wedding gowns. It almost disappears under the elegant wig he wears for the occasion with black curls covering much of his forehead. He is carrying the portfolio under his arm. Prince William has never actually met this man whom he admires and asks him right away for his most current pictures. No protocol seems to be observed this evening. The palatial environment belies the family atmosphere. Everyone bends over Monsieur Delamarche's exquisite etchings with praise coming from all quarters.

The Prince turns to Aunt Marianne. "How lucky are you, Madam Schweitzer, to have such an artist of natural philosophy under your roof. His renderings are spectacular. Is this what it truly looks like?"

Marianne nods, proud of the baronet. "Monsieur Delamarche draws exactly what he sees. He just has a much more accurate eyesight than we do."

"Uncle Billiards is the best," Maximo exclaims. "He can see everything. I've seen it too, but his eyes are better." My son looks at his gentle tutor with deep admiration.

His Excellency looks at Monsieur Delamarche's eyes with the look of an experienced observer.

"I've had an illness which left me with deformed eyes," the latter explains barely audibly.

"They look like the eyes of a fly," Johanna blurts out. "We put a fly under the microscope and his eyes were just like Uncle Billiards's." Her complete innocence makes all the adults laugh.

Maximo looks puzzled. "She's right, you know," he insists.

"Yes she is indeed," Monsieur Delamarche concurs in a louder voice.

Everyone begins to talk at once and in the following melee I notice that Susanna has come up to my uncle and is whispering to him. Helvetius then goes over to Christiaan and the two of them talk with serious looks on their faces. I note my husband gravitating toward them and I wish to be part of their three way conversation. But the Ambassador requests my attention.

"His Excellency Constantijn Huygens has told me remarkable stories about your little daughter," he corners me. "He says that music flows from her hands like honey. You know that our Emperor Leopold has a passion for music?"

I nod. The Habsburg Holy Roman Emperor's love of the harpsichord spinet is known all over Europe.

"You must come to Vienna," he insists. "And not just to show off your daughter," he adds mysteriously. I have no idea what to make of his words.

The servants have filled our glasses: gin for the men, sherry wine for the ladies and warm ale for the children. Prince William raises his glass: "Before proposing a toast to our illustrious guest Imperial Count Karl Ferdinand and his great Master, Holy Roman Emperor Leopold of Austria, I want to remember my grandmother Princess Amalia van Solms. Her spirit pervades this North End Palace which was her home together with my grandfather for many years." He raises his glass.

"Hear, Hear!" we all respond in unison.

Constantijn Huygens bows deeply. "Princess Amalia was one of the great spirits of the age, Your Highness. She would have so enjoyed this gathering." Prince William smiles, a gentle expression on his face. Old Constantijn had served both his father and grandfather and had been a good friend to Princess Amalia.

"And now let's hear music before I welcome everyone officially."

I am grateful for his order of the evening, since everyone
can see that Johanna has been fidgeting nervously.

Constantijn Huygens accompanies my daughter to the high
stool behind the keyboard of Zenti's magnificent blond wood
spinet. The top of the almost triangular instrument has been put
vertical to free the sound of the strings, and on the inside a colorful bucolic scene with frolicking dogs and dancing maidens
enlivens the instrument. The right side of the triangular spinet
curves inward to allow for the different lengths of the strings,
creating a warmly elegant bay.

Old Constantijn helps his pupil onto the stool and as she
sits down I see the world around her vanish. Only music remains. The love for my daughter is so vast that my heart hurts
because it cannot contain it. I notice myself sighing and taste a
tear I hadn't noticed.

Johanna briefly runs her fingers over all the keys to become
acquainted with the instrument, which twangs back at her with
light metallic vibrations.

Then music begins to flow. I have never heard this. It
springs directly from the fountain of this particular moment
through her hands into the strings that joyously respond to her
mastery. I notice how Johanna disappears, eyes closed, entering
into sound like a mist over water. Every last one in the room is
riveted. The servants in all corners barely breathe as Johanna
rushes from minor to crescendo in waterfalls of echoing waves.
The room becomes a single heart with common strings uniting
us all with the music played by the pure soul of a child. I feel
tears filling my chest as I inhale and exhale my love for my
daughter and for God who gave her to me.

When finally she stops the silence she leaves behind is filled
with our collective adoration of beauty. The spell is broken by
Maximo who begins to clap loudly. Then we all chime in and
applaud Johanna. As she returns from her world of music she

looks surprised that an audience has followed her on her journey.

"You *must* come to Vienna!" His Excellency exclaims, unaware that his voice is booming.

❧

I am seated next to Imperial Count Karl Ferdinand von Waldstein, who sits to the right of the Prince of Orange presiding at
the head of the rectangular table set with sumptuous linens and
glittering silver. Aunt Marianne sits to the Prince's left as an acknowledgment of their remarkable closeness. His Highness has
honored The Twins with a seat at the table. They are between
old Constantijn, seated to Aunt Marianne's left and his daughter
Susanna Doublet-Huygens, whose husband is traveling on business leaving his lonely mother, Susanna's aunt nee Gertrud
Huygens, with his hapless wife. She, her father, and The Twins
are instantly conversing vividly about geography. Christiaan
Huygens sits between his sister and my uncle, diagonally across
from me, engaging Count von Waldstein in scientific conversation, the Count being a lover of natural philosophy. I notice
that, on a golden chain around the nobleman's neck, there hangs
the tiny golden sheepskin, sign of the order of the Knights of
the Golden Fleece, the most powerful and highly select order
of knights in Europe. His Highness the Prince of Orange pays
him homage well beyond his rank as a mere ambassador. Count
von Waldstein will soon be off to Whitehall to become Permanent Ambassador of Emperor Leopold to the court of Prince
William's uncle, King Charles of England. We are in illustrious
company. My husband to my right, seated beside Monsieur
Delamarche, is in an involved conversation across the table with
Helvetius and the baronet about the remarkable microscopes by
Leeuwenhoek. Helvetius insists that under a microscope the
blood of a person with a malady looks different from that of a
healthy person. Now the conversation centralizes and Count
Waldstein inquires about Helvetius' assertion. Christiaan

Huygens seems to forget that he is at death's door and listens intently. Prince William is beaming, thoroughly enjoying intellectual conversation, a chance he rarely gets now that he is primarily a soldier.

"There are many whitish *animalcules* in the blood of a sick person," Helvetius tells us, using Leeuwenhoek's nomenclature for the microscopic beings he has encountered.

"They look like little fish that gobble up other *animalcules*," Monsieur Delamarche clarifies.

"So are we being eaten by these whitish *animalcules*?" asks Christiaan, open to any answer.

"I don't know," Mundanus replies. "It could also be that they are the army defending us against foreign invasion."

"In that case I want to learn strategy from them," Prince William exclaims. "Nature is very clever, much more so than us generals."

Count Waldstein laughs heartily. "Your Highness, that's why you're one of the great Field Marshalls of our time. You're always ready to learn." The Count has a wide face with inquisitive eyes looking into the world with caution. His jaw is set and he looks like a man one would rather have as a friend. The shape of his face is rounded and smooth with the polished shine of the diplomat. His majestic wig flows down to well below his chest.

"Have you ever looked through the microscope at what happens to blood after you have given the patient your famous medicine?" asks Christiaan.

"No, I have not. But it would be an excellent idea," Helvetius concurs. I remember the time nine years ago when we sat across a round table in Princess Amalia's quarters upstairs in this same Palace and we were divided between alchemist and scientist. It seems that today we're all on the same side and the distinction no longer matters. It seems that we are all experimentalists now.

"Speaking of illness, is Vienna still in mourning?" Prince William asks the Count, referring to the death about six weeks

ago of the 22-year-old Empress Maria Josepha, briefly the second wife to Emperor Leopold. "I would like to express our condolences to his Majesty from all here assembled." We raise our
glasses: "To His Majesty the Emperor." Count Waldstein bows
to receive our condolences in His stead. Then he replies:

"No, Your Highness, the days of mourning are over. In fact
they have been replaced by days of joy and anticipation. The
Emperor has decided to remarry to the incomparable Countess
Palatine of Neuburg, Eleonore Magdalene.

"Of Dusseldorf? I know her family. They were friends of
Grandmother's," says the Prince.

The Count nods. "They will wed in December. I hope you
can be part of the wedding."

Prince William bows, noticeably pleased to be invited to the
wedding of his powerful ally in the fight against King Louis. I
reflect on the shortness of time between the death and the wedding. For ordinary souls it would have been unseemly. But all
the Emperor's children have died before the age of two and he
much needs a successor. I feel sorry for the young Countess.
The pressure upon her to produce a living heir must be terrible.
However, like everyone in our social circles, I know that her
family is noted for their great fertility. So the choice is under-
standable and the immediacy of the wedding excusable. I am
woken from my musings when Count Waldstein turns to address me.

"It has been the Emperor's special request, Madam Dolfin,
that you create the future Empress' wedding gown. As I said,
you must come to Vienna; and bring your daughter to perform
at the wedding."

Everyone looks intently at me. The silence is suffocating.

"She'll do it!" Maximo exclaims. "We'll all go to Vienna to
help her."

"I'll go," Johanna concurs, as if it were a matter of her decision.

Everyone laughs.

"Not only are you a great artist, Madam," Prince William says proudly, "But your children are true patriots. There is no greater service you could do for the Dutch Republic!" Emperor Leopold rules the Habsburg Netherlands to our south and is the only force standing between us and King Louis XIV and his desire to be Emperor of Europe, the second Charlemagne.

The decision has been made; history has decided. All I have to do is but consent.

My husband looks at me with unabashed pride: "We will all accompany you to Vienna, my Darling." Aunt Marianne nods vehemently. An atmosphere of celebration circulates around the table like rolling fireworks.

"The Emperor is a very wise man," Susanna enthuses towards the Count, "May all his decisions be as good as this one!"

Count von Waldstein keeps looking at me. The response of my husband and of my sovereign the Viceroy is not enough. I am grateful to him for waiting for my personal consent. He is a man who understands the pride of a woman.

"It would be the greatest honor to have ever befallen me," I solemnly express my agreement to his imperial offer.

A broad smile breaks through his cautiously diplomatic face. "Vienna will adore you, Madam Dolfin. Of that I can assure you." Then he turns to Prince William. "I hope for the Dutch Republic that you will get her back. Madam Dolfin and her daughter will be idols of the court at the Hofburg."

"I trust her love of the Fatherland," Prince William replies coyly.

"Why don't you come with us, Aunt Susanna," Maximo asks. "You so want to see the world!"

A painful silence ensues. Susanna fumbles. Christiaan comes to her aid with a clever diversion. He takes a gold coin from his pocket and shows it to the Count.

"Have you seen this?" he inquires as he hands the coin to the imperial envoy.

"Most certainly," Count Waldstein replies. "It was made from the gold of Wenzel Seyler. I was present at the transmutation as one of the official inspectors."

"You were?!" Mundanus exclaims unceremoniously. Helvetius looks riveted. Every other concern has vanished and the subject has explosively been changed. I am glad the spotlight has moved away from me.

"You know that Dr. Helvetius here has been involved in one such transmutation ten years ago. As a natural philosopher it has been hard for me to accept the evidence, if there is any to begin with," Christiaan Huygens explains.

"Oh, but this transmutation certainly occurred. It was in front of some of the main natural philosophers at the court and the gold withstood all the tests. Only after this, Emperor Leopold consented to have his image on the coin. It was the most excruciatingly tested gold ever to have been assayed in the Austrian Empire. And I was there through all the assays from the moment of the transmutation, after having satisfactorily ascertained through all the necessary tests that the initial material was indeed tin. The gold stayed in my possession until it was minted, so no foul play could occur. His Majesty trusts me. I can assure you Mr. Huygens that this was a true transmutation from tin into gold."

"Who is this Mr. Seyler, Your Excellency?" Aunt Marianne inquires with avid interest.

"I know Robert Boyle believes he is not an adept but that he has true red powder for transmutations," Christiaan interjects.

"I know," the Count expounds. "I'm in correspondence with the illustrious Robert Boyle himself. I'm looking forward greatly to meeting with him and with Isaac Newton when I'm in London a short while from now. They are both very interested in this transmutation. I believe they both experiment with the art of alchemy."

Christiaan nods. He has written to me that he doesn't understand the interest of these two greatly admired natural philosophers in a discredited art.

"By now Mr. Seyler has been elevated by His Majesty to a knighthood of Reinberg and he has been made Mint Master of Austria."

"But what about Robert Boyle's assertion that Seyler is a charlatan who just happens to be in possession of the so-called philosopher's stone?" Christiaan insists.

"We had him investigated by one of the other inspectors at the transmutation, Johann Joachim Becher. I'm sure Mr. Boyle's information comes from him. What he uncovered was most alarming. I have warned the Emperor to distance himself from Mr. Wenzel Seyler. But for now the man is still our Mint Master."

"I would so love to hear his story," my husband beseeches the Ambassador.

"Let's hear the story in the music room where we shall have desserts," Prince William suggests. I think his grandmother would have approved of this excellent hosting move. The Prince has certainly matured. He gets up, indicating us all to follow him to the adjacent room.

Once we are seated around the fireplace where a cozy wood fire crackles in the most welcoming of ways, Count von Waldstein begins his story about the life of Wenzel Seyler as told by inspector Becher. The twins are sitting at his feet, as always eager to hear tales. The Count gives them a kind paternal smile and tells the story directly to them. If they had looked tired some moments ago, that has vanished entirely.

"Johann Joachim Becher told me this very strange story. The furthest he could trace Wenzel Seyler back was as an Augustine monk called Brother Wenceslaus sometime in the late '60s. He went to the friary at Bruno in Moravia, where the other friars told him that Friar Wenceslaus had always been different. It was said that there was a treasure buried in the monastery and that Brother Wenceslaus had become a friar only for that reason. They said that he became a friend of a practicing witch who lived at the edge of town. Every free moment he would go and help her. For this she gave him a ball made of wax with numbers and symbols on it. This ball would roll by itself to places of treasure. So he tried it out in the monastery, hoping he would find the treasure, but nothing happened."

The children's eyes are glowing with transport while Christiaan Huygens is rolling his.

"It is said that Brother Wenceslaus sought out one of the old monks who was an adept in alchemy and magic and together they tried out the witch's wax ball to no avail. Then there was a great storm that threw over much of an old section of the Bruno monastery. And then the magic wax ball rolled to an ancient pillar where they dug to discover a box. Brother Wenceslaus was very disappointed to find it filled with a red powder. He had expected gold and diamonds. So he left it to the old monk. One night the old monk called him in and told him to get some pewter plates from the refectory. These he melted in his alchemy pot and then projected them with some of the red powder. The content of the pot turned to gold in 15 minutes. The old monk told one of the other young friars and that's how we have the story. Soon after the old monk died under mysterious circumstances and Brother Wenceslaus disappeared. The box with the red powder was never found again. Then in '73 a man looking like a description of this friar, now calling himself Wenzel Seyler, came to the Hofburg Palace boasting that he can turn any metal into gold. He was scorned by the alchemists at the court who said that gold had not been made in this way for centuries. But then one of the goldsmiths let himself be convinced, and gave Seyler the opportunity to demonstrate his art. And he succeeded. He sold his gold and started living an extravagant lifestyle, transforming more and more tin into gold to pay for his squandering. That's how I met him in 1674 at the behest of His Majesty himself to check out the veracity of Seyler's claims. I found they were true, every and each one of them; but Becher and I are both convinced that he does not know what he is doing. The story at the monastery may have been embellished by the young friars with whom Becher spoke, but essentially it must be true that Seyler somehow found this red powder and didn't manufacture it himself."

"Or maybe he stole it from the old friar who was an alchemist!" Maximo exclaims.

"Or from the witch!" Johanna suggests. The twins are thrilled by this marvelous story, which is obviously some kind of subterfuge spread by Seyler himself to obscure the source of the red powder.

"But you are sure this powder is real. Have you seen it?" Helvetius asks. Count Waldstein nods.

"By day or by night?" Helvetius inquires.

"A few times by day and then once at night."

"And does it glow green in the dark?"

Count Waldstein looks at Helvetius with obvious surprise.

"Does it?" Aunt Marianne asks.

"It does indeed. How did you know?" the Count mutters astonished.

"Because when this Doctor Mundanus first showed me his box with the Red Sulphur he had us close the curtains and it glowed green in the dark," Helvetius explains.

"Like what they lately have been calling phosphorus," Christiaan Huygens suggests. "I have been corresponding about this with Robert Boyle who has made this light emitting substance from urine mixed with sand. He said he hoped to use it as a basis for making gold."

My husband can't hold himself back anymore. I have seen how he almost erupted several times but he clearly doesn't want to give himself away as the fabled Dr. Mundanus. I'm sure he is not going to talk about his own experiments with phosphorus. I remember him telling me about it when he spoke of his encounter with the crescent dagger phantom.

"It is said in alchemical texts that gold is made of very pure urine," he suggests.

The twins begin to giggle in the way children laugh about urine and excrements.

"Robert Boyle sure seems to think so. He's been discussing urine as the basic substance of the philosopher's stone with Isaac Newton," Christiaan Huygens concurs. He obviously is no longer as opposed to alchemy as he had been a decade ago. "He has already been able to add phosphorus to sulfur-tipped wooden splints that ignite when you scratch them on a rough surface. It is a completely new way of making fire. He told me he will publish his discoveries sometime in the near future."

"I can't wait to meet Robert Boyle in London!" Count Waldstein exclaims with uncharacteristic enthusiasm. Then he turns to my husband. "Well Signor Dolfin, when you come to Vienna with your family I will make sure you get to personally inspect Wenzel Seyler's red powder."

Chapter Twenty-Three

December 1676

Christiaan Huygens moved into his father Constantijn's home across the street and became a frequent visitor to my atelier, often accompanied by his sister. Uncle Johann began treating him – primarily with the Red Sulphur Medicine – and his health returned slowly. He did not go back to France, to my secret joy; I was beginning to feel a great deal of affection towards him, which confused me to an unexpected degree. It made me feel guilty toward my husband while knowing full well that his tenderness towards Aunt Marianne freed me from the usual restrictions. But these matters are different for women. Men take mistresses while we are supposed to remain loyal – not that I thought of Aunt Marianne as my husband's mistress. Our situation was quite unparalleled, with our three-way marriage, and Uncle Johann as a much forgotten afterthought. But my growing affections for Christiaan, now that I saw him almost daily, began to bother me. I wished I could talk about it with someone and finally decided to take Aunt Marianne into my confidence.

I had expected her to be upset with my adulterous feelings, even though she herself lived in a vortex of multiple adulteries. Instead she took me into her arms and held me close without saying a word, making it clear to me that no one could advise me in these matters and that she would love me whatever my decision was to be. We felt close.

Christiaan installed his twenty year old telescope – with which he had discovered the moon around Saturn and its mysterious ring – on the roof of his father's house and invited me and the twins to come view the stars.

One crisp moonless night I came up to the observatory all by myself. I wore my mother's soft white lynx fur and was ready to fall for him. With Saturn sharply visible, as was its orange moon, I listened to Christiaan explaining the Copernican heliocentric principles to me while I was seduced by the loveliness of the night sky. Had he been more forward I would have kissed him. But he shyly held my hand as I looked away from him to the stars. That was as close as we came. Then I left for Dusseldorf to meet with the future Holy Roman Empress, Eleonore Magdalene of Neuburg, so as to take her measurements and discuss her tastes.

I met the 21 year old thin blond woman with very sad eyes and a determined yet obedient mouth who would have been a nun, had it been her own choice. She should have married in black, I thought, though of course I didn't tell her that. I showed her the glow cloth and she instantly had visions of the Holy Virgin with Child, which convinced her of the viability of a marriage with ample offspring. I was sorry for her, a bird in a cage ready to hang at the heart of a faraway court, and felt guilty about the immense freedom my own life granted me.

❧

We have our quarters at the new wing of the Hofburg Palace in Vienna that Emperor Leopold had built for himself. It connects two sections of the old Palace. It is white and austere, built to imperially impress and unsuccessfully compete with Versailles in a Germanic kind of way; not to warmly welcome a young bride. Our suites are close to the palatial rooms for the bride, so it is easy for her to visit my workshop where I am completing the finishing touches on the wedding gown aided by seven Austrian seamstresses who love to giggle.

Count von Waldstein has not yet been able to make good on his promise to Mundanus that he could inspect Wenzel Seyler's red powder. The Mint Master has been asked to leave Vienna during the wedding festivities, his lascivious behavior having become an embarrassment at the Catholic court of the Holy Roman Emperor where all is allowed but scandal. His Majesty himself is on his best behavior, having been warned about the extreme piety of his future bride, and everyone who might give cause for her disapproval has been asked to enjoy the countryside. It has made my husband restless, his eagerness to speak to Seyler increasing by the hour.

We have been given a special music room where Johanna is playing all day long while a gaggle of various high ranking dignitaries and their Ladies enter our chambers under feeble pretexts just to hear her practice.

The Prince of Orange has arrived some days ago and is spending as much time as is seemly with Aunt Marianne between hunts. He has marriage troubles of his own, being now set on a course towards proposing to his 14 year old cousin Princess Mary of England who despises him. Aunt Marianne is a great listener, advising him in matters feminine.

Having just instructed the seamstresses about the fitting of the bodice, set with a sea of pearls, I am in my private room weaving the last material for the sleeves dawning with a pale glow of rose to offset the white gloves giving off a faint suspicion of blue. The sleeves are elegantly crumpled in a ruffled manner so the rose-white glow cloth will reflect kaleidoscopically.

Aunt Marianne enters unannounced. I am startled, having gotten lost in the sumptuous demands of the cloth.

"I am so sorry to disturb you, dear Clara," she begins, a bit embarrassed, sitting down on a low cream colored settees usually occupied by one of the twins. "But I have a question that is very private I need to discuss with you."

My hands pause, giving me permission to look carefully at her. She appears distraught. Has the same thing happened to her and the Prince of Orange as had happened between Christiaan and me? I instantly dismiss the thought. Her relationship to him is purely maternal, though he has been taken with her in a boyish romantic way since the age of 16. Their conversations, she had told me, had until recently been primarily about botany.

"It is about the Prince," she begins. "What I am about to tell you is a state secret."

I nod. No matter the torture my mouth shall remain silent. Aunt Marianne knows.

"Princess Mary is refusing to receive his proposal. She seems to be of a very independent mind. A young woman after my own heart. She is resisting both her father the Duke of York and her uncle King Charles to accept a fiancé. It is rumored that her affections have been absorbed by a girl called Frances who has confessed about the matter to her father, Sir Allen Apsley. Young Frances has been instructed to have their correspondence be more formal. Princess Mary seems to be like Donna Lucia Solario who responded to you in this particular affectionate manner." I shiver, remembering Venier's mother.

"Prince William has come up with a plan only men could conceive; and strategists at that. He has asked me to discuss this with you."

Now my curiosity is peeked.

"Let me first tell you that I think this plan ludicrous. I'm conveying it in obedience to my sovereign."

I don't believe a word she says and smile. She knows I have taken her cover-lie as an inconsequential envelope for the letter of her message. Aunt Marianne grins shyly.

"After Prince William spoke to me of his would-be fiancée's romantic leanings, I told him that you had once been approached in this manner." Seeing my obvious disapproval of her revealing such private matters to a stranger she lowers her gaze in a gesture of apology.

"Go on," I say after a moment of silence, my curiosity outweighing the effects of the offence.

"He suggested that you might befriend the Princess while making a wedding gown for her if she were to consent to his advances. Actually he asked if you could go to London with a mock-up of a gown to show her and sway her mind."

I laugh at the absurdity of this suggestion which could only make sense to a soldier. Aunt Marianne joins me in my giggles and we enjoy the complicity of women in our common surprise over the stunted sensitivity of men.

"He meant that since you had experienced such advances before they wouldn't frighten you if they were to happen again," Aunt Marianne explains after our interlude of mirth has passed.

"This is not a request," Aunt Marianne clarifies. "He gave you an order. He explains that this marriage is crucial for the future of the Dutch Republic in its relations to England and Scotland and he orders you as your Viceroy to bring this proposal to England. His uncle, King Charles leans towards marrying off Princess Mary to the Dauphin of France to strengthen his relations to the Gaul. Our Prince of Orange getting Princess Mary for himself is currently the most urgent matter of state. She of course wants neither him nor the Dauphin. She pines after her beloved Maid of Honor. Prince William has agreed with the Holy Roman Emperor that His Majesty Leopold shall rave vociferously to King Charles about the spectacular nature of his bride's wedding gown. Not that it will make much of a difference to the King, but it might make the Princess curious. King Charles is as yet undecided and easily influenced by the voices of women. At this moment the weight of a feather will decide the fate of Europe. Between your sorcery and the divine talents of our daughter that feather might be found."

I laugh even louder. "It sounds as though he wants me to refuse. He knows me well enough that I would never follow orders such as these."

"I reminded him of that and then he laughed as well. He said: 'Van Os women make terrible soldiers. They don't follow orders.'"

"Tell him that this terrible soldier will consider his request. But as a request only."

"Oh, he knows – of course. But he hopes you will oblige. Anyway it might be fun to go to a wedding in London. I've never been there myself. He has already commissioned a painter to make a portrait of the current bride in her gown which the Emperor has agreed to have sent to Princess Mary's father, the Duke of York."

"So it seems that everything has been decided then," I gently sneer.

"Let's say there are strong hopes," Aunt Marianne placates me.

"If I were Princess Mary such subtle pressure tactics would make me run towards the Dauphin."

"Her decision is not entirely essential. The Duke of York is Catholic and wishes a French Catholic wedding for his daughter. But King Charles is still an Anglican Protestant, though there are strong rumors that he has made an agreement with his cousin King Louis to convert towards the Church of Rome." Her lecture to me sounds like a lesson in statecraft given to her by Prince William in the style of his reluctant mentor Johan de Witt. "The King knows his people would prefer a marriage to a Protestant and will never abide by having the Catholic son of the hated King of France insert himself into the line of succession. King Charles painfully remembers his exile during Cromwell's Puritan revolution and he fears the mob. But he is biding his time. A push from Princess Mary, who despises her father's Catholicism and his new Catholic wife who is barely any older than she, still might decide the matter in one direction or other."

"But most likely, in the end whatever I do makes no difference," I conclude.

"Probably not. But the young Princess is a devout Anglican despising Rome and would thus tend towards the lesser of two evils. And we know that her piety does not prevent her from an outspoken love of garments." Aunt Marianne allows her last sentence to trail like the sounds in an echo chamber.

"If it makes no difference, I'll do it. I would love to show London to The Twins. And Mundanus has been speaking about nothing else but Robert Boyle and Isaac Newton during these last months." My mind is set. Aunt Marianne kisses me on both cheeks and I throw my arms around her neck as I used to do when I was little.

"How did we get ourselves involved in these global politics?" I ask. "Do you think these are the doings of Red Sulphur?" The imagery of alchemy is full of Kings and Queens.

Having no answer, Aunt Marianne kisses me with maternal tenderness.

℘

"I know no man is allowed to see the wedding gown, Madam Dolfin," Count von Waldstein addresses me in the anteroom to our suites. "But I'll be honest. His Majesty, who abhors surprises, has sent me as a spy. He wishes me to report on the appearance of the gown. Speculations at the court are running wild, with some superstitious Ladies calling you a witch trying to enchant the future Holy Roman Empress." He grins broadly, obviously amused by such far-fetched nonsense. I am not going to disabuse him of his conviction that sorcery is the stuff of fairy tales and medieval lore. I know the Ladies to whom he is referring to be correct but for my motives. I have no interest in gaining power over Princess Eleonore Magdalene. But Princess Mary shall be another matter altogether. In her case the Ladies at the court might have been correct. I wonder if I will encounter the same reception by the Ladies at the English court.

"I hope indeed that my gown will enchant everyone who sees it. What dress maker would not?"

The Count bows in agreement, awaiting my decision. It is a heady feeling to momentarily hold power over an Emperor.

"It would feel like a betrayal of the Empress to be," I counter.

"Your loyalty is greatly valued," the diplomat responds. "Of course His Majesty would hope you'd reply in this manner." He lets a silence linger the exact number of beats observed by a consummate musician. "His Majesty insisted however that an advance viewing by me as his eyes would certainly encourage his enthusiasm in the matter of King Charles."

To my surprise I realize that I do enjoy politics.

"I cannot show you the dress since it has not yet been assembled. But I could show you the sleeves, gloves and bodice so you will have some impression. Would that do?"

Count von Waldstein smiles: "Madam Dolfin, you should consider a career in diplomacy."

"It has been suggested recently," I concur. I take the Count to my personal fitting room where I'm working on attaching the glow cloth sleeves, with their rose undertone, to the pearled bodice. The gloves are positioned next to them to accentuate the barely perceptible contrast. It is a sunny room with large windows looking out on a courtyard, just high enough that not even a tall equestrian can glance in. But just in case, the translucent white curtains are drawn. I had asked that every wall be painted egg shell white in order to not have to deal with false colors.

Count von Waldstein stands in the door opening, transfixed.

"The Ladies are right," he mumbles, "you are performing witchcraft."

"Come in," I invite him to view the sections of the wedding gown closer up.

Playing absentmindedly with his Golden Fleece on its gold chain – he must just have come from an official encounter where he was dressed to impress – he enters with trepidation, as if in the presence of a religious icon. He has been silenced.

"What do you think?" I ask him informally.

He stares at me with incredulous admiration. "You may ask the Countess von Waldstein and she will tell you that I am not interested in the esthetic beauty of the clothes people wear. And she is right. I look at clothes for clues to perform my diplomatic mission. They reveal the intricacies of rank. But this is different. Words fail me."

"That must be an unusual occurrence," I tease him. I feel very comfortable with Count Waldstein. His behavior towards my children has melted my mother-heart and ever since we arrived at the Hofburg he has been our gallant liaison. His Majesty had postponed the Count's Ambassadorship to Whitehall until after the wedding.

"Of course you are right, Madam Dolfin. Such a thing rarely happens. It has to do with the quality of the cloth. It appears to be alive; I would swear I could see it breathe. The illusion is perfect."

"You are very perceptive, Your Excellency," I compliment him. "I made it that way in order to create the effect you notice."

"It reminds me of the days when I was a child and our Governess would tell us fairy tales from our native Bohemia. There was one that made me dream of countries far away. It was about a cloak that could make the owner fly as high and as far as he wanted. I dreamed of that cloak. I think the cloak made me a diplomat, traveling far and wide. But I never thought I should see the cloth that can make you fly. This cloth makes me fly." He sounds like a young boy and I feel motherly towards him. Maximo could have spoken just like him. Suddenly he looks at me, embarrassed over his effusion.

"It's alright," I say gently. "The cloth has that effect on people. My weaving teacher calls it glow cloth. Not just because it glows, but because it sets people aglow when they look at it."

"How did you make it?" he asks. I hesitate. I have never told anyone outside of our triad about the Red Sulphur. Elspeth has asked me many times. But for some reason I feel that I should include Count von Waldstein in our secret. I don't know if it has to do with the fact that he has been the primary inspector of Wenzel Seyler's Red Sulphur powder, or that I trust him in an avuncular way. Something tells me that his heart is true.

"I trust that you will never tell anyone what I am about to tell you. Swear it on the Golden Fleece." The Count looks at me with consternation, our vast difference in rank suddenly establishing itself. For a person without aristocratic lineage to demand an oath on the Golden Fleece is close to sacrilege. Then, suddenly, a large grin breaks through.

"Madam Dolfin, you are certainly one of the more remarkable people I've had the privilege of encountering." He takes the Golden Fleece off his neck and holds it in his right hand upon his heart. "I swear," he says solemnly with a twinkle in his eye.

"It was made of the same kind of Red Sulphur Wenzel Seyler is using. That's why we were so eager to come to Vienna. We have never before met someone else who possesses the Red Sulphur."

"Do you have it?" he asks in awe.

"No, but my husband does. He is the famous Doctor Theodore Mundanus everyone in Europe has been looking for." Count Waldstein sinks down on a chair. "I understand why you made me swear on the Golden Fleece. It was justified. Any lesser oath I might have broken. I believed Theodore Mundanus to have been a legend."

"Like you believed the cloth that makes you fly to be a fairy tale," I compare.

The silence in the room makes the textiles even more present than they had been.

"Will you tell Signor Dolfin that I know his true identity? I'm under oath and cannot do so."

I nod, certain that Mundanus will be glad to cast off his incognito for a man of the Count's caliber.

"Please tell me more about the Red Sulphur textile," he implores.

I explain to him how glow cloth makes the true imagination come to life, allowing it a stage upon which to manifest as clear as in a dream. The Count is hanging on my every word.

"Just look into the cloth," I say, pointing at the sleeve. "What do you see?"

He is quiet for some time.

"I see a little boy – that must be me – listening to my Governess and flying through the world on a magic carpet in the way the Ottomans tell their tales; and landing right here at your feet."

"But my story is no fairy tale. It is as true as is Wenzel Seyler's red powder."

ॐ

"How could you?!" Aunt Marianne asks in a most accusatory manner. "We have never told anyone. Not even Helvetius!"

"Calm down, Marianne," Mundanus tells her. "I'm sure Clara had good reason. Why did you tell him, Darling?"

I'm befuddled, not knowing what to say. I had told the Count in a sudden ebullition without a particular reason. "I don't know. I just felt I should trust him. He knows the Red Sulphur is true. He has seen it with his own eyes."

"But that is not the same as betraying Mundanus' identity!" Aunt Marianne fulminates.

"Maybe it will be useful for our journey to England," Mundanus ponders. "He will be the Imperial Envoy there. It could be practical."

"We could have befriended him without telling," Aunt Marianne insists, annoyed.

"I am sorry Giovanni. But I suddenly could no longer keep it a secret. That's why I had him swear upon the Golden Fleece. He will never betray your identity. His honor as a nobleman will prevent him from ever telling anyone. Not even his Emperor. The Golden Fleece has priority over all other allegiances," I conclude. Everyone knows this for a fact.

"Well, now at least he knows why I am truly here: to meet this Wenzel Seyler. I want to talk to Seyler, see him face to face and ask him about his Red Sulphur and where he got it from or how he made it."

"We could ask the Count to invite him back to the Hofburg Palace and meet with us. He has enough power to circumvent the decree that all subjects who might cause disapproval from the Empress to be should stay away," Aunt Marianne suggests in a conciliatory tone, regarding my indiscretion from this moment forward to be mere matter of fact.

"He is eager to meet with you, Giovanni. He would love you to invite him," I concur.

"Clara, why don't you invite him for one of Johanna's rehearsals? Tell him that I shall be there. We'll have a private soiree. Then we can discuss the Seyler matter."

℞

The next few days all I can think of is the train. I have created a very long gossamer train for the wedding dress. I have been experimenting with a new material, a mixture of glow cloth and silk dyed in the last remnants of the *lunaria* dye which created the original batch of glow wool. It has had the same effect on the silk and once we obtained a starter batch of silk thread it could be used as sourdough for other raw silk. We had imported large amounts of silk from Venice and this was my first attempt at a hybrid material that was even lighter than the woolen glow cloth, the filaments finer than spider web thread. Even the slightest breeze would cause it to float. Yet it was sturdy as fibers ten times its circumference. The train could be many yards long and the bride would barely feel it. It would look like a luminescent cloud magically floating behind the gown. The train bearers only needed to keep it on course. Only the very end of the gossamer veil weighted down by a plethora of pearls would touch the ground. I had draped it lengthwise in the workshop revealing any unevenness in the weaving so I could work on the final touches. It looked like a long misty transparency as it hung down from specially constructed scaffolding taking up the entire length of the atelier.

I had only spoken briefly to Count Waldstein who promised he would bring in Wenzel Seyler and his red powder so Mundanus could meet him and inspect Seyler's Red Sulphur.

The meeting has been set for this evening.

The Count comes by himself into the music room where Johanna is playing her heart out after dinner.

"I asked the Mint Master to come in later after the court has gone to sleep so as to attract less attention," he whispers close to my ear in order not to disturb my daughter. I appreciate his thoughtful gallantry towards a child. Mundanus sitting next to me has heard and smiles with the same sentiments. He gets up and bows; Aunt Marianne curtsies. I quickly get up and do the same, having forgotten all about protocol. The Count bows back in acknowledgement. Johanna stops playing and gets up from her high stool in front of the keyboard to curtsy as well.

"Hi Count," says Maximo who seems by nature incapable of understanding etiquette. He treats everyone with the same courteous disrespect. It must be Mother Marianne's influence. Blindness towards rank is a dominant strain in her character. It makes no basic difference to her if someone is our coachman Hendrik or an Emperor. She is only impressed by knowledge.

Count von Waldstein grins boyishly at Maximo. I see a faint flutter of magic carpets in my mind. "Hi Maximo," he responds jovially.

After some light banter we leave the children in the music room where Johanna resumes her music while Maximo lies on the floor in total concentration constructing intricate machinery from scraps he has scavenged from all over the Hofburg grounds where he is free to roam, causing smiles on the faces of even the most formal courtiers. He is particularly popular among women folk of all ranks.

We withdraw to the adjacent workshop room so we can keep listening to Johanna's virtuosity while staying out of earshot and sit down on the hardly comfortable chairs used by the seamstresses. The Count admires the train looking like a giant opalescent silkscreen. The candlelit silver candelabras confer a dancing flamboyance to its surface. But he is distracted, obviously waiting for Mundanus to start the conversation.

"My wife has told you about my true identity," Mundanus begins at last.

"Yes, Your Excellency," Count Waldstein replies in perfect French. I have never heard my husband being addressed as 'Excellency' before and am shocked.

Mundanus smiles, turns to Aunt Marianne and me and says in French, making self-deprecating fun of himself: "That's how they talk about me in England. I should have warned you. I'm held in high esteem there."

"That's putting it mildly," the Count continues in French. "Isaac Newton has been searching for you, as has Robert Boyle. It is said that you correspond with Dickinson through friends in Paris. It is rumored that you are the only man alive who can make gold from other metals and actually knows what he is doing – not like Seyler, who must have obtained the Red Sulphur by other means. They say you are French, but I hear you have a slight Italian accent, which would correspond to the knowledge I have about you as Signor Giovanni Dolfin VII from Venice." A turbulent waterfall of words flows from the great nobleman, as from a man meeting his idol. "You performed a transmutation before Isaac Newton which changed the course of his life and made him into one of the great adepts in England. Indirectly Robert Boyle came to chemistry through you as well. But how do I know that you truly are this legendary Theodore Mundanus?"

"Because I saw with my own eyes how he transmuted lead into gold," Aunt Marianne states firmly in words that leave no doubt as to their veracity.

"It was his Red Sulphur that created the famous Helvetius transmutation of 1666," I support my aunt.

"With all due respect, Madam Schweitzer, Madam Dolfin, Theodore Mundanus has been the object of an extensive

European manhunt which included not only Johan de Witt and the Prince of Orange, as you must know, but also King Louis of France, the Duke of York and the Royal Society in England. Mundanus is said to possess knowledge no one else has any longer. It is hard to believe that I am suddenly sitting in a room with this grand Magus right here in our own Hofburg. I was asked by His Majesty to be an inspector in the Seyler case because I myself am an aspiring adept, corresponding with most of the other aspirants in Europe. We are all more than eager to talk to Theodore Mundanus. So please allow me a moment of suspicion. You look barely thirty five years of age, Signor Dolfin, and it is said that Theodore Mundanus was already well into his forties when he performed the transmutation before Isaac Newton in '65 in Woolsthorpe, eleven years ago."

Both Aunt Marianne and I nod simultaneously. His suspicions are fair. Mundanus should answer them himself.

"I wasn't aware that King Louis was looking for me," Mundanus replies with an affable smile.

"Since it is rumored that Theodore Mundanus is a French subject the King wants his chrysopoeia all to himself. He wants Mundanus' gold to throw after the treasury disaster he is building at Versailles. But please answer my questions, Sir." His voice is stern. This is the first time I hear him speak in this tone. The personal urgency he feels in this matter has peeled away his smooth diplomacy displaying a more prickly fruit.

"What if I told you that even the fabled Theodore Mundanus doesn't know how to make Red Sulphur; that the art was lost over a hundred years ago."

"Then I would know that you are not he," the Count retorts.

"Oh, but yes, I am he," Mundanus replies with a broad grin. "It is your hope that makes you believe that there must be a man who still knows the secret. But it got lost. The stars by which the Stone was made no longer rise at night. We are now in the age of matter and the future of matter will astound us. We may fly to the moon in flying machines Master Da Vinci has already imagined. However we have become blind to bodies that are extracted from matter, but are themselves non-material. They are made with the oil with which the Lord anointed life itself. That's what the Stone is, and we can no longer fashion it."

"But Newton says that Theodore Mundanus showed him a projection and I saw Wenzel Seyler do it right in front of my own eyes. Then where does the Red Sulphur come from?"

"I don't know where Seyler obtained it, but I can tell you about mine. I brought it to show you, for I knew you would not believe me." Mundanus gets up walks around the long silk-screen train and disappears behind it. He returns with his mother's ivory box and asks me to snuff all candles in the room, which I do by lowering the candelabras. When the room is dark, lit only by the candles in the adjacent room where Johanna is playing in ever more entrancing phrases, Mundanus opens the box before Count von Waldstein's hungry eyes. As the box opens the room is lit by the green radiance exuding from the two clumps of Red Sulphur inside. "You told Doctor Helvetius that once you saw Wenzel Seyler's Red Sulphur by night. Do you recognize the glow that Christiaan Huygens likened to Boyle's phosphorus?"

Count Waldstein looks at the box in jaw-dropped astonishment.

"This is Red Sulphur," Mundanus tells him solemnly. "It was made by my ancestor the great Salomon Trismosin, teacher of Paracelsus, around the year 1500." He hands the box to the Count who is overcome with emotion, knowing that he is in the presence of both the Red Sulphur and of the fabled Theodore Mundanus. As he gazes at the miracle before his eyes, stunned, Mundanus briefly tells him the tale of Trismosin's legacy. At the end of the story Count Waldstein has regained his speech and asks Mundanus: "So you mean to say, Your Excellency, that these stones do not consist of matter?"

"Indeed," Mundanus replies. "They're like the wax of honey combs, but the honey itself isn't visible. The honey of the Stone is pure inspiration. What we see is not really the Red Sulphur, what we see is the messenger. That's why it is made from alive Mercury, the seed on earth of the great Messenger wandering the skies. In order to make it potent and run smoothly from the honeycomb we have to activate it before projection."

"How much Red Sulphur did Wenzel Seyler use for the projection you witnessed?" Aunt Marianne asks him.

"Very little," the Count replies. "Only a heaped teaspoon."

"A teaspoon!" Mundanus and Aunt Marianne exclaim simultaneously.

The Count looks confused. "It may have been a little more than that. But it wasn't much."

Mundanus turns to Marianne. "He doesn't know what he is doing. He must be using the Stone inactivated."

"I don't understand," the Count says, still staring at the contents of the ivory box. "I might have been wrong about the exact quantity. But it certainly was no more than a dessert spoon."

"A dessert spoon?!" they erupt.

"A dessert spoon of activated Red Sulphur is enough to transform just about a thousand pounds of lead into gold of the highest degree. He is squandering the Stone!" Mundanus looks aghast.

"What do you mean?" Count Waldstein asks.

"The Stone can transmute up to 18,000 times its weight into gold," Aunt Marianne explains.

In our amazement we have not noticed that Johanna has stopped playing.

"You can hand that box to me, Count von Waldstein," a familiar voice tells us from the other room. At first I can't quite make out to whom the voice belongs, just that I know it very well and that all my hair stands on end. Terror grips me. Then I see it.

A man stands behind my daughter pointing a pistol to her head.

"Venier!" I scream.

"Master Seyler," Count von Waldstein calls out. "What the Hell are you doing?"

"You're making the same mistake again, Clara. I am Mantis. I told you not to have a child with Giovanni Dolfin. You disobeyed me. Your daughter will die if you don't give me the box. You've come just in time to bring me a fresh supply of your magic stone. I've just about run out of the red powder. Thank you for coming all the way from Holland to bring it to me," he sneers.

"This man stole the Stone from me," Mundanus hisses at Venier for Count von Waldstein to hear. "He is capable of anything. He is a man possessed by a demon. Look!" He points at the glow cloth behind us. For a moment we are all transfixed, Venier Solario/Wenzel Seyler included. On a cosmic stage where the silkscreen train used to be a giant green insect stands on its huge hind legs with a widely opened beak about to devour an angel made of transparent golden light. I cower, knowing what this means. Whether we give him the Stone or not, he is going to kill Johanna. There is nothing I can do, nothing any of us can do. It is just a matter of moments. My heart shatters.

"No!" Aunt Marianne screams, realizing the same thing.

"Don't do this Seyler," the Count gets up. "Here is the box. Don't harm the girl."

"He is going to kill her no matter what," I whisper hoarsely.

In the glow-cloth world Mantis' eyes glow brightly as his beak begins to close in on the golden being of light. I look back at Venier and notice his trigger finger tensing. Johanna has her eyes closed, knowing full well what is about to happen. Mantis is more interested in the kill than in the Red Sulphur.

Suddenly I see Venier shudder, looking at the world behind us. I'm afraid his shaking will cause him to fire the pistol.

We all turn. Behind the giant Mantis a blinding cloud of golden light explodes, overtaking the entire cosmos.

"Take your hands off my sister!" Maximo commands in a voice of absolute authority. I know instantly that the spirit of Red Sulphur is speaking directly through his mouth, incarnating in this little boy who is my son. Its power is immense.

Venier looks overwhelmed with awe as his weapon sinks down. The bullet rolls out of the barrel and bounces several times with the clear staccato of a lead ball on a parquet floor. The echo dies away into an unnatural silence.

A magnificent eruption of a thousand silent suns consumes Mantis.

Venier and Maximo collapse at the same time.